The Heart By Which We Live

author@djamesthen.com

ISBN: 978-1-62646-672-2

Library of Congress Control Number: 2013916231

Printed in the United States of America; Hebron, KY

Booklocker.com, Inc.
2013

First Edition

The Heart By Which We Live

D. James Then

Also by D. James Then

That Tender Light (2011)

For:

Jenny Glassburn Then
Lisa Robertson Then
Trudy Then
Anthony & Theresa Harenda
Larry Szantor

†

Thanks to the human heart by which we live,
Thanks to its tenderness, its joys, and fears,
To me the meanest flower that blows can give
Thoughts that do often lie too deep for tears.
—*William Wordsworth*

PROLOGUE

Pittsburgh, PA, 11:58 p.m. *January 6, 2012*

V*oices! Why would I hear voices in a snowstorm?*

Manny Tobias listened intently but the voices, if he had heard any, had disappeared. The only sound was the din of his labored breathing. *It must be my muddled mind,* he thought. *It does cartwheels when I want heroin.* He forced himself to steady his breathing, leaned against the rear wall of the smaller of two garages behind JUMPIN' JOE'S SALOON, and waited for the frigid air to cull his aspiration for 'H'.

Tobias, clean for a year, occasionally cheated with beer and bourbon, which inevitably fueled an urge for *magic in his veins.* Fortunately, Tobias' desire to stay clean trumped his avidity and the rapid inhalation of cold air stilled his predatory lust for heroin. *No more needles, ever!*

He relaxed and looked skyward, letting snowflakes tickle his face. He reached for a smoke and was about to light up when two voices rode the wind again. For sure, a couple was in a nearby alley and a male voice cut a nasty edge.

Tobias, a bit of a snoop, evaded two garbage cans, braced himself against the wall, inched sideways, and peeked around the corner. Surprisingly, because a wall buffered the wind, line of sight was clear.

A man and woman stood thirty feet away, near the alley's entrance on East Carson Street. Tobias tossed the cigarette, rotated his ball cap, and silenced his cell phone. He placed it on a nearby stack of bricks and pressed record.

"What did you hear me say?" the man demanded.

"Nothing," the woman said. Her coat was on the ground, she stood in a sleeveless cocktail dress, shivering. "I was just leaving the restroom. Take your hands off me."

She punched the man's chest, albeit weakly.

"My husband is there," she added, "in the carriage house."

She pointed down the alley toward the front of the larger garage where, above a sagging wooden door, an amber light bulb swayed its lonely vigil in the falling snow.

"Jack," she yelled. "Help me! I need you. Where are you?"

The woman studied the light bulb and, when her gaze happened upon Tobias' face peeking around the corner, she shouted, "I see him. He's right there!"

Tobias crouched behind the bricks and held his breath, ready to grab his phone and bolt if the man made a move.

"I don't see anyone," the man replied. "It's only a garage. Tell me what you heard. I will let you go. I promise."

Tobias exhaled softly. *Jesus,* he thought, *that was close.*

"Tell you what?" The woman seemed confused.

"What you overheard," the man demanded.

"Twenty kilos," the woman stated. "You have twenty kilos for sale." Slurred words indicated too much alcohol.

"Damn it," the man said. "I *knew* it."

"I saw Jack," the woman said, still on a tangent about seeing her husband. She looked down the alley again. "Jack, I've got the money you wanted for the real estate."

She almost fell, clutched the man's lapels, and steadied herself. He squeezed her elbows tightly.

"Hey, you're hurting me," she shouted. "Where's my coat?"

"God, I wish you hadn't heard me. We could party," the man said. "You are one *beautiful* woman."

"Twenty kilos," she repeated. "That's what I heard and I would *never* go with you. Where is Jack? I have the money."

She attempted to free herself but the man's grip was firm.

"How much money?" he asked, sensing a score.

"I have hundreds, no thousands," the woman said, slurring her words. "I have a key, too, the money's in a..."

Did she say locker? The wind muffled her voice.

For the first time, Tobias saw the man's full face.

I'll be damned, Lieutenant Aaron Cooper, Pittsburgh PD! That smug fuck is a dirty cop.

"Jillian," Cooper demanded, "How much money?"

"I prefer Jill, I told you that," she said.

"End the bullshit. Tell me about the goddamned money!"

"I won't say another word. Stop hurting me! You said if I told you, I could go. I did! Let me go, you creep."

"I guess I lied," Cooper replied. He checked the street and alley. The glare of a streetlight angled a few feet away.

Tobias studied Cooper's expression.

The bastard is going to kill her!

"Let me go," Jill shouted and, as she stooped for her coat, she struck Cooper flush in the face with her elbow.

He swore, wrapped Jill's head in his arms, snapped her neck, and let her fall. Her skull cracked against concrete.

"Fuck you," Cooper said.

Instinctively, he looked around. The snowfall was heavier. The street and alley were as empty as an old man's ambition. He lifted the woman's purse and rummaged inside. He moved to the edge of the alley and examined a key in the glare of neon. He slipped it into his pocket, threw the purse beside the woman's coatless body, and walked away.

Quickly, Tobias pocketed his phone and dashed in the opposite direction. He jumped over garbage cans, ran behind the larger garage, vaulted a fence, found the sidewalk, and slowed to a nonchalant pace. The snow muffled his footsteps as he approached JUMPIN' JOE'S side entrance on South 19th.

Minutes later, inside the bar, waiting for an espresso, Tobias watched the recording with the sound off and wrote down everything he saw and heard.

He underscored one line: Aaron Cooper is a dirty cop!

"I'll be goddamned," he said, slapping the bar.

"Excuse me?" the bartender asked. "Is something wrong?"

Tobias shook his head, pocketing the napkin and phone.

He sipped his drink and revisited the scene from the alley: *Cooper will find the money! How difficult is that for a cop? However, the bastard does not know I recorded everything.*

Tobias did the math. Twenty kilos of coke was roughly forty-five pounds. A quick calculation revealed the cocaine would be worth a fortune on the streets. He smiled. *Maybe I can figure a way to help myself to some of that money. I could really use it.* He downed the espresso.

Outside, nothing moved as the storm's intensity grew. The streets remained empty. Snow swirled in the wind. Ice particles stung his skin.

Tobias turned into the alley, crouched in the shadows, and retrieved the woman's purse. Hiding it beneath his coat, he re-entered JOE'S, found the men's room, and took a stall.

He counted eighteen hundred dollars and change. He stuffed all but a few hundred bucks into his pocket, wondering how much the woman had actually stashed away.

He searched her wallet and found several business cards: one was hers for a lawn-care business and one was for a man named Jack Redding. *Must be her husband,* Tobias reasoned. They had the same last name and the woman had called out to a man named Jack.

Tobias put the business cards into his pocket with the money. Still holding the wallet, he froze when he considered his fingerprints. He quickly uttered a sigh of relief. Thankfully, he was wearing calfskin gloves. The cops would never know. Good, he could not afford stupid mistakes!

"Stay cool," he whispered, exiting the nightclub.

Outside, the city was now in the grip of a blizzard and a snowdrift covered the woman's lower body. Soon, she would disappear completely. Tobias tossed the purse onto her chest and disappeared into the swirling snow. He knew what he wanted to do; he wanted *to jam* a crooked cop. *That should be piece of cake,* he thought, *just play it smart.*

Pittsburgh, PA, 1:27 p.m. *December 4, 2012*

Frank Kropinak opened a desk drawer in his Mount Washington office. He withdrew the still-folded envelope Manny Tobias had given him back on St. Patrick's Day. With gloved hands, Kropinak used a wet wipe to eliminate any fingerprints. He quickly fanned the envelope dry.

His first thought, after Tobias' tragic death in July, was to burn the letter. He had not done so because of a promise. Frank's word was his honor.

Instead, he hid the letter and waited. Neither the cops nor anyone else nosed around with questions. No one cared or knew about his connection to Manny Tobias. Now on this day, Tobias' birthday, Kropinak decided to fulfill the commitment he made, as he and Manny drank a few beers...

...After work, Manny and Frank were in MURPHY'S TAVERN on the Southside to honor St. Patrick. They watched two women in their twenties, in tight green skirts, shooting pool. After a blonde-haired beauty sank the *four-ball*, Tobias turned and smiled at his friend and mentor.

He removed a folded envelope from his jacket and slid it beside Frank's half-empty pint of green lager. Curiosity wrinkled the older man's brow.

"What," Kropinak asked, "your last will and testament?"

"It's an insurance policy, Frank," Tobias whispered. "If anybody jams me up, wait a few weeks and mail it."

"Why wait?"

"I want the son of bitch to think he's off the hook. He'll get complacent; it'll catch him off guard."

Kropinak did not unfold the envelope or note its address, although he did feel something hard, small, and square on the inside. As he buttoned the missive in the breast pocket of his checkered shirt, his curiosity deepened.

"What gives, Manny?"

"Nothing to worry about, Frank," Tobias replied. "If something happens to me, drop the letter in the mail."

Kropinak nodded.

The chic woman with the blonde hair ran three straight balls and, as she leaned over the table, Tobias smiled.

"You could crack an egg on that ass, Franklin."

"At seventy-four, I can only dream," Kropinak replied, admiring the woman's tight backside. He sipped his beer, turned to Tobias, and asked, "You in trouble, kid?"

A red-haired server passed in front of them.

"Her ass is nice, too," Tobias added, hoisting a pint in approval. Tremors in Manny's hand spoke volumes about his twenty-year, love-hate relationship with heroin and other drugs. Beer he could handle; more drugs would kill him.

"Are you in trouble, Manny?" Kropinak repeated.

Tobias shrugged as if to indicate it was no big deal.

"No trouble," he replied, "no drugs, no needles."

"If you're on thin ice, be careful."

"Actually, I'm onto a no-good pug who stole a lot of money from an innocent woman. I have proof. He jammed me up a few times in the past. It is payback time. The letter is an ace in the hole. If the pug does not do me right, I'll ruin him."

Wisely, Tobias did not mention witnessing a murder.

"What if this *pug* takes you down, first?" Kropinak asked.

Tobias smiled. "He might try, but he'll back off after he learns what I have on him. If he does not help me clear my pendings, I will ruin him. The Feds will get my evidence; pretty slick, huh? I hate crooked pugs, Frank." Wisely, Tobias did not indicate he wanted a piece of the cop's action.

"Did you keep me out of it?" asked Kropinak.

Tobias looked at the old man with a pained expression.

"Sometimes I'm dumb, Frank, but I'm never stupid," Tobias stated. "You ain't involved, not even remotely."

"Good, because I'd worry," Kropinak replied.

"I know," Tobias said, watching the women.

Kropinak whispered, "Is what you're doing smart, kid?"

"I think so," Tobias replied. "If it helps my pendings, I save a shit-load in legal fees."

Tobias also hoped he could get a few hundred thousand dollars. That kind of money would solve all his problems.

"Don't screw things up, Manny. Your life is turning around. With union papers, you will be a full-fledged plumber. You're headed toward a life better than anything you've ever known, kid."

"I thank you for that," Tobias said. "I never dreamed I'd start at fifty bucks an hour. I got a kid and a life. I want to clear my record. I just want some of the bullshit hanging over me to disappear. This pug can do it."

Tobias swallowed half-a-glassful of beer and motioned to the redheaded server for another round. He lit a cigarette with a match and blew the flame out as he exhaled. He studied Kropinak's face for several seconds.

"Trust me, Frank," Tobias added, "The lowlife will do what I want, especially when he knows *I know* he's dirty."

"It doesn't sound good, Manny," Kropinak replied.

"Stop worrying," Tobias whispered. "It'll work out. Crooked pugs got nowhere to turn for help."

He touched Kropinak's shirt pocket.

"Please, do what I ask," he stated.

Kropinak nodded.

"You got my word, kid. I can't tell you what to do, because you won't listen, but watch your ass."

"I'll be fine," Tobias said, giving the server a ten spot...

...As it turned out, Tobias was not *fine*. Kids found his bloated body in an empty warehouse near the steel mills.

The police ruled his death accidental, due to an overdose.

They found a needle in his arm and too much heroin in his blood. "A lethal overdose," a small news article reported. Because of their prior conversation and because of Manny's envelope, Kropinak thought otherwise.

Tobias said, "I hate crooked pugs." Those were his exact words. In Manny's vernacular, *pug* meant a cop or anyone else in the legal system with an official capacity.

Kropinak believed a cop killed Tobias. If true, that meant murder and it scared him.

He shivered and considered unfolding the envelope to read the address. He hesitated. He had never read it; why do so now? The less he knew the better, especially if he was dancing on the fringes of a homicide. His answers would be honest, if anyone ever questioned him.

He rescored the fold, put the envelope in his hip pocket, and walked down the hallway toward the kitchen.

"Where are you going, Frank?" his wife asked when he entered, surprised to see him with his hat, gloves, and heavy coat. "It's cold and snowing outside, sweetheart."

Ruth Kropinak stood at the counter making hot chocolate. Chicken soup was boiling in a big pot on the stove.

Frank considered telling his wife about the envelope; however, that notion quickly faded. If Tobias was murdered, then it was because of something bad. The less Kropinak told his wife, the less she would gossip. If she did not gab, they would both be safer. Kropinak was not scared but it made no sense to pour gasoline on dying embers.

"I'm going to the post office," he replied. "I want to get the office mail. I am going to DUKE'S SMOKE SHOP, too. I want a few cigars in the humidor."

Ruth Kropinak smiled at her husband of fifty years.

"The brand Manny used to bring to you," she said.

Kropinak nodded.

"You miss him, huh?"

"Yeah, Manny was really trying. He would have made a good plumber. He had a remarkable memory. I never had to tell or show him anything twice. He memorized things instantly. He was good that way."

"It's awful, him killing himself."

Kropinak nodded absently.

"Yeah, we'll never know what he was thinking."

The pull of the letter against his hip told him that somewhere someone *did* know Manny's thoughts.

~

Twenty minutes later, after receiving his mail, Kropinak handed the folded envelope to a postal clerk who weighed it as Frank turned to leave.

"Excuse me, sir," the clerk said. "You need more postage."

"I'm sorry," Kropinak replied.

"The letter, it will cost thirty cents more for first class, more if you want it to arrive sooner."

"First class will do," Kropinak said.

He handed the clerk a buck, awaited change, and noticed the clerk detect something inside the envelope.

"Do you want to insure the contents?"

"No, just send it," Kropinak said.

"I will," the clerk said, making the correct change. "Sir, your letter should be in Buffalo the day after tomorrow."

Buffalo!

Kropinak was surprised.

Why Buffalo?

Manny Tobias never mentioned knowing anyone in Buffalo. Kropinak decided it was none of his business.

He nodded to the clerk, exited the post office, and buried his favor for Manny Tobias deep where only he could find it.

Now, he thought, whatever happens is with God, or fate, or destiny, or whatever-the-spiritual-force that moves people to do the things they do.

Kropinak started his car, letting the engine warm.

He pulled out into traffic and watched his wipers sweep away accumulated snow.

A few moments later, he entered DUKE'S SMOKE SHOP, saying a prayer for Manny Tobias' tortured soul.

East Las Vegas, NV, 3:35 p.m. *January 11, 2013*

Gordon Shaw entered his mother's suite, alone. He walked to the far wall, pressed a button behind a bureau, and watched a full-length mirror slide sideways.

Before entering the previously concealed alcove, he studied his image in the mirror. He appeared drawn. Sorrow filled his eyes; a haggard expression distorted his face. Louise Shaw's death had hit him hard.

One minute they were laughing; the next his mother was gone, sitting dead beside him on a sofa. Her death was shocking, unexpected, and utterly devastating.

He walked to a shelf at the back of the alcove and removed a necklace and earrings from his suit coat. The priceless diamond ensemble was insured for two million dollars. It might be worth more. He arranged the teardrop diamonds in a velvet pocket and exited the alcove, waiting until the mirror locked in place to hide the secret niche.

He turned off the lights and exited the suite. Before descending a staircase, he made a mental note to take the diamonds to the bank in the morning. They had to be secure. For now, he needed a double scotch and lots of rest.

A stiff drink and a good nap might help ease his anguish and soften his deep sense of loss.

He had no idea what he had just set in motion, that the ramifications of his actions would be devastating to his family or that an unknown man from Buffalo would touch his life and that of Shaw's first born son, Kyle.

Book 1

January 2013

Resolution

A heart to resolve, a head to contrive, and
a hand to execute
—Edward Gibbon

1

Jack Redding, I know who killed your wife! Eight simple words altered my life, forever. As I fought the tug of sleep in Buffalo on a cold January night, I formed a plan. First, get the money. Second, kill the bastard who murdered my wife and took the money. Third, take the money and start life anew. As for the cops, they would never know.

Specifically, I would leave Buffalo, drive to Santa Fe, find Aaron Cooper, and recover the $390,000 he stole from my wife, Jill, after he broke her neck in a Pittsburgh alley.

With money in hand, I would take Cooper into the desert, put bullets in his head and heart, bury his body, and vanish.

Maybe I would work, or write, or do something else. Whatever it was, Cooper would be a memory, a diversion, a nightmare I had to endure to jettison the misery that tried to camp permanently in my heart.

As for my penalty for taking a life, if any were due, that was up to God. From what little I knew about His mercy, God just might extend compassion rarely seen in a human court of law. I know His commandment against killing does not feature a *what-if* clause. Still, I hoped God would soften His blow in light of Jill's death and my broken heart.

In my mind, sin does not exist when avenging an innocent life. I recognize the rationalization but I held that killing Cooper was justified. Maybe God would agree and in His profuse kindness excuse the deed instantly—a prompt allocation of divine absolution, if you will.

God knew Jill was innocent. He knew she died horribly. He knew she was in the wrong place at the wrong time. He knew how deeply I loved her and how much I suffered. He knew I despised the memories of her death.

God also knew that Aaron Cooper was a son of a bitch.

Moments later, I was sleeping.

2

Amanda Cassidy's emotions burned as fiercely in Las Vegas as Jack Redding's did in Buffalo, but for a different reason. Gordon Shaw, Amanda's future father-in-law, had just called her a dirty whore. At that instant, a friendship she believed robust crumbled into a thousand grains of sand, never to be re-assembled.

I am so damned naïve. He only cares about money, position, and people he considers his equal. As for Kyle, Gordon's lame excuse for a son, I will never marry that rotten bastard. He stood idly and swallowed all the vehemence his father spewed, and not once did Kyle fight for me.

Amanda, invited to have cocktails, could not avoid the heated whispers she heard coming from Gordon Shaw's library. The fiery litany stopped her in her tracks. She stood paralyzed.

"She has your grandmother's teardrop diamonds?"

"I didn't see any harm in it. It's for a photo shoot," Kyle Shaw explained. "She has the knockoffs, the cubic zirconia. She'll return them in a few days."

"Bullshit, she'll return them tonight! She has the actual diamonds, worth millions."

"That's wrong," Kyle said. "They were in grandmother's suite with the other knockoffs. Recall, you removed them before her burial. The real ones should be in the bank vault."

"Sadly, they aren't," replied Gordon, icily. "In her Will, your grandmother stipulated that she would wear the real diamonds in her casket, in honor of my father. However, she wanted them returned to the family to become an asset of our foundation. Only I, and the funeral director, knew about her private request. She took the knockoffs to her grave.

"It was a private directive for me. It was important to her. The knockoffs were my father's very first gift to her.

"He had one of his engineers fabricate them. They were mere trinkets but she cherished them. When his wealth grew, after he helped develop this city, my father replaced them with real diamonds, which cost him a bundle sixty years ago. The clarity of the real diamonds is unsurpassed.

"Mother liked the real diamonds but, in her mind, the knockoffs were more precious." Gordon paused. "We have everything money can buy, we live like royalty, and she favored chunks of glass over the real deal. It baffles me.

"Anyway, the day we buried her, the funeral director switched the real for the fake. I planned to tell you and your brother about the donation to the foundation after the fact.

"Upon return from the cemetery, I placed the real diamonds in the alcove with the other knockoffs. I intended to return them to the bank, but never did. Kyle, Amanda has the actual teardrops and they are worth a king's ransom."

"I'll just get them back," Kyle replied, recognizing the issue at hand. "It's not a problem. Amanda will understand. After all, we are in love and I am going to marry her."

Gordon downed a scotch, his fourth, and told himself to bite his tongue. Sadly, he did not follow his own advice.

"That's another issue. In my opinion, Amanda is a common whore. Screwing some show-business tart is not love, Kyle. What you two have is raw sex, a transient fancy. Amanda is not like us. She is a loose woman. I have had her investigated. Perhaps, you should look elsewhere. Find a woman with a pedigree comparable to ours."

Amanda heard Kyle mumble something incoherent, which was clearly not a resounding endorsement of his love for her.

"If you go public," Gordon replied, "I'll disown you. Now, get the diamonds and stop wasting time. Stop being a gullible fool, Kyle. She is a floozy, a bump-and-grind artist. She's been fucked more than the common man."

"She's a classically trained dancer," Kyle offered, weakly.

"Amanda studied at Julliard, headlined on Broadway. She's won two Tony Awards," Kyle added.

"And now, she's in Vegas," Gordon Shaw noted, "like a dancehall queen shaking her titties. I've had her checked out. She has no real money to speak of, she owns a modest art collection, she has had three abortions, and gonorrhea. Rumor persists about a sex tape. She is *not* qualified to be a Shaw. If she were a dog, she'd be a mongrel."

"You son of bitch," Kyle shouted.

"I've been called worse. Your family duty is to get the teardrop diamonds. If you choose not to do it, our friend Honey will get them. Either way, I want the teardrops vaulted this evening. The bank president will open for me."

"I gave them to her for her photo shoot," Kyle reiterated, Amanda thought he was crying.

"So, *ungive* them; the diamonds *must* be returned. Get them back. They are far too valuable, end of discussion."

Amanda did not wait to hear Kyle's response. In haste, and with growing anger, she rushed to her car and drove away, taking her broken heart along for the ride.

As she drove home, Gordon Shaw's words pounded with a ferocity Amanda had never experienced. Her head throbbed, she felt clammy, and the left side of her face tingled.

Tears filled her pretty eyes, as her rage grew. Amanda was a fighter. *Mongrel! Whore! Bump and grind artist! That prick, I'll make him squirm!* She checked the rearview mirror. Headlights! *Kyle's Mercedes is coming fast. Daddy's little errand boy.* She hit the accelerator.

Amanda knew the Shaw diamonds could never be hers. Still, she decided to maintain possession until she could huddle with her attorney. It was now a matter of principle. Had Gordon talked to her nicely, had he and Kyle explained it properly, she would have returned Mrs. Shaw's teardrops, without question, but not now! Now, she would fight.

That old bastard, Gordon Shaw, will have to take me to court to get the diamonds. He'll rue the day and it was not gonorrhea, it was a near-deadly yeast infection.

A few minutes later, she parked her Lexus and ran up the sidewalk to her condominium. She unlocked the door, intent on hiding the diamonds. Kyle, his father, or anyone else they might send would never find them. She would see to it.

If she lost the diamonds, she would lose what little advantage she still had. *No money to speak of, fuck him! I'll make him pay.* Possession, she knew, was nine-tenths of the law. Her attorney would settle it. In the meantime, she would hide them, and she knew exactly where!

She rushed into her office, opened a desk drawer, removed the diamonds, and went to a nearby bookshelf, standing before a pair of lucky T-strap dance shoes. They had brought her fame. Years ago, after placing a four-leaf clover in each shoe, she had worn them for every performance of her first Tony Award-winning role on Broadway.

Amanda peeled back the insole of the left shoe, tossed the dried clover away, and dropped the diamond necklace and earrings into the hollow above the arch, nearer the heel. She pressed the insole back into place. Her experience said the strong adhesive would hold. She repositioned the shoe beside its mate. Kyle or anyone else would never find the jewels.

Tomorrow, I'll visit my attorney. I might walk away with something. This tart will show Kyle and his dick-of-a-father her true mettle. Screw them, their family, and everybody they know. As for the sex tape, yes, but I destroyed all the copies.

She glanced out the window. Kyle was in the cul-de-sac. Amanda smiled and actually clapped her hands. *Eat shit, Gordon. This round is mine you putz.*

She walked into the kitchen, thinking a cup of Earl Grey might ease the pounding in her head. She heated a kettle of water, placed a teabag in a cup, and went to her front door.

She knew Kyle, incensed and obedient, would demand the diamonds. *This will be fun, a sheer pleasure!*

As she turned the knob, a jarring pain behind her left ear forced Amanda to her knees.

"God, no," she whispered, collapsing at Kyle's feet.

A white flash, a searing agony rendered her unconscious. A massive hemorrhage destroyed Amanda's delicate brain. She would be dead in less than four hours.

"Amanda, no," Kyle shouted, "Someone, help!"

He flipped his phone open and dialed 911.

Ramon Lopez, the facilities manager at EL CORAZÓN CONDOMINIUMS, saw Amanda on the floor, as he walked toward his office.

The ex-Army medic rushed in to give her CPR. As he worked on her, he knew she would never awake again as a whole and functioning human being. He had seen it before. This is sad, he thought. Miss Cassidy is a lovely person.

~

Kyle Shaw and Ramon Lopez had no idea that, in time, Amanda's tragic death would have a residual effect.

The former would become a killer; the latter would mourn the loss of friends.

Amanda's death would also affect Jack Redding, who at that precise moment was sleeping soundly through a snowstorm more than two thousand miles away in Buffalo, New York.

As for Jack Redding, he would eventually come to understand that a first act of revenge often primes the well for a second.

3

EMTs rushed Amanda Cassidy to a Las Vegas hospital as Sister Margaret Bosko prayed in a small rural Baptist Church in New Cordell, Oklahoma. She needed guidance on this cold night. Her January fund-raising trip was a bust. For example, the orphanage's best benefactor gave her a tenth of his annual five-thousand-dollar donation.

"It's the economy, Sister. I'm truly sorry; it's all I can do."

The old woman bowed her head. Had a prayer bench been available, she would have been on her knees, begging.

A few prayers into her rosary, a hand touched the nun's shoulder. The old woman did not jump. Instead, she turned toward the handsome face of a minister in his mid-thirties.

"I saw your headlights," he whispered. "I must admit I've never seen a Catholic nun praying in a Baptist Church."

"Any port in a storm; the Gospels link us," she replied.

He nodded. "I agree. Do you need sanctuary, sister?"

"No, I stopped for God's solace and to ask His help."

"May I ask what's troubling you?"

"My Order cares for orphans in Los Alamos, New Mexico. I am in the midst of my annual fund-raising trip. It is a failure. I had hoped to raise nearly fifty thousand dollars to see us through the year. I have barely four, which might sustain us for six weeks, if we stretch. I need help, fast."

"I wish I could give you what you need."

"We who serve the Lord sometimes have a rough road," she replied, sadly.

"Still, I can join you in prayer?" the young minster asked.

"Another voice can't hurt," she said, adding, "Rejoice in hope, be patient in tribulation, be constant in prayer."

"Romans 12:12," the minister whispered.

"You paid attention in Divinity School," she said, smiling.

The minister patted her delicate hand and began to pray.

4

Sometimes life is a big pile of shit, Emma Cassidy thought, as a Baptist minister and a Catholic nun joined hands in prayer in New Cordell, Oklahoma.

Tomorrow, Emma would close a 60-year-old newspaper and release her staff. The day would surely be dark but at this late hour in Ft. Mitchell, Kentucky, her boyfriend's rebuff was the issue. He had just slammed the door on their relationship, a union Emma thought would last.

"You're leaving?" she asked, completely surprised.

"My run at THE PLAYHOUSE is over. I have a major role in a new Broadway musical. They liked my audition. My performance should be my sole focus."

"Pidge," Emma argued, "you know I'm closing the newspaper tomorrow. I'll join you in Manhattan."

His back stiffened as he locked his suitcase. Her reply surprised him. It was unexpected. He had to level with her.

"Emma, I really like you but I do not love you."

He lacked the courage to look at her.

"Did you ever?" she asked, shocked.

He lifted the suitcase to take his leave.

"The sex was great, until you blew out your knee."

"You son of a bitch," she said. "It was all about sex?"

"Mostly, but we did have a few laughs and some good times. You liked it, too. I must go; they're sending a plane."

"A bit late in the day, isn't it?"

"Rehearsals begin at eight a.m."

She sat on the bed, forcing herself not to cry. He tried to kiss her goodbye, but she turned away.

"I hate to ask," he said. "Do you have any twenties?"

"Cabs take credit cards."

"I guess," he said. "Whatever, I'm out of here."

"Fuck you, Pidge," she whispered. "Break a leg."

5

Finally, a trucker stopped. As Emma Cassidy showered away her sorrow in Kentucky, Sam Toliver hustled down a road near Toledo, Ohio, hopped onto the running board, and opened the cab door of a bread hauler.

The driver, a middle-aged man with a graying beard, seemed cordial. Toliver took a seat inside the warm cab, placing his knapsack beside his feet.

"Where you headed?" the driver asked.

"Fayetteville, North Carolina...Fort Bragg. They got a program for vets of the 82nd Airborne...jobs and rooms, an opportunity to restart my life."

"I can take you north of Columbus, how's that?"

"Beats the shit out of walking in January cold and snow," Toliver said, fishing a cheese sandwich out of a pouch.

"Hot coffee is in the big thermos, if you've got a cup."

"I have just the thing," Toliver replied. He found an empty canteen. "I usually have water, but I'll add coffee, thanks."

"Looks like you're a seasoned traveler," the driver noted.

"I've been *on the road*, off and on, for fifteen years. I work some and travel some, and sleep where I can find a warm spot. I've been lucky and my health is reasonable."

"You don't have a family?"

"I had a wife and daughter long ago; they died in a house fire, bad space heater. I had a small farm, too, but I was no good on the land. Sold the place and hit the road, thinking I might do it for the summer. I've been at it ever since...traveling, seeing new places, avoiding shadows."

"Shadows, what does that mean?"

"All the evil shit we face in life."

The driver nodded, saying, "I can understand that. Most of us face a boat-load, huh?"

"You betchy," Toliver replied.

6

Two men stood in darkness at three in the morning just off the Las Vegas Strip. Far to the east, in Ohio, a trucker dropped a lonely hitchhiker off near Columbus.

"I didn't find the diamonds," Kuba *Honey* Pszczoła said. "She had a safe. I cracked it. No stones."

Louis Shaw nodded. "Maybe you should ring her neck, Honey. Put needles through her nipples. I don't care, do what you got to do but get my grandmother's diamonds."

"You haven't heard, Louis?" Honey countered.

"Heard what?"

"Amanda died…of a brain hemorrhage."

"Jesus, does my brother know, what about my old man?"

Honey shrugged. "I haven't called either one."

"Kyle and the old man had a real dust up. Apparently, Amanda heard it. Kyle finally grew a pair and told the old man to piss off."

"Your old man could anger the Pope. Anyway, Amanda is toast. My contact says she died about thirty minutes ago."

"Damn," Louis said. "The pot of goo thickens."

"The scars of others teach us caution," Honey whispered.

"Who said that?"

"St. Jerome, a doctor of the Catholic Church," Honey replied. "In essence, we should learn from the bloody mistakes of others. Tell your father I'll get the diamonds. I'll take another run at Amanda's place before sunup. No one will see me."

"Honey, do you think Amanda went to heaven or hell?"

Pszczoła shrugged. "I'd say heaven. Why do you ask?"

"Paradise just got one great piece of ass."

Louis Shaw laughed, entered his Jaguar, and departed. Honey walked to his Harley. What a fucking mess, he thought, but they pay me well. He needed strong coffee.

7

I decided to leave Buffalo and execute a retired Pittsburgh police lieutenant about five seconds after I read Manny Tobias' letter and watched a recording from a memory card.

There was never a doubt that Aaron Cooper would die or that I would kill him. The key to success was timing and planning. I had to prepare, ease out of my job, sever ties in Western New York, and do it all without raising suspicion.

As I showered that morning, I remembered my initial reaction. I held my breath when Cooper broke Jill's neck. I screamed when he tossed her aside like a bag of bones. When he found that key in her purse, I knew he would find Jill's and my money. Rage boiled in my blood.

When I could breathe again, when the jackhammer stopped pounding in my head, the bone-deep sorrow I felt morphed into a fiery vengeance.

My dear, sweet, flawed Jill made four poor choices. She withdrew two-thirds of our money from a joint account. She took it to Pittsburgh. She mentioned the money to a crooked cop. She admitted hearing that cop's private conversation.

Even though I would never grasp her distorted logic, Jill thought she was helping me. Tobias' recording revealed that detail. She knew I needed money to purchase real estate. The fact that she took it to Pittsburgh while I was hundreds of miles away in Central New York will forever remain a nagging and unresolved mystery.

Thankfully, fate intervened.

For some inexplicable reason, Tobias witnessed Jill's murder. Because he did, Cooper stood in my crosshairs. I can think of no other logical reason for Tobias to be standing beside that snowy alley in Pittsburgh on that particular night at that specific time except to help me.

Because of Tobias, Cooper was a doomed man.

I wanted revenge. I could taste it. I embraced it as a mother hugs her child.

In his letter to me, Tobias asked that I give his information to a responsible authority. He did not know that I would be the only authority he would ever need.

I chose to become judge, jury, and executioner. To me, my choice made perfect sense. I knew how to kill. I had done it many times for my country. I had the skill and the experience, and I could handle the residual emotions that haunt a man after he ends a life, especially in cold blood.

I understood revenge. I would do it secretly. I could manage the psychological waves that try to turn a man into mush. I also knew that revenge grants but one chance to get it right. I knew if I screwed up, I would either die or end up in jail. Consequently, I prepared and did my homework.

Postings on Pittsburgh Web sites defined Cooper as a caring and thoughtful cop, a knight exemplar of a modern age. Informative on-line articles and interviews lauded his sterling public service. The consensus: Cooper was a shining star, a diamond of rare clarity, the best of the best.

Remarks from the chief of Pittsburgh's Police Department and the head of its Narcotics Division defined Cooper as a meticulous officer, a leader, the crème de la crème.

Others in authoritative positions, like prosecutors, criminal defense attorneys, and fellow police officers, offered similar sentiments. A few ex-cons plugged Cooper's skill and fairness. One reformed addict actually described him as a mentor, a man who transformed lives from bad to good.

Reporters described Cooper as smart, modest, and affable, an irreproachable public servant. Collectively, police leadership agreed that Pittsburgh's loss was Santa Fe's gain.

It was all crap. Tobias' recording disclosed another, darker side of Cooper that his adoring public had never seen.

I spent hours studying on-line digital streams.

I studied Cooper's expressions, inflections, and non-verbals. He was oily and vane, his persona a façade, with something deeply askew in his eyes and nuances. He covered it well, but not completely. It was there. I saw it. I was sure of it. I knew he was corrupt.

Despite my bias, I honestly understood why authorities in Pittsburgh placed Cooper on a pedestal. His arrest rate was unrivaled. He brought down hundreds of addicts and dealers, and thwarted scores of drug shipments into and out of the metropolitan area.

He and his team had captured tons of heroin, cocaine, meth, oxy, hash, speed, and other drugs, which men, women, and kids ingested like Halloween candy. As Vince Redding, my brother, liked to say, "We live in a dumb fucking world, and it's getting fucking dumber all the time." Obviously, Cooper lived and thrived in the midst of that stupidity.

Sadly, the inexorable demand for drugs had tainted the police veteran. According to Tobias, in his twenty-five years of service Cooper had skimmed untold drugs. His position and reputation offered the perfect cover to amass a fortune.

Cooper was a fox. Until he dropped his guard with Jill, no one ever tied him to wrongdoing of any kind.

According to news features, Cooper's morals and reliability scores were off the charts. He was the kind of cop people admired and colleagues tried to emulate, the sort of wily detective that public affairs minions readily select to motivate recruits, rookies, and aging veterans.

Cooper, a master of deception, had fooled them all!

Pittsburgh officials had not read what I read; they had not seen what I saw. They did not know that Cooper had profited from illegal drugs for decades. They did not know the dirty son of a bitch snapped my wife's neck and stole our money as an afterthought to murder. They did not know Manny Tobias was a source, my witness for the prosecution.

I knew! Cooper would die and I would kill him.

The Internet is an amazing resource. A quick search gave me Cooper's Santa Fe address, with street and aerial views. I obtained a plan view of his condominium from the complex's Web site. I knew the layout, the trees, the open areas, the parking facilities, and the surrounding landscape. I would get him, and do it easily.

As for reacquiring Jill's and my money, I had to rely on commonsense, which told me Cooper would have it, and much more, stashed nearby. Most likely, it would be in a safe deposit box or some other venue that Cooper thought secure. The latter might be easier for me to pilfer. I could only hope. Somehow, I would figure it out.

Cooper, hardened by years of deception, had to be extremely reticent. He would stay away from recordable investments, aware that financial flags would destroy him.

Logic told me that Cooper's vanity would negate overseas accounts. He would want to feel and smell his fortune. It would give him a sense of power, satisfaction, dominance, accomplishment, and perhaps sexual arousal. The need to feed his ego would eliminate complications.

Cooper would have his money nearby, stacks of cold, hard cash: not diamonds, or gold, or silver, just unmarked bills and plenty of them.

I smiled as I shampooed my hair.

The bastard would never see me coming.

He would never enjoy his ill-gotten gains.

That was fate, too!

I smiled.

It was but a matter of time.

It was a matter of choice.

It was my cold decision.

I had what I needed: a heart to resolve, a head to contrive, and a hand to execute.

8

As Jack Redding rinsed his hair in Buffalo, Theodora Jefferson was in Tulsa, Oklahoma, fighting an old ennui. Again, she felt empty and on the edge of a precipice. She needed a warm light to take away a chilly darkness.

Theo checked the clock on her wall. She was early. If she left now, she would be on campus an hour before her first class began. She could review student papers and get ahead of the curve. It would certainly ease her load. No, to hell with the papers, she thought, I need help.

She had to quell her uneasiness. Was it the lack of love? Was it a need for a physical relationship? Was it guilt for having left her religion's ministry? Was it her uncle's illness? Was it racial? Was it something entirely different?

If she departed now, she would have time for a cup of coffee with her good friend Lillian Ayers, a Princeton-educated physician/psychologist.

Maybe Lily can point me in a better direction.

Theo put on boots, a hat, and her winter coat and, before leaving for the university, spread salt on her porch and sidewalks. A storm was coming. The salt would prevent ice.

She opened her jeep, started it, and let it idle in the cold.

She made the sign of the cross, thinking a prayer was in order. She still prayed for guidance and inspiration.

Theodora Jefferson, professor of history, knew prayer was a powerful antidote, that it would help take her mind away from her burden.

She finished her prayers by saying aloud, "Hear my prayers, oh Lord, come to me in this moment of my distress."

Next, she selected a CD. A moment later, she pulled out into traffic, listening to Wes Montgomery's BUMPIN' ON SUNSET as she drove to the University of Tulsa.

Music was a powerful antidote, too.

9

Ever since childhood, Tulio Garcia arose before dawn. Tulio was the maintenance man at EL CORAZÓN CONDOMINIUMS, in Spring Valley, west of downtown Las Vegas. His sainted mama told him he would live a happier, more productive life if he arose early and he believed her. He had a good job, with good pay, and a wonderful family.

As Theodora Johnson entered the University of Tulsa campus, Tulio lifted his tools and walked to the day's first job, strolling along happily in the soft light of dawn.

Tulio had a work order to replace the switches and wall sockets on the patio behind Amanda Cassidy's condominium. He had hoped to get to the assignment the evening before, but a family issue forced him away.

He took the walkway that led around Amanda Cassidy's condominium, unaware of her stroke or subsequent death a few hours earlier in a Las Vegas hospital.

This will be an easy job, he thought. All I have to do is exchange two switches beside the patio door and the two all-weather sockets beside the grill and I will be on my way. Maybe, the job would take ten minutes, maybe a few more.

He set his tools down and stooped to flip the breaker that controlled the condominium's external electricity. Having been shocked twice before, Tulio always heeded the owner's advice: "It's risky, Tulio. I installed circuit breakers outside of each unit. They control the external electricity," Bill Hawkins said. "For outside work, we won't bother the residents or worry about lighting up like a Christmas tree."

As Tulio reached for the breaker the patio door opened behind him. Thinking it was Amanda Cassidy, he started to turn to greet her.

A winged insect surged past his eye. Tulio attempted a feeble swat, smelled sweet flowers, and passed out.

10

Based on Jill's comment on Tobias' recording, Aaron Cooper had twenty kilos, roughly forty-five pounds of coke, the night she died. Presumably, he had a lot more.

From my research, twenty kilos of pure cocaine could fetch some six hundred thousand dollars in a dealer buy. I did some simple math, spread it over twenty-five years, and realized Cooper probably had gobs of money.

I had to assume Cooper was still moving drugs. If so, it could be a complication and I had to be ready for it.

I turned off my shower in the converted carriage house in Buffalo where I had shared a life with Jill. I opened the glass door, and dried myself with a large red towel. Jill loved red towels. It was yet another reminder of my loss.

As I hung the towel on a hook and slipped into a pair of shorts, I remembered Cicero's words from Roman History in my academic days: *The life of the dead belongs in the memory of the living.*

Jill, once my life, now only filled my memories.

I ran my fingers through my damp hair, reached for my razor, and studied my face in the mirror. A hard and determined man stared back at me: cold eyes, fearless heart.

What was Cooper doing at that precise moment? Did he feel immense release? Did he think he had made it? He had to believe he defeated the system. Did he even remotely consider that a hellhound had his scent, that I would eventually track him down and kill him?

If he dropped his guard, it would make my task easier.

"For you, Jill," I whispered as I wiped steam from the bathroom mirror. "Despite a few hard days, you were my joy and my love."

Soon, I would be the hunter and I was a damned good one. I would take him down. I would end Cooper's life.

11

An untraceable, throw-away cell rang in Detroit, Michigan, as Jack Redding rinsed his razor in Buffalo. Tony Sarcusi, rolled over, noticed the time, and answered on the third ring. Only one person had this specific cell number.

"C," he said, "it's not even six-thirty in New Mexico. Get a life, man. Why are you up this early?"

"I take it you were sleeping," Cooper said, laughing.

"As a matter of fact, I was. I stayed late for inventory. I hope you're on a disposable."

"Yeah, it's clean. How's business?"

"Booming, because the economy sucks people tend to nest, which means they buy more of our meats, cheeses, pastas, and sauces. Our produce is the best in Michigan."

"Traditional sauce still the big seller?" asked Cooper.

"Nobody's tops it. Why you calling; aren't you living the good life out there in the high desert?"

"I have some Quesillo, are you interested?"

Sarcusi, Cooper's former partner, became immediately attentive. Quesillo was their operative word for pure Colombian cocaine. Without saying it, Cooper wanted Sarcusi to find an interested buyer and arrange a deal. Sarcusi quickly slipped out of bed, moved to the bathroom, and closed the door to prevent his wife from eavesdropping.

"How much you got, bud?"

"Fifty K, topline, primo, the best," Cooper replied.

Sarcusi whistled, fifty kilos! "What's the bottom line?"

"I want thirty a kick; COD, with a hand-off at the taste test. The buyer must assume immediate ownership.

"Does my usual commission apply?"

"I'll make it twelve, because it's my swan song. It's time to retire and live quietly. I've been doing this a long time."

"It's got to be a broad," Sarcusi said, chuckling.

"Yeah, I've met an incredible woman. I'll do one final transaction. Then, she and I will live a special life."

Sarcusi did the math, fifty kilos at thirty grand a pop was a million five. He would clear a hundred eighty thousand for the hook-up, a tidy return for minimal effort, and tax-free. All he had to do was find a serious buyer.

Sarcusi quickly went through a mental checklist. He eliminated a bunch of names because they were punks. Then, the names of two very important men surfaced.

"Let me ask around. I'll get back to you."

"You have my number. You'll call in a couple of days?"

"Sure," Sarcusi said, adding, "You against delivering?"

"If I deliver, the price is thirty-five and your commission reverts to six percent. It's risk-related. It's a better deal if you or someone you trust picks it up."

Sarcusi thought briefly about third-party drivers, but quickly decided that option was too problematic.

"I'll do it," Sarcusi agreed. "We need proper safeguards. Besides, I like the twelve percent and tight control."

"It's a more responsible way to go," Cooper stated.

"C, the outfit I'm considering will be very unhappy if you screw with them, in any way. They'll be taking a huge risk for which they'll expect an excellent return."

"We're cool," Cooper said.

"Listen C, they'd be angry with me, too," Sarcusi added. "Do you get my drift?"

"Sure, I do and, as I said, we will not have problems. I'll keep the cheese dry and await your call."

"I'll get back to you. We'll talk soon."

"I'll be waiting. Incidentally, can you send me a case of the traditional sauce second-day delivery and, please, throw in assorted boxes of pasta? I've begun to cook and the woman I'm with loves Italian."

"Consider it done," Sarcusi said, ending the call.

12

As I packed my bags in Buffalo, latent skills bubbled up inside from a syrupy abyss, where fragments of covert jungle incursions prowled like bottom feeders.

One skill I favored was circumstantial analysis, an analytical method I used when my Army Ranger Red Robin Teams secretly entered South American countries. The technique forced me to consider iffy situations, anticipate twists, and have solutions ready. It minimized Murphy's Law because in combat, as in life, shit always happens.

I had some two thousand miles of cold road and a handful of days before I would try to take Aaron Cooper's life. Conditions could not spiral out of control. If shit happened, I would be ready. I would live. Cooper would die.

"Cooper murdered Jillian Redding," Tobias wrote. *"He's a lowlife Pittsburgh narcotics cop. He's not a hero. He's as dirty as dog shit. The bastard skimmed drugs and cheated the system for twenty years. I watched him kill her; I heard her skull crack. Make him pay, make that bastard pay!"*

Indeed, I would. My brand of justice was swift, and final! My way eliminated mistrials, appeals, and verdict reversals. Maybe it would heal my disdain for the Pittsburgh Police.

Early on, my gut told me someone had killed Jill and stole our money. I told the cops, hoping they would agree. They did not. They did not have a clue and, without a clue, a cop's guess is as empty as the wisps of desert wind that would eventually slide over Aaron Cooper's unmarked grave.

The cops did not care. Calling Jill's death accidental made their job easy. Now, that I possessed evidence, my gut told me they would be greatly pissed if I rubbed their noses in their insularity and incompetence.

As for the money, I believed the boys-in-blue stopped searching immediately and were too embarrassed to say so.

Sure, they would call me if they happened to find the money or if someone walked in with it. Realistically, how often does some mook trot in off the street with gobs of cash? Try never. Even if I hand-delivered Tobias' evidence and the cops did leap into action, some high-dollar district attorney or crusty old judge could torpedo my proof.

The reasons seemed obvious: too grainy, not verifiable, altered photographically, no time code, obscure faces, and so on. Typical bullshit from people who would not try if they thought they could not win. For all my effort, I would end up right where I was, mired in icy mourning and on my own.

Instead, I would clean the slate.

First, I'd get my money. Second, I'd kill Aaron Cooper. Third, I'd bury his body. Fourth, I'd live a damned good life.

I looked in my bedroom mirror. A wry smile crossed my lips. Revenge is best when it seasons a guilty man's bile. I knew how to pull a trigger. I had done it before. I would do it again. I felt it morally wrong to allow Cooper to live knowing that he killed Jill and stole our money.

I opened my bedroom safe and removed a handgun—a vintage 1911 U.S. Army Colt .45. I checked the chamber and removed the clip. I wrapped the weapon and three clips in separate plastic bags and placed everything in a duffel bag.

I pilfered the .45 in a covert operation a number of years ago. I never thought I would use it for anything, not even target practice. The well-oiled weapon, a memento of a clandestine war, was now a means to an end. That it was unregistered complemented my intent. No one could ever trace the handgun or bullet characteristics back to me.

I placed my grandfather's fixed-blade hunting knife next to the old Colt and packed several red hand towels around each weapon to secure the fit in the duffle bag.

Ammunition, binoculars, and a 12-gauge five-shot pump were in a bin behind the seats of my pickup truck.

My suitcase and my duffel bag would be there, too. A silencer lay hidden in the suitcase. I had packed tools, too.

I took every bullet I owned because I would not buy ammunition *on the road.* Clerks asked too many questions and I did not want strangers having an edge: no paper trails, in-store cameras, or memories of customers or counter staff. If my private arsenal of roughly four hundred rounds could start a small war, it was enough to kill one bad cop.

I lifted my *Cooper file* and placed it in my suitcase. It was thicker than I realized. I had gleaned a lot of information from the Internet.

Tobias' memory chip was in a spare phone in a side pocket. A copy of Tobias' letter and a copy of his recording were on a DVD, and sealed in an envelope with detailed instructions. I would give the envelope to my brother, when I visited him later in the day. I trusted Vince completely. He would do what I asked, no questions asked.

Vince was my fallback on the off chance that Cooper killed me. In the instructions, which I hoped he would never read, I asked Vince to give everything to the FBI. I wanted the Feds to know that Cooper moved drugs; that he killed Jill; that he took our money; and that he most likely killed Tobias and me to cover his tracks.

I paused, swallowed my anger, and forced myself to calm the throbbing rage that seemed to creep up on me when I least expected it. As a diversion, I concentrated on Cooper. The retired cop spent his entire career in the narcotics division. It gave him the perfect cover to lift drugs and accumulate a fortune.

An enterprising cop could pocket a kilo of coke or a bottle of pills before the confiscated drugs hit inventory. He could figure a way to sell the stuff via lowlifes. Repeat the process often enough and an immoral man could make a bundle.

My take: Cooper was wily, cautious, patient, and smart.

I was not worried. I was wily, and cautious, and patient, and smart, too. I was also resourceful. Cooper had no idea how much pain I would rain down upon him.

I rummaged through my nightstand for a sewing kit and saw a stack of outdated day timers. Sorting them, I found one from 2002. I sat on the bed and opened it to June 14.

Jill is lovely; she warms my heart.

I wrote the simple, truthful observation the day I met Jill, Jillian Wellington. My life changed that day and hers did, too. Unfortunately, too much alcohol eventually killed her. It destroyed her from the inside out.

Before the booze, everything fit together perfectly.

After the booze, nothing aligned.

Square edges, round holes, broken hearts, and shattered dreams. It all seemed evil and so damned wasteful.

I swallowed a bitter lump. Jill was dead. I could not bring her back to life. I could only do the right thing. I would find our money and kill Cooper. The cops would never know.

Goddamn it! Jill deserved better than she got.

I lifted Tobias' letter off the bed and reread the opening paragraph for probably the thousandth time:

Jack Redding, I know who killed your wife. I know who took her money. I know where you can find him. He is a drug-dealing, crooked cop. If you are reading this, most likely I am dead or, if I got lucky, back in jail…

"I miss you, Jill," I said, looking at her photograph on the nightstand. I lifted it and touched the glass by her cheek. "You broke my heart, kid. You didn't mean to, but you did." Tears came. "Maybe I broke yours, too. I'll kill him, Jill. The others were for my country; Cooper is for you."

I slid Tobias' letter between Jill's photo and the backing, tossing the day-timers into a wastebasket.

I set my sewing kit and the framed photograph between two folded shirts in my bag. Hiding the letter was my only mistake. Eventually, I would come to believe that it destroyed a very real and honest possibility for a new life.

I was about to close the duffel bag when a thought hit me. I removed bottles of Jill's tranquilizers and sleeping pills from the nightstand. They might come in handy. I packed them in with socks, jeans, slacks, sweats, underwear, and several nylon pullovers. I zipped the bag with finality.

Life moved on; I would, too!

I forced the fact that I would soon kill a man into the dark recesses of my mind. Although it was a daring choice, I would not dwell on it in the short-term.

Instead, I focused on a deep yearning for change. Something stirred my soul and pushed me forward. I needed space and room to breathe.

I needed dry air, hot days, high skies, and wide horizons.

I yearned to cleanse my spirit, soften hard memories, and burn away hours and days of raw and unwanted emotion.

Jill did not ask for any of it and neither did I.

I would do what I had to do and start a new life.

I would wipe the slate clean.

13

Not unlike Jack Redding, Liza Mercer also thought about a fresh start that very day in Santa Fe, New Mexico. She was in love with Aaron Cooper. Something about the man made her heart do cartwheels. She saw intrigue in his eyes and found his animal magnetism appealing.

Mercer, an exquisite portrait artist, was at work in her studio. She loved to paint early in the morning, when the world was quiet and seemed at peace. Because of Cooper, her concentration was slightly off. She put down her brush and walked to the window. What was happening to her?

Liza never thought she would fall in love again. After the death of her first husband, she decided to go it alone. She built her life on her talent, educated her children, and was pleasingly independent. She had male friends and physical relationships, but always she was overly reticent. Then, unexpectedly, Cooper asked her to dance, they talked and laughed, and her self-imposed restraint disappeared.

He was sexy, caring, humorous, and yielding, everything a woman with her independent flair found appealing. Money never seemed an issue; in fact, they never discussed it. He told her about his pension, luck with investments, and several inheritances. Financially, he seemed sound.

With her wealth and his, they could do what they wanted, when they wanted. The freedom and adventure of it seemed terribly appealing, too.

From her studio window, shades of pink on the horizon fascinated her. Even though clients demanded her portrait skills, she loved to paint landscapes, especially if she could capture nature's variant colors. Quickly, she went back to palette and canvas.

Liza smiled; this landscape was for her new love.

Aaron Cooper was a rare gift of nature, too.

14

Rosemary Tomasulo paused at a magazine rack in the narthex of St. Paul's Roman Catholic Church, in Kenmore, New York, not far from her Buffalo home.

The morning mass she had attended ended at about the same time Liza Mercer was working feverishly to capture the irregular hues of dawn on her canvas in Santa Fe.

Rosemary thumbed through several publications and then picked out a copy of GUIDEPOSTS MAGAZINE. She loved the heartwarming stories and the recipes.

"I was at your concert the other night, Mrs. Tomasulo," a young priest said.

Rosemary looked at the assistant pastor and smiled.

"Did you enjoy the music, Father Stephens?"

"I did…I especially liked the Ellington selections you played. I love jazz, I didn't realize…"

"That an old bitty such as I would play those marvelous selections," she said, chuckling.

"I didn't realize you played jazz. I thought you were devoted to classical compositions; the jazz was a breath of fresh air, it was a wonderful experience for me."

Rosemary put a few dollars in a coffer for the magazine.

"I want a cookie recipe," she said, with a twinkle in her eye. "Father, I've played the music of many diverse composers for more than sixty years. It keeps me young."

He nodded. "Indeed, young you are, let me know when you are performing again."

"I shall."

He blessed her and exited the church.

As Rosemary followed, she made a mental note to send a plate of the cookies to the jazz-loving priest. She would also give a plate to Jack Redding, who lived in her carriage house. His wife's death had hurt him deeply.

15

My first day with Jill was a like a rare jewel. I thought about that day more than all others because of its pure promise and the hint of a new, unblemished life.

Sitting on my bed in Buffalo, preparing to leave my life there behind, I remembered that the early years were sweet; I also remembered how the years soured over time.

Jill did not cope with the miscarriages or deaths of loved ones. Booze became her chapel and her refuge.

In the end, the gin, vodka, or whatever-the-hell she swilled at any given moment of any given day did not provide one ounce of consolation. It masked Jill's pain, deepened her depression, and destroyed a beautiful woman. It nearly destroyed me, too.

Much-too-much alcohol consumes everything in its path; it defies nature, darkens souls, crushes love, and ends lives.

If the alcoholic years, as I call them, provided any solace, they emphasized the resiliency of the human heart. Never once did I stop loving Jill. I loved her unfailingly. I never sought another woman, even as Jill unraveled before my eyes a layer at a time.

I always thought or foolishly hoped she would come back to me, full and strong. The way she was in the beginning, on that very first day, when I felt her life's force seep into mine and suggest limitless joy.

I rubbed my forehead and scanned the room.

Everything whispered Jill's name: the books, the clothes, the pillows, the artwork, the perfumes, and the furniture. Even the rich reds and dark greens on the walls taunted me. Like a Greek chorus, they chanted about shattered dreams, broken hearts, and unfulfilled promises.

The lack of Jill's presence permeated everything, suspended everything, and redefined everything.

I recalled the scent of her favorite perfume. Without too much effort, I also remembered the sour-sweet scent of booze on her breath.

I considered leaving Buffalo about a year ago, a few weeks after a police detective called to tell me about Jill's frozen body in a snowdrift in Pittsburgh. I wanted to run away.

Because of my anger and confusion, I did not. What would I do? Where would I go? I held everything deep within a very fragile heart, hoping life's natural evolution would assuage the pain.

I thought nature, and prayer, and good deeds, and hard work would make the next day and all subsequent days, better, easier, faster, and more palatable.

It never was. They never were.

Then nearly a year after Jill died, Manny Tobias' letter arrived like a siren's song. Consumed by an intense hunger for revenge, I made a commitment to understand Jill's killer; I compelled myself to learn as much as I could.

Thinking back on it all, my desire to settle the score actually helped save my life. A Chinese proverb says, "If you seek revenge, dig two graves."

I paid to have a grave dug for Jill a year ago. The time had come to open a second for Aaron Cooper. Only after he was in it would I turn the page.

Professionally, too many budgets, deadlines, media plans, commercials, and insignificant meetings fueled my weariness. Interest in my profession soured.

My position as chief operating officer at the city's top advertising agency, once challenging, seemed entirely inadequate. The same was true for many of the people who worked with and for me.

Writers could not write, designers could not design, account managers could not manage, and photographers believed their work rivaled Jesus' beckoning of Lazarus.

As for clients and their attorneys, words like meddling and intrusive seemed apropos, although quite disruptive in a customer-friendly business.

At night when alone, images from my life with Jill lingered like evil spirits. *Should haves, would haves,* and *could haves* swirled like obstinate and ill-mannered ghosts. No matter how hard I tried, I could not wish, or shake, or dream, or pray the apparitions away.

Heartaches grew.

Disappointments festered.

Emptiness rambled.

Memories lingered.

Tender moments. Rich laughter. Wondrous expectation. Unfulfilled potential. Sexual intimacies. Bitter tears. Sad miscarriages. Tragic deaths. Constant drinking. Continuous denials. Retched lies. Chilling screams. Vicious arguments. Deep sorrow. Brutal hurt.

Compounding all of it was our missing money, which added its own sense of loss and confusion.

I first learned about the money a few hours before I boarded a flight for Pittsburgh to identify Jill's body.

For reasons only Jill knew, she withdrew two-thirds of our savings from a joint account. According to her claim on Tobias' recording, she was bringing the money to me. I would go to my grave never understanding her logic. The property we planned to buy was in Buffalo, not Pittsburgh, and I was away on business in Syracuse. It was baffling.

My wife's death and the disappearance of hundreds of thousands of dollars were two big hits to take in one day.

Jill failed.

I did, too.

The marriage was over.

Life, as I knew it, stopped.

Our world spun madly away.

Jill was dead.

Our money seemed lost, forever.

A year of reflection defined my life in awkward phrases when, at my age, robust paragraphs should have been the norm. I could not remember the last time I felt eager about anything, and I yearned to feel excited again. Unexpectedly, in December, Tobias' letter turned indolence into resolve.

Because Tobias had been dead for months, I have often wondered who mailed his letter to me. Perhaps it was my guardian angel.

Thereafter, I resigned my position. My reason: I wanted to leave bad memories behind and create a new life. Of course, it was a deception. My military pension would hold me until I found something else, if I ever worked again.

I planned to kill Cooper. The remainder of my life would take shape afterward. I did not think about it.

Looking out of a frosty bedroom window at eight inches of overnight snow, I decided I would finally depart. This was the day. I would shake off the past, take my dog Bailey, gather up whatever money remained, say goodbye to my landlady, leave Buffalo, visit my brother, and head southwest to end a man's life.

I would travel roads never traveled; see country never seen. Maybe, eventually, I would write books. Maybe I'd gamble some. At one time, I was very good. Maybe I'd meander. Maybe, I'd find work. Maybe I would not. I really did not think much about my life beyond Cooper, only that I wanted it to go on. Whatever I would do, it would begin after I put a bullet in Cooper's heart and another in his head.

My image in the nearby mirror revealed age lines and flecks of gray hair. I was thin, perhaps too thin for my height! Still, I felt strong and in perfect shape.

Jill's death had chiseled hard edges and I misplaced much of my appetite.

In an attempt to diminish my grief, I exercised feverishly. Closer inspection showed regret lingering in my brown eyes, mixed with a significant amount of guilt that seemed to darken the edges of my irises. I had tried to help Jill. My best was not good enough. I doubted anything or anyone could mend the breach. Still, I could even the score.

"You have things to do," I whispered, checking the time. It was 9:24 a.m.

I opened a tattered address book and thumbed through yellowed pages looking for one specific name: William Hawkins. When I found the number, I wondered if I should call this early. It was not yet seven-thirty, Nevada time.

It was not too early. Hawk would be up.

I dialed the number, and waited for the connection.

"EL CORAZÓN," a man's voice announced.

"Bill Hawkins, please."

"Speaking."

"Hawk, this is Jack Redding."

A slight hesitation preceded a surprised reaction.

"Midnight, is it really you?"

For a moment, hearing the nickname from my days as an Army Ranger took me back to covert operations in Mexico and in South and Central America, and the pungent smell of burning bodies.

"Yeah, Hawk, none other," I replied.

"Man, it's good to hear your voice. What's it been, colonel, three years?"

"Less than that, you still own the place, Hawk?"

"Sure do. I added twelve units and paid off the mortgage last summer. Las Vegas is suffering some because of the economy, but my business is booming. People have learned they can still enjoy Vegas if they book a place a few miles out of town for a third of the money."

"That's good for you, huh?" I said.

"It sure is. Some folks live here full time, too. My condominiums are beautiful. Are you headed this way?"

"I've been thinking about breathing some desert air," I replied. "Does your offer still hold…about a place for me?"

"Damn right it does. I have the perfect place." Amanda Cassidy's empty unit flashed in Hawkins' mind. "One just opened up, we'll have to move some furniture, personal items, artwork, and repaint. It won't take long."

"That sounds like a lot of work, Hawk."

"No, it's not, really. I have to do it regardless. Six rooms furnished, plus a kitchen, big closets, a full bath, a half-bath, a small yard…it has a lovely garden and a carport. It's yours, and it's on me."

"I can pay my way, Hawk."

"Let it go my way for a few months…we'll talk about some other arrangement down the road," Hawk replied. "I'm alive because of you. Giving you a place to stay is an honor." Several questions followed a slight pause. "Are you gambling again? I thought you had an arrangement with Jillie?"

Hawk always used the diminutive *Jillie*, which Jill despised. She wanted people to call her Jill.

"Last time I saw you I had and I did."

"I trust things have changed," he said.

"Yes, some. Most of all, I want the feel of new country."

"Sounds like a winner, when should I expect you?"

"It's about twenty-three hundred miles. I plan to visit Ted in Tulsa. I might make a few other stops along the way. I think it will take me about ten days or two weeks. You never know about the weather this time of year. My dog'll be with me, is that a problem?"

"Nope," Hawk replied. "Take your time. Is Jillie coming with you?"

The image of Jill's bloated and bluish body on a gurney in a Pittsburgh morgue peppered my memory.

"No," I said. "Jill died last year, Hawk."

"I didn't know. I'm sorry to hear that," he said.

"I'll tell you more when I see you."

"Still, it's damned sad. When are you leaving?"

"Today; if I get delayed along the way, I'll call."

"That sounds great. I'm always here. It will be good to see you again. The beer is always cold."

"I'll see you in a few weeks, Hawk."

"Roger that, colonel," Hawkins replied. "Roger that!"

I hung up.

Hell, if it was that simple, why hadn't I gone sooner? It really did not matter; I was going now.

My grief and my desire for revenge had finally evolved into a desire to change my life, to find a new course.

I shivered, thinking about Jill's swollen death mask.

I hoped hours of open road, winter winds, cold air, and the ultimate quiet of the western desert would blanch those memories or at least push them far enough away to allow me to begin to feel normal again.

Normal?

I never thought a yearning to be normal would matter to me as much as it did.

16

Ray Lopez studied the distant skyline of Las Vegas and then walked into the office at EL CORAZÓN a few minutes after Bill Hawkins ended his conversation with Jack Redding. Lopez sported a puzzled expression.

Hawkins looked up from his desk and said, "What's up?"

"Bad karma over at Ms. Cassidy's place, I found Tulio out cold on her patio."

"Did he shock himself again? I *told* him to use the breakers. He has to start listening."

"It's not that. I had one of the boys drive him to Urgent Care. He doesn't know what happened. He said he was in the process of pulling the circuit breaker. The last thing he remembers is swatting at some sort of insect and then I was standing there beside him.

"I'll be darned," Hawk said. "Tulio's not a drinker, is he?"

"No, never," Lopez replied.

"Hey, let me know what Urgent Care says."

"Will do."

"Ray, I just talked to an old friend who's coming for a visit. He'll be here in about ten days. We need to move Amanda Cassidy's things into storage. Put everything in the corner of the warehouse and schedule a crew to repaint. I want my friend to have that particular unit."

"Should I refurnish or is a moving van coming?"

"Refurnish."

"The western motif?" he asked.

Hawkins nodded. "Sure, we have everything, let's use it."

"You got it, boss," Lopez said. "I'll get on it right away."

"Before we do anything, I want to call the police. Just to make sure we are good to go with Cassidy's unit. Because of her boyfriend's call to 911, I want to check to make sure the authorities do not have an ongoing investigation."

17

Las Vegas Detective Jacob Stola was searching for his address book when his telephone rang. He took a quick sip of coffee, answering the call on the third ring.

"Stola," he said. His voice, almost a whisper, was a contradiction to his persona. He was 6' 2" and mostly muscle. A man many people tried to avoid.

"You have a call from Bill Hawkins at EL CORAZÓN. He has a question about the death of the woman that occurred there the other night."

It was Marlene, the administrative assistant, a real tease. If I were fifteen years younger and twenty pounds lighter, I might try tapping some of that, Stola thought.

"Put him through," Stola said.

"You got it, big boy," Marlene whispered, huskily.

He smiled, shook his head, and heard a clicking sound.

"Lieutenant Stola," he said, his voice was calm and polite, as it always was with a taxpayer.

"Hi, Bill Hawkins here, I own EL CORAZÓN."

"Yes sir, how can I help?"

"I am looking for some direction," Hawkins replied. "It's concerning Amanda Cassidy's death, the woman who had a stroke and died. Do you remember the 911 call?"

"Certainly," replied Stola.

"We want to begin to repaint and refurnish her condominium. I am just checking to see if we can proceed. No investigation, right?"

"Nothing," Stola said, "She died of natural causes. She was pretty and relatively young. Life moves on, huh?"

"Yes, it does." Hawkins said goodbye and hung up.

Harry Stanton, Stola's partner, looked up from the financial pages. "Anything?" he asked.

"Just routine," Stola said, picking up his address book.

18

Gordon Shaw met Honey Pszczoła in a café, east of Las Vegas on Lake Meade Boulevard. Shaw requested the face-to-face because sons and cell phones were problematic. At precisely that same moment, Jack Redding was in Buffalo contemplating another telephone call.

"Did you find the diamonds?" Shaw asked.

Honey dabbed an egg yolk with toast. "I did not. She hid them well. For a woman close to death, she was alert. Her brain worked fine until the moment it exploded."

"However, you went in again?"

"I took another run. Getting in was easy. I flipped the lock on the patio door the first time I was there. I checked everything I could lay my hands on. She had her act together. Is Kyle sure she had the diamonds in her condo?"

"Yes, he gave them to her. He claims she put them in her desk. He said she was going to use them for a photo shoot. Then, they left for the day. In his defense, he thought they were the knockoffs. He's pissed at me."

"Do you blame him?"

"Not really, she heard us arguing and stormed out."

"I thought it might be something like that."

"I said some stupid things about her."

"That's too bad."

"Yeah, it is. Kyle and I were in my library. She must have heard me. How long were you inside her place?"

"Two hours, the diamonds can't be far from the front door. Amanda was inside only minutes before she collapsed."

"I need the diamonds back," Shaw said, emphatically.

"I know."

"With her death, if those diamonds become part of Amanda's estate, I cannot prove they weren't a gift. I do not want a legal fight. That is my real concern."

"What about the serial numbers? Aren't they registered?"

"Did you hear me? No court...if I sue, issues surface that I must avoid at all costs. I could kick Kyle's ass for a month."

"Don't be too hard on him."

"Jesus, what was I thinking? This mess is my fault; I should have taken the diamonds to the bank. I should never have argued with Kyle or demeaned Amanda."

Honey studied Gordon Shaw's expression.

"Don't worry. I'll get the diamonds. No one will know."

"It has to be that way. There's something else."

Hearing Shaw's tone, Honey waited.

"In the 1980s, my father was broke. He sold the teardrops illegally, under the table, avoided taxes, and kept his business afloat. It worked. When he was financially able, he tried to buy the originals back. They were gone, cut for smaller settings. So, he did the next best thing."

"Black market conflict diamonds," Honey whispered. "Does Kyle know?"

"Maybe," said Shaw. "He and my father were close. Who knows what that senile old fuck told him? The originals had ID; the Black Markets did not. My father never fixed that; I will. If this goes public, I will have insurance issues and the feds and activists will be all over my ass. Let's avoid that. Are you with me on this...there's a bonus in it for you."

"I'll do what I can," Honey said. "Oh, I had to chloroform a maintenance man as I was leaving Amanda's place. I always carry the stuff. He was stooping to fix something. He never knew what hit him. I put him down like a stone monkey."

"I find no self-aggrandizement in that statement," Shaw said, reaching for the sweetener.

Despite the fact that both men laughed, the worry and cold concern evident in Gordon Shaw's eyes could have chilled a small house for several days.

"Either you get the diamonds or you help Kyle get them."

19

Before loading my pickup truck in Buffalo, I flipped through my directory, found another number, dialed it, and learned the phone was not in service.

I dialed Tulsa information and requested a listing for Theodore Jefferson.

"Sir, I do not have a listing for Theodore Jefferson. I do I have a listing for Theodora Jefferson at 15 Parkside Lane," the operator replied. "That is in Tulsa."

I authorized the connection and, after five rings, heard an automated voicemail. I left a message, wrote down the address and phone number, tossed my address book into my carryall, and looked at my dog.

"Bailey, you need to go outside. We'll be in the truck a while. You go out and shake things loose."

My yellow lab barked and slipped through his pet flap. I watched him descend the porch steps and find a workable spot in the backyard.

Lots of fresh snow; unmarred mounds were everywhere. Icicles hung like gnarled fingers from gutters. The frost on nearby windows made them appear translucent. Tree limbs hung low from the added weight.

The affluent neighborhood, bordering Buffalo's Delaware Park, was picturesque. A heavy truck rumbled by on the parkway just down the hill, and a horn blared in the distance, somewhere out beyond a line of blue spruce. The sky was gray, threatening more snow. The storm had yet to dissipate and Western New York would get more snow. So be it, in a few hours it would all be a memory.

I looked at smoke curling upward from a nearby rooftop. Several birds with feathers puffed, maybe mourning doves, sat next to a furnace vent pipe, longing for warmth.

Behind the big houses, deep snow created a barrier.

The drifts were chest high. I imagined they were similar to the drifts that covered Jill's body the night it froze solid in Pittsburgh...

...As he entered the U.S. Air Terminal in January 2012, Jack Redding spotted Casmir Kwiatkowski, a police detective. His rumpled trench coat, white shirt, dark tie, and alert eyes announced his presence conclusively. The big Polish cop, with thinning hair and the build of a professional wrestler, smiled slightly, as Jack approached.

A firm handshake accompanied strong eye contact.

Despite the kindness in his eyes, everything about Kwiatkowski's expression said he had seen too much bad in his good life. His tired clothes suggested he was biding time, saving his money to enjoy a well-earned retirement.

"Mr. Redding," the big cop said. "I'm sorry we have to meet under these awful circumstances."

Jack nodded, saying, "You can't change it, detective."

The cop's nod indicated he concurred.

"Still it's tragic," he said.

Jack added, "I guess you've seen your share of tragedy."

"I've seen too much in my nearly three decades," Kwiatkowski replied.

"That long?" Jack replied.

"Yeah, good years and bad...I retire if a few months when it hits thirty. I have a car waiting, do you have luggage?"

"Just what I'm carrying, I won't be here long. I booked a room downtown. I'll leave tomorrow afternoon, after I identify...," Jack hesitated, "...after we finish."

The two men walked side-by-side, maneuvering through a crowd of late-afternoon travelers, none of whom cared a tinker's dam about Jack's visit to identify his dead wife.

As they exited an outer door, another detective stood waiting in the twilight and softly falling snow.

He flicked a half-smoked cigarette into an inky puddle.

"My partner, Sergeant Tom Miller," Kwiatkowski said, making the introduction. "Tom, meet Jack Redding."

The younger cop, maybe in his mid-thirties, shook Jack's hand as they nodded to each other. Miller had an earnest face in an otherwise insincere and contemptuous world.

In unison, the three men entered a black Ford Crown Victoria parked at the curb with its flashers blinking.

Jack sat in the back by himself ostensibly preoccupied with drops of moisture sliding down the side window. He was really thinking about Jill's pretty eyes, realizing he would never see them again. He remembered how warm Jill felt the last time he hugged her. He shivered thinking about her frozen, coatless body beneath a snowdrift.

As they drove away, Jack turned to the detectives and asked to see the spot where Jill died.

"You sure," Kwiatkowski turned, surprised. "I mean it's just an alley."

"I know, but her life ended there and I want to see where she took her final breath. We won't be long."

"We'll go." Looking over at his partner, Kwiatkowski said, "Tom, you know JUMPIN' JOE'S on the Southside?"

"I think so, Caz."

"2000-Block of Carson."

~

Twenty minutes later, they stood in front of a nightclub. By this time, darkness had consumed twilight.

"JOE'S is one of the more popular watering holes in Pittsburgh…good food, too," Miller said, "Great steaks."

Jack noticed Kwiatkowski's embarrassed expression.

"Jesus, Tom, we're not on a sight-seeing tour. Stop with the routine," the older detective scolded. He looked at Jack and shrugged apologetically.

"Sorry," he said.

Jack held his hand up and said, “It doesn’t bother me. I’m not offended. He’s merely making conversation. This is awkward. I’m sure it’s a decent place. Jill would never drink in a dive. Where did the work crew find her body?”

In the background, Rod Stewart’s muffled voice filtered through the restaurant’s walls. A nearby neon sign blinked in perfect rhythm with the beat of the music.

Bring over some of your old Motown records

Jesus, Jack thought, Jill loved THE MOTOWN SONG.

He swallowed his anger to avoid vomiting.

Kwiatkowski removed a flashlight and said, “The spot is this way, Mr. Redding,” pointing the way with white beam.

A few yards later, they turned into a narrow alley, walked a few paces, and stopped.

Listen to the Miracles echo to the alley down below

Jack turned instinctively.

At the end of the alley, he noticed a garage where a single yellow bulb hovered above sagging doors like a votive candle in a darkened chapel.

In the dull amber light, Jack saw snowdrifts nearly as high as the garage-door windows. He nodded, instinctively understanding why Jill chose that particular alley.

“Tell me about the snow,” Jack said.

“Heavy for three days prior to the removal crew finding your wife,” Miller began. “Our theory, she probably left the bar alone, paused here, slipped, fell, and hit her head.”

There's a soul in the city watching over us I swear

“Who watched over you, Jill?” Jack whispered.

"Pardon me," Miller said, turning to Jack.

"Nothing," Jack replied, "Just a prayer."

"She hit her head pretty hard," Kwiatkowski added. "It must have broken her neck. She was on her back against the wall, with her elbows up and head angled toward the gutter near the basement window of the adjacent building."

Jack closed his eyes briefly, shaking his head in disbelief.

"My guess, lieutenant, she thought she was home. The building in the back with the solitary yellow light resembles the garage beside our carriage house, remarkably so."

"It does?" Miller asked, adding, "That might have merit."

Questions were running in Jack's mind. Were you coming home, Jill? Did you think this was Buffalo? I hope you were looking for me. I hope you wanted me. I know you loved me.

"No one saw her through the window from inside the other building?" Jack asked.

"No, that basement room is rarely used. The gutter was snow-filled," Kwiatkowski replied. "The snowfall was heavy. It would have covered your wife quickly. As you can see, it's dark here at night. In a storm and under a drift, no one could have noticed your wife. The crew found her when they plowed. Two converging drifts were waist high. Her purse was on her chest. It's a terrible accidental death."

"This happens a lot in bad weather," Miller added.

"Then, right now, Sergeant Miller, a lot of people feel as desperate as I do. They can't feel any worse," Jack said. "When you called you ruled out foul play. Are you absolutely sure it was accidental?"

"Yes, sir," Kwiatkowski replied, "No evidence otherwise."

Luck is believing you're lucky

"The medical examiner checked her thoroughly," the big cop added. "She broke her neck and fractured her skull."

"She hit her head on the curb," Miller added.

The cop pointed to a spot with the tip of his wet shoe. The black residue might have been a stain from Jill's blood.

"Which break killed her?" asked Jack.

"Both, but the M.E. said the skull fracture imbedded bone in her brain," Kwiatkowski replied.

"Hmmm," Jack replied. "When you called, you said she wasn't wearing a coat? That's odd. Why would she do that in a blizzard, unless she was in a hurry? Was she assaulted?"

"I can't say about the coat. There is no sign of an assault. We think she just fell. She probably tried to brace herself and slipped. Our techs found her coat in the snow."

"You sure she wasn't attacked?" Jack asked.

"Nothing indicates an assault of any sort," Kwiatkowski continued, "When we spoke on the phone, you mentioned she didn't have family or friends here. Why Pittsburgh?"

Jack shrugged as he studied the big cop's sad eyes.

"Jill drank, Detective. Who knows what goes on in a drunk's mind when a bottle's handy? I'll never know how drunks connect the dots. The Panthers played the Bulls on Saturday; maybe she came with someone to see her alma mater. She was a graduate of the University of Buffalo.

"She liked basketball, but I don't really know. I was in Syracuse on business and the weather forced me to stay through the weekend. She'd been dry for five months, a long time for Jill. I thought she turned a corner. I was wrong. When she drank, I'd expect anything and still be shocked."

"We haven't found her car."

"You won't; we sold it because of the booze, maybe a rental?"

"Nothing has turned up."

"The airlines?" asked Jack.

"She wasn't on any flights, and nothing has shown up in bus or train records."

"Most likely, someone brought her here," Jack replied. "Someone she met or knew...another goddamned drunk."

"Can you name anyone?" Miller asked.

"No," Jack replied.

Kwiatkowski added, "That would really help us."

"I doubt we'll ever know," Jack replied. "The person she came with might not even remember. Jill was a beautiful woman, very friendly, more so when she drank. Acting off-the-cuff, she did that a lot."

Jack remembered the first time he saw her. Christ, it was magical! The thought of it still made him breathless.

"You didn't know she was out of town."

"No, she forwarded our home phone to her cell. She was hiding her drinking from me. Drunks know how to deceive."

He heard Rod Stewart's voice again.

I got plans for us playing like a skip on a record through my head all night long

Sadly, Jack and Jill's plans were gone, forever.

"Was she...did she have sex?" Jack asked.

"No signs of sexual activity. No semen, vaginal bruising, or irritation."

Jack nodded, grateful that those demons would not play in his mind continuously.

"How long was she in the snow?" he asked.

"At least three days, maybe closer to four," Miller replied. "We checked with the restaurant staff and a bartender remembers serving her two or three nights running. He thinks the last time was Friday, but it could have been Thursday. He isn't sure."

"It must have been Friday night, I spoke to her that afternoon, and she seemed happy when we talked."

Miller nodded.

"The bartender said your wife wasn't intoxicated, just very happy, almost effervescent," he said, adding, "The snow crew found her Tuesday, mid-afternoon."

"Jill wasn't a sloppy drunk," Jack noted. "She got happier with every sip. The booze hid the things she hated; that's why she drank. Did the bartender mention any friends?"

"He and a few servers said she was with several couples, none of them regulars. Several people, men and women, wandered in and out of the group. We called as many as we could, using credit card receipts. Several people remembered her, but she didn't arrive or leave with them. They said she was unattached," Kwiatkowski offered. "The servers think she left the restaurant alone, but aren't completely sure. The bartender says she was *definitely* alone. We talked to as many patrons as we could. We haven't much to go on. Of course, like your wife, a few paid with cash. We can't follow up with them. She wasn't with a man, if you're asking."

"Do you know where she stayed?"

Miller studied Jack's eyes and Jack was reasonably sure the cop saw sorrow and deep regret.

"We checked the major chains and all of the mom and pops in the area. Nothing, we didn't find a room key in her possession or a reservation in her name. She must have stayed with some nameless someone."

"Not a very fitting end to a beautiful woman's life," Jack whispered to no one in particular. He thought about the missing money. Why did you take our money, Jill? Kwiatkowski had not mentioned it. Did the police even know? Surely, they would say something, if they did. Maybe they were waiting for him to bring it up. Would they mention it, if they suspected robbery?

Jack tried to interpret Jill's logic, tried to understand why she withdrew nearly four hundred thousand dollars. He wished he never went to Syracuse to pitch that new account.

Leaving Jill by herself immediately after Christmas was a mistake. When she did not answer his call on Saturday, he began to worry, but with the storm, he could not leave. Even if he had, nothing indicated she would be in Pittsburgh.

It was futile to try to sort it all out. She seemed fine when he called. Then, she stopped answering.

Goddamn it, Jill, a snowdrift; did you even know where you were? Did you even think about what you were doing? Did you think about me before you died? Did you think our house was at the end of the alley? You said you were fine. You promised you would stop. You broke your promise.

Put the speakers in the window

"No drugs?"

"Drugs were not involved," Kwiatkowski added. "Due to the freezing conditions her blood alcohol was still above the legal limit. The bartender said she never ordered food."

Jack nodded and asked, "What did she have with her?"

"Her purse, her watch and rings, some keys, a cell phone, several hundred dollars, credit cards, some cosmetics, a few odds and ends, and her driver's license. We used it to track you down. She was terribly unlucky."

Jack felt the same way.

"No room key, locker key, anything of that sort?"

"No, sir," said Kwiatkowski.

Listen to the Miracles

"Damn," Jack whispered. "I've seen enough. Let's leave."

His hope for a miracle had vanished.

~

Footsteps echoing down a hallway announced the arrival of two men at a small suite of offices in the morgue.

After introductions, Kwiatkowski ushered him into a small viewing room. Jack stood before a curtained window, his mind numb, his breathing shallow.

He detected movement on the other side of the glass and he noticed shadows through a thin curtain.

A green light flashed twice above the window and the curtains opened automatically.

"They're ready for you, sir," Kwiatkowski whispered.

Jack nodded to the attendant.

Jill's bluish face contrasted against the white surgical sheet scared the hell out of him. He was immediately dizzy.

At least they had the decency to close her eyes.

Indignation swept through his body.

"It's Jill," he whispered.

Aside from some bloating and discoloration, her face was clean and sans makeup. Jill hardly used any. She did not need it; her face got prettier as the years passed—until now.

Jesus, he thought, why go out this way. What was going through her mind? What made her regress?

He remembered the first time he saw her...about twelve years ago, in a library in Buffalo, checking out a book on roses. Great eyes and a warm, inviting smile snared him quickly. If he did not fall in love with her immediately, love blossomed quickly afterward. Six months later, they were married and happy—at least for a while.

Jack was a successful advertising executive and Jill's business thrived. She was a landscape architect. About six years into the marriage her mother died. Quickly thereafter, her father passed. In the mix were miscarriages, accidental deaths, and the bombshell that they could not have children.

Afterward, Jill lost interest in her business and sold it.

Jack did not know it at the time, but she added vodka to everything she drank. When he discovered it, she told him the booze dulled the pain.

He got her help and everything seemed normal, for a few weeks. Then, her sister and her niece died in a freak accident and vodka became Jill's only reality. Thereafter, it became whatever liquor she could find.

Damn it, he did not want to remember her this way.

"That's Jill," Jack repeated. "Close the curtain."

"My sympathy, Mr. Redding," Kwiatkowski said. "You have to sign a few forms and we can release your wife's body. If we learn anything else, I'll contact you."

Jack nodded.

"I'd appreciate that."

~

"Minutes later, they sat in a conference room drinking hot coffee and Kwiatkowski listened as Jack talked.

"So," he continued, "earlier today, before leaving for the airport, I went through my mail and discovered about three hundred and ninety thousand was missing from our savings account. She withdrew the money the same day I went to Syracuse. I phoned the bank right away, hoping it was a mistake. It wasn't"

"If it was a joint account, why did they write to you?"

"It wasn't a letter. The bank sent the withdrawal receipt to my home because Jill left it on a bank manager's desk. My guess, she was probably stiff when she did it. She took the money in cash, thirty-nine stacks of one-hundred $100 bills, enough to fill a good-sized suitcase.

"Was she leaving you?"

"I don't think so. But, I don't really know."

"Why did you have that much money in a joint account?"

"I had consolidated a good portion of our holdings. I was negotiating the purchase of rental property, as an investment and second income. I put the money in our checking account temporarily. We were to sign the papers when I got back from Syracuse.

"Jill received about two hundred thousand, after taxes, for her landscaping business a few years ago. The remainder I saved from bonuses and my pay."

Kwiatkowski raised his eyebrows.

"I know what you're thinking," Jack replied softly. "I didn't do this. If you have to check me out, do it. I will understand. I was in Syracuse when this happened and I can prove it. We were snowed-in. I'll furnish names, addresses, receipts, my cell phone, whatever you need."

"We will check," the cop said, "because of the money but I know you're clean. She stashed it somewhere, most likely."

Jack nodded, adding, "I don't understand why. I have nothing to hide, except a broken heart, unfulfilled promises, and a ton of remorse. Do what you have to do. You will find I had nothing to do with Jill's death..."

...I called Bailey back into the house and dried him with a bath towel.

"You need to be tidy," I said, "when we visit Rosemary."

Rosemary Tomasulo owned the converted carriage house where Jill and I had made our home. She lived in a grand white house atop a hill some fifty yards away, on the other side of a hedgerow.

Rosemary was an angel, a rare human being that all men and women should encounter at some point in their lives. She was a beacon and a rock, the warmth of heaven. She liked Jill and me, and we adored her.

Rosemary understood life and the elation or turmoil that drives its varied emotions. She loved Jill like a daughter and treated me with kindness and respect.

I never saw Rosemary angered by any issue or enraged at any time. She had a charitable and compassionate heart. Had she known I was leaving Buffalo to kill another human being, she would have been devastated.

20

Emma Cassidy stirred a cup of coffee in her Covington, Kentucky, office as Jack Redding wiped his dog's fur in Buffalo. This was D-Day; a day she had dreaded for more than a year, a day deeper and blacker than a virgin tar pit.

THE COVINGTON STAR, the newspaper her father founded, was on the scrap heap. Emma had failed to turn it around, something she promised her dying father that she would work hard to accomplish.

Unfortunately, Emma failed and, riddled with debt, she acquiesced to the obvious.

Moments ago, Emma had released the newspaper's staff, save for a few who would stay to help her shut things down. Forty people were 'on the street' looking for new jobs. In a matter of days, Emma would join them.

Despite an intense effort, her Ivy League business education, and outstanding reportage, THE STAR could no longer compete. The villains were free on-line news, a big-city competitor, and the poison of a down economy.

She coughed and turned toward a knock on her door.

"Emma, some good news, I think."

Her operations manager, Rich Conley, smiled.

"I could use some," she confessed.

"CINCINNATI PRESS took your offer for the printing press, systems, archives, and accounts receivable...however they'll only pay forty-two cents on the dollar.

Emma nodded, doing a quick calculation.

"What is that, two hundred thousand dollars?"

"I figure two hundred three," he replied. "At least you'll have the cash and can stop worrying about those issues."

"Take the deal. That means I'll only have to come up with about four hundred and seventeen thousand to satisfy the full debt."

"Do you have that much money, Emma?"

She nodded. "I do. I'll give the bank the deed to this building, the equity in my house, and I'll sell my car and my jewelry. When the dust settles, I'll walk away with about thirty grand. Not much, but enough to start over."

"You can always choose bankruptcy protection."

"I owe the money and I'll pay it. I'll be able to sleep at night. Thank God, I don't have a husband or children. I'll find something. What about you?"

"I'm good," Conley said. "I have investments and a 401K."

He paused, noticeably uneasy.

"What is it?"

"THE PRESS likes what I did with the on-line version of THE STAR. They've asked me to manage their Web site."

"That's wonderful," Emma said, slapping the desk. "That's the best thing I've heard today."

"Same pay…still, I feel like a traitor."

"Nonsense, at least one phoenix will rise from THE STAR'S ashes. I'm happy for you, truly."

"Thanks."

She wiped her eyes with a tissue. "Sorry about the tears," she added. "They come and go. The stench of this current failure has replaced the sparkle of hope I felt five years ago. Our reporting was superior. No matter how hard we all tried, we couldn't get advertisers or subscriptions. I failed and it's damned painful."

"The economy's bad; competition's stiff," Conley noted.

"Yes, still it's a bitter pill to swallow," Emma said. "My father put his heart and soul into this business."

Conley nodded and moved aside for Theresa Hogan, THE STAR'S long-time office manager, who stood in the doorway.

"Emma," she said.

"Hi, Terry."

"Are you going to make it, honey?"

"So far," Emma replied. "I'm not happy, but I know I can't continue to suffer. I tried. Hell, we all tried. It was not in the cards. Closing the business is the right thing to do."

Hogan shrugged. "*C'est la vie.* Emma, an attorney from Las Vegas is on line one, something about your aunt. Do you want to take the call?"

"A call about Amanda, what is it?"

"I don't know. He asked for you and I didn't probe."

Emma took a deep breath and lifted the phone.

"Good morning," she said.

"Miss Cassidy, my name is Lucas Finch. I represent Amanda Cassidy, whom I've learned is your aunt."

"That's correct; she's my father's younger sister."

"Ms. Cassidy, I have the unfortunate task of telling you that your aunt suffered a stroke and died about three this morning, Las Vegas time."

"Amanda is dead?" Emma's hand went to her brow.

"Yes, massive brain damage...the doctor told me she never had a chance."

"A moment, please, I need time to digest this." Emma put her hand to her mouth and wept, inhaling deeply.

Hogan handed her a tissue and Emma dried her eyes.

"I'm sorry, Mr. Finch, this day is shitty and it just got shittier."

"I've had them, too. Sorry you did not know sooner but the police eventually connected Amanda to me. I handle her legal matters and review her contracts. Your aunt is with a local funeral home in Las Vegas. She signed a power of attorney a while ago, for emergencies. I have authority over her estate until you take its reins, as her executor. Since you are her only living relative, her estate is yours and that means you must make a decision on the disposition of Amanda's remains. Will you plan a service in Las Vegas?"

Emma was shaking and felt cold.

Briefly, she saw her aunt in 42ND STREET on Broadway. She remembered how they danced like chorus girls to the music of WEST SIDE STORY, once when her aunt visited.

"I'd like her body sent back home, where she grew up. Many local people will remember her. Can you make the arrangements?"

"Nothing here in Las Vegas?" he asked.

Amanda thought about the expense.

"Have a one-day viewing, please. When we finish this conversation, my assistant will come on the line to provide all the pertinent information. I would like a call back when everything is confirmed and I'll give you a credit card number for any charges."

"That won't be necessary. Amanda was not rich but her estate will cover her final disposition. She collected art and had many valuable pieces. You'll have enough money."

"Just a moment please." Emma covered the mouthpiece and gave instructions to Terry Hogan. "I'm back," she informed the attorney.

"Miss Cassidy, you will need to sign documents as we settle her estate and we can do that via overnight mail. But the art work is extensive and requires personal attention."

"Mr. Finch, I'll come to Las Vegas, to settle everything. I'll need a few weeks. I'm in the midst of shutting down my business. I have legal and financial obligations."

"I'll give all my personal information to your assistant and you can call me at your convenience," he said.

"That will work, thank you. I'll talk to you soon. Please stay on the line. Theresa Hogan, my office manager, will pick up shortly."

As Emma punched hold, more tears flowed.

"My aunt, my parents, the newspaper, Pidge, broken promises, it's all a big fat mess," she said.

"Emma, I'll take care of everything," Terry Hogan said.

"Thank you," Emma replied, adding, "If I've had worse days than this, I do not remember them."

"Sorry for your loss, Emma," Conley added. "I'll be down the hall. Call me if you need anything."

Emma nodded, stood, and went to the window.

Despite bright sunshine and a blue sky, she felt shadows descending all around her.

"Why did this happen," she whispered.

For a moment, she watched a crow picking up scraps of French fries someone had tossed or dropped. Then her mind drifted to her aunt. She tried to remember the last time she saw Amanda. The answer came quickly.

It was her father's funeral.

Families tend to meet at weddings and funerals: a bushel, a peck, and a hug around the neck.

She shivered and returned to her desk. She needed to get back to work. Emma always felt better when she was working and using her mind.

~

As she sat and wiped away more tears, Emma was unaware that her life would change dramatically in the coming weeks and that her current disappointments would fade away and that others would replace them.

Fate whispered in Emma's ear in Covington, Kentucky, but she was too distraught to hear the call.

Still, as is always the case, fate would persevere.

Emma Cassidy would eventually face the toughest test of her life, one that would challenge her courage, resolve, and moral foundation.

21

On this blustery day in late January, before stopping to see Rosemary Tomasulo, I called the Pittsburgh Police to cover my tracks. Not doing so might seem suspicious.

"Kwiatkowski," a voice said.

"Detective, Jack Redding up in Buffalo."

"Hello, Mr. Redding. It's good to hear your voice again," the cop said. Then, somewhat apologetically, he added, "I don't have anything new for you, sir. I'm sorry."

"I know you would have called if you had something new," I said. "That is the reason for my call to you. I'm leaving Buffalo today and I doubt I'll come back. I have a phone number, in case you ever need to reach me.

"I already have your cell number, Mr. Redding."

"That was my business phone. I left my job and turned that phone in with my office keys. I'll get a new phone along the way and, when I do, I'll call."

"Good," the cop said. "Sometimes we catch a break when we least expect it. We still might recover your money and apprehend the person who took it. In this business, you never know."

Sadly, I did know. They would not find a damned penny. I gave him the phone number at Hawk's place in Las Vegas.

"Correct?" The cop asked, after repeating the number.

"Sure is."

"What will you do?"

"Something new, a friend from the Army, lives out west. We served nearly twenty years together. Leave a message, if you get anything. I'd like to hear from you."

"I will, Mr. Redding. Be safe."

"Thanks," I replied and hung up. Seconds later, I shut the door on the home I'd made with Jill. I stowed my items and laptop, and Bailey and I walked over to the main house.

22

Vince Redding had no idea his brother had just talked to the police in Pittsburgh; however, at that moment, he was thinking about him. Jack was the reason Vince invited his attorney to a meeting on this snowy morning in Jamestown, New York.

Unfortunately, Vince did not have long to live, maybe six months, a fact his brother did not know. He wanted to change a section of his Will regarding a lake and woods purchased nearly a hundred years ago by a relative, land that Vince owned through inheritance.

"You look pale, Vince," the attorney said after they chatted for a while.

"I know, Bernie, that's why I asked to see you. Doc says if I have six months, if I'm lucky. Hell, a man has to go sometime, right? Anyway, did you bring the documents?"

"Yes, I have everything right here," the attorney replied, opening his satchel and removing Vince Redding's file.

Vince turned in his chair and lifted a copy of his Will, which had one notable modification outlined in red ink.

The attorney read the changes.

"I have it," he said. "You want to give the cabin, lake, and land to your brother, Jack. In the event Jack is not alive, you want me to sell it all and give half of the proceeds to the Vietnam Veterans of America. The other half goes to the Wounded Warrior Fund."

Vince nodded, asking, "When will the change take effect?"

"Today, as soon as I print it out, you'll sign it and I will, too. The administrator is a notary. He'll witness and stamp it. Then, it is current and you are protected."

"Good," Vince said, nodding. "That acreage has been in my family since the 1920s; a relative bought it after the world war. It should stay with my brother."

23

Rosemary Tomasulo beamed as she opened her back door. She patted Bailey's head and motioned us in from the cold. Bailey sniffed the air, immediately aware that Rosemary was in the midst of doing morning baking.

"Typical Buffalo weather we're having, huh? It makes us hardy. Why don't you and the pooch sit and have a few cookies with me," she said. "I just made coffee, too."

When I smiled, she shrugged knowingly.

"A fresh pot, it's an Italian thing, you know."

"I do know and I like it."

Rosemary pointed toward a coat rack.

"Hang your jacket on a hook."

As I did, she walked to the table with Bailey in tow.

Rosemary, in her mid-eighties, seemed much younger. She was petite, exceedingly pretty, and fiercely independent. A housekeeper came twice a week, but everything else Rosemary did by herself. On this particular morning, she wore a dark blue, long-sleeved jersey dress, a white apron, and beige slippers. Nylon stockings formed rolls around her thin ankles. The silver luster of her gray hair, fixed in a single braid, hinted of expensive pearls. A lacey, silvery hairnet held the intricate braid in place.

"You boys will like these cookies. Peanut butter and oatmeal, with almonds and walnuts," she said, smiling. "I found the recipe in a GUIDEPOSTS MAGAZINE I picked up after morning mass. It sounded delicious." Her eyes filled with joy as she pointed to dozens of cookies on a counter top.

"They smell wonderful," I said. "Will you eat all these cookies; you have hundreds?"

Her giggle was that of a little girl and she blushed slightly. Crimson in her cheeks accented her beauty.

"Don't be silly, they're for the parish kitchen.

"I have a dozen meatloaves in the freezer downstairs, too. My housekeeper will take it all to St. Paul's tomorrow."

Rosemary pulled a chair away from the table for me and returned with a decanter of coffee and plateful of cookies. She broke three into bite-sized pieces and put them on a paper plate on the floor beside her chair for Bailey.

Next, she filled two cups and sat down across from me. From a bottle of Crown Royal already on the table, she added a splash to her cup and, after a nod, some to mine.

"Good for the heart on a cold day," she beamed.

She casually chose a cookie, placed it on a napkin, and broke it in half. As she chewed, I watched the muscles in her elegant jaws and the sparkle in her remarkable eyes. The color reminded me of rare emeralds Jill and I had admired years ago as we 'window-shopped' Cartier on Fifth Avenue.

"You're not working today?" asked Rosemary.

"No."

I removed a gray monarch envelope from my shirt pocket and placed it on the table. Rosemary picked it up and held it in her hands. The same beautiful hands that baked cookies and meatloaves also played jazz and classical piano.

"What's this?" she asked.

Surprise wrinkled the soft skin across her aging forehead.

"Rent for six months," I replied.

Her expression darkened a bit as she studied my face.

"You're leaving," Rosemary whispered intuitively. "You said you might. I hoped it was talk. It's because of Jill?"

I nodded.

"It's time," I added.

"It's sad, you know," she replied.

"The bloom's gone. Jill is in every place I turn, in everything I see and touch. You should rent the carriage house quickly, but if you don't, the money keeps you whole, until you do. You won't be caught short."

“So, then, it’s a permanent move?”

“I think so. I might come back, I don’t know. If I do, I won’t live here, although I would visit you.”

She nodded understanding.

As I tasted a cookie, sadness fill Rosemary’s eyes.

“Delicious,” I said, trying to extend a bit of cheer.

A slim smile whispered her silent thank you.

“Would you do a favor for me, Rosemary?”

“Of course,” she replied.

“When you find time, sell my furniture, clothes and anything else I leave behind, keep twenty percent for yourself, or give it to the poor. Send the remainder to me. An address and a phone number are with the rent money.”

She smiled and nodded.

“I will and with a tracking receipt,” she added. “You know how I am, I like to know people receive the things I send, especially money. I’ll send a money order for whatever I sell. What about your personal mail?”

“I filled out a change-of-address form, it’s in the envelope. Would you give it to the mailman?”

She nodded, opened the envelope, and saw the address.

“Spring Valley, Nevada, is that near Las Vegas?”

I nodded.

“For now…please, keep it to yourself. I don’t want calls from my former employer.”

She touched her chest near her heart and blessed herself.

“My promise to you and God, Jack,” she whispered. Her complexion was virtually flawless. She remained a strikingly beautiful woman who had turned many male heads in her day; maybe she still did.

“I’ve a friend in Vegas,” I explained, “We ate some dirt together in the Army. He’s encouraged me to visit for years. I never found the time to go. Now,” thinking about Jill, “maybe a change is best.”

"You left your job?"

"I resigned a few weeks ago but finished all my assignments. I won't work for a while. I have my military pension, which is a direct deposit. I have my savings, too. If I need more money, I'll find something out west."

"Are you sure? It's a tough economy."

"Rosemary, if a man knows how to write, he can always make a buck. I have money; I'll be flush for a long time."

"You have healthcare? You're getting older." She studied my humorous reaction and shrugged apologetically. "Hey, I'm a mom, a grandma, and a great grandmother. Life's little details worry me."

"I was wounded in the service and because I received the Purple Heart I have the V.A., so, yes, I have coverage."

My comment seemed to ease her concern.

"Are you going to gamble again, Jack?"

I knew her heart would break if she knew I was leaving to kill the man who murdered Jill.

"I doubt it, certainly not like before. Actually, I have the urge to write. I feel a book or two in me. I was a good writer at one time. I only stopped..."

"Because of Jill's drinking," she said, finishing my sentence.

"Yeah, it was too hard to concentrate."

I sipped my coffee, feeling the whiskey's warmth spread in my throat and chest. I gestured at the whiskey bottle.

"It's ironic, booze means nothing to us. She couldn't control the stuff," I said.

"Too bad our beautiful Jill lost her willpower," Rosemary said. "Alcoholism is truly a terrible addiction."

She must have noticed my shoulders sag.

"It hurts," she added.

"Yes, it held her tighter than I realized."

"I know."

Tears glistened in Rosemary's eyes.

"So tight, it killed her," I whispered.

"A senseless way to die," she added.

She pushed the envelope aside and leaned toward me. Rosemary had something important to say and patiently selected the proper words.

"I saw Bailey every day," she began. "I didn't think Jill was gone. I forgot about the pet flap you installed so he could get out on his own. I didn't worry about not seeing her because of the weather; it was cold and snowy. I called her twice every day and she seemed fine." Rosemary wiped her eyes. "Then, I went to visit my daughter."

"It's not your fault," I said. "She forwarded the phone and made sure Bailey had food and water. She fooled me, too."

"She must have left soon after I did," Rosemary replied, fidgeting with a corner of the envelope. She sighed. "I don't need this money, Jack," she said, changing the subject. "I have plenty. Dominic left me with enough and I have my pensions from the symphony and Uncle Sam and the money I make from piano lessons. Money is never a problem. When you get my age, time and keeping warm matter most."

She laughed lightly.

"You were kind to Jill," I told her. "I couldn't have coped if you had not helped us. She loved living in the carriage house. I could never get her to move." I paused, adding, "Six month's rent, it's the right thing to do."

Rosemary Tomasulo's eyes embraced mine.

"You're special, Jack Redding."

"How so?" I asked. Her next statement surprised me.

"You're the only man I know who always does the right thing, regardless of the consequences. Others try, you do. My big-hearted Dominic was the same way."

"It's usually the best way, Rosemary."

I thought about killing Cooper. That was best, too.

She smiled as she folded and tucked the envelope into her apron pocket.

"You're the son I never had; Jill was like one of my daughters. I take it Bailey's going with you?"

I nodded.

"He goes where I go."

She looked at the big dog. "I'm going to miss you, handsome," Rosemary said. Bailey wagged his tail.

I nodded.

"Life evolves, things change," I said.

"Shit happens," she added.

"Yes, it does."

She nibbled a piece of cookie and gave a bite to Bailey.

I took another mouthful of coffee and stood for my jacket.

The old woman came around the table and hugged me, kissing each of my cheeks twice. Her perfume filled my nostrils. I wiped her tears away with my thumbs.

"So, we say goodbye, huh?" she asked, looking up at me.

"For a while, anyway…Bailey and I might be back."

"I hope so. I'll miss you. Write or call from time to time to let this old broad know you're well."

"I will."

"Things move fast with you when you make up your mind, don't they?"

"They always have."

"You'll be in my prayers, Jack."

"And you'll be in mine; you are a uniquely wonderful person, Rosemary Tomasulo."

I hugged her tightly and kissed her forehead. I smelled the fragrance of her shampoo, something vanilla.

"Be safe, Jack," she replied, her voice quivering. Unexpectedly, she added, "The angels and I love you."

She noticed my reaction and shrugged, saying, "I always told the same thing to my Dominic whenever he'd leave."

"I believe it kept him safe," she added. "I trust it will work for you, too. We need angels and love in our lives, as guides."

She kissed my cheek again, patted Bailey's head, went to a cupboard, and returned with a small bag of dog treats and a dog collar with built-in GPS.

"Use the treats on your trip," she whispered. "The collar has a tracking gizmo and a button you set to beep after a specific distance. Don't ask me how it works. I bought it before Jill died. I never found a good time to give it to you."

"Did she want this?"

"No, it was an impulse buy. I thought it would be good for Jill to have, just in case Bailey found a girlfriend and decided to go roaming."

I nodded, took the items, tucked them under my arm, and blew a kiss in her direction. Then, Bailey and I departed.

The last thing I saw in the rearview mirror, as we drove away, was Rosemary Tomasulo standing at her front window, waving goodbye, her face filled with sadness.

A moment later, Rosemary was back at her kitchen counter, preparing another batch of cookies.

What I did not see was her teardrops falling softly onto the cookie dough as she went about her chores.

24

Ted Jefferson was fighting a recurring nightmare in Tulsa, Oklahoma, at the same time Rosemary Tomasulo slid a sheet of cookies into her oven in Buffalo. The same irritable dream had given Jefferson fits for weeks...

...Jefferson waited in the Colombian jungle, anxious for the signal to advance on the Munoz Cartel's compound. The intense heat and humidity pulled sweat from his body and he could feel it trickling down his spine. Fifty feet away, in either direction, his fellow Rangers waited for the same command. Even though he could not see them, they were there. He toggled his radio switch.

"This is Teege," Jefferson said. "What is causing the delay? Why's Midnight waiting?"

"Hold your position, Teege," Hawk replied.

"Hawk, this is bullshit. The bandits will get away."

"I repeat, hold your position," Hawk said.

"Roger that," Jefferson replied.

As he looked off to his right, he felt the tip of a knife prick his skin beneath his Adam's apple. Quickly, his assailant put him in a strangle hold. Jefferson's impatience was about to cost him his life.

"You are a stupid man," the Munozista said. "Why are you here? You must have comrades, no?"

The man smelled of spiced ham, stale cigarettes, and rum.

"Answer or die, tomcat," the Colombian whispered.

The blade sliced Jefferson's skin. Jefferson felt a burning sensation as perspiration entered the wound. Both blood and sweat rolled down his chest. He tried hard to free himself, but the Munozista held firm.

Jefferson was about to stand and try to fall backward onto the man, when his assailant grunted.

The man's grip loosened and he hit the ground hard behind Jefferson's boots.

"Aren't you a lucky fuck," Jack Redding whispered.

"How did you know he had me?" Jefferson asked.

"I saw him in the moonlight," Jack said. He took the Munozista's silencer, slipping it into his pocket. "A vintage Colt .45, I've always wanted one," he added, examining the man's weapon and tucking it into his belt.

Jefferson nodded and said, "Thanks, Midnight."

"It was either issue the order to advance or watch you die, dipshit. Since I need you for interrogations, I decided to save your sorry ass. Next time, stay focused..."

...Jefferson awoke shaking. He almost died that night in Colombia. He smiled at the irony. He was close to death on this day, too. Why, then, did the nightmare bother him so?

He groaned, wiped his forehead, and heard movement at his door. His niece, Theo entered.

"Were you sleeping, Uncle Ted?" she asked.

"No," he lied, grateful to sidestep his own vulnerability.

"I thought I'd stop by before my afternoon classes begin, as I had a prescription filled in the pharmacy."

"Is everything alright," Jefferson asked.

"Just a pick-me-upper," Theo replied.

"God, I'm happy you came." He squeezed her hand.

He watched his niece exchange dried red roses with pert yellow carnations, his favorite.

"How do you feel, today?" she asked.

"About the same...it won't be long now."

"Stop that talk, you have to fight hard every day."

"Why should I?"

"Because things can change with new scientific discoveries," she replied, adding, "I've some news for you."

"Oh?"

"You had a phone call, today," she added, matter-of-factly.

"Who would have called me?" he asked.

"A man named Jack Redding; he'll be here in a few days."

Her uncle's demeanor brightened immediately.

"I take it you know him," she said.

"I do. He is the finest man I ever met. You'll like him. Did you tell him about my cancer?"

"No, he left a message. You'll have to tell him yourself."

"We called him Midnight," Jefferson said, chuckling.

"He didn't sound like a black man."

"No, child...although he told me he had some Indian blood from one of the Iroquois tribes. Midnight is just a nickname."

"Why?"

"We called him that because he believed midnight was the best time to take down an enemy."

"Is he the man you always talk about, the colonel who saved your life?"

"Yes, the very same, and he saved it more than once."

"Then, I *would* like to meet him."

"He's the toughest, bravest man I ever met. He is as hard as steel, and he can be deadly, but his heart is made of gold. Ain't no man better, nowhere. That's the god-honest truth and it's the best compliment I can pay him."

"It sounds good me," Theo replied.

"What are you teaching, today?"

"We're discussing Lincoln," she replied.

"He was a good man, too. We could use him today. Yes, we could. He'd be good for all of us."

"The problems facing our country, how would he do?"

"He'd fix them," Ted Jefferson stated. "He wouldn't worry about the polls or vote present. He had a heart of gold, too."

"On that point, I think you might be right!"

25

Emma Cassidy admired Lincoln, too, but unlike Ted Jefferson in Oklahoma, Honest Abe was not on Emma's mind this day in Ft. Mitchell, Kentucky.

She was thinking about her mom and dad. They had built their newspaper from the ground up with hard work and lots of sweat. Now, she had shut the newspaper down, forever.

Emma parked her car on a side road in Hillside Cemetery and walked across the frozen ground, stopping by two graves marked with a single stone.

She picked up several pieces of wind-blow debris and shoved them into her pocket.

"I needed to stop by and talk to you guys," she said. "I tried, I honestly tried. Nothing I did was enough. We were bleeding money. I had to stop while I could cover the debt."

She paused to wipe tears from her eyes.

"Daddy, I even tried to sell it, I tried hard. No takers, the industry is dying. It's the Internet. I thought about becoming Web-based, but I'm too far behind and I'd never make up any ground. The ad revenue structure is completely different. I have to find something worthwhile.

"I want to tell you that Amanda died, too. Her body is coming back home and I made arrangements for her to rest here beside the both of you.

"By the way, mom, you were right. That son of a bitch Pidge turned his back on me, just as you said he would. I never thought he would turn against me. Anyway, my romance is in the shitter, too. These have been a rough couple of days."

She stooped and placed a bouquet of carnations on the grave, said the Lord's Prayer, picked up a rusting soda can, and walked to her Volvo, for which she already had a buyer.

She was crying; she was hurting; she was lonely.

26

Helen Smith watched her dad playing with her children, unaware of Emma Cassidy's blue day in Kentucky. On the contrary, it was a glorious day in Wichita, Kansas.

Helen loved to see her father, a bear of a man, enjoy his time with her twins. Fred Adkins was a great dad and a special grandfather. Ken, her husband, thought so, too.

Helen noticed her mom, smiling. Her mom nodded, as if to confirm her daughter's recognition.

"I wish we could see you more often," Helen said. "The boys need to get to know their grandparents. It'd be wonderful to be able to do things as a family."

Her dad stood. "Helen, we have something we want to share with you before we leave for Flagstaff tomorrow."

Fred Adkins nodded to his wife, Madison, who removed a document from her purse and handed it to her daughter.

"What is this?" Helen asked.

"It's the deed to a condo your mom and I purchased a few miles away. We intend to visit in the summers and during the holidays. We'll lease it out the rest of the year."

"Are you kidding me?" Helen shouted.

"Nope, it's paid in full. We want to see the boys more often, too," Madison Adkins added.

Helen hugged her parents, adding, "This is wonderful news. When did you think of this?"

"Actually, on the drive in...we were in our usual restaurant in Elk City when your dad broached the subject."

"Yes," Fred Adkins added. "We called Ken at his law office, he put us on to a realtor, and the rest is history. We told her what we wanted and viewed properties when you took the boys for their checkups. Are you surprised?"

"Flabbergasted," she replied, "and happy, too."

"Good," Fred Adkins said, smiling.

27

My brother Vince whistled. "Damn Jack, four hundred grand is a big jar of ginger snaps." He sat in his wheelchair, across from me, with his back to a window. "I had no idea. Did Jill wipe you out?"

I shrugged. "She took about two-thirds."

The drive to Jamestown, New York, from Buffalo took about an hour and we'd been talking for ten minutes.

Outside, because of a break in the storm, vivid sunlight bounced off white fields. To the west, far beyond barren oak and maple trees, a cobalt sky darkened by the minute. Bailey and I would encounter more snow when we eventually departed the Veterans Administration Hospice.

My brother lifted a pack of unfiltered Camels in his right and only hand. Army doctors had amputated Vince's left arm and two legs nearly forty-plus years ago in Vietnam. He jerked the pack deftly and caught an unfiltered cigarette between his yellowed teeth.

"It was a big portion of our nest egg," I added. "I lost my wife and a fortune on the same day."

"Talk about a kick in the nut sack," Vince said. "The cops don't have a clue?"

"No," I said. It was not a lie. The cops did not know, but I did. Fortunately, Vince had not asked me that question.

I studied my brother's aging face. I had several reasons for not telling Vince about Aaron Cooper. First, it served no purpose to divulge my plan to kill a man in cold blood. Second, I did not want Vince to perjure himself if the police ever knocked on his door. Third, Vince might try to stop me and I wanted to avoid a confrontation.

I made my decision; I would not change my mind. The less anyone knew about it, the better my prospect of success.

Killing Cooper was my resident obligation.

It was my life, my soul, my wife, my decision, my responsibility, and maybe my destiny.

Vince continued shaking his head in disbelief. His next question registered in his eyes before he spoke the word.

"Why?"

"I have no idea why Jill took the money," I answered.

"No, not that," Vince countered. "Why did you have all that money in a joint account? Christ, Jack, you should've known better, especially with the way Jill swilled booze. What were you thinking?"

I shrugged, saying, "It was only supposed to be in that particular account less than a week. We planned to purchase an apartment building and had an appointment to sign the documents after I returned from my business trip. The money had to be in my account at least three full business days. The bank wanted it free and clear. They required thirty percent down."

Vince adjusted his cigarette and listened.

"Here's the odd part," I added. "I never told Jill it was in the account. My guess, she needed some traveling money, went to the bank, and took it out. Why she did that will always be a mystery. Anyway, the money's gone."

Of course, because of Tobias' recording, I knew more than I let on. Jill thought she was bringing the money to me. I withheld that tidbit from Vince. It would generate questions that I did not want to answer.

"You're absolutely sure she didn't stash the money in your house? Maybe she put it in a lock box."

"No, nothing, and there are no keys," I replied.

"Maybe she trusted it with a friend or relative, did you check? What about emails?"

"Nothing," I replied. "I've been through everything."

Vince's stare seemed to penetrate to my soul and I struggled to maintain my demeanor.

Vince had always been able to sense my thoughts. For obvious reasons, I remained silent. He was smart. If he got wind of Cooper, he would connect the dots quickly.

"I haven't a clue," I reiterated, which was a half-truth. I believed my money was in Santa Fe, but I did not know where, specifically. "It wasn't in the house and she didn't leave notes or emails. The Pittsburgh cops are clueless. I doubt they'll ever find it."

I hated to mislead Vince but, under the circumstances, I thought it the best way to go.

Vince whistled, still wrestling with my revelation.

"Three hundred ninety grand is a major-league kick in the beans. What would you do, if you knew who killed Jill?"

I wondered. Did he suspect something?

"I'd kill the son of a bitch and get my money back, but not in that order," I answered, directly.

Vince nodded.

"I would, too." He lit his smoke with a Zippo lighter he bought in Da Nang. "Yes, indeed. If I knew, I'd get the money and kill him." After exhaling, he studied my face. "Say, why're you here on a work day? It's not because of Jill or the money, something's up?"

I nodded. "I've decided to head west," I said. "I resigned my job. I'm going to Vegas and I stopped to say goodbye."

Vince contemplated the burning end of his cigarette. As he exhaled, he asked, "You've thought this through?"

"Sure."

"You said Jill took about sixty-five percent." He did the math mentally. "You must have nearly two hundred grand left. That size poke should carry you for a while."

"It will," I said. "Plus, I have my pension. I had about five thousand in my checking account and a bit more than a hundred and ninety grand in my credit union account."

"That's where you should've parked the coin Jill took."

"Goddamn it, Vince," I replied, "hindsight's visionary. Don't you think I know that? I've kicked myself every day."

He smiled, removing a tobacco shred from his upper lip.

"Sorry, Jack, sometimes I get carried away."

"It doesn't matter," I said, calmly. "I've racked my brains trying to understand. The rental property was for our retirement. Then, she goes and dies in a damned snowdrift."

Vince nodded and changed the subject.

"Will you gamble again?"

"I don't know, maybe. If I do, it won't be much. I don't have the passion I once did, and I'm rusty. I could easily lose it all."

"Hell, you don't need to gamble. You can go pretty far with two hundred grand and a military pension."

"That's the way I see it…why be foolish?"

Smoke curled outward from Vince's smile and hung above his shaved head like a translucent halo.

"Being a fool is a choice; a lot of people forget that."

I laughed.

"Sage advice…yeah, I guess they do."

"Let's go over to the sofa, you'll be more comfortable."

I nodded, stood, and pushed his wheelchair.

Since he returned from Vietnam nearly forty years ago, Vince had lived his life in veterans' hospitals. He had spent the past five years in the VA's Jamestown Hospice, counseling terminal patients and their families. He also did internet research for a variety of companies.

I was a boy when Vince went to Vietnam. I was still a boy when he came back, forever changed by a war that meant nothing but death to thousands. Seeing him without limbs broke my mother's heart and embittered my father until the day he died.

I straightened the blanket covering the lower portion of Vince's ravaged body.

In addition to three limbs, Vince lost a testicle and a major portion of his intestines in a mortar attack during the Tet Offensive.

Vince was thinner, his face hollowed, with dark circles under his eyes. The stubble of his beard was almost white.

Vince noticed my scrutiny.

"I won't win any beauty contests, will I?" he asked. "I used to be a good looking guy. Girls liked me. A few days of war, a couple of bursts of mortar, and I'm fucked for the remainder of my life. Jesus, talk about wide right."

"Seriously, how is your health, Vince?"

A tight smile crossed his lined face.

"On average, the arrows are down rather than up; I have good days and bad. Doctors say my kidneys are failing. Truthfully, I'm losing my appetite, too."

Before I could comment, Vince asked, "Why Vegas?"

"You remember Bill Hawkins?"

"Tough little pisser, from Missouri, he was on your team."

"That's him. He owns apartments and condominiums. He's been after me for years to visit. I never went because of my job. Of course, Las Vegas is not a town for drunks. It would not have been good for Jill. Anyway, he has this place and, at least for a while, it's gratis. I'll also visit Ted Jefferson in Tulsa. He was on my team, too."

"Your interrogator, black guy, one hardnosed hombre," said Vince.

"Yes. As for Vegas, I like the desert, always have. I might write a novel or two, try something new."

"You've talked about writing books for years," he replied. "Ma always thought you would. I'd love to see it."

"I know...other things got in the way."

"Jill?"

"My work, too...Jill chewed up a lot of hours. I never had the 'thinking time' needed to write books."

"You know, you might never get over her."

"I know," I said.

"It's a tough piece of leather," he added.

"I hope getting away helps me, although Jill was too beautiful and precious to ever forget," I replied.

I knew I'd never forget but I hoped I could bury much of my hurt with Cooper's body in the New Mexico desert.

"Maybe I can find a way to push it far enough away to begin to feel normal again," I said. "I need a change. Everything I see reminds me of Jill and," motioning toward the glare beyond the window, I added, "I'm tired of snow, too. Without Jill my life is bitter."

"I pulled a rose from off its tree and my lover stole my rose but left the thorn with me," Vince whispered.

"Robert Burns?" I asked.

Vince nodded and then chuckled.

"You know I'm sixty-five years old and I haven't been laid since Saigon. What's that, forty-six years?"

I nodded.

"I can still remember it like it was yesterday," Vince added. "If I think about it long enough I could get hard. It might take a day or two."

His laugh was deep and guttural. "Goddamn, it would be good to feel a woman's skin against mine."

"It's a gift," I said. "Too bad it's fleeting. It's one hell of a loss once it disappears."

"More than we know. Hey, you want to get some coffee?"

"Coffee would be good," I replied.

28

"Fifty kilos of pure coke nets about eleven million on the streets, after cuts. That's nearly a seven-to-one ratio," Tito Claroni said, sitting in an office in Oakland Hills, Michigan, a Detroit suburb. In New York, Jack Redding pushed his brother's wheelchair toward a coffee shop in the Veterans' Hospice of Jamestown.

Claroni, rail thin, had a voice like sandpaper rubbing against dry wood. "That's a hell of a return," he added.

"Yeah, I did the math, too. You think we can trust Sarcusi's guy?" Patsy Domico replied.

"Tony is solid; his word is tits. We use him and our people to pick it up. Nobody knows we're involved. It's tight as a nun's tweeter."

"Tony could hurt us bad?"

"Why would he? He'd ruin his family, his business, and a damned good life. He knows his place. Tony understands and appreciates business. He won't slice off his own dick."

"I suppose. The buy's a million five," the boss noted.

"Does that bother you, Patsy?"

"I keep thinking we should negotiate."

"If the sniff is pure, why nickel-and-dime the deal?"

Domico shrugged. "I never pay sticker, it's a principle."

"We get a back-end return," Claroni said. "The market is good. The tutsoons and slants down this shit like candy."

"The world is full of idiots. Would you snort that powder?"

"I did once and said never again," Claroni replied.

Domico smiled and, after reaching for his wine glass, said, "Same for me. Okay, if it's good, we score big."

"Yes, we do…who goes with Sarcusi?"

"Sarcusi and Tommy Jax will drive to New Mexico. Send two of our best men, for muscle. We'll control the risk," the boss said. "Also, call Julie. Tell her we need her in Santa Fe.

"Six random bag tests, and her best effort," Domico added. "She gets thirty grand and half a percent on the back-end."

"That's nearly a hundred grand," Claroni said, surprised.

The boss smiled. "I like Julie, she's a sweet kid."

"Are you schtupping her, Patsy?"

"She's like a daughter," he smacked Tito's shoulder.

"Do we do anything for Tony, for bringing us the deal?"

"I imagine he's getting a decent commission. Give him a dime to show good faith. It'll bring him back to us."

"Ten grand," Claroni replied. "Which stash?"

"The Southfield banks, let's hope the sniff ain't spoiled."

"It won't be. Sarcusi likes his nuts too much."

"Tito, talk to him; I want assurance that this guy in Santa Fe is a player. Make sure he knows I hate fuck-ups."

"He knows," Claroni said.

Before Claroni could depart, Patsy Domico raised a finger.

"Something else on your mind, Patsy?" asked Claroni.

"Lucasi guards their backsides."

"He's a shooter."

"Jelly's good to have in your corner, in case shit happens. Only you and Tommy Jax will know he's trailing behind. Julie, Sarcusi, and the other boys are not to know, capisce. Tommy keeps Lucasi informed. Jelly calls you."

"Absolutely," Claroni replied, "and I'll call you. Why do you always call him *Jelly*, he's a grown man."

"Did you ever see that son of a bitch eat toast?"

"No," Claroni replied.

"Watch how much jelly he spreads, at least half an inch." Work out the details and get with Lucasi."

"You want to know what we decide."

"No, too much info jumbles my mind," Domico said. "Just make it happen, no mistakes, it's a big deal. Tell Sarcusi to tell his contact in Santa Fe that he can trust us, tell him we won't fuck with him. Tell him he better not fuck with us."

29

Vince took a second sip from his coffee cup and popped another cigarette out of the pack.

"When did they put a coffee shop on the third floor?"

"A few months back, a local Jamestown contractor donated it. We've never come here when you've visited. I work here a lot on the Internet, we have Wi-Fi."

"The computer's good, then?" I asked.

"Yeah, a lifesaver, thanks."

Vince lifted the pot, added more coffee to his cup, and blended in vanilla-caramel cream. He stirred several times with a spoon. His hand shook noticeably.

"You remember the ninety acres of land and the lake Joe owned north of Allegany?"

Joe was Vince's nickname for our grandfather, Anthony Goodwin, our mother's father. Allegany was an hour away.

"Where we used to hunt and fish? Sure."

"I've updated my Will. When I die, it's all yours."

Vince saw surprise in my eyes and smiled.

"That's a big shift," I said. "You always said everything would be sold and proceeds given to veterans' charities."

Vince inhaled again and nodded.

"I've changed my mind," he said, exhaling. "I've been thinking about it. It's been in our family for about ninety years. Joe's father bought it for twenty bucks an acre. Eighteen hundred bucks was a lot of money back before the depression. I had it assessed."

"And?"

"The lake is clean and I own a decent amount of valuable hard wood—oak, maple, hickory, and other varieties."

"You're a proverbial robber baron."

"I'm told the pine is good, too. The trees should be thinned and sold sometime, and new trees planted."

"You keep it," I said. "What if I don't come back?"

Vince laughed.

"Jesus, Jack, I don't think they've made a wheelchair that can maneuver through dense woods or deep water. I can't walk the land. I wouldn't be able to see what's going on. I've decided it should stay in the family and since it's only you and me, you get it when I die. What you choose to do with the place is your call. Besides, you'll come back. I don't know when but you will, some day."

I shifted uneasily in my chair.

"You seem awfully sure about that," I said.

"It's a fact of life, sooner or later mooks like us return to our roots, after we wander all over hell's half acre."

"I might break the mold," I stated.

"You won't. Something always pulls us back. Think of the land and the lake as your anchor, maybe they'll make up for what Jill lost."

"And, if I die first?" I asked.

"You might but I'd bet money you won't."

Vince realized that I found the conversation troubling.

"You're uneasy about my decision?"

"I'm uneasy about a lot of things," I said. "I'm not over Jill. I think about Joan sometimes, too."

"Joan, our sister, why?" he asked.

"Her death crushed ma and dad," I continued. "They never recovered from that or from what happened to you. You were recuperating in San Diego. Sis went to mail her college registration and never returned. I can still hear Ma's screams when the police came to our door."

Vince nodded.

"I live with the fact that you sit in a hospital with no visitors except me on Sundays," I continued. "I served for twenty years, was in numerous firefights, and came back in one piece, wounded twice, but in good shape.

"You went to Vietnam and, in only three weeks, lost everything. It plays on my mind sometimes and I cannot do anything about it."

Vince leaned forward in his wheelchair and looked squarely into my eyes.

"Get over it, ace," he said emphatically. "I don't sit here mired in self-pity. So, stop yours." He paused to sip coffee and said, "I learned a long time ago that worry and heartache drain the human spirit. It might be sinful, too."

He rubbed his stubble and scratched his cheek.

"Life's what we make it. We can't change what's happened. If we fail to make the most of what we *do* have, it's our own faults. Who was going to take care of me? I remember when I couldn't take a dump, clean myself, or get dressed without someone assisting me. It was awful."

"I know," I said.

"If not for advances in technology, I'd still have to rely on others," he added. "A hospice is best for a man with an overused right arm. My kidneys are failing and I'm beginning to leak. I even piss myself. Sometimes I have to wear a diaper, a damned diaper with blue ties! Tell me that isn't evil? I wouldn't impose my condition on anyone.

"I didn't want ma and dad doing it, and it wasn't your responsibility. You were much younger and had a life to fulfill. I got over my problems years ago." Vince paused for more coffee. "I'm happy Jack, I really am. I spend my time reading and dabbling in the market. Hell, I'm on-line most of the day. I do research for a few private companies.

"I'm good at it, too. I earn a few extra bucks and it keeps my mind active. I have a knack for it. Other than the land, my bank account, and the few stocks I have, I don't own much, but my mind is still active. I go to the hospital wing and counsel vets who are far worse than I am. Some are dying. I talk to them and their families."

He looked out the window, turned to me, and said, "I try to make a difference and contribute." He scratched his ear and asked, "How old are you now?"

"I'll be fifty-one in August."

Vince nodded.

"That's what I thought. You have twenty-five or thirty good years left. Don't spend them alone. Jill had a problem, you tried to help, and it didn't work."

"So?"

"So, grab hold of a new life and run with it."

"What do you mean?"

"Don't become the booze's next victim. You say you're leaving for something new. I'm smart, Jack. I suspect there's more to it than that, but I won't pry. It's none of my business. Whatever the issue is, go and flush the poison out of your system. Then, move on."

He paused to watch a distant car negotiate an icy road.

"Get on with your life," Vince continued. "I'll be fine. Jill and her problems are gone, but you need to heal. I know it takes time, but you'll do it just as everyone else does it, one minute at a time.

"The minutes add up to days and the days to years. Things change. We don't forget, but we heal and it doesn't hurt as much. Maybe, that's by God's design. Make the most of what's coming and, should you find another woman, don't let Jill's memory stop you from falling in love.

"The feel of a woman's skin is a wonderful thing, if I remember correctly. Women are smarter than men are. You deserve to have a smart woman, Jack. She'll make you a better man. After what happened to Jill, you deserve someone who will love you and comfort you as easily as waves lap against a shoreline."

I patted my brother's hand. Tears welled in his eyes.

"I hear you," I said.

Vince observed the western sky for a moment.

"More snow's coming," he whispered. He turned and studied my face. "As I said, Jack, I don't want to know your business but I do have some advice."

"You have advice for me?" I asked.

Vince nodded, became reflective, and spoke firmly.

"You are a tough and determined son of a bitch, Jack. I wouldn't want to go up against you. You are the sort of man who likes things tidy, a man who hates loose ends. Whatever you're getting yourself into, think it through thoroughly and, when you're ready to act, don't hesitate, go in fast, end it quickly, hide your trail, and get the hell out. Don't back off and no second-guesses. Also, I want you to say a few prayers."

"Prayers," I asked, confused, "for what, my soul?"

"No, the prayers are for the man you're going after; it won't be his best day when you've finished with him."

30

Henry Bosko, a leathered old cowboy, had driven and worked the rodeo circuit for years. He loved it. Sadly, as often happens, age and arthritis sat him down and Hank retired to his family's farm in Clinton, Oklahoma.

While not confined to a wheelchair like Vince Redding in Jamestown, Bosko was barely ambulatory.

His legs, arms, and spine had been broken or cracked many times. He spent his days idling on the porch when the weather was warm or in his living room when it was not. He walked short distances: to the parlor, bedroom, kitchen, and bathroom. Mostly, he remained immobile.

On this day, he was drinking lemonade in his kitchen, waiting for his sister. Margaret came to visit him this time of year; she had for ten years running. Hank was one of the reasons she still made her fund-raising trips through the Texas and Oklahoma panhandles.

He lifted his binoculars and watched the highway. She had called twenty minutes ago and should be close.

Sure enough, her car turned onto his dusty driveway.

This was their childhood home. They had grown up on this land and she always visited—at least, twice a year.

When his sister exited the car, he noticed how gaunt and worried she looked. He thought he detected sadness in her voice when she called, but seeing her face confirmed it. She must be having some problem with the orphanage; it was her life's passion, her reason for living.

"How are you, Maggie," he said, as she entered. He took her in his arms and gave her a kiss and a big hug.

Sister Margaret Bosko smiled. "Hank, you're as handsome as the day is long. You got a drink for a starched old nun?"

"Fresh pot of coffee's on the stove," he said.

"You got anything stronger?"

31

A young nurse brought Vince to the front door so he could see Bailey. I hugged my brother, kissed his cheek, and slipped two envelopes into the pocket of his robe.

"One envelope has an address and phone number, and a few bucks for you," I whispered in his ear. "The second has instructions and a DVD if you don't hear from me before the first of June. Please, do not open it until then."

"And, if I do hear from you?" asked Vince.

"Burn the letter and break the DVD."

Vince nodded.

"Word of honor," he replied. "I won't read it until the first of June, count on it."

"Thanks, I appreciate that."

I kissed Vince's cheek again, told him I loved him. I was anxious to get going and hoped highway crews would be spreading salt and sand.

After I buckled in, I waved, gave a thumbs-up, and drove away with Bailey by my side.

We departed at three-thirty in the afternoon. Within five minutes of our exit from the hospice, Bailey and I drove into the advancing storm.

The wind was freshening and the snow was wet and heavy, the sort of snow that gathered moisture as the storm passed over the open waters of Lake Erie.

If the snowfall intensified, traffic would be at a crawl.

As for my brother, I doubted I would ever see him again. Something told me that either he or I would die soon.

If I knew Vince, he watched my pickup disappear behind the trees, wiped tears from his eyes, and said a prayer for my hurting soul.

He was probably in his room, getting his laptop.

Ultimately, he would go to the coffee shop or an annex.

He would visit men who gave their blood and tears to a country that often seemed smug and ungrateful for their sacrifice and service.

Because of the mystical firing of synapses that link siblings together, I truly believed Vince had examined my soul and my thoughts, looked into my heart, and knew what I intended to do. I also believed he realized that my intention was none of his business.

An unspoken and indescribable understanding had passed between us that afternoon.

Something told me he knew I was going to kill the man who murdered Jill.

I said a prayer for Vince and asked God to protect him, to give him comfort in the winter of his life.

I loved my brother fairly and deeply, and he knew it.

I also know he loved me, too, but realized I had to leave.

His parting words to me were his blessing, a form of approval. Vince was saying he agreed with me, in the deepest recesses of his strong and vibrant mind. That brought a warm sensation and gave me much needed consolation. Vince had a habit of doing that.

Men who have fought in war have an instinctive respect for duty, for obligation, and for what is just and honorable.

At heart, Vince and I were warriors.

Warriors fight the good fight.

They run the good race.

They understand how much blood and sacrifice is required on a field of battle.

They do the right thing, regardless of pain.

They quiet their fear and hide it deep within their competitive spirits.

The never back down.

They never give up.

They figure out a way to win and they move on.

32

Aaron Cooper stood on his balcony in Santa Fe as Patsy Domico poured another glass of wine in Michigan and Vince Redding logged onto his computer in New York.

A pleasant breeze brushed across Cooper's face. His adopted city stretched for miles across the brown New Mexico plateau. Not far away, sunlight drenched the spires of Saint Francis Cathedral. From somewhere nearby the invigorating scent of enchiladas drifted upward.

Cooper looked westward. Mt. Taylor, snowcapped and dominant, stood its ground against the advances of westerly winds. Somewhere, high up in the hills behind his condominium, two coyotes howled a lonely love song to each other. In the background, a radio announcer spoke of temperatures in the low sixties for the entire week.

The day had a Georgia-O'Keefe ambiance. Cooper liked what he saw, heard, and smelled. Admittedly, it took a few months to settle in but he felt relaxed, the tranquility was energizing. His new life was a dream-come-true. He had money, freedom, independence, and Liza Mercer.

If Tony Sarcusi found a buyer, the money he would make, added to the stash he already had, would fund an exceptional lifestyle. His cop's pension would cover day-to-day expenses; the remainder would be for fun and good times with Liza.

The backdrop of his new life was much better than that of his old. His precautious past lay far behind him in an old-and-worn eastern steel town. Finally, he could enjoy life.

In Santa Fe, no one cared about his past or asked probing questions. His very presence and residency validated his qualifications to live there. He liked that...a lot.

The balcony door slid open behind him and he turned with a smile for a remarkably beautiful woman.

"Here you are," she said.

Her voice, with a southern lilt, was as soft as the wind, her smile reminiscent of the warmest of sunshine.

"I'm enjoying this splendid view," Cooper said, gesturing toward the distant mountains. "You're early; did you finish?"

She nodded.

Liza Mercer, a portrait artist and a distant cousin of a famous lyricist, Johnny Mercer, stood beside him and placed her hand over his. The charge of electricity was thrilling. The native of Savannah, Georgia, placed a cup of coffee on the railing, looked into his eyes, and kissed Cooper's cheek.

"You smell good," she said.

"You smell better," he replied, kissing her fully.

Mercer was the gold at the end of Cooper's rainbow, an unexpected treasure. She was a smart, sexy, and effervescent woman, and an extremely talented artist.

He enjoyed spending time with her: no questions, no commitments, just fun. Surprisingly, of late, emotions seemed to be growing, and new doors were opening.

Back in Pennsylvania, women like Liza Mercer rarely glanced Cooper's way. Maybe it was his recent weight loss. Maybe it was because he stopped smoking cigarettes. Maybe it was because a natural vulnerability had supplanted his made-up, tough-guy persona. Whatever it was, he liked it.

The sex was superb but emotions that went beyond the physical were stirring. Liza and he fit together as hand fills glove, an uncommon sensation for a man who was always too busy building his illegal fortune. Love? What was that? Women pleasured his body; Liza Mercer touched his mind.

Cooper studied her remarkable face, Audrey Hepburn's twin but with a fuller and more inviting body.

Cooper loved Liza's smile, her radiant brown eyes, the dusting of freckles across the bridge of her nose, and the tender slope of jaw to a very delicate neck.

Her rich, southern drawl was equal parts sex and refinement, and her informal style masked an astute mind.

Liza's nonchalance hid her immense talent and profound intelligence. Cooper stood constantly amazed as he watched her apply brush and paint to canvas. She transformed and authenticated reality.

"It's February," he added. "I guess I expected as much snow as I would normally see in Pittsburgh. Certainly, I thought it would be as cold."

Cooper put his arm around her warm, firm waist.

"Sometimes it will be as cold," she observed. "We've been lucky this year. The snow has stayed in the mountains."

As she leaned against him, the fragrance of her perfume filled the air.

"I have to tell you something," he said.

"Which is?"

"I love you."

She kissed his cheek and she tightened against his body. "I've wondered if you'd say it," she replied. "I love you, too."

"So what do we do about it?"

"We live each day like it's our last and go from there."

"I want you with me all the time," he added.

"I'd like that."

"What time is it?" he asked.

"A few minutes before three," she replied. "Why?"

"I'm thinking about a nap, you want to join me?"

He yawned.

"You're tired," she said. "It's mid-afternoon."

"I was up early to call Tony Sarcusi, a friend, back east before he left for his office," Cooper said. "He says he's interested in my '58 Thunderbird. He might visit, buy it, and drive it back."

"Really?" she replied, with apparent surprise.

"Yeah, it's his for twenty-five grand," Cooper lied.

He felt a twinge of guilt, a new sensation. He did not like lying, but he could not tell Liza he hoped to sell cocaine. His dark past would surely destroy their bright future.

"Do you think he'll buy it?"

"For sure he'll come for an inspection."

"What does your friend do?"

Cooper kissed Mercer's cheek.

"At one time, Tony was my partner. He left the department six years ago, after twenty years, and went home to Detroit to run his mom's and dad's business. His family owns three very popular Italian markets."

Cooper rationalized his deceit about the Thunderbird as a 'white lie.' Fifty kilos of cocaine lay hidden behind a faux panel between the T-Bird's rear seat and its trunk. The automobile, in a secure and well-lighted self-storage facility, was a few miles away. Three extra security locks, an anti-theft system, and cameras discouraged intruders.

"It's a magnificent automobile, why sell?" Liza asked.

"I've had it for a long time, it's time for a change," he replied, leaving it at that.

"Will you ever tire of me?"

"How could I?"

As he kissed Liza, a piece of Cooper's history jabbed him in the ribs like a middleweight's punch. The memory of a dead woman in a Pittsburgh alley filtered through his mind. It came at him at the oddest times.

In fact, that very memory had awakened him in the early morning gloom. It was the real reason for his dawn call to Sarcusi. In Cooper's dream, he actually believed the woman was alive and coming for him. He awoke drenched in sweat.

He had to kill her. She could have destroyed everything he planned. He was too close to the perfect ending of twenty-five years of deception. She might have ruined it all.

Cooper shivered noticeably.

"What is it," Liza asked. "Someone walk over your grave?"

"Just an odd memory," he replied, "nothing of real concern." Another lie, he thought.

Liza Mercer squeezed his hand.

"Good," she said. "The past will go away. It's the magic of the high desert; it cleanses one's soul."

"I hope so."

He sipped coffee from the cup on the railing.

"Why Santa Fe?" she asked.

"I was stationed in Albuquerque at Kirtland Air Force Base. I liked the area. I visited periodically and knew I'd retire here when I left the department."

"Do you miss being a cop?"

"Not at all," he said.

"Good."

"With each passing day, it dims, despite random thoughts. I thought *I would* miss it. Once I turned the page, it has started to disappear quickly."

He watched Liza unbutton her blouse, letting it hang loosely around her waist. For a woman of forty-six, with two grown children, she was exquisite, a gift he did not deserve.

She moved against him.

"Let's celebrate," she said.

"Celebrate?"

"Our love for each other," she replied.

He fondled her breast.

"Hey," she said, "I have a six o'clock appointment in Albuquerque with a client. Come along for the drive."

"I'd feel like a fifth wheel."

"You can have a drink while I'm meeting. We'll spend the night; I know a quaint hotel east of the city."

"Good restaurants?" he asked.

"Several nearby are fantastic. Let's go. We'll make an adventure of it; it will be fun."

He smiled and kissed her throat.

"I like adventure," he whispered

"My river of love runs to thee," she said, nibbling his ear, breathing hot air on his neck.

He loved the way she often quoted literature.

"I am your love. Any Italian restaurants?" he asked.

"One very good Mediterranean spot," she replied.

"Close enough," he said. "How's the wine selection?"

"I'm told it's one of the best."

She placed her hand on his abdomen and her fingers drifted lower. She lifted her face to his and kissed him passionately.

"Come inside me," she whispered.

"Right here and right now?" asked Cooper.

"We'll start the adventure early."

She slipped her hand beneath his clothing. Thoughts about his career, and money, and a dead woman in an alley, disappeared from Cooper's mind. A warm, fluid, and tender motion replaced his hidden anxiety and then washed it completely away.

His eyes were on those of a beautiful woman who liked to look deeply into his eyes when they made love.

At that intimate moment, Cooper could not have imagined the wrath he would ultimately experience.

An old demon would awake, surface, and introduce panic into his life. It would be terrifying.

Aaron Cooper was very near to learning about the real meaning of hell-on-earth. He would come to hate the moment he confronted a misguided woman outside JUMPIN' JOE'S in a snowy Pittsburgh alley.

As Cooper died, he would see the face of that woman, the face of Manny Tobias, and long for Liza Mercer's touch. Sadly, the crack of Jill's neck and Tobias' choking sounds would echo in Cooper's mind as his heart stopped beating.

He would never again hear Liza Mercer whisper sonnets, or poems, or the lyrics of songs in his ear.

The last image he would see was not the face of his new love. Rather, he would see the image of revenge personified in the anger and sorrow of a man who seemed to have lost his very soul.

The hurt and heartbreak about to descend on Cooper would be the composite of all the pain he had ever inflected upon innocent people.

He had hurt, wronged, and misused many individuals, and his accumulated burden would be profound.

Cooper's fate was rapidly approaching because Frank Kropinak decided to fulfill a promise made to his friend Manny Tobias and mail a letter to a man in Buffalo, New York, a man he did not know and would never meet.

That is how life works, simple actions create monumental shifts, and few of us ever realize the resulting implications or importance.

Jack Redding knew.

Cooper had no idea that Jack Redding was heading toward Santa Fe and hunting him like a hungry and desperate animal from hell.

33

After leaving Vince, I took I-90 out of New York. In time, it would merge with I-71, south of Cleveland, for a straight run into Columbus. From Ohio's capitol, I would go west on I-70, cross Indiana and Illinois, and steer toward St. Louis. In Missouri, I-44 would take me to Tulsa and my visit with Ted Jefferson.

After Oklahoma, Bailey and I would drive across the Texas panhandle on I-40, running straight to Albuquerque. Then, we would go north to Santa Fe. Altogether, we would see roughly two thousand miles of cold winter road. After I killed Cooper, the trip to Las Vegas would add another six hundred miles. I hoped that would be an easier drive.

I refueled at a combination truck stop/outdoor store on the backside of Erie, Pennsylvania. I also topped off a five-gallon gas can, which I carried in the pickup for emergencies.

Inside, I browsed the aisles for items that might come in handy: batteries, soft drinks, bottled water, a fleece blanket, a loaf of bread, a jar of peanut butter, two disposable phones, several packs of dry dog food, and half-a-dozen assorted canned goods.

The food would hold Bailey and me for several days, if a storm forced us to *hunker down* for a spell.

On an end cap in the Outdoor Section, I noticed boxes of parabolic dishes with headsets. The promotional blurb indicated hunters or birdwatchers could hear animals from up to 200 yards.

Cooper! The listening device might give me access to some of his conversations. On impulse, I dropped one in the cart

I added two canisters of pepper spray, a small portable heater with a jug of kerosene, and selected two quarts of motor oil and a gallon each of antifreeze and window-wash.

At the checkout counter, I said, "Gas at pump three, too."

A slight, but lovely, young woman with a pretty face totaled everything. "That's $383.15, with tax."

A gut feeling said she knew the mean side of lonely.

I gave her eight fifties.

"Keep the change for a movie," I added.

"That is so kind," she replied, smiling. Her eyes sparkled.

I would carry her expression with me for many miles.

After Bailey and I were moving again, heading through steady snow about seventy miles east of Cleveland, I turned to him and said, "If the weather strands us, we'll stay put for a while, no worries."

Bailey seemed to understand my comment, panted a few times, touched the side window with his nose, curled on the seat, and went to sleep. For Bailey, sixteen hours of sleep in any given day was never nearly enough.

Several hours later, heavy snow had accumulated under the wipers and along the edges of the windshield. I stopped, brushed it away, and drove on into the darkness, watching traffic and listening to swipe of the wipers. Two thousand miles seemed an eternity but it would pass quickly enough.

Aware of the hum of the tires on the wet pavement, my thoughts went to Cooper.

Besides his life, did I want anything else from him?

Yes, I did.

I wanted Aaron Cooper to admit he killed Jill.

I wanted him to show remorse.

I wanted him to say he stole Jill's and my money.

I wanted to look in his eyes and see the same sorrow that I had seen in mine for more than a year.

I wanted him to beg for his life.

I wanted to smell his fear emanating from his pores.

I wanted Cooper to feel as defenseless as Jill felt when he snapped her neck as easily as a child snaps a twig.

I wanted him dead!

34

Kyle Shaw opened the door to his home in North Las Vegas and waited patiently until his brother seated himself. Kyle studied Louis Shaw's face for a moment and took a deep breath.

"What did you find out?" Kyle asked. His heart was beating rapidly. Louis thought his brother looked disheveled, as if he had not eaten or slept.

"A viewing will be held tomorrow locally at Brewster Funeral Home. Her burial will be in Kentucky in a matter of days. Does that seem odd?"

Kyle shook his head. "No, it makes sense," he said, "she grew up not far from Cincinnati."

"Will you go?" Louis asked.

"I will attend the local services. I will not go to Kentucky. Have you talked to the old man?"

Louis nodded. "He's sorry as hell about this."

"He should be; he killed her."

Louis shook his head. "He didn't kill her, Kyle."

"He started it," Kyle shot back. "Now, he and I have to live with it. Jesus, Louis, he *had* her investigated."

"I'm not siding with him, Kyle, but he did it for you...it was all for you."

"I didn't ask for any of it. I accepted Amanda and I loved her. He stole that from me."

Louis was about to contest his brother's observation but held his tongue. Instead, he asked, "What will you do?"

"I'm going to get those diamonds and I am going to shove them down the old man's throat. Then, I'm walking away from him, forever. I have enough money. He threatened to disown me if I married Amanda. That says an awful lot about his position and all the other bullshit he holds sacred. He is a Class-A son of a bitch!"

35

Bailey snoozed as we approached Cleveland and I thought about the media articles I had compiled that portrayed Cooper as courageous. Most likely, he would need some encouragement to say the things I wanted to hear. I smiled. Ted Jefferson would help me.

Regarding interrogation, Ted was an expert and he understood torture. He had used it for many years and knew how to push buttons. As a member of my Red Robin Teams in the steaming jungles of the Western Hemisphere, he cracked strong minds quickly and proficiently.

Many in our country argue that torture only makes a man or woman say what respective captors want to hear.

Jefferson did not believe that, neither did I.

He could make a bad man plead for death and remain ever grateful to go on living. Ted made evil people do good deeds and the information he gleaned was always accurate.

I considered the political and moral outrage I had read about in the news. Many displayed shock and outrage that their country could 'water-board' a few terrorists.

"We're better than this," was the often-heard argument.

I laughed inwardly, thinking if they only knew the real cost of freedom. If faced with the life or death of their child, I believed those same individuals would gladly stick a needle in a man's eye to get him talking.

I did not care about moral implications. If I needed to torture Cooper to avenge Jill's death and get my money, I would do it. I did not think about sin, or wrongdoing, or immorality, or illegality. I would do what I needed to do and kill Cooper for killing Jill.

As for my everlasting soul, it and my heart had dried and crumbled. The remnants blew away like dust in the wind.

Losing Jill seemed to have ruined whatever faith I had.

Everything I held sacred had slipped away.

I flicked my lights and passed a slow moving auto carrier.

After arriving in New Mexico, I would empty my mind of extraneous thoughts. Cooper would be my sole focus.

I would study his routine: Basic Recon 101. Never hit an enemy until you know everything about his habits, his location, his condition, and his fortifications.

I would study his condominium complex. I would learn where and with whom he spent his time, where he dined, the roads he traveled, the places he shopped, and the clubs he frequented. I would know everything!

It would be the only way to assess the best time to take Cooper out. It would be when he was most vulnerable. That moment would surface and, when it did, I would be ready.

My men called me 'Midnight' because of my preference to attack at that particular hour. It made no difference with Cooper. I would kill him whenever I had the advantage.

I envisioned Jill's swollen face. I knew I would unravel easily, if the emotion I felt continued to swell. I would have to bury my feelings in some unused segment of my mind. I would become a cold and calculating killer. Sentimentality could come, but later, as I drove toward Las Vegas.

What would I do with Cooper's body? I would scout the desert near Santa Fe and find a secluded place, some spot easily accessible by day or night, maybe some old mine shaft. I would bury the son of bitch so deep that the devil himself would have a hard time finding Cooper's body.

I made a mental checklist of things I needed to do. I forced myself to believe Cooper would be smarter, faster, talented, and more alert than any foe I had ever faced. Then, I addressed each possibility—twice!

Afterward, I gave a handful for dog food to Bailey.

As I scanned satellite radio, a Michael Feinstein song, MY FAVORITE YEAR, gave me pause.

I had to go so far without you, now it's clear,
You were my favorite love; that was my favorite year

Thereafter, the past settled over me like a net. Again, I ached for the magic of Jill's and my first day together...

...The young woman wearing jeans and a yellow polo shirt approached the librarian's desk. Her extraordinary beauty offset her casual manner. Her persona brightened the room.

Jack studied her pretty face for a few seconds before he realized she was not wearing makeup.

"May I help you, Miss...?" the librarian asked.

"Wellington. Jillian Wellington," Jill said, smiling. "Everyone calls me Jill; you should, too."

Wholesome warmth filled Jill's voice and her smile. Her teeth were even, extremely white, and perfectly formed.

Jack failed to fight an immediate attraction.

"I'd like GROWING GOOD ROSES by Reddell."

"And the call number?" asked the librarian.

"Right here," Jill said, showing a card.

Jill spoke slowly, as if from the south. Her voice lacked the nasal quality typical of Western New Yorkers.

The librarian studied the reference number.

"In the back, I'll be just a minute, Miss Wellington."

"I'm not a miz, miss, or missus, I'm Jill, remember."

The librarian smiled, "Yes, of course, Jill...sorry." She walked away with an air of professional efficiency.

Jill fidgeted with her pencil and, as she turned, she noticed Jack seated at a nearby table.

"I think people should just say what's on their minds," she said sensibly. "It's easier that way, no pretense."

Jack nodded.

"Everybody gets too hung up; too many people dance around an issue," Jill continued. "I like directness."

Jack nodded, again.

"Open and honest expression is seldom used," she added.

"I agree. My name's Jack, how about a cup of coffee?"

"Under used by everyone except you," she responded, with a wider and more appealing smile.

"Just popped into my mind," Jack replied. "When you said you like honesty, I thought I'd give it a shot and go for the gold. After all, *Jack and Jill* has a certain ring. How much pressure is in a cup of coffee and a conversation?"

Jill held her smile, listening, anticipating more.

"You know," he continued. "I thought I'd take a chance, roll the dice, and break away from the pack." He hesitated. "It's the first time I've tried this approach. How am I doing?"

Jill nodded. Her eyes sparkled.

"Better than most," she replied. Jill studied his face, assessing him. He liked the scrutiny. Her smile poked at his heart. "*Jack and Jill...*coffee could be fun."

Twenty minutes later in a small café after two cups of coffee, a minor discussion about roses, and a few laughs, a door opened to romance, and ultimately to enduring love.

Their passion was always honest and intense but, as the pendulum swung, it ultimately turned bittersweet.

"So you're a twenty-year Army officer and you write advertising messages and jingles," she said, sipping a decaf latte, repeating what she heard. Afterward, she giggled.

"I like advertising; what's so amusing?" he asked.

"Don't misinterpret my laughter, Jack. Nothing's funny, I'm actually laughing at myself. I'm terrible when it comes to guessing a person's profession. I never *ever* get it right."

"What did you imagine for me?"

"I thought maybe a doctor or lawyer."

"Did my cutoffs, tee shirt, and sandals point to those professions? Doctors and lawyers have gone casual, but I doubt my style fits hospital wards or mahogany offices."

"I don't know, those professions entered my mind."

"I don't have the patience or discipline. I'm a retired Army officer comfortable in advertising. What do you do?"

"I took over a relative's grass-cutting business and branched out into architectural landscaping, which was my major in college. I have forty-three commercial clients and two crews. I make good money and I have lots of fun."

"An independent businesswoman," Jack said.

"Yep, the people are good and I get to work on my tan."

"Thus, your request for the book about roses," he added.

She smiled.

"You don't have a Western New York accent," Jack stated.

She giggled again.

"My turn to be wrong?" he asked.

"Yes, I'm a native Buffalonian and I really haven't traveled much. A few trips," she replied.

"You like it here," Jack observed.

She nodded. "Yes, I do, very much, even the snow. You write jingles and can connect the dots. I must learn more."

"About arbors and trellises?" he asked.

"That, too," she said.

He glanced at her exquisite pink fingernails, and said, "Your hands don't indicate they're in the dirt all that much."

She glanced about, seemingly to see if anyone was listening. Then, Jill leaned toward him as if to tell Jack a deeply guarded secret, all the while teasing him with her magnificent eyes.

She liked him and he knew it. He liked her, too. He was surprised by how much and how quickly it had happened.

She pursed her lips as she thought.

"Did you ever hear of gloves?" she whispered.

"Sure, I own several pairs. I even wore them in the Army."

"I own them, too," she replied, giggling. "They're part of my secret. Gloves, a nail file, and polish."

Unexpectedly, she reached across the table, taking his hand in hers. The sensation was exhilarating. The fragrance of her perfume hinted of warm days and warmer nights.

"Your hand is soft and warm," she whispered.

"Is that good?" he questioned.

"I think so," she replied.

She paused, thinking, then asked, "How about dinner tonight at my place? I'll cook and might even bake a cake."

"What's the occasion?"

"Soft and warm hands," she replied.

"What if I'm involved with someone?" he asked.

She hesitated for just a second before answering.

"If you are," she replied with a distinct air of finality, "You won't be for long. What did you do in the Army?"

"I was an Army Ranger."

"Did you have a white horse?"

"That's the Lone Ranger. He was a cowboy."

"Did you ever catch bad guys," she said with flirty eyes.

"A few."

"Ever married?"

"No. It never fit my profession. I guess I'm unlucky."

"Luck can change," she said.

He scratched his chin with his free hand. The word *astounding* entered his mind.

"You seem to be a woman who is damned sure of herself."

"Remember, I know how to grow things."

"Dinner would be wonderful," Jack replied.

Jill smiled, wrote on the back of a business card, and handed it to him.

"It's my home address. I live near Delaware Park."

He read it. "I know the street, about seven?" he asked.

She teased him with her eyes once again and toyed with the second button on her shirt, and said, "Let's make it seven thirty. I should be finished playing in dirt by then."

That night, when Jack kissed Jill the first time, her mouth tasted of ginger spice; the second kiss had the same distinct flavor.

"You taste like cake," he whispered in her ear.

Another purse of her lips indicated humor.

"I stirred in an aphrodisiac of ginger extract before I put it in the oven...it's a part of my master plan."

"Really, you have a master plan?"

She nodded.

"Yes," she replied, "And this is a part of it."

She leaned against him and kissed him deeply, probing his tongue with hers.

Jill's third kiss did it. He laced his fingers in hers to stop from falling off the edge of the earth and she moved his hand to her breast.

"You're sure about this?" he asked, pausing to breathe.

"Right now, I can't think of another place I'd rather be. It's Friday night. You don't have promos to write, do you?"

"Nope," he said softly.

"What about in the morning?"

"I usually read on Saturday mornings. What will you do?"

"When I awake, I'll roll over and say good morning to you," she said. A nibble on his earlobe taunted him.

"That means we'll be together."

"Now, you're catching on, kemosabe," she said...

...Several large trucks passed and the whine of their wheels pulled me back into the present. In the glare of oncoming headlights, I noticed a brisker snowfall. I glanced at the outside temperature gauge: twenty-four degrees. We were running south of Cleveland and the traffic was heavy.

I changed lanes, gunned the engine, and passed two mini-vans and a slow-moving Volkswagen.

Jill had a way of wrapping our souls together.

I again looked at Bailey. He was asleep, curled, and comfortable on the passenger seat.

I reached for my thermos of coffee, opened it, and drank. Immediately, the aroma of fresh brew filled the cab. Jill loved the smell of coffee. I loved the smell of Jill.

A Greyhound bus passed in the opposite direction and its lights angled across the interior of the pickup. For just a moment, I was back in Jill's bedroom...

...When they made love, the only light in the room came from the moon and the headlights of traffic passing on the street behind Jill's carriage house.

After his eyes adjusted to the silver light, Jack watched Jill move on top of him.

She placed her hands behind her head and he saw her prominent tan lines and her taut breasts with tight pink nipples, her skin pearl gray in the semi-darkness.

He lost track of how many hours he spent inside Jill or how many times they made love. They explored and tasted everything about each other.

No fear. No caution. No concern. No inhibitions.

He was hers and she was his...completely!

Sometime after three in the morning, they finally fell into a deep sleep, and as he drifted off, he smelled the fragrance of roses in her hair.

He hugged her through most of that night, spooning his body against hers, breathing to the same indescribable rhythm as she did, content in the exciting bond of new union and the residual pleasure of complete sexual release.

Several times during the night, he awoke only to experience the joy of knowing that he was with the most remarkable woman he had ever met.

He thanked God for bringing them together and he asked God to keep it that way into eternity.

The next morning Jack was in love with Jill, and Jill was in love with Jack...

...In our early years together, we had many similar days and nights like that first one. That was before the drinking, before Jill's and my heartache.

Nevertheless, in my mind, that first day would forever be the most precious and revered of all our days together.

It was perfect and unblemished, a dream come true, the answer to a lifetime of yearning and empty searches.

I remembered that first day often because of its purity, because of its excitement and newness. Despite all the subsequent issues, nothing could ever change the magic of our first day together.

Twelve years in advertising seemed too much; ten years with Jill had not even scratched the surface.

I paused and swallowed a deep sense of loss.

I changed the channel, found an all-news station, passed several slower vehicles, and drove on into the stormy night, unaware of the snow and ice swirling behind my pickup.

Eventually my thoughts landed on Aaron Cooper.

"I'll get him, Jill...I will take him down."

As my pickup bore through the night toward Columbus, not one person who passed in either direction knew I was destined to kill another man.

It was my secret and I would never tell another soul.

Jill always told me secrets are for the heart and not for public consumption. I would follow her advice.

God, I missed her and the hurt was bone deep.

36

The snowstorm that blew across Oklahoma had intensified throughout the day. As Theo Jefferson pulled into to her driveway, Jack Redding drove toward Columbus, Ohio. Theo was grateful to be off the streets and at home. She had departed the University of Tulsa at just the right time. She was now safe and soon she would be warm.

In a matter of minutes, she gathered up her groceries and briefcase, and was out of the car and into her house.

Theo's day had been a good one. The classes she taught went well, as did her meeting with her friend Lillian Ayers.

"You have a mild form of depression," Lillian told her. "Millions go through it at one time or another in their lives. You did the smart thing by talking to me."

"What causes this?" asked Theo.

"Any number of things," Lillian replied. "It's best summed up by saying things build on us and sometimes our bodies change and we experience chemical imbalances. The pills I have prescribed are not addictive but they are powerful. In about a week, you'll feel content and confident again. Nothing will bother you, problems will seem less taxing."

"Happy pills," Theo whispered.

The doctor smiled. "In a way, yes, they are. Nevertheless, depression is nothing to fool with; if unchecked, it can cause severe problems. So, you did yourself a favor."

"At times, through the years, I've felt like I've been in a deep hole and escape seemed impossible."

Lillian nodded. "Those sensations will subside. Just knowing what the problem is should help turn it around."

Theo was surprised. She felt relieved to know it was not something more serious. She unpacked her groceries. Because of the storm, the university would be a ghost town.

She would make several kinds of soup, instead.

37

The miles and hours merged and I settled into the comfortable rhythm of driving and listening to news radio. I only talked to Bailey when I wanted to sort out some issue concerning Cooper.

We paused at a rest stop north of Columbus and shared a can of cheese ravioli and pieces of French bread.

As Bailey romped in the snow for exercise, and to do his duty, I went to the restroom. On my way out, I stopped at a vending machine to purchase a cup of hot chocolate.

"Hell of a storm out there ain't it, pard," a voice scratched from somewhere in the darkness behind me.

I turned and saw a bearded man, red-faced, thin, and in his mid-sixties. He sat in a corner of the small concourse. He wore a frayed Army fatigue jacket, jeans, and scuffed jump boots. A ratty Tigers ball cap sat atop a worn knapsack. A faded name was on his fatigue jacket.

"Cold, too," I replied, asking, "You a vet, Toliver?"

"How do you know my name?"

"Name's on your field jacket," I replied. "I was a Ranger."

"Oh, yeah, I forgot. I went to Nam, 82nd Airborne…a long time ago. I was Third Brigade at Phu Bai, up in I Corps. There've been lots of shadows since then."

"Shadows, what does that mean?"

"Losses and heartaches, man…losses and heartaches."

"You need a lift somewhere?" I offered.

"No, I'm warm and happy right here. I could use a few bucks to buy one of those vending machine sandwiches. I've missed a few meals lately."

I gave him a handful of tens, a fifty, and all my loose change. He smiled happily, showing yellow teeth. Then, tears formed in his eyes and he wiped them away with the back of his hand. I knew immediately how grateful he was.

"You're a saint, brother."

I thought about my goal to kill Aaron Cooper and said, "Far from it, I've been called many things but never a saint. I'll never be one."

"They come in all shapes and sizes, pard, and in places you'd least expect. Thanks for helping' me, I'll pray for you."

"Where you headed?"

"Fort Bragg

Thinking of my brother, I said, "Friend, the Veterans Administration can help you."

"I know, but I'm not on the dole and that has meaning."

"You sure you don't need a lift?"

"I'm warm. I'll hitch a ride in the morning from a good-hearted trucker; they're always willing to help. Watch out for those shadows, man. They put dark holes in your life. Thankfully, one life usually touches another with kindness. The type of kindness you just showed me. We don't really notice it, but the things people do, touch our lives all the time. They're angels, man...real angels."

I nodded and departed, realizing I was trying to extract a few shadows from my life.

I whistled for Bailey, brushed the snow off his fur, and opened the pickup door. He curled on the seat beside me and yawned.

By the time we were up to pace on the highway, my big dog was sleeping. I turned the radio to background music, tromped the accelerator, and sped off into the snowy night.

I would do my best to avoid shadows.

38

The State Trooper's patrol car came into the EL CORAZÓN Complex in Spring Valley, Nevada. It was a slow and routine drive-through. When the trooper saw two men removing furniture from one of the units, he stopped and waved to Ramon Lopez.

"Just a moment," Ramon Lopez said to Tulio Garcia.

He jogged over to the patrol car. "Can I help you, Lieutenant Stola?"

"I heard the woman died. Sorry about that, seems sad."

Ramon nodded. "Yes, very. The way I understand it, she didn't have a chance. She was a good person, a pretty woman. I saw her dance once. Man, she was hot."

The trooper smiled.

"I never had the pleasure, my friend." With his chin, he motioned to a trailer loaded with furniture. "Did you lease the place already; you must have a hell of a backlog."

Ramon chuckled.

"No, we're moving everything into storage out back, where the boss keeps his boats. Ms. Cassidy's niece is going to come and sort through everything. As for the unit, we'll repaint and put in new furniture. A friend of the owner is coming for a visit. He'll stay for a while. After that, we might lease it."

"Life goes on, huh, amigo?"

"You got that right, boss."

"I was merely passing through for a routine check. Be good and keep your left up."

Ramon, a golden-glover, nodded and the cop pulled away.

Back near the trailer, Ramon bent to help Garcia lift a big brown sofa."

"Who was that Ray?" Garcia asked.

"Lieutenant Stola...he used to come and watch me fight. He is a good cop and a good man. He likes to spar."

39

My focus on driving silenced, at least temporarily, the memories and speculation about what I might have done differently for Jill. The hum of tires on the wet pavement, the passing traffic, the road signs, the falling snow, and the business of travel dulled my preoccupations.

That night at nine o'clock, I passed miles of farm country where tall silos stood vigil over snow-covered fields. At the edges, patches of woods blended with the deep black sky that blanketed the eastern edge of America's heartland. Two words came to mind: beautiful desolation.

Approaching Dayton, Ohio, a traffic accident forced a slight detour. A reroute, north of Enon, a nearby town, forced all westbound vehicles onto county roads.

As I wound my way back toward I-70W, I passed a farmer on a wagon pulled by a brown draft horse. Quickly, long-ago shadows inundated me. The sedation of a long drive vanished and Jill and I were sitting on a carriage, riding through Central Park.

Snow fell that night, too, as Jill curled against me for warmth. She seized my heart in ways that seemed endless. The clip clop of a horse was our music and, for just a moment, winter in New York was akin to heaven.

Thereafter, memories poured into my troubled heart, holding me captive...

...The trip to New York was their first together, the first of many for Jill and Jack. No place on earth is as magnificent as Manhattan during the Christmas holidays. For a man and woman in love, the elegance of the Plaza added a special ambiance.

A gentle snow fell each day. The air carried the sweet, roasted scent of pretzels and chestnuts.

People chattered happily on the sidewalks as they pushed into restaurants and out of retail stores.

The steam from manholes spiraled upward in the wind.

Music from street musicians filled many corners and decorative lights brightened almost every window.

The hustle of Chinatown and the flavor of cannoli from an Italian bakeshop on Mulberry Street became treasures.

The rhythm and blare of the horns of city traffic added a unique symphony. A Broadway play and a quiet, candle-lit dinner redefined intimacy and tightened their bond.

Hot cocoa and cheesecake after window-shopping on Fifth Avenue enhanced a Saturday afternoon. An impromptu ride through Central Park on a carriage drawn by a horse named Lester, driven by an old man named Johnnie, was ideal for lovers. Somehow, the presence of Lester and Johnnie made the ride more romantic.

Sunday Mass at St. Patrick's reinforced their faith in God, in the world, and in each other. They cherished the pomp and circumstance of a Mass concelebrated by a cardinal and bishop. A tenor from the Met sang with the choir.

The weekend emphasized the special 'together' things a man and woman deeply in love shared before buckets of booze washed good parts of that special life into the gutter.

The specific hours of early Sunday morning stood out in Jack's mind. He had returned from a night of playing cards at a very private Manhattan gaming room.

Jill wore a pink satin robe and sat on a king-sized bed reading the Sunday NEW YORK TIMES when he entered their suite at the Plaza. The robe's sash was untied and provided candid glimpses of Jill's naked body beneath.

"It's barely six in the morning, I thought you'd be asleep," he said, kissing her. He smelled powder and perfume, and tasted toothpaste.

She smiled and returned his kiss, saying, "Hi."

"Back at you," Jack replied.

"It's the magic of the city, Jack. I awoke. I couldn't sleep anymore. So, I ordered coffee, croissants, and a newspaper."

"I'll bet the room service guy appreciated your robe."

She giggled. "I'm sure he would have liked it very much, if he'd seen me. I requested a knock and told them to leave the service cart at the door. I peeked to make sure he was gone." She placed the paper aside. "So, tell me, did we win?"

Jack nodded, removed his billfold from his vest pocket, and set it on the bed beside her. He stifled a yawn and said, "I don't really know the final total but I finished ahead."

"Did you play Blackjack?"

He nodded and whispered, "Yes, that's all I ever play."

He removed his shirt, sat on the bed, and untied his shoes. Jill's eyes studied several scars and the blue and gold diamond tattoo on his left bicep.

As he slipped off his pants, her robe fell off her shoulders.

"You always win playing Blackjack. You want to join me?"

"Yes, I do," he replied caressing her chin and brushing his hand across one of her nipples. "I need to wash first. I'll be right back."

He went into the bathroom and turned on the shower. He shaved, brushed his teeth, and stepped into the spray. The warm water beat against his smoky skin and, after a shampoo, he felt normal again.

He liked Blackjack. Jack was a card counter but he never told Jill or anyone else his secret. His grandfather taught him how to do it and, with years of practice, he had refined the talent. "Certain things are best if they remain unsaid. It makes life easier and less complicated," his grandfather cautioned. "Always keep it to yourself and be restrained."

He poked his head out of the shower and saw the reflection of Jill's legs in the mirror. The notion of her lying semi-naked on the bed was breathtaking.

That she chose him always amazed Jack. Jill would turn her head, move a certain way, brush her hair aside, or smile just so, and his heart would tumble.

"While I'm in the shower," he shouted, "Do the honors, tally everything up."

She pulled the robe back onto her shoulders, removed the money, and began separating the bills by denomination.

"What'd you start with?"

"Three thousand...everything else is ginger and spice."

~

The hot shower beat on his skin and Jack watched water spiraling down the drain. The intense focus needed to win always drained him. He had to use all his skill to avoid discovery. Dealers and owners hated card counters. The hot water was a perfect way to empty his mind and massage the stiffness out of his shoulders.

Jack breathed in the steam, trying to unwind. Instead of relaxing, the water dripping from his nose and chin reminded him of the terror-filled night in the Colombian jungle. That memory rushed at him with full force. He tried, but could not shake it.

He lowered his head, wanting his mind to go blank. Sometimes it worked; sometimes it didn't. In a matter of seconds, Jill and New York disappeared. He was back in the jungle, where he and others did trigger work for the CIA...

...The deputy director conveyed the message to impart its severity. The Munoz drug cartel had captured a senator's daughter, a medical doctor working in remote Colombian villages. They demanded ten million dollars or they would start shipping fingers and toes via express delivery.

Twelve hours later Jack, three of his men, and a local agent huddled under ponchos. He commanded five groups of four. Twenty men had volunteered to rescue the doctor.

They would also unleash untold misery on the cartel.

Officially, they were to rescue the woman and her associates. Unofficially, they were to send a clear message that the United States would not accept the specified terms. Translated that meant they would kill as many members of the cartel as they could, and burn all facilities. Red Robin's actions were to be 'definitive.'

A trusted operative named Carlos was their boots-on-the-ground, reporting directly to Jack.

"The Munozistas love the heavy rain," Carlos whispered. "They believe the rain protects them and deters enemies because it makes it more difficult to find them."

"They're idiots," Bill Hawkins whispered.

Carlos nodded, opened a waterproof map, and pointed to a specific sector. "They are here, opposite this ridge."

"We'll hit them hard," Jack said. "They won't expect it."

"The cartel's primary manufacturing facility is here," Carlos added. "This is where the doctor is being held. She is with other physicians and nurses."

As a cartel runner passed in the distance, the team newbie, Willis, flinched noticeably. Knowing Jack saw the recoil, Willis leaned in and said, "I'm a bit uneasy, sir."

Jack studied the fear in the man's eyes and nodded, saying, "Me, too, but you can't beat the rush. Now, shut up or you'll get us killed."

Bill Hawkins and Ted Jefferson, sitting next to Willis, smiled. So, did Jack and Carlos.

"How far do we have to go?" Jack asked.

"Two kilometers," Carlos replied...

...The shower door opened and Jack was back in New York. Jill's hand on his hip pulled him away from an unwanted memory. As her caress moved across his skin to his pelvis, the terror-filled night in Colombia disappeared.

He turned, found her mouth, and kissed her.

"Did you count the money?"

She nodded.

"You did fine," she whispered in his ear. "We have an unexpected windfall."

"How much did we win?" Jack asked.

"Twenty-two thousand," she replied, caressing him with her fingers. She loved to touch him and feel his response. She giggled.

She lifted her leg around his waist and her eyes widened as he entered her. He heard Jill moan.

"Not a bad night's take," he said, kissing her cheek. "It's a pretty big haul," he added.

"I'll say. It's also one hell of a double entendre," she replied. "You have a way with words."

"Maybe I should write love stories," he whispered.

"An excellent choice," she said. "Now, stay focused."

For ten minutes or so, they were one in body and motion, wrapped in an embrace designed by God to overwhelm the spirits of those deeply in love.

Later, as Jill breathed softly and rhythmically beside him, Jack lay awake. He had tried to fall asleep, but old memories kept jabbing him. He remembered the doctor's cold comment after the Colombian rescue.

"What took you clowns so long?" she shouted. 'We were without food and water for two days. My father will hear about this and he will respond accordingly."

"Is that supposed to scare me?" asked Jack.

"It should," she said. The doctor was spoiled and self-centered, and showed no concern for the member of Jack's team who died to attain her freedom.

That mission, Jack's last, was the reason he retired from the military. Jack and his Rangers gave the woman a gift.

She never had the class to say thank you.

Thank God, he had Jill, his refuge and his strength.

He pulled Jill close, pushed the bad memories aside, and fell asleep believing nothing could taint their love.

Years later, miscarriages, family tragedies, and far too much vodka proved Jack Redding wrong...

...I took the ramp onto the interstate, drove through a slight skid, and continued on, into the night.

I liked the good memories and hated the bad. Of late, they comingled, coming at me all at once.

I took a piece of bread, chewed it, and wondered if killing Cooper would really take my pain away? I hoped so but I really did not know.

A road sign indicated the Indiana border was nearby.

I checked the time: 9:40 p.m.

Bailey and I would stop. Eventually, I hoped the memories would stop, too...at least the bad ones.

I needed a chance at a new direction. I needed something that would pull me out of the hell I had known since learning that my wife died in a cocktail dress in a snowstorm in Pittsburgh.

40

East and a bit north of Albuquerque, Aaron Cooper and Liza Mercer sipped wine beside a warm fireplace as Jack Redding crossed the Ohio/Indiana border and swerved to avoid an adventurous deer.

Through the window, over their shoulders, a light snow was falling. In the distance, lights dotted Sandia Peak and a nearly full tram of people descended toward a nearby lodge.

"Was your meeting a success?" Cooper asked.

Mercer swallowed wine and nodded, "I think so. My client wants portraits of his two daughters as a birthday gift for his wife. It should be relatively easy."

"Good."

"What did you do while I was meeting?"

Cooper set his wine glass on a nearby table and smiled at his new love.

"I did a lot of thinking, about my life, about what I want, and about us."

"Good thoughts?" I hope.

"For the most part, yes, they were. When you're a cop, you do and see things that are far from the norm and sometimes the memories return. You have to live with many bad things, it comes with the turf."

"Do you want to discuss it?"

He shook his head, indicating he did not.

"I'd like to travel and see the world, and I'd like you to go with me, in a permanent way. I have money, I've been lucky with investments, and we could work it around your portrait assignments. I'm hoping you'll find that exciting."

She arched her eyebrows, "Aaron Cooper, are you asking me to marry you?"

He smiled. "Would you? I'd like that very much."

"That would be wonderful," she said, kissing him.

41

Sergeant Amos Talley had marriage on his mind, too. Tonight was the night he would pop the question.

The sergeant had never heard of Jill Redding nor had he met Jack Redding. However, the sergeant's actions would eventually link the two men. In a few hours, Jack would glance at the load of rocks that Talley was taking to the northern edge of Fort Leonard Wood in Missouri. That glance would reopen a troubling memory.

"Why are we taking the rocks out this late, Sarge?"

Talley looked at Corporal Devon Johnson and laughed.

"I'm taking them, Dev. You're along for the ride."

"What I meant, we can take them in the morning...why do it tonight? We can't repair the fence. It's almost dark, besides it's snowing like hell."

"I promised the major I'd do it. He let me drive to St. Robert this afternoon to pick up Loren's engagement ring."

"Did you ask her?"

"I will, tonight, when I'm off duty."

Johnson smiled. "You know," he said, "getting married is a lot like building a fence, Sarge,"

"You think of that on your own, Dev?"

"My daddy did, in one of his sermons. He said if you build a marriage proper, like you do a fence, it lasts a lifetime."

"I'll remember that, here's the turnoff. It leads to the fence line. We'll unload the trailer in the morning."

He slowed the truck and turned. Out on the interstate, a steady stream of headlights streaked by in the twilight.

Devon watched the traffic and said, "Man, the world is full of hustle and bustle, ain't it?"

"Hey, hustle and bustle, let's unhook the trailer, I've got a date with a pretty woman."

"Sarge, you are a lucky man!"

42

The last swallow of coffee, which I bought in Erie, went down in the snug comfort of my pickup at a rest stop west of Richmond, Indiana. The weather this far west and south of Buffalo was warming; snow was turning into sleet.

I watched traffic pass a road sign on I-70, which indicated Greenfield was fifty miles away. We would arrive by eleven.

"We should stop for the night and get some sleep," I said to Bailey, whose ears lifted at the sound of my voice. "We should eat something. I believe you're as hungry as I am."

Bailey lifted his head briefly, panted several times, and settled back into the warmth that his body transferred to the passenger seat. I studied his handsome face.

"You know, Bailey," I whispered, "You were Jill's boy from the moment she saw you."

At the mention of Jill's name, Bailey cocked his head and the tip of his tail began to wag.

"From the moment she first saw you," I repeated...

...They were in a kennel.

"You can have any dog you want as long as he looks like OLD YELLER," Jill said, as she browsed the cages. In front of them, hundreds of dogs barked and yelped. It was as if each said, *"Choose me, please; choose me!"*

"That limits the field, sweetheart," Jack replied.

"I loved that movie," she said. "OLD YELLER was a noble dog, and that's exactly what we need."

"Noble," Jack repeated. He looked at the kennel master and said, "The lady wants a noble dog."

"Our yellow labs are this way," the man whispered.

Moments later, after opening a cage door, Jill stooped and lifted a male puppy, which immediately cuddled against her shoulder and fell sound asleep.

"Look at him, Jack."

Jack smiled and shook his head. Jill found her dog.

"How much?" asked Jack.

"Five hundred dollars," the kennel owner replied.

"Did you hear that, Bailey," Jill said, jostling the puppy's chin, "You're coming home with us."

"Bailey?"

She looked at Jack and shrugged.

"I grew up on Bailey Avenue and always thought Bailey would make a great name for a dog."

"Do I have a say in the matter?"

"Sure, you can sign the check,"...

...A big auto hauler carrying Cadillac Escalades passed on my left, covering my windshield with mist. I hit the wipers.

"That man is definitely running late." I rubbed my dog's head. "She had a way about her, our Jill; she had a way."

Bailey whined several times.

"I feel the same way, bud. We both feel cheated."

Up ahead a neon light flashed *Vacancy* at a small mom and pop motel. When I saw a *Pets Welcome* sign, I exited the interstate.

Half an hour later, we were in a comfortable room eating peanut butter sandwiches. We shared a quart of skim milk.

When I turned out the lights, I took the bed against the wall, and Bailey hopped on the twin near the window. He was asleep almost instantly, but I lay awake and thought about God, Cooper, and things I needed to do. The surprising sound of thunder over the motel, took me back to the Colombian jungle and the face of an irate female doctor...

...Operation Stone Cold had two primary objectives.

First, Jack and his Red Robin Team went in to rescue an American medical crew, including Dr. Joanna Stone.

Second, they were to inflict whatever damage they could to the Munoz Cartel's cocaine production facilities.

Dr. Stone was the daughter of Joseph Stone, an ultra-liberal United States Senator from New Hampshire.

Senator Stone, a descendant of a long line of New England progressives, often denigrated U.S. military efforts, especially its clandestine activities.

His daughter, with an Ivy-League pedigree, was a chip from the same block of New Hampshire granite. She went to Colombia as a medical volunteer with the international relief and humanitarian organization Put People First (PPF). Like her father, PPF was often critical of U.S. Foreign Policy, especially in the Third World.

About eleven thirty, the final growl of thunder dissipated, the rain subsided, the cloud cover broke, and moonlight brightened the Colombian jungle.

Hawk reached out and shook Jack's shoulder.

"It's time, Midnight."

Jack opened his eyes and nodded.

"Do you think they know we're here?"

"Not a chance in hell."

"Did you check our back trail?"

Hawk nodded.

"Twice, we're clean."

"The sub teams, Hawk, are they ready?"

"Yes, waiting for you to flip the switch," Hawk replied.

"Is Willis listening?" Jack asked.

"He's had them hot for about an hour. The woman is there; other docs and nurses, too."

"Good."

He studied Hawk's expression.

"Something's bothering you, bud?" Jack asked.

"Her old man criticizes the very air we breathe, but turns to us to rescue his daughter. This stinks."

"It is what it is. He and his family can say what they want. They're Americans, free speech and all that important stuff. We still have to help them."

"Damn it, I don't have to like it."

"Us 'liking it' is not in the equation; we do our job."

Jack and Bill Hawkins moved down a hill to a natural indentation in the slope. They crawled in beside three men. Jack adjusted his hat and looked at Willis, his radioman."

"What are you hearing, Sarge?"

"Chatter mostly, but Carlos thinks he's got something."

Jack turned to the narrow-faced Colombian. Despite six hours of constant rain and intense heat and humidity, the lenses of the Carlos' glasses were bone dry.

"Let's have it."

"A man was talking and he said Salada *took food to his kitten and the others*."

"Meaning what, that Salada and Dr. Stone are lovers?"

"That's my interpretation."

"We saw a light in a window in the second building," Hawk added. "I studied it with my scope. The shade was half-drawn. Stone did embrace a man, maybe Salada."

"Salada, really…Jesus, is this all a hoax?" Jack asked.

"It might be," Hawk replied.

"So," Jack added, "extending the logic, this kidnapping could be a scam?"

Hawk nodded, "If so, it's tied to the money."

"Maybe to fund the doctor's projects," Carlos noted.

"Proof?" asked Jack.

"Other than us knowing Salada runs the cartel, we got bupkis," Hawk whispered. "But, it wouldn't surprise me."

"Why am I not shocked?" Jack asked. "The doctor wants money for something. Let me have the field glasses."

Jack studied the building: no movement.

"Do we know how many men?"

"Ten, for sure, that we've counted," Hawk replied.

"Manageable," Jack said. "We should be ready for more. Where's the production facility, Hawk?"

"Underground, and to the left, it looks like a shed. Men and women moved in and out at five in the afternoon, and at eleven. Each time the count was twenty."

"Shift workers," Carlos explained. "They have assembly lines and employ modern production processes. A newer facility is under construction. We don't know where exactly."

"Henry Ford would be proud," Jack whispered. "Did the cartel guy really refer to Joanna Stone as *Salada's kitten*?"

"Si, mi amigo," Carlos whispered.

"I'll be damned," Jack whispered.

"Do we still rescue her?" Hawk inquired.

"Sure, we don't scrub the mission based on speculation. I want Jefferson to tape the interrogations. They might prove invaluable. For now, it's game on. We get her out."

Jack turned to Hawkins and said, "Red Robins Two and Three will hit the production facility. They go in hot, burn it, and get out. Tell them to use tear gas to drive out the workers. Red Robins One and Five will extract the doctor and others. Robin Four guards our six. Robin Five secures the Landing Zone, after we have the doctor. Robin Four retains the work crew. I want Jefferson chatting them up. I want that second production facility burning before liftoff. Is all that clear?"

"Yes, sir," Hawk replied.

"What's your take, Hawk?" Jack asked.

"Midnight, these aren't the sharpest nails in the barrel."

Jack nodded, smiled, and spoke. "You should know, Hawk, about 'Midnight,' I hate that fucking name. It doesn't fully capture my true persona."

"I know, sir...but me and the boys, we love it as much as you love to kick ass in the first hour of the day."

Jack nodded. "Well, there is that. Call it in, I want choppers airborne and ready to extract upon my order."

"Five square, Midnight."

~

The assault went smoother than expected. The Red Robin Teams hit with surgical precision and in less than five minutes Dr. Stone and the others were secure, and the known production facility was ablaze.

"We're out of here in one zero minutes, after your order, sir. Robin Five caught a bandit and he might be a good one."

Jack nodded. "Bring the choppers in," he ordered, "and hustle Jefferson up here with Carlos pronto."

Two minutes later, Jack and three of his men had the cartel man spread eagle on the ground with his pants around his ankles. Terror filled the man's eyes, tears rolled down his dirty face.

"You've got one minute, Teege," Jack said. "I want this man singing an aria."

"Where's the other facility?" Carlos asked.

The man shook his head. He clearly was not going to reveal the location without an impetus.

"Choppers in eight minutes," Hawk said. "We need the location now, if you want that facility burning."

Jack looked at Jefferson and said, "Do what you do best, I need that location."

Jefferson removed a thin, five-inch long hypodermic needle, showed it to the cartel guard, and inserted it through one of the man's testicles.

He screamed immediately, shouting to Carlos.

"He says it's very close but not yet operational. A tarp covers the entrance."

"The direction," Jack demanded.

Carlos asked and was told it was due south of the complex, about two hundred yards.

As Jack gave the order, a delicate hand grabbed his shoulder. It was an angry grasp.

"What in the hell are you doing?" Joanna Stone asked.

He turned and looked at a petite woman whose nostrils flared with condescension.

"Hawk, move this woman to the LZ," Jack ordered.

"I expect an answer," she said

"No," Jack said, flatly. "It's what we do; you don't like it take it up with your daddy." He turned to Hawk. "Get her out of here, now, before I lose my temper."

She slapped Jack hard across the face.

"You're a war criminal," she said.

"Lady, you don't know the half of it," Jack said, smiling.

"My father will hear about this," she said.

"I'm counting on it," Jack replied. Turning to Hawk, he added, "Get her out, now."

~

A week later, Colonel Jack Redding and Senior Master Sergeant Bill Hawkins walked into a private office in the Dirksen Senate Office Building in Washington, D.C.

When they entered, Senator Joseph Stone was at his desk. His daughter sat on a nearby leather couch, with another man beside her. The reception was cool.

"They look like they want red meat," Hawk said sotto voce, as he stood slightly behind Jack.

"These are the men, Joanna?" The senator began without any introduction.

"Yes," his daughter replied.

The senator turned to the man on the couch, "Tom, my daughter witnessed these men using torture. They must be brought up on charges and taught a lesson."

The eyes of the man on the couch immediately shifted to Jack and Bill Hawkins.

"Torture?" he asked. "Did you really use torture?"

"Your name, sir?" asked Jack.

"Thomas Kindred, chief counsel for the senator's subcommittee on military affairs."

"I wouldn't call it torture," Jack said. "We were moving fast and required information to complete our mission."

"You shoved a needle through an innocent man's testicle," Dr. Stone said. "What *would* you call that?"

"Innocent, Dr. Stone? He helped produce drugs for our streets. Your response is ungrateful and unwarranted. You are a deceptive woman and you are playing to your father's position and power," Jack stated, calmly and clearly.

"Easy Colonel Redding, as an attorney, I advise against unfounded accusations, they could be construed as slander."

"Mr. Kindred, with respect, we had orders and we executed those orders. I'd say we handed Senator Stone and his daughter a diamond, and they're bitching because they found a piece of lint on the velvet."

"You call *torturing a man* a diamond?" the Senator asked.

"I refer to Dr. Stone's rescue," Jack said with an edge in his voice. "I had hoped to see some gratitude. I was wrong."

"And, I was hoping you'd show a sense of civility," the senator replied. "I am a U.S. Senator."

"BFD," Hawk whispered. "That can end quickly."

"What did you just say?" the Senator's eyes were icy.

"You heard me," Hawk replied.

Jack looked at Stone's daughter and at the attorney. Then, his eyes shifted to the Senator. "Senator Stone," he said, "I've been carrying water for the U.S. Army, the CIA, and do-gooders like you and your daughter for twenty years. I think the time has come to stop and find a new life. At this moment, I am retiring from the United States Army."

"Me, too," Hawk added.

"I'll still bring charges against you," Senator Stone said.

Jack smiled. "You can try. You can also go to hell."

"Colonel," Kindred said, "Mind your tongue."

"Or what?" asked Jack, removing a pocket recorder from his vest pocket and hitting play. On the tape, Ted Jefferson interrogated Salada's second in command.

"What is this?" Kindred asked.

"Dr. Stone was screwing the leader of the Munoz Cartel. Her capture was a deception to raise money for PPF causes in Colombia, and elsewhere. Salada agreed to match the payment. Because her daddy is a U.S. Senator, she and Salada actually believed they would get the money."

The attorney shifted his position uneasily.

"You are a piece of shit," the doctor whispered.

"Yes, but a smart one," Jack replied. "How does it feel?"

"Is this true, Joanna? Were you after money? Jesus, such treason and imprudence could ruin us," the Senator said.

Dr. Stone's bowed head and silence emphasized her guilt.

"We've got other eyewitness testimony, and several photographs have surfaced," Jack said. "If you call me or any of my men before your committee, I'll ruin your reputation, your daughter's, and your family's." Jack paused. "Then, you'll learn what many Americans really think of you."

"I suspect this information is safely tucked away in several places?" the attorney asked evenly.

"You'll never find the originals or any copies."

Kindred turned to the doctor and the senator and said, "It's time we let these men leave to enjoy retirement." He looked at Jack. "Your word of honor, none of this leaks?"

Jack pointed at the senator and said, "That's up to him...

...I awoke at seven on Friday morning to find Bailey licking my hand. He needed to go out. At the sink, I splashed water on my face and then peeked through the curtain.

At least four inches of new snow covered the landscape and every object in sight, with more snow falling.

A quick check of the weather channel indicated that we would drive in snow all the way to Tulsa.

I pulled on my jeans, slipped into my heavy boots, and lifted my coat. While I went to the office to settle the bill and get coffee, Bailey found a friendly tree. I also picked up two fresh biscuits, and, after we ate them, Bailey and I took a walk on a snow-covered trail behind the motel. Bailey spooked two rabbits after his morning dump.

Back in the room, I fed Bailey a package of dry dog food, took a hot shower, and finished my coffee.

Before leaving, I made a quick call to the Tulsa number and left another message. I was beginning to worry that something was wrong with Ted Jefferson. No one ever answered the telephone, which seemed odd.

On our way to the Interstate, I stopped at a fast-food restaurant, bought a breakfast sandwich and two large cups of coffee, which I added to my thermos.

I checked the directions on the GPS. I had about six hundred miles to get under my belt and wanted to be in Tulsa before nightfall. It was doable.

"February first," I said to Bailey. "Everything is coming together and I'm glad you are with me, bud. We still have a few miles to go and a battle to fight."

43

On Friday morning, as Jack steadied his cruise control on I-70 in Indiana, Tito Claroni walked into a private office at Sarcusi's Italian Markets of Michigan in Detroit. The snowfall there was heavy, too.

Tony Sarcusi, beside his desk, greeted Claroni warmly.

"Tito," he said. "Do you want coffee? It's our private blend and very tasty. I'll send you some, if you like it."

The slender man nodded, closing the door.

"I assume your visit means good news?" Sarcusi asked.

"Yes, indeed."

"Patsy will take the deal?" Sarcusi inquired. He poured a cup of coffee from an urn.

"First, a few questions about your guy: can we trust him, does he deliver, and does he keep his mouth shut?"

"Yes to all. I've known him for twenty years."

"You know what happens if you're wrong?" Claroni asked.

"Sure, but he's good. I trust him. Here's your coffee."

Tito sipped the brew, nodding his approval.

"Primo," he said. "We take it with stipulations. You join Tommy Jax, make the connection, and bring the stuff back."

"I can do that, anything else?"

"Our chemist does six random tests to verify quality. Tommy's in charge; he'll have the money."

Sarcusi nodded. "Agreed, when do we leave?"

"Probably late next week," Tito said, drinking. I'll call with the exact date. I like this coffee. Also, Patsy's giving you a dime for bringing him the deal."

"That's not necessary," Sarcusi said.

"I know, but I don't argue with Patsy. Why should you?"

"I guess I won't." Sarcusi smiled.

"Good choice," Claroni laughed and departed. He topped off his coffee and took the cup with him.

44

Bailey and I skirted the northwestern edge of Ft. Leonard Wood in central Missouri, running steady at seventy miles per hour on I-44. Afternoon traffic was light in moderately falling snow.

As we came over a rise, off to our left in a misty haze, I noticed a huge pile of stones next to a breach in an old fence. Somewhere in my mind, a switch flipped, memories swirled, and I was with Jill a few months before our wedding.

If I could take back one day, it would be that one. I believe I could have reshaped Jill's life and eased her burden. I will go to my grave believing that was the day that Jill discovered how easily alcohol dulled her sadness. Years later when her problem grew exponentially, I remembered that day. I know I could have helped her, I just cannot prove it.

We were at her parents' summer place in Eden, New York, preparing for her grandmother's funeral on a warm day. As expected, Jill was sullen.

We had known each for a few months and were just getting past the mystery. The awkward moments, the flecks of diffidence that tend to surface with new love, had yet to disappear; luckily, we were gaining on them.

We had shared coffee and muffins at breakfast. After my morning run and a shower, her father mentioned Jill's desire for a long walk...

...Jill exited a large cherry orchard and ascended a slight grade, pausing where a dirt path forked. Either direction led back to her parents' rambling farmhouse.

Hearing persistent singing off to her right, Jill took that fork. The voice was Jack's; she wondered what he was doing that required a song. Curiosity quickened her pace.

That particular stretch of path paralleled a meadow and a

century-old stone fence, a section of which had crumbled due to the push of too many winter snowdrifts.

Nearing the fence, she paused in the lee of several birch trees to listen and observe.

A few yards away, Jack Redding worked steadily, sorting large stones, chipping away debris with hammer and chisel, and mortaring them into position at the base of the break in the old fence.

That she found him mending a broken fence on his own initiative surprised Jill. Jack wore a tattered shirt, ratty with holes and soaked with perspiration.

As he worked he sang Neil Young's HARVEST MOON.

But there's a full moon risin', Let's go dancin' in the light, We know where the music's playing let's go out and feel the night

He paused, sorted stones from a pile, placed them next to the fence, turned to a wheelbarrow, added a tin of water, and began mixing another batch of mortar.

Halfway through, he lifted the front of his shirt and wiped his brow. Jill noticed muscles ripple in his forearms and saw an elongated purplish scar on his left side, above his hip. Even though she had seen it before, the scar never seemed as garish as it did in the intense sunlight.

He let the shirt fall, added another half-tin of water to the mortar, and continued mixing.

Because I'm still in love with you;
I want to see you dance again…because I'm still in love with you, on this Harvest Moon

When the mortar reached the proper consistency, Jack began to whistle the song and continued fitting stones along the base of the break in the fence. He worked fast, moving from bottom to top.

"You know," he said, moments later, without turning toward Jill, "This makes us even."

Caught, Jill stepped out from behind the birch trees.

"Even," she repeated. "How are we even, Jack?"

"Yesterday, you said I was being nosey that day when we met in the library. If I remember, your exact words were, 'Jack, you were snooping and you know it,' and then you laughed. Who is snooping now? We're even." He laughed.

"Touché," she said. "I'm guilty as charged. I'm heading back to take a shower, I'll be there when you finish."

She started for the house.

Jack, focused, smoothed mortar around a large stone, and thumped it into position with the trowel's handle.

When he finally glanced her way, he said, "No critique about my impression of Neil Young or my masonry skills, no offer to help the man you love?"

"I should get back, my mom might need me."

"Your dad was here not long ago, she's napping. I know, you're hurting, Jill; we're all hurting."

"You're hurting, too?" She asked.

His statement clearly surprised her.

"Sure, that's why I'm out here."

She seemed puzzled.

"I didn't know your grandmother well," he continued. "I sense she was a good person. I feel sad, for you, for your parents, for her family."

Jack paused and rubbed his hands on his jeans.

"Jill, I've lost and killed men in battle. It took a while to figure it out but I learned how to ease my sorrow and guilt.

"Singing and working with my hands relaxes me. I find something spiritually reparative about the combination; it soothes the pain.

"If I were a betting man, I'd wager some sacred and mystical link connects the two, that it's part of heaven's design for humanity," he concluded.

"You really believe that?"

He nodded, adding "For years, religions the world over have highlighted the therapeutic value of song and touch. People sing when they are sad and healing powers are associated with *the laying on of the hands.*

"Jesus and his disciples healed with their hands. The context typically refers to helping another person. I've come to believe men and women can help themselves with song and by working ardently with their hands.

"I saw the break in the fence during my morning run. I talked to your dad and he said if I wanted to fix it, stones were here and the equipment and mortar were in the barn. He said have at it. Therefore, here I am. Come, help me."

"Do I have to sing?" Jill teased.

"Only if you choose."

"Good. I don't think I will."

"Wisdom knows it's limits; I've heard you sing, Jill."

"Wiseass," she replied.

"Spend a few minutes working with your hands, sweetie. You will feel better. I believe it."

Jill knelt beside him in the grass.

"You're carrying a burden," Jack whispered. "Use your hands to work out the pain. Just a moment, I have to do something before you begin."

Jill was sure Jack would kiss her. Instead, using his fingertips, he brushed crumbs away from her shirt collar, residue from her breakfast muffin.

"A snoop and a sloppy eater," he noted.

"Oh, shut up," she replied, laughing and jabbing his ribs.

Briefly, he watched the wind caress her dark hair. Her eyes were emeralds, her smile sunshine.

"Have you ever built a stone fence?"

"No."

He pointed to the wheelbarrow. "That goop is mortar, these big things are stones. Together they form a damned sturdy fence that will last a long time."

He gestured toward the pile on his left.

"We'll put these big boys in a nest of mortar and when it dries," he snapped his fingers, "voila, we have a union that verges on the miraculous."

He struggled against the draw of her body.

"It's basic, honest-to-god work. In this case, it mends a broken fence, but it also repairs a damaged heart. The *laying on of hands* does the trick. It's a remedy, a silent song sung unto thyself. Here, let me show you."

He whistled again, took her hands in his and demonstrated the proper way to repair the fence. She felt the muscles in his arms. His hands were simultaneously tender and powerful. Jill was actually disappointed when, realizing she had the hang of it, he let go.

He offered her a spare trowel.

"You have the left side; I'll take the right," he said. "The base is ready on your side. Let's see who finishes first."

"You're on, buster."

~

Forty-five minutes later, after they had repaired the breach, he and Jill walked back to the farmhouse. He teased her as he pushed a wheelbarrow filled with tools. At least for a few minutes, he knew he had diverted her thoughts away from her grandmother's death.

He kissed her before she went into the house.

"Do you feel better?"

"I do. My family, we're very close," she whispered. Jill lowered her head and cried softly.

Jack quickly hugged her.

He handed her a clean handkerchief and she wiped tears from her cheeks, nodding her gratitude.

"I should be with my mom," she whispered. "Thanks for helping me. Jack, I *did* like your singing."

He kissed her again.

"You'll feel better. I know from experience. We all heal. Just give it time, Jill."

She nodded and started to leave for the house.

"Jill, if I do something, promise you won't be angry."

She paused, looked back at him, and said, "It depends on what you intend to do but I doubt it will anger me."

"Good."

He walked to her and again Jill thought of a kiss.

"May I have my handkerchief?"

"Sorry," she said.

He took it and wiped several specks of mortar off the bottom of her chin and the side of her nose.

"So, what were you going to say that you thought might disturb me?" She asked.

"You are as sloppy with mortar as you are with your food."

She giggled and he kissed her.

"I love you, Jill."

"I love you, too, Jack. Stay with me always."

"That's my intent; are we going to go to the next step?"

She nodded, "I believe we should. You make me happy."

"Good."

"The next step," she repeated, "I'd like that very much."

"You should smile more, Jill" he said.

"I should?"

"Yeah, it warms my heart,"...

...Later that day, I believe Jill sowed the seeds of the alcoholism that ruined her life. I am as sure of it as I am of the air we breathe to sustain our existence.

It chills me when I think of it.

It was a naïve mistake not to have recognized it.

After the funeral service, I believe Jill found her own way of soothing her sorrow. I did not think anything would emerge from the three cocktails she had before dinner or the two glasses of merlot she drank with her partially consumed meal. They were not on my mind when she kissed me good night and went off to bed.

Knowing what I know from experience, and having lived with her daily struggles, Jill ignored my observation about song and *the laying on of the hands* to ease personal pain. She much preferred the numbing effect of alcohol. It masked her deep sorrow quicker and delivered a softer, but unsustainable, reality.

Maybe it was too hard to follow my suggestion. My way took time, work, and practice. Vodka gave her an instant fix, but a fleeting one. To prolong it, she had to consume ever-larger amounts. Then, the booze trapped her and she could not exit from the downward spiral!

Thinking back, I believe Jill found what she thought was a better solution, albeit a hollow one. She tucked it away to nurture it as if it were a treasure. She guarded it and opened its lid when she needed comfort.

In her life, as in all, burdens arose. She tried damned hard to drown them with booze but she failed.

I can still see her that evening staring absently out a window, wineglass in hand, biting her lower lip, and fighting tears, her sorrow a bitter memory that would not go away.

Of course, the real damage came much later when one miscarriage after another made her spin out of control, day after day after day.

I passed an older couple in a 90-something Cadillac. They were laughing and gesturing, and seemed very much in love. Seeing them brought a wave of melancholy.

I had hoped to grow old with Jill but that never happened. That pleasure, and many others, had dissolved in a vat of alcohol and not a goddamned thing was ever the same. I know I could have done more but that is the flaw of hindsight. It always provides a clear focus and a succinct solution. Hindsight never eliminates hurt as deep and as wide as a stormy sea.

I think about that day at her parents' farm often. I wish I could peel back time and wipe away Jill's sorrow. Things might have been different. That I cannot hurts deeply.

Of course, drinking led Jill to Pittsburgh to die at the hands of a stranger. I could do something about that. I would kill him for Jill and for what he took from me.

When I think about things I could have done differently, when these thoughts roll and flip in my mind like little imps, I played a game of *if only*.

If only I had done more.

If only I had known sooner.

If only I was smarter.

If only I had done things differently.

If only she had not gone to Pittsburgh.

If only Jill had talked to me about her problem.

If only she had conquered it.

If only I had not gone to Syracuse after Christmas.

If only *Jack and Jill* had not gone up the hill! My crown would be unbroken and Jill would not have tumbled down.

If only.

But now, it's gettin' late and the moon is climbin' high
I want to celebrate, see it shinin' in your eye

I missed Jill's shinning eyes. It would cost Cooper his life. He destroyed any chance Jill and I had of growing old together and dancing beneath a harvest moon.

45

The yellow Cadillac, driven by the old couple in Missouri, was a distant image in the review mirror of Jack's pickup truck when Emma Cassidy met with her banker in Ft. Mitchell, Kentucky.

"I don't like the fact that we have to meet but..."

Emma held up her hand to stop the man in mid-sentence.

"Don't say it, Charlie; don't tell me this is business and not personal, because business is always personal. I believe I've satisfied the loan, would you agree?"

"Yes, for the most part...we might need a minor correction, when your house sells."

"How about we agree to end it right here, no minor corrections. My family has conducted business with this bank for fifty years. Let's just move on and call it a day."

"Emma, we need the exact amount."

"No, we don't," Walter Kurnik, the bank president, said as he entered the room. "Sorry, I'm late." He smiled at Emma. "Emma's right, Charlie, we'll write off any shortfall, and if there's an overage, we'll forward it to her. Emma's father and I always worked on a handshake and we'll do that now."

Kurnik reached across the table and extended his hand. Emma Cassidy shook it and nodded.

"What's next for you, Emma?" Kurnik asked.

"A job, I hope. Before I begin my search, I have to go west. I still have to sort through my aunt's things in Las Vegas."

"I knew Amanda, a wonderful entertainer; she could really dance. Have you made your travel arrangements?"

"Not yet," Emma replied.

"Call my secretary when you decide, she'll handle the trip and the bank will buy your airline ticket."

Charlie Lox, the manager, just nodded. He would always remember how embarrassed he was by Emma's smile.

46

Emma Cassidy shook hands with the bank president in Kentucky as Tony Sarcusi made a call to New Mexico. He used a disposable cell phone in his Detroit office.

Tony was excited. He would see his old partner and make almost two hundred grand, all because of a few phone calls and the answers to a few simple questions.

"I hope this means we have a deal," Aaron Cooper said, answering the call.

"What happened to hello?" Sarcusi replied, chuckling.

"Hello, is it good news?"

"Indeed, everything is cool."

"When does it go down?"

"The end of next week, C," Sarcusi said. "They'll take ownership after they test the product. Their man will hold the money. They have a chemist who will do random testing. You need to make sure things are secure on your end and that the product is pure as driven snow. I mean that sincerely, bud. You cannot screw this up."

"I won't. It is extremely pure and I'll be ready."

"I'll call with details. I'll tell my wife it's about your car."

"Good," Cooper replied and ended the call.

Cooper smiled as Liza Mercer exited the bathroom, wearing only a towel. They were still in their suite in a quaint hotel overlooking Sandia Peak.

"Who was that?" Mercer asked.

"My friend, he called about the Thunderbird."

"Does that mean you'll sell it?"

He wants to see it, before making a final decision.

"I'd like a ride before you do," she said, tossing the towel.

He smiled. "I'll give you a ride," he whispered.

She did a sexy twirl showing her fully naked body.

"I knew you would," she replied. "Let's enjoy."

47

A few minutes prior to six in the evening, I stood on the front porch of a grand Victorian house in Tulsa, Oklahoma. Behind me, the bare branches of large maples snapped amidst strong winds and swirling snow.

Here and there, drifts of varying sizes formed against any obstruction, in between parked cars, and in narrow driveways beside neighboring houses.

A big plow passed and the driver waved, another solitary figure braving the heavy storm. I blew into my hands for warmth as the lock turned. An attractive woman, perhaps in her late thirties, smiled at me.

"May I help you?" she asked, keeping the door chained. Her smile was pretty. Her eyes were dark, her skin flawless, her warm voice a notch above the rush of the wind.

"I hope so. My name is Jack Redding." I held up my ID as a courtesy and she perused my name. "I called yesterday morning for Ted Jefferson. I'm heading to Nevada and stopped to say hello. Do you know Ted? Is he here?"

She nodded her head. Her smile seemed warmer.

"Yes, I do know him but he is not here. I received your messages. Just a moment, please."

She shut the door briefly, removed a security chain, reopened it, and invited me inside with a friendly gesture.

"Please come in out of the cold; it's pure misery outside."

"I agree," I replied, nodding appreciatively as I entered the warmth of her house. The woman wore tight jeans and a crimson Tulsa sweatshirt. She was slender but ample in the proper places. The scent of spices hung in the air.

"The storm turned out to be worse than forecasted," she continued. "Have you been driving in it long?"

"Since breakfast, we hit the full brunt of today's storm just after Ft. Leonard Wood over in Missouri."

"I was looking off at a fence," I added, "rounded a curve, and then the storm nailed us. Snow has been steady since we left Buffalo, yesterday morning. I'm glad to be out of it."

"We?" she asked.

"My dog, Bailey, he's out in my pickup. My guess, he went back to sleep."

The woman smiled.

"This is just the beginning of the bad weather," she said. "I heard the forecast on the radio a moment ago. A second, larger storm is crossing the plains from Canada and coming fast behind this one. It will hit us later tonight. Most businesses and schools are closed and probably will be for the next few days."

"Other than a plow or two," I said, "not much traffic is moving on city streets."

She locked the door behind us.

"Ted said you were married. Your wife isn't with you?"

"No," I replied, "Jill died about a year ago."

"Oh, I'm so sorry to hear that."

"Thanks. I'm sorry about it, too."

The woman studied my expression. I probably looked as sad as I felt. I watched her dark eyes. They reminded me of polished pieces of black onyx. I did not see their pupils.

"If you wish, you can bring your dog in," she said cheerfully, changing the subject. "I don't mind."

"He's fine. I put a blanket over him. I'll get him later."

She nodded.

"What breed of dog?"

"A yellow lab, he's been with me about eight years. He goes where I go."

"Seems like a good arrangement. So, you and Ted served together in the military?"

I nodded, saying, "We shared time together, yes, some good days, and some bad. We drank and gambled some, too."

She smiled again.

"Blackjack, right?"

I nodded.

"Ted mentioned you're an excellent player."

"Not much anymore...I haven't played in years."

She held out her hand; its warmth and softness tendered reassurance. Her grip was stronger than I expected, comfortable and friendly, too. I noticed a gold crucifix around her neck.

"I'm Theo Jefferson," she said, "Theodora Kay actually; Ted's my uncle.

"Your uncle?" I hated to hear the disbelief in my voice.

For a moment, she was puzzled. Then, she smiled. "I get it...he's black and I'm not."

"I didn't mean anything by my dumb reaction."

I could do nothing about the flush I felt in my face, except hope it disappeared quickly.

"You are not the first. My mother is Caucasian. I inherited her skin color. She married Ted's brother, William. Uncle Ted's name and mine honor my great grandfather who relocated to Tulsa many years ago from St. Louis, when the railroads spread across the country. He was a chief porter. Since my dad died, I've handled my uncle's affairs. I'm his closest blood relative. Ted never remarried. My mom lives in Florida. She married an old college chum after my daddy passed. She's living the good life, as they say. I have a cousin or two in Tulsa but they only come around if they need money or some other handout."

"Unfortunately, families tend to be that way," I replied. "Does Ted know about my visit?"

A pretty smile broadened Theo's face. Her black eyes were flirty. I noticed two freckles on her left cheek. She resembled someone famous, but who? Maybe it was Dana Delaney but with darker hair.

"Yes," she said, "I told him you were coming. He's in a local hospice."

"I did not know that."

"Pancreatic cancer, he's quite ill. Although, I must admit, the mention of your messages cheered him. His face lit up."

"Isn't pancreatic cancer fatal?"

"Almost always, he's suffering...some days he really hurts, other days not as much."

"I had no idea. We haven't talked in a few years."

She shrugged and wiped her hands on a towel slung over her shoulder.

"The cancer crept up on him about three months ago. It's getting worse. In his case, there is no chance for recovery and he knows it. My dear uncle will disappear, forever. Families disappear, I guess. It's evolution."

"Jesus," I whispered, "I am sorry to hear that."

"Jesus is the only one who *can* help him. Doctors can't."

She blinked hard several times, fighting back tears. She inhaled, regained her composure, and cleared her voice.

"Forgive my manners, you must be chilled...how about a cup of coffee? I have a fresh pot."

"Coffee sounds great."

She motioned toward the kitchen and I followed her down a long hallway. Our footsteps were loud on a polished hardwood floor. As I followed, I found the sway of her hips appealing and quickly glanced away.

"Pardon the mess, I'm making soup. I teach American History at the University of Tulsa. Because I have the day off, I decided to make three kinds: ham and bean, chicken noodle, and minestrone. My uncle loves the former. I prefer the latter. We both like chicken noodle."

"They smell delicious. Where is Ted?"

"The hospice is about twenty minutes away in a facility managed by the Holy Cross Fathers. I'll take you there."

"In this weather?"

"I have a jeep with four-wheel drive. It's great in the snow. We'll have a straight shot up this road. One signal, one right turn, and we're there."

"I'd love to see him. I'm staying in town only one night. I want to leave in the morning. Perhaps you could recommend a hotel nearby. Maybe I could use your phone to make a reservation?"

"Why don't you stay here? I have plenty of room and would enjoy the company."

"I don't want to impose...besides I have my dog."

"I like dogs and I'm sure your dog will like me."

I nodded, saying, "As long as it's not a problem."

"I assure you, it is not."

"In that case, Bailey and I will stay."

"Good," she said, smiling. "You bring in your dog and I'll transfer the soups to crock pots to let them simmer. Then, we'll go to see my uncle after we have our coffee."

A few minutes later, Bailey was inside, eating his supper.

"He's a handsome dog," Theo said. "Uncle Ted loves dogs, too bad Bailey can't go with us to his room."

"Are you taking soup to your uncle?"

"Yes, ham and bean. Now, tell me about your wife and your travels to Nevada."

48

Theo Jefferson tightened a thermos filled with soup in Tulsa as Sister Margaret Bosko opened an envelope in Clinton, Oklahoma. The last thing the nun expected was money from her brother. It would not make up her deficit but it would help. Every dollar did, and she needed fifty thousand of them.

She was completely surprised and tears filled her eyes.

When she walked into the kitchen, her brother Henry was making a pot of tea. He turned and smiled at her.

"Hank, you're an angel," she said, hugging him.

"All broken and bent," he replied.

"You don't have much; can you afford a thousand dollars?"

"I have enough and, to tell the truth, I don't need much these days. I have my rodeo pension and my Social Security. I don't go anywhere, other than the grocery store. I'm good here. If it helps you, then that makes me happy."

She smiled and kissed his cheek.

"You're a kind man to help me."

"There's a few of us left, tea?"

"Yes, I'd love a cup. I see it continues to snow outside. It makes me want oatmeal, how does that sound?"

"Good...did you decide when you'll leave?"

"I think tomorrow. One of our benefactors lives in Elk City. I'll see her and then I have a few stops on the way back to Los Alamos."

He nodded, "God will provide."

"I hope so," she replied. "He always has but this time, with the economy and the orphanage's true need, it's going to have to be a miracle. Do you think God might still work miracles for a tired old nun?"

"Miracles I don't know about, sis; but I hope so. I don't like to see you feeling so damned low."

49

Despite the warmth of the Tulsa hospital room, all of Ted Jefferson's body, except his arms, was beneath a warming blanket. The room was nearly dark; the only light came from a small lamp on a nightstand beside the bed.

Outside, very near the window, snowflakes swirled in strong winds. On a distant hillside, snowplows worked under streetlights, trying to clear a road. The second storm was blowing into Tulsa.

"He's always cold," Theo said, referring to the room's heat. She gazed at her uncle as we stood just inside the doorway. Remembering something, she added, "I'll be right back," and turned to leave.

"Aren't you coming in with me?"

"A supermarket is only a block from the hospital. I noticed it was still open when we pulled in. I want to check its bakery before the store closes. I'll be gone maybe twenty minutes. I promise." She gave me the thermos of soup.

"See you soon."

I watched her depart, entered the room, set the soup on the nightstand, and sat beside Jefferson's bed. His face was thinner, his cheeks hollow; the man I saw was a shrunken version of the vibrant soldier I once knew.

He heard movement, opened his eyes, and a faint smile cracked his dry lips. He offered a weak wave.

"Midnight," he said. "Give a dying man a sip of water, would you?" His eyes moved toward a pitcher on the nightstand. I held a glass and he sipped through a straw.

"Thanks," he replied. "Have you been here long?"

"No," I replied.

"Where's Theo?"

"She had a stop to make, she's coming."

"Good…man, you are far from home," he whispered.

"Yeah, I am."

"It's good to see you; it's been too damned long."

"Yes, it has."

In the next few minutes, I explained Jill's death. I mentioned her alcoholism and told him that my job and the memories in Buffalo were a burden. I spoke of my need for a new venue and clarified why I was on my way to Vegas."

"Are you going to reside there permanently?"

"I don't know, honestly. I want to see Hawk. At least I'll have a base for a while, until I can sort things out. I might write novels, crafting fiction from real life, drawing on some of our field experiences."

"We do have some tales to tell," he agreed.

"I think so, some truly hard days."

"That would make the stories good. Lord, we went through some shit together, didn't we?"

"Yeah, we did, probably ate too much of it, too."

"Yes, indeed. These books, are you going to tell it the way we did it? That would be unique, based on the crap most authors turn out. They don't have a clue."

I nodded. "That's the plan. I'll talk it through with Hawk to make sure everything's five square."

"That'd be good," he said, "Hawk knows most of it."

"Yes, he does."

"Don't jaw too long, get 'em written," he advised.

For a while, we talked about missions, tactics, and situations. Then, purposefully, I led our conversation to Ted's peculiar specialty—interrogation.

"I won't pull punches about getting bad guys to talk. Some people won't like what I write but, at least, I'll be honest. Some people won't like reading about torture."

"Good for you, I'd expect as much."

"The books I'm thinking about will deal with many forms of torture: the water, the knives, and the needles."

"Guilty as charged," he whispered, grimacing.

I thought about Cooper and my intentions, and considered what I needed from Ted.

As cautious as I'd been up until that point, because of his terminal illness and if he pressed me, I was prepared to tell Ted the truth. I'd show cause and get him to understand. I'd have to hope that he would not repeat it.

A moment later, I crossed a very precarious line.

"You always told me about the power of a thin needle. From my research, experts say needles are the best way to get a man to crack, especially if all other techniques fail. Are they? Do they work the fastest with the extreme pressure of time? I'd like your insight on that."

He stared at me for what seemed like an eternity.

"I know you came to visit, if you didn't want to see me, you wouldn't be here. Nevertheless, I sense an ulterior motive. You came hoping I would answer *that* specific question." He winced. "Am I right?"

Silence filled the short space between us. Finally, I spoke. "Yes, I did. I need it because I intend to..."

He held up a frail hand, interrupting me.

"Midnight, I don't want to know; don't tell me."

I was embarrassed.

"If I've offended you or if it seems I'm using you, I'll stop and leave. You should know I trust you implicitly. You're the only man I know who's actually proficient in these things." I waited. "Do you want me to leave?"

"Hell, Jack, I'm trying to forget all that horseshit," Jefferson coughed, taking in several deep breaths.

"I'm sorry, Ted. I feel obligated to do something that requires attention to detail. It has to do with Jill. As I started to say a moment ago, I'm going to..."

A wave of his hand stopped me again.

"Don't say it; don't put an evil thought in my mind."

He coughed again and I wiped his lips with a tissue.

"I'll tell you but you keep the reason to yourself." He closed his eyes, thinking. When he reopened them, he said, "If time is a pressure, a highly corrosive acid is best and works the fastest. Use the strongest concentration you can find." His voice was a notch above a whisper. "Show the son of a bitch how corrosive the acid is; let him see it bubbling on something that makes him think of his skin."

"How hard is it to get that kind of acid?" I asked.

Jefferson was thinking.

"Theo's house used to be mine. In the basement, there's a bottle of highly corrosive sulphuric acid from my business on a shelf to the right of the stairs. It'll work. There's a sedative there, too, with needles. It was for my horses. Take it, in case you need to put someone down fast."

"Acid really works?"

"You want a man to admit something he's seen, or done, or talk about something that will happen, tie him down and hold corrosive acid above his face and tell him you're going to begin pouring it into one eye and then the other until he coughs up the answer. Believe me he'll reveal so much you'll have to stuff stones down his throat to shut him up."

"And, if he refuses," I asked.

"I'd hit his belly or his inner thigh near his crotch with a few drops and tell him it's eating into his stomach or nut sack. It won't be but from the sensation, he'll believe it. For some reason, threats to the eyes, stomach, and genitals scare men shitless. Trust me, the acid will make him sing the truth, 'cause if he lies, he'll know you'll be back for him. The threat of losing his sight or his manhood will play on his mind for a long time. I know it will."

"I understand."

"Of course, colonel, irreversible consequences always surface with acid," Jefferson continued.

"Which are?"

"Using acid means no going back, it has lasting physical damage." He winced again and hit a thumb button for morphine. "The pain...my doctor says it won't be long now, maybe a week," he sighed.

"I'm sorry."

"No more than I am; where was I?"

"Consequences," I reminded him.

"You have to be prepared to kill the person, especially if you actually use the acid. Consequences surface when you push a man hard with acid. Either he limps away, forever humiliated, or he hunts you like a big cat, wanting to kill you. At that point, it's either kill or die, ain't no room 'tween the two." He cleared his throat. "If you lack a strong constitution, it will really screw you up, too, Jack. I mean psychologically." He paused. "Do me a favor."

"Sure."

"It ain't my business why you want this stuff. My soul is already black enough; I can't make it any blacker. Maybe it's for books, maybe not. I already forgot you asked me, if you get my drift," he whispered, closing his eyes. When he reopened them, he said, "We all have reasons for doin' the shit we do. Whatever yours are, keep them deep and silent. They won't help me or anyone else."

By *anyone else*, I knew he meant his niece.

I squeezed his arm and said, "My word of honor."

"Mine, too," he replied, smiling weakly. "As you can plainly see, my burden is big enough. I don't want another."

His eyes closed and I thought he might be asleep. Then, he said, "Damn, Jill's been gone a year? I wish I'd known."

"Actually thirteen months, she died horribly."

"Bad?"

"Bad enough, she passed out drunk in a snowdrift, broke her neck, and froze solid."

He shivered and said, "Ain't that a motherfucker."
"Yeah," I replied.
"I thought my way of dyin' was bad. We just never know."
I took his cool hand in mine.
"Your hand is warm, colonel," he stated.
"The doctors can't do anything for you, Ted?" I asked.
"I'm near the end of the rope," he whispered. "I hope I go sooner than they say. This waiting is miserable."
"For Theo?"
"For me, too," he continued. "I've actually thought about ending it all, but I can't do it, I've killed too many men in my life. I can't commit suicide after asking God to forgive me for the things I've done. I can't mock Him, not when I want Him to forgive me."
He held up his hand.
"If it wasn't for this button and morphine, I couldn't take the pain. It's awful. Two weeks, at the most," he noted. "You know I was thinking about us, you and me, and the rest of Red Robin, yesterday when Theo told me you called."
"How's that?"
"I was dreaming about that mission in Mexico, my first. I can still hear the screams and see faces made blue in the flashes of lightning in that storm. Here's what I want to know, were we lucky or good?"
"Probably some of each," I whispered.
"We killed a lot of people that day and many more in the days that followed. Command said they were bad people but we did the shooting. I wonder, do you think we damaged our souls irreparably back then? They said the cause was good, that our actions were justified. Was it God's cause or did we drink from a big fucking jug of phony grape juice?"
"I believe our cause was just and you should believe that, too," I said.
His uneasiness was obvious.

"You know what I fear?" he asked.

"No."

"I fear a spot in hell is reserved for me when I die. I've confessed my actions to priests and I've received absolution each time. Do you think the absolution will hold?"

"Maybe forgiveness isn't even required."

"Oh," he replied, surprised by my perspective.

"We fought to protect the innocent, to protect a nation."

"Did we?" he said. "I often wonder if we were soldiers of deceit. Politicians spew too much bullshit. Hell, from what I've read, Vietnam and Iraq were frauds. There've been others. Were we pawns, Jack; were we duped, too?"

"I really can't say," I replied. "If we were duped, then we *are* innocent." I thought about Jill. "Innocents are never accountable. The way I see it, any sin transfers to those who lied. The people who should worry about hell are the men who create it here on earth. The blame is theirs, not ours."

As he glanced at the ceiling, tears inched from the corners of his eyes.

"We could have said no," he whispered.

"Unfortunately that water is long gone."

I wiped his cheeks with a tissue.

"Every once in a while, when my mind is tight, things squeeze my thoughts," he said. "I used to be good at getting them out; now, with the cancer, they linger."

"Don't beat yourself up, Ted. Think about how good you were after the service. You loved a wonderful woman, helped your brother, and you have a caring niece. You helped poor people here in Tulsa. I know you helped the disadvantaged and the disabled, and were active in your church. Kids loved to ride your horses. Think of those things. Fill your mind with that. God knows you're sorry, I believe that."

He nodded and glanced out the window. The snow still swirled near the pane.

In the distance, the two snowplows drove away, leaving mounds of snow in their wake.

"Thanks," he whispered. "You miss Jill, huh?"

"With every beat of my heart," I replied.

He nodded.

"It was that way for me with Gerri. I take it Hawk knows you're headed to Vegas for a visit?"

"Yes, I called. He knows that I planned to see you. He doesn't know about the questions I've asked."

"What questions?" Ted replied, smiling, "Haven't heard any questions from anybody. If I did, I forgot 'em."

"Thanks," I replied.

"Say 'hey' to Hawk for me. You think you might play a little 'jack' in Vegas?"

"Not much...I've lost the passion."

"It's there, it never goes away. Hawk's place is on the edge of the city. I've visited him several times and enjoyed myself, won a little coin at the tables, too. I'll never go back. Jesus, life turns to shit sometimes, huh?"

"Yeah, it does. Do you need anything, Ted? Anything I can do for you before I leave. Do you need money?"

"I do worry about Theo."

"Your niece seems like a nice woman, she said she teaches at the university. From what I have seen, she's very strong."

He hit the morphine again.

"You know, she's one step away from becoming an ordained Anglican priest. Left her order about three years back after her father, my brother, died. She said she'd been having doubts and it crept up on her, but she didn't want to hurt him. He was deeply proud of her. You know, because of her mama, she looks Caucasian. Behind her back, people still say racist things about her. That hurts."

"I imagine it would. Hate likes to nest in the human heart; it always has and probably always will."

"Some people live inside dark shadows," Ted replied.

I immediately thought of the old veteran I met in Ohio. He believed evil resided in shadows.

"Please, will you do me a favor?"

"Sure, Ted."

"Check on Theo, maybe a visit or a phone call."

"You want me to check on your niece?"

He nodded.

"Do you want me to call anyone else, maybe Hawk, or some other guys you know?"

"Nope, they have their own lives, their own crosses. They don't need to carry mine. About Vegas..."

"What about Vegas?" I replied.

"If you do play some 'jack,' don't let them catch you counting, they'll run your ass out of town faster than darkness disappears when you turn on a lamp."

"You knew about the counting! You never said a word."

Jefferson nodded.

"That's because I tried to do it, too," he replied. "I was good; you were a master."

"But, you never said a word," I repeated.

"Why should I, it was your secret. It was fun to watch you win. You lost some and I know you did it on purpose; most card counters fail to do that often enough. They get greedy, but not you. I respected the hell out of you for doing that...it took real discipline."

"It's a part of the play."

"Jack, at her core, Las Vegas is a two-timing whore. Just when you think she is yours, she will gouge your heart out. If you win big, quit fast." Ted smiled. "Remember, it's their house, their game. You have to promise me. Win big, quit fast. I mean it."

"I promise."

"Say it!"

"Win big, quit fast."

"That applies to whatever else you plan to do, too."

Our eyes locked and I nodded. He did, too.

At that precise moment, the door opened, and we both smiled as Theodora Kay Jefferson entered the room.

"Are you two enjoying your chat?" she said. "The storm is getting ugly again. Major highways are closing as are many side streets, too." She turned to me. "We should go in about twenty minutes. They are closing all city streets in an hour to let the plows through."

"I hope you have a place to stay in Tulsa tonight," Ted whispered.

"I do."

She kissed her uncle's cheek and looked at me.

"He's staying with me, I insisted. I have a surprise, Uncle Ted. I made soup today. You're having some before we leave. I think you will like it."

"Is it ham and bean?"

She nodded, reaching for the thermos.

"Maybe a spoonful or two," he said. "That's about all I can handle." His eyes sparkled. She was good for him.

"I have cornbread, too," she added, "I bought it warm at a nearby supermarket, from their bake shop."

"A morsel or two would be wonderful," Ted added.

Despite his troubled soul and ravaged body, Ted looked at me and winked.

~

At her house, Theo said, "I'm taking soup to a neighbor. Can Bailey come with me and romp in the snow?"

I nodded; her leaving was fortuitous. I quickly found the acid and sedative. A penlight did the job. I put the items in my duffel bag. As promised, Theo never knew.

When she and Bailey returned, I was asleep on a sofa. I was very tired; the cushions were very cozy.

50

Kyle Shaw poured a scotch in Las Vegas as Theo Jefferson kissed her uncle goodnight in Tulsa.

Shaw glanced out the window. Far to the west, a line of pink at the base of the horizon was the only remnant of sunset. Hearing someone enter the room, he turned.

"Good news?" he asked, hopefully.

Louis, Kyle's brother, shrugged and said, "A source told me Amanda's things are now in storage at EL CORAZÓN. It's a metal building, at the back of the property. I did a drive through. Two, well lighted garage doors face the road. An access door also faces the road.

"Four cameras on poles monitor the doors. I didn't know this but Hawkins reconditions and sells vintage cabin cruisers. According to my source, he has five boats worth millions. The remainder is storage for the residents."

"No windows or back entrances?" Kyle asked.

"There's a fire door, it only opens from the inside. It's on the side, flush with the outside of the building, covered by one of the cameras. No handles or hinges."

"Amanda's condo is completely empty?" Kyle asked.

"Yes, I assume the diamonds are with her possessions in the warehouse protected by those high-speed cameras."

"So, there isn't an easy way in, huh?"

"Not that I could see.

"I have some research and homework to do. Keep quiet about this. You want a drink?"

Louis declined.

"Where's the old man?" asked Kyle.

"I saw his car at the gun range, he's shooting."

"You think his targets have my face on them?" Kyle noted.

"You'll have to ask him, Kyle. I don't know."

"I will, when I toss the diamonds at him."

51

The wind howled and the furnace popped through the heating vents. Near the bedroom window, tree branches scraped against the side of the house in Tulsa. The clock on the nightstand displayed 12:15 and I was wide-awake.

At 12:16, the bedroom door opened and Bailey growled.

"Do you have a problem?" I whispered.

"No," Theo answered, entering. "Are you warm enough?"

"Yes, very, thank you."

"Not me, I'm chilly."

She coaxed Bailey out of the room with a few treats and closed the door. She switched on a nightlight atop a bureau, turned away slightly, and removed her robe. She stood beside the bed to reveal her fully naked body.

"Why?" I whispered.

"Jack, I've missed out on a lot of things in my life. Sometimes, I get lonely. Not too often, but I do. I sense you are lonely, too. My guess, you've not made love to a woman since your wife died."

"No, I haven't," I replied.

"I have a gift for you. Let me take Jill's place for one cold winter's night in Oklahoma. You can fantasize that I'm your wife. I won't mind."

She pulled back the covers, leaned over, and kissed my lips. Her nipples brushed against my naked chest.

"Theo, I'm not prepared, I don't have protection."

"Trust me, we don't need it…not shush, let's enjoy this."

She smiled and her hand tickled my abdomen and crept beneath my sleep shorts. I responded immediately and she smiled pleasantly.

"So far, so good," she stated.

She made me lift my hips and removed my shorts. Next, she used her saliva as a lubricant and mounted me.

"Wow," I whispered.

"Does it feel good," she said huskily a few minutes later. "I love it. I am thrilled, are you?"

"Yes."

"Good."

She resumed her considerate movements until we both climaxed and then she fell softly onto my chest, kissing my neck. Her hot breath quickly replaced many empty nights.

I pulled her body tight against mine, kissing her mouth, which was warm and rich, and remarkably talented. Her kiss was similar to Jill's but different at the same time, certainly as bold, definitely as hungry.

After an hour, she rolled on her side and I entered her, kneeling beside her on the bed. She was warm and willing, moist and receptive, and smooth and tight.

This time the sex was fierce and enthusiastic.

"Lord," Theo whispered. "You fill me completely."

Later, we made love again, softly at first, enjoying the steady movement. After a while, her breathing thickened and I felt her shutter a third time; then, I shuttered, too.

"Wait, please, don't move," she whispered. She rocked slowly against me, enjoying the sensation.

Our intimacy seemed to erase every wound from the past year. It was as if our sex had magically cleansed my soul and, finally, I had come home from a long and dark journey.

Moments later, we were sleeping.

~

I held Theo in my arms through most of the night. When I awoke about nine the next morning, she was gone. Flecks of sunlight told me the storm was now off to the east.

For just a moment, I wondered if the sex had been a dream. When I noticed fresh towels on the edge of the bed, next to my folded shorts and laundered clothes, I realized it was very real.

As I stood and stretched, classical music filtered into the bedroom. From somewhere below, I heard a voice, probably coming from the kitchen. Theo was talking to Bailey. Her muffled words were unintelligible, but her tone was caring and I knew Bailey had a new friend.

I closed my eyes, remembering Theo's warmth, the smell of her breasts, her dampness, and the way she shuttered when she climaxed.

For the first time in months, my initial thought of the day was not about Jill's death. I yawned and did fifty pushups and fifty sit-ups. Surprisingly, I did not feel guilty about having sex in the wee hours of morning. I used to think I would. I thought it would feel like cheating if I ever made love to another woman. It did not, not for a second. It seemed to have lifted a millstone.

I smelled coffee brewing as I gathered my clothes and toiletry bag, and found the bathroom down the hallway. I turned the water on and stepped into the medium-hot shower, letting the heat penetrate my muscles.

I had just finished a shampoo, when the shower door slid open. Theo stepped in beside me, naked. Her eyes glowed, her face and breasts quickly moist from the splash of water. My eyes consumed her body. Nicely tapered legs, a thin waist, breasts firmly proportioned. I noticed more freckles on her shoulders.

"You like what you see?" she asked.

"You're a lovely woman."

She touched me.

"How about one for the road," she said, nibbling my earlobe. "I would like that."

I touched her nipples lightly. They hardened instantly.

"A breakfast thrill," I said.

"Yeah, why not," she whispered. "I, for one, think we've earned it and I hope you agree."

"I do," I said, lifting her bottom in my hands. She hugged me for support and our passion was as warm as the water splashing upon Theo's freckled skin."

~

After breakfast and, as we shared another cup of coffee, Theo looked at me and smiled.

"So, you'll be leaving."

I nodded. I had to find to Cooper.

"Wouldn't you like to stay another day?"

"I don't want to wear out my welcome."

"Fair enough," she replied. "Radio says the weather will break for a while. The roads from here to Vegas are clear. There is a threat for more bad weather."

I nodded, refilling my cup.

"Did my uncle ask you to look in on me?" she asked.

"How did you know?"

"He asks everyone to do that. He thinks I'll be lonely. I really don't need anyone. I'm very independent."

"I know you are."

"Did he mention the black thing or the minister thing?"

"Both," I stated.

"That's my Uncle Ted."

Out the kitchen window, I saw an older man starting a snow blower.

"Peter, my neighbor," she said, following my gaze. "He'll do his driveway and walkways and then he'll do mine."

She reached out, resting her hand on mine.

"Jack, there's no obligation here. I want you to know that. We both needed someone and it was the right thing to do. I don't expect to see you again. I want to thank you. I wanted the feel of a man. I hope you needed the feel of a woman."

"I did," I replied. "My first thought this morning was different than those of the past year."

She smiled.

"A good sign, huh?"

I nodded, "Yeah, it's been a while. It was a complete surprise. I didn't know how I would react."

"You did just fine. I still tingle. I liked it. I will continue to like it. Our union was wonderful."

I felt a blush.

"Don't be embarrassed, what we did was amazing, we gifted human pleasure to each other."

We laughed and Theo motioned toward the counter.

"I packed a lunch for you and Bailey...a few sandwiches, a thermos of chicken soup, and crackers, too. An old thermos; toss it when you've finished. I hope you like the soup. It is my great grandmother's recipe. She grew up on a plantation in Alabama"

"I appreciate your thoughtfulness." I paused, adding, "In every way, and I mean that."

"I know. I can see it in your expression."

She handed me her business card.

"It's for my office; my cell is on the flip side. You have my numbers. If you ever decide to pass through Tulsa you have a place to stay and a heart to thrill."

"And, if I don't?"

"We'll always have the memory of the tingles."

"Yes, we will have the tingles."

"How long does that memory last?"

"Because we conducted ourselves properly, forever," I replied.

"That's good to know."

52

Five hours later, Bailey and I approached Elk City, Oklahoma. A road sign bragged about the Ackley Park Carousel. Maybe in another time I would have shown an active interest.

For hours, the sky had been a vivid blue but now in the distance, gray clouds hung in the far horizon over the Texas panhandle. I switched to a local radio station and heard an announcer say a strong storm was pushing across the land toward Amarillo, which was not too far away. As if on cue, drops of icy rain hit the windshield of my pickup.

"Sleet," I said to Bailey.

I pulled into a truck stop, took Bailey for a relief walk, refilled the gas tank, refilled the pickup's window-wash reservoir, and went inside for coffee.

As I sat at the counter, a server near the kitchen window saw me. She gestured that it would be a moment. I checked her out—in her sixties, a bit plain, probably a grandmother.

I removed my jacket and looked around the restaurant.

Another sixtyish woman, wearing a nun's headpiece and a devotional scapular, sat a few stools away. She removed an airline-size vodka bottle from her purse and smiled at me.

"Nuns have an occasional snort," she said.

"I try never to judge, sister," I replied.

"More folks should be like you. I've had a few bad weeks."

"How so?" I asked.

"I've been trying to raise money for our orphanage in Los Alamos, St. Therese of the Mountains. In this economy, it's damn tough...pardon my French"

"I've heard much worse," I stated.

She eyed me for a moment, adding, "I had hoped to raise fifty thousand dollars to get us through the next year.

"How'd you do?"

"I've only raised seven and change. It is already in the bank. I've prayed and hoped until I can't pray and hope anymore. Not long ago, a Baptist minister prayed with me."

"How many orphans do you have?" I asked.

"Twenty children and six nuns, we have twenty-six souls. It's tough. The vodka calms my nerves."

"Not too much," I cautioned, thinking of Jill.

"Don't worry, I cannot afford it and I know about the evils…but once in a while, how can it hurt?"

I watched her add the vodka to her tomato juice. She tossed the bottle into a waste can behind the counter and added a bit of pepper.

The aging nun with the sad face stirred her drink and soon her hands morphed into Jill's…

…They were on Elmwood Avenue in Buffalo having breakfast. As Jack returned from buying the BUFFALO NEWS, he saw Jill pour vodka from a pint bottle into a glass of tomato juice. She quickly hid the bottle in her purse. She took a large gulp and at least half of her makeshift Bloody Mary disappeared.

Jack felt guilty standing and watching but his concern for his wife's drinking at breakfast trumped his guilt. It was the first real inkling that Jill had an issue with alcohol. When he sat down, she smiled, as if nothing was wrong.

"Why the booze, Jill?" he asked, his tone serious.

"Booze?"

"Don't lie to me, Jill. I saw it. It must have been four or five shots. What the hell is going on?"

She glowered and her eyes grew defiant.

Jack ignored her moue.

"Jill," Jack repeated her name emphatically.

"It helps me forget the babies, the deaths, and my sister's accident, all the bad that has happened to me and to us."

The server returned with their food and set the plates on the table. Seeing a dark cloud forming between her two customers, she retreated to take another order.

In a few startling minutes, Jack fit the pieces together and it all made sense. Jill selling her business; the way she seemed to sleep later and later each day; the sporadic lethargy in her voice; her sometimes-disheveled appearance; and the unplanned weight loss. She had a drinking problem.

"We have to talk about this…how long?"

Tears replaced Jill's pout of defiance.

"I'm hurting," she tried to reason. "I just need a buffer."

"How long?" he repeated.

She shrugged, afraid to answer.

"How long, Jill?" he demanded.

"It started after the first miscarriage," she said, crumbling. "It grew worse after the second and the loss of my parents, and then my sister died."

Jack did the calculation.

"Jesus, that covers years."

Her curt nod poked a searing pain in Jack's ribs.

"How much?"

She was silent.

"Jill," he pleaded, "Tell me how much."

"Maybe two pints a day, maybe more," she whispered. The tears were dripping onto her cashmere sweater.

"Jesus Christ, Jill," Jack whispered…

…A door slammed and I was back in the restaurant.

"You want a cup of coffee, hon?" the older server asked. I was wrong. Up close, she was a very attractive woman.

"Actually, can you rinse and fill my thermos?" I asked.

"Sure, I'll have to charge you for two cups, though."

"Not a problem."

"Where you headed, handsome?"

"Las Vegas."

"You want anything to eat?"

I thought about my ever-hungry dog and nodded, saying, "How about two fried egg sandwiches on whole wheat toast."

"You got it, anything else?"

"I'd like a couple of apples."

She smiled and toyed with a silver heart hanging around her lovely neck.

"Coming right up."

Jill always wore a heart, too. I remembered how tightly she held it that morning when I confronted her.

We left the restaurant with anger anchoring our silence. In the car, Jill fidgeted with her necklace as she cried.

"This isn't right, Jill," I said.

"I know," she whispered, looking out the window as if she were afraid to look at me.

"You have to stop, Jill."

"I've tried, Jack," she whispered.

When she did look at me, I thought of a shattered child. The woman I loved seemed to have disappeared. In her place was an awkward, hesitant, terrified girl. I asked myself how I could have been blind to all of it. I wondered how I could have missed everything.

"I can't stop, I've tried," she continued. "The memories are bitter and hurt so much, the booze helps me cope."

"Jill, constant drinking is not coping!"

~

"Damned memories," I whispered, slapping my hands loudly in the restaurant.

"Pardon me," my server said, placing the thermos, apples, and egg sandwiches on the counter in front of me. "Are you having a bad day, honey?"

"Sorry, sometimes old memories rear up and bite me where it hurts," I said.

"Like right in the ass," she noted. "I hate some of mine, too. For example, I wish a few men never saw me naked."

She put the food in a bag.

I looked at her and smiled.

"Although, I imagine they liked what they saw."

"You're a kind and thoughtful man."

"Thanks, I guess I was sitting somewhere back in the past. I apologize for the outburst."

She nodded. "I know the feeling...here's the bill. You pay at the counter." She pointed toward the entrance.

I took the check, nodded, and handed her a ten.

"That's for you, sweetheart, sorry for the flare up."

"Ah, forget it," she said.

"I bet you were a sight to see, back then, huh?"

"Still am," she said, smiling and patting her backside.

I looked at the nun, who raised her glass to wish me well.

I tipped my hat, nodded at each woman, and started to take my leave.

"Let's hope something better down the road presents itself," the woman behind the counter added.

I looked over my shoulder, smiled at her, and recalled the warmth of Theo Jefferson's body.

If Theo could make me feel happy, maybe a better life *was* coming. That would be good.

"One can only hope," I said.

At the cash register, I gave the attendant a twenty and waited as she made change.

She opened the cash drawer and paused, pursing her lips.

"I'm sorry, sir. I have to run in the back for singles."

"Not a problem."

I watched her go and saw a credit card paper-clipped to a driver's license for a man about my age. Some customer had obviously left his identification behind. I looked around. No one was watching me.

Murphy's Law popped into my head. Maybe it would be good to have an alternate identity. I checked for the attendant and palmed the driver's license and credit card.

If I needed to do so, I could add my photo and re-laminate the license. The credit card was not an issue. I would use cash for all purchases; still, it might help to have it, to reinforce my bogus identity.

A few moments later, the attendant returned, opened the register drawer, and made the proper change. I turned to leave, took a few steps, and thought of something.

"Say, miss?"

She looked up.

"Yes, sir."

"While you were away, a man came in and said he was looking for his credit card and driver's license, he said he left them behind. I guess he saw it next to the register and took it. He told me to tell you, he said his wife was all over him because they were way behind schedule."

"Good," she replied. "I intended to mail it and, now, I don't have to do that. He must *really* be off schedule. He left the restaurant sometime around ten o'clock."

"At least you know and it saved you some effort."

She smiled.

"Oh, will you do favor for me?"

"Sure."

"The woman at the counter," I said, motioning.

"The nun?"

"Yes."

"Give this to her for me, would you?"

"Sure."

She walked over and handed the nun five one-hundred dollar bills.

As soon as the money was in the good sister's hands, I departed the restaurant. I did not wait to see her reaction.

Maybe I was trying to buy some peace but then that thought slipped away. It is never wrong to help people.

Moments later, Bailey and I were on the Interstate. I checked the time. It was nearly three o'clock. The customer left his credentials at ten, some five hours ago.

I checked the man's address in Flagstaff, Arizona. My guess was he was nearing his home state and might not even know he forgot his personal items. I doubted he would ever return for them; however, to be safe, I pulled into a nearby gas station to make a quick call.

Using a pay phone, I called Flagstaff information, gave the name and the address, asked to be connected, and deposited the needed coins. I watched traffic and, a moment later, a young woman answered the call.

"Hello."

"Yes, my name is Tom Weaver," I lied. "I just came out of a restaurant in Elk City, Oklahoma, and found a driver's license and credit card in the parking lot."

"Okay."

I gave her Fred Adkins' name and address, and the type of the credit card.

"That's my dad," she said. "When I talked to my mom recently; she didn't say he'd lost anything. Can you wait, while I call them on my cell phone to check?"

"Sure."

Seconds later, she was back on the line.

"They're his; he didn't even know he'd misplaced them."

"Tell him not to worry, I'll find a post office and send these items to him."

"I'll let him know, I still have them on my cell."

"Good."

She came back on, "Mr. Weaver that would be wonderful and it's very thoughtful. My dad wants to send you a gift, what's your address?"

I thought of my brother.

"Tell him to make a donation to help our wounded veterans. I'm going to find a post office."

I heard her relay my message.

"He'll do it," she said. "May he have your phone number?"

I immediately played possum, pretending I was losing the connection.

"Hello, miss; are you there? For some reason I cannot hear you. If you can hear me, I'll say goodbye and mail these things to your dad right away."

Before she could say anymore, I ended the call, started the pickup, and joined the rush of traffic.

Bailey and I were moving through late afternoon sunlight, heading into a possible storm spreading itself wide across the Texas panhandle.

I would definitely mail the items I palmed but only after Cooper died in Santa Fe.

I knew Fred Adkins in Arizona would never know that I would use his identity. For sure, he would never know that the man who pretended to be Tom Weaver, the man who had spoken to his daughter, would eventually kill another human being.

That was my burden, not his!

It was my obligation, not his.

It was my decision, not his.

I silently thanked my benefactor Fred Adkins and drove toward the Texas Panhandle.

Regarding Aaron Cooper, his hours were numbered and the clock was ticking.

53

Cooper had just finished working out at Santa Fe's STRONGER BODIES when he heard the chirp of his throwaway cell phone. He checked the number, saw it was Sarcusi, and answered on the second ring.

"Hello, Tony."

"I have an arrival date," Sarcusi stated. "We'll be there one week from today. I have more detail about their testing, also. They will conduct six random checks. Their private chemist will make the call. With her approval, it's a sale."

"I have to ask, Tony, do you trust these people?"

"Yeah, I do, C. Some advice, do not tease these men. Give them what they want, take their money, and forget you ever met or heard of them. If anything goes wrong, they will not care about your happiness, your retirement, or the woman you love. They won't care about me, either."

"Are they paying you?"

"A dime," Sarcusi answered.

"Good, that tells me they like you. When do we do it?"

"Friday, February one five, we'll arrive the night before. I'll call when we get in. Is this stuff stashed away tight?"

"Foolproof," Cooper replied, "it is in a perfect location."

"Good, keep it that way. Does your girlfriend know?"

"No, she thinks you're coming to check out the T-Bird."

"That's what I told my wife, too."

"We're on the same page, bud."

"After it goes down, I'll tell my wife I decided the salt in Detroit would turn the car into a piece of Swiss cheese."

"I'll use that, too," Cooper replied.

"C, remember," Sarcusi said to reemphasize, "Don't cross these guys or you and I will be Swiss cheese, too."

"Not to worry," Cooper said. Sadly, he had no inkling of the terror coming toward him from Oklahoma.

Cooper was feeling smug and invincible.

He believed he had finally won; he believed he beat the system, one of the few to do that in this or any other lifetime. He considered it a grand accomplishment.

He sat and thought about all the deception, about all the lies. However, he did not think about the people he hurt or the lives he ruined. In his case, it was out of sight, out of mind. Of course, that is how Cooper lived his life.

All he had to do was deliver the drugs to Sarcusi and the people who were coming with him to Santa Fe.

Then, his former life would be history.

After that, he could live a very happy and fulfilling life.

Cooper liked a drink or two but he seldom drank during the day. However, on this day, he thought a minor celebration was in order.

He stopped for a drink at a nearby bar.

He asked the bartender for two fingers of whiskey with a beer chaser.

"You look like the cat who just ate the cheese," the man behind the bar said, serving the drinks.

"Quesillo," Cooper said. "The finest you can get in South America. It's really tasty and very expensive."

Book 2

February 2013

Revenge

Let every eye negotiate for itself and trust no agent.
—William Shakespeare

54

One week later, Gerard "Jelly" Lucasi, driving a white nondescript Nissan Sentra, lagged behind Aaron Cooper's burgundy Cadillac STS and Tony Sarcusi's silver Suburban on a highway leading northwest out of Santa Fe. He wondered where they were going.

After another half-mile, the forward vehicles slowed and turned right onto a newly paved road. A road sign indicated *No Outlet*.

The road, built for future development, seemed to extend several miles into rolling and barren hills.

Lucasi said aloud, "I wonder if this is what they call urban sprawl. Who would store drugs out here?"

He glanced to his right. Not too far away, he observed a self-storage facility with maybe fifty units. The parking lot was vacant so early in the day.

A 15-foot-high fence, topped with razor wire and a series of security cameras, encircled the typical complex. Lucasi looked for, but did not see, other buildings in the immediate area. As for traffic, all roads were virtually empty this early in the morning.

"I've seen the middle of nowhere," Lucasi whispered.

Jelly did not follow the other vehicles. Rather, he drove through the intersection, pulled onto the shoulder, grabbed a briefcase off the back seat, and ambled up a wooded hill.

He was in position within fifteen seconds, even before the vehicles entered the storage facility. He knelt, assembled a rifle, locked a scope into position, and checked his watch: 6:28 a.m. To the east, the horizon was brightening.

The exchange was going down. This was it. He removed his cell phone and set it in the crook of a tree.

Down the hill, an electronic gate swung open and the two vehicles entered the storage complex.

After the Suburban's bumper cleared an infrared beam, the gate closed quickly.

Although he was slightly elevated and some distance away, Lucasi heard a loud snap as the gate relocked.

Seconds later, Cooper exited his STS beside a unit in the middle of the complex and entered a series of security codes for three separate systems.

Sarcusi, Tommy Jax, and Julie Adams waited patiently and entered the facility with Cooper. Tommy Jax held a black suitcase containing one million five hundred thousand dollars in unmarked bills. He did not turn to look for Lucasi.

Two muscle men, Patsy's boys who accompanied Sarcusi and Jax from Detroit waited beside the Suburban, casually watching the street. Jelly knew each man was armed.

Twenty seconds later, Muscle-One jabbed Muscle-Two's arm. He gestured toward a cyclist turning into the miles-long cul-de-sac. Lucasi followed their glance and scoped the cyclist: road suit, iPOD, fanny pack, but nothing else.

"No guns," Lucasi whispered, as if Patsy's boys could hear him. "Don't be careless, lads. Some hump is getting his morning exercise. Stay cool."

The cyclist went by at a decent clip, intent on his heart rate. Focused on his routine, he never glanced at the storage units. As a precaution, Lucasi used his scope and followed the rider until he was confident the man was not a threat.

The cyclist peddled faster, shifted gears for a slight incline, and headed into the rolling hills toward the cul-de-sac's roundabout several miles away. The cyclist, moving at a fast pace, made Lucasi feel uncomfortable. A twinge of guilt told Jelly he should drink less and exercise more.

After the cyclist faded from view, Lucasi rechecked the road, scanned the storage facility, and pushed his guilt aside. His reflexes and shooting ability were unsurpassed. He yawned. No cars, no people, nothing; everything was cool.

Jax and the others should be out in ten minutes or less, he thought. He set a timer on his watch, lifted his cell phone, flipped it open, pressed a speed-dial number, and waited for Tito Claroni to answer. The sky was getting lighter.

"Tito, Jelly here, they are inside doing the deal."

"Good, is everything copacetic?" asked Tito.

"It's as quiet as a hungry mouse stealing bread crumbs in a bakery, not a peep."

"How many men does the guy have?"

"Zero, none, nada...he's either stupid or very trusting."

"You're shittin' me?"

"The guy must really believe in Tony S."

"That's a good sign. Did you talk to Jax?"

"Yeah, he called me last night. He told me they would roll before dawn, but he did not know where. Apparently, Mr. Santa Fe is a cautious man."

"Wouldn't you be vigilant?"

"Yeah, I guess."

"Did you have a long drive?"

"Maybe ten miles; I thought we were heading out of town but then we turned into an area staked for development. It's a dead-end street leading into a bunch of vacant lots, rolling hills, and sparse woods. They should be back out in," he checked the timer, "nine minutes, max."

"Are you timing them?" Tito knew Lucasi like a book.

"Of course, I am," replied Lucasi.

"Keep me posted."

"You got it."

~

With a few minutes to go, the cyclist rode by on his way back to the main highway.

"Lord," Lucasi whispered, "that guy is kicking ass."

Again, he watched through his scope until the cyclist turned onto the main thoroughfare and disappeared.

The two muscle men watched the rider disappear, too. Thereafter, the door for Cooper's storage unit opened and Jax and the others exited. Tommy carried a large brown suitcase and he pulled his right earlobe after he placed the luggage in the rear of the Suburban.

Immediately, Jelly Lucasi understood Jax' signal. He scoped Cooper, standing nonchalantly in the doorway. Mr. Santa Fe was no great shakes, just an average chump.

Cooper unlocked the gate with a remote and watched his guests depart. Lucasi chuckled to himself. Cooper actually waved as Jax and the others drove away. What a schmuck! It would have been a piece of cake to pop him.

Again, Lucasi pressed speed dial.

"Trade closed; deed given," he said. "Sun's coming up."

"Bring 'em home, Jelly Bread," Tito Claroni said.

"You got it."

Lucasi watched Aaron Cooper enter his storage unit and close the door. Cooper was now a very rich man.

Lucasi disassembled his rifle and lit a smoke. He allowed himself two each day. He smiled. He just made a cool fifty grand. Tito and Patsy paid him well but he knew he was worth every penny. He locked his briefcase, returned to the Nissan Sentra, and drove away.

In a few moments, he would settle in behind the Suburban for the long ride back to Detroit.

First, they would stop in Albuquerque so the little broad Pasty liked so much could catch a plane. Deep in his heart, Jelly believed the old man was humping the cute little chemist. More power to him, he thought.

Lucasi did not see the cyclist hiding a few hundred yards away, standing in a thicket of box elders. The man stood stone still until Lucasi drove away.

Then, the cyclist turned his attention to Aaron Cooper and the revenge he would inflict.

55

Delta Flight 412, bound for Las Vegas, departed from the Greater Cincinnati-Northern Kentucky International Airport as Jack Redding waited near Aaron Cooper's storage facility in Santa Fe.

As the aircraft banked to the southwest, Emma looked at the Ohio River, following it east to Cincinnati and Covington, and the shattered dreams she left behind.

She sighed, trying hard to push away the fog of failure, hoping to set aside the past troublesome years of her life.

The break was clean. Still, it was a struggle to get past months of intense work, her dismal failure, and the loss of virtually everything she owned. She had about thirty thousand dollars. The rest of it, six hundred grand, went down the tubes. Somehow, she had to find a way to rebuild.

Thirty-three, she mused, very few possessions, some money, no car, no home, and a simple gold necklace. Still, I am alive, she thought. I have my health, my talents, and my education. She cringed. She sounded like her mother.

"Are you traveling for business or for fun?" a voice rasped.

When she turned away from the window, Emma found an older, gray-bearded black man seated beside her.

"Personal," she replied. "My aunt died. I need to settle her estate. I buried her beside my parents yesterday."

"I'm sorry. I don't want to pry, just making conversation. I get queasy when I fly, talking helps my nerves."

Emma held out her hand and introduced herself.

"Nice to meet you," the man replied, shaking her hand. "I'm Ike Turner, but not the fool who did Miss Tina wrong."

His big hand was strong, his grip firm.

"Hello, Ike," Emma said. "Are you on business or fun?"

"I'm heading back to Vegas and my little café. I was in Atlanta visiting my sister and old dance partners."

"You're a dancer. My aunt danced in Las Vegas."

"What's her name, child?"

"Amanda Cassidy."

"I know the name, never met the lady. I've been off the stage for years."

"So, you did dance professionally?"

"Yes, I did, until my knees said: *Please, no more!* I danced all over: New York, Miami, Chicago, L.A., U.S.O. tours, Europe, and hundreds of places 'twix and 'tween. I worked with Will Mastin and Sammy Davis, Jr. I made enough money to buy a café, and I set some aside. Show biz was good to this old hoofer."

"If you don't mind my asking, how old are you?"

"I'm pushing ninety-one."

She seemed surprised, saying, "I would have guessed you'd be in your mid-sixties."

Ike smiled gratefully.

"Ain't you a peach," he said, making Emma laugh.

It was the first time she laughed in a week.

"You have a pretty smile. You should use it more often."

"Ike, I haven't had much to smile about lately. I just closed my business. I failed miserably."

"We all have crosses," Ike said. "Most of the time, today's failure is tomorrow's wisdom. Things work out."

"You sound so sure."

"Been there, done that, got the double-x tee shirt," he replied. "I failed more times in my life than you got hairs on your head but I landed on my feet. I'm a happy man. God and life have been good to me. In time, stones become diamonds. For all things, there's a season."

"Are you a religious man, Ike?"

"Spiritual and truthful, where are you staying in Vegas?"

"I've taken a studio apartment at EL CORAZÓN."

"Hawk's place," he said, surprise filled his eyes.

"Bill Hawkins, indeed, do you know him?"

"I surely do. This big world is but a small neighborhood. Hawk and me, we fish at Lake Meade; sometimes we go up toward Reno and Tahoe. That man owns some beautiful boats. He reconditions cabin cruisers, the variety I will never afford. He and I have a ball; we tell more fibs than we catch fish, big fibs, too."

"I've only talked to him via telephone."

"Hawk's a good man. He's a former Army Ranger and he's been successful. A little gung ho, at times, but he's as solid as they come. Fair minded, too. My café ain't too far from his place. You'll have to stop in for coffee and a piece of pie. I bake tasty pies. A pretty woman like you is bound to improve my business."

"Do you say that to all the girls?"

"Just the pretty ones," he replied, laughing.

Inwardly, Ike felt a warm glow. He was happy to have relieved some of Emma's obvious burden.

A flight attendant requested drink orders.

Ike wanted coffee; Emma opted for hot tea.

"What flavors of pies?" she continued.

"My specialties are apple and lemon meringue. My pecan and walnut are tasty, too. "

"I'm partial to pecan," she said.

"A heavenly treat," he responded.

He knew he would get to see Emma Cassidy from time to time and, for that, his life would be brighter.

Things were definitely looking better.

What he did not know was that two of his friends would die doing Emma Cassidy a simple favor.

56

Aaron Cooper heaved a sigh of relief, and was actually so animated that he waved goodbye as Sarcusi's Suburban departed the storage facility in Santa Fe. Although he had been extremely nervous, Cooper held his cool as the young woman quickly tested random samples of cocaine.

"Tommy, this is some of the best I've seen," she said, "and extremely pure. Buy it."

Tommy Jax nodded, shook Cooper's hand, and the exchange occurred.

Tony Sarcusi had guided Cooper every step of the way. When they met privately the day before, his former partner told Cooper not to worry, that he had his back, and that the deal would go down without a hitch...and it did.

The cocaine was pure gold. Tommy Jax consummated the deal. Sarcusi got his commission. Julie Adam's eyes sparkled. Cooper smiled. In fact, he was so pleased that, as the Suburban disappeared, tears actually filled his eyes, something that had not happened since he was a child!

They were tears of joy. Cooper's former life was over, forever! The plan he conceived as a rookie cop, the plan he executed masterfully, had delivered a fortune.

Goddamn it, he thought, twenty-five years. I pulled it off.

This day marked a new beginning. The drugs, the tough-guy persona, and the deception were history, stepping-stones to a very comfortable but private lifestyle.

He vowed not to do anything that would draw anyone's ire or attention. He would live actively but smartly. Wisdom would be the rule.

He closed the storage unit door, turned the dead bolt, slid two iron bars into position for added security, and went to the suitcase sitting atop a small table.

Here it is, one million three hundred thousand dollars!

The money, sans Sarcusi's commission, brought his total fortune to nearly seven million dollars. He was a rich man, with freedom to do whatever he wanted to do.

Cooper clapped his hands and did a spirited jig. The movement, completely foreign to his character, was a delightful twist for a guarded, reserved, and practiced man.

"Free at last," he said. "Free at last," he repeated.

The irony of his words was lost in his elation. All he knew, and sensed, was release. The burden of the past was gone. Twenty-five years of planning, sacrifice, patience, deception, and living-on-the-edge disappeared with Sarcusi's vehicle.

Cooper smiled. His great fraud was over and gone, water under the bridge, or whatever-the-cliché that seemed most appropriate. The faces of the people he hurt and killed dissipated quickly. Manny Tobias, the woman in the alley, and numerous dopers meant nothing to him and never would. He would never think, or dream, or consider them again. He would *will* it. If he had just scaled Everest, he could conquer a few bitter memories.

He removed two new and large briefcases from the T-Bird's trunk, splitting the 'million three' evenly between them. One for each bank he would visit.

As he divided the money, he hummed MOON RIVER from BREAKFAST AT TIFFANY'S, the movie. Liza Mercer and he had watched the classic several days ago. The song stuck with him because Liza said her cousin wrote the lyrics.

They would emulate the two vagabonds in the song: off to see the world. Because of his money, their *someday* was *today*. They could cross any river they chose, at any time.

The song was beautiful, the day was beautiful, Liza was beautiful, and their life together would be beautiful, too.

He checked the time: 7:32 a.m.

The banks opened in about an hour. They were nearby. He would lock the money away and be home free.

Excitedly, but off key, he sang a few lyrics from the song:

There's such a lot of world to see. We're after the same rainbow's end, waitin' 'round the bend

An idea hit him. He paused, pressed a number on his cell phone, and a moment later, Liza answered.

"Hi, Aaron," she said. "Did you sell the T-Bird?"

"No, he was worried winter salt would destroy it. Say, are you still going to Albuquerque this morning? If so, I thought I'd tag along, maybe we can stop for breakfast."

"That would be wonderful...what time?"

He glanced at his watch, did a mental calculation, and said, "I'll pick you up in about two hours. Is that good?"

"I'll be here. You don't like stores, you don't mind?"

"Usually, I don't, but not today. Today is different. Today, I'm the king of the world. Whatever you want is my treat."

"Aaron! What has gotten into you?"

"You...I love you. Let's stop at a jewelry store."

"For what?" she asked.

"An engagement ring," he replied. "I want to spend the rest of my life with you."

"I love you," she said. He heard her crying.

"Don't cry, Liza, you should be happy."

"You continue to surprise me."

They said goodbye and hung up.

Of course, he would never tell Liza about the money. His cover would remain that he had been lucky with family inheritances and investments. Eventually, after some homework, he would move his fortune, maybe into gold and silver, maybe into overseas accounts. For now, safe deposit boxes did the job and were entirely confidential.

He locked the briefcases, sat down at the table, opened a newspaper, and scanned the sports pages.

The cup of coffee he carried in earlier from his car was lukewarm, but it would suffice. It tasted fine.

"You gotta love Starbucks," he said.

He needed to kill some time. He checked on the Pirates, the Yankees, and read all the box scores. Then, he read all the local news and actually looked at the real estate section, thinking he would buy a house, after the wedding.

As he promised himself earlier, he did not think about the laws he broke, the money he stole, or the people he killed. That was another man, another life, a different time.

~

Surprisingly, the time passed quickly.

At 8:20 a.m., Cooper double-checked his .38 and peered through a peephole. The parking lot remained empty. He ventured that no one had entered or exited since Sarcusi departed. He opened the door slightly. Nothing moved.

Good.

He chirped the trunk of his STS, opened the door of the storage unit fully, and holding his .38 in his right hand, placed each briefcase quickly into the trunk of his car, one after the other in a precise pattern.

After locking the trunk, he set the security codes for the storage unit, and started the Cadillac's engine.

Seconds later, he drove to the gate, opened it, exited, and watched the gate close in the rearview mirror.

He was on his way to a new life, a new world, a new love. As in Johnny Mercer's song, his love Liza was waiting just around the bend.

We're after the same rainbow's end, my Huckleberry friend...

57

Jack Redding never thought about fate until he discovered Cooper's Santa Fe storage facility was at the start of a long, winding, and rarely-traveled cul-de-sac. Fate extended a helping hand. Cooper had to exit the same way he entered.

As he waited, Jack moved for a better view. After nearly an hour, Cooper stepped into the sunshine. He seemed buoyant. Jack watched as Cooper placed two briefcases in the trunk of his car and locked the storage unit. *He has the money*, Jack realized. *I thought he would leave it; this is my lucky day.* Cooper's mistake would be Jack's gain.

Jack noticed a small pistol, maybe a .38, in Cooper's right hand. It did not scare him. He watched Cooper pass through the gate, saw it close, observed the Cadillac make a left turn to exit, and drive slowly toward the main highway.

Jack looked left and right. A car went by, but no other traffic was visible. Chance favors the righteous. He told that to his men in battle and he actually believed it.

Jack had analyzed the situation as he waited. He knew Cooper's awareness would be acute; he would be watching for the extraordinary. If Cooper expected an attack, he would be ready for it. However, Jack believed Cooper would not expect the mundane. That is why Jack believed his plan would work. In fact, it was so silly it could not fail.

Cooper had to be feeling immense relief and jubilation. His heart would be racing believing he *beat the system*. He had to be thrilled with his grand deception. Of course, he was wrong.

In a few seconds, Cooper's life would go from dream-come-true to nightmare-in-hell.

Jack placed a vial of pepper spray in his left hand and a lump of wax, filled with theatrical blood, in his mouth. It was show time! He was ready and surprisingly calm.

As Cooper's STS slowed to stop, Jack made his move. He jumped on the 10-speed, rolled down the hill to the sidewalk, took a slight turn, and drove into the right front fender of the Cadillac. The 10-speed's front wheel hit hard, Cooper slammed on the brakes, and tires squealed.

Jack intentionally rolled onto the pavement. As he hit the asphalt, he bit into the wax. He waited for Cooper, as make-believe blood filled his mouth. It would be very realistic when it oozed out from between his lips.

A moment later, the driver's door opened and, peering under the car through squinty eyes, Jack saw loafers as Cooper exited.

As for Cooper, he moved cautiously toward the front of the vehicle, his .38 readily accessible in his left hand and pressed against his left leg. Cooper paused. He wanted to make sure the accident was not an attempted ambush.

Jack's eyes followed Cooper's steps as he rounded the STS. As Cooper approached the front right fender, Jack let the blood spill from his mouth, threw the wax under the car, and played to his injury.

Jack moaned, tried to sit up, and fell backward. Blood trickled down his chin. His acted disoriented.

Jack knew what would happen. He believed when Cooper saw the blood his whole demeanor would change. As expected, it did.

Jack lifted his head briefly, role-played his confusion, and glanced at Cooper, babbling, "Didn't see your car…chest…I have a heart prob….bad pain…" He fell back hard, his helmeted head bouncing on the pavement.

"Fuck me," Cooper whispered.

As Cooper leaned down cautiously, Jack noticed him pocket the handgun. Jack moaned but did not move.

"My chest, bad heart…," Jack whispered.

"Jesus, I'll call 911," Cooper said. "I didn't see you."

"My fault, it's my fault, I..."

As Cooper reach for his phone, his eyes drifted. Quickly, Jack grabbed his collar and slammed the ex-cop's head against the asphalt. Then, hit Cooper with pepper spray.

Cooper, confused and vulnerable, was an easy victim. Jack rendered him unconscious with a chokehold, lifted him into the back seat of the STS, and bound his hands and feet with plastic ties. He force-fed a combination of sleeping pills and orange juice down Cooper's throat. With tape from his fanny pack, Jack wrapped Cooper's mouth.

He removed the 10-speed's front wheel and tossed it and the remainder of the bicycle into the trunk. Finding a blanket there, he decided to cover Cooper's body. Then, he drove away, as if nothing had happened.

~

About thirty minutes later, Jack turned onto a dirt road that led to his final destination: an abandoned tin mine, ten miles away. Bailey was out there, waiting in the pickup, hidden in an arroyo. A length of black thread that Jack had stretched taut across the entrance remained in place. No one had entered.

After passing large rock formations, he stopped the STS facing a pit, some 20-by-20-feet square and fifty-feet deep, not far from the mine's entrance. The car idled in park.

Before pulling Cooper out of the Cadillac, he popped a briefcase open with his knife. He found neat stacks of used and worn currency of varying denomination.

"I have our money, Jill," Jack whispered.

Jack stashed the briefcases, 10-speed, and the Cadillac's license plate in the pickup. Then, he dragged Cooper to the mouth of the mine. He doused the driver's side of the STS with bleach to dilute DNA. Then, reaching in, he put the car in drive, stepped aside, and watched the STS disappear into the pit. Killing Cooper was next.

58

Two small boys were the first to see Sister Margaret's car turn onto the orphanage's potted driveway in Los Alamos. In their innocence and naïve young minds, they had no idea that far to the south, Jack Redding would lead a man to a rendezvous with death.

"Sister Margaret's home," the younger of the two boys shouted, clapping his hands.

Hearing his voice, all the children turned and raced toward the approaching car.

The oldest of the orphans carried a newly arrived infant as he escorted Sister Marie Elizabeth down a walkway.

"Do you think her trip was a success, Sister?" Joseph asked the middle-aged nun.

"We'll know by her demeanor as soon as she steps from the car. Perhaps our prayers have been answered," the nun replied. In her heart, because she had not heard from Margaret, Sister Marie assumed the worst.

Sister Margaret parked near the front of the orphanage as the dust settled on the ground behind the car.

As she opened the door, two children hopped into the tired Buick and onto her lap.

Quickly, the three were laughing.

After giving and receiving kisses, Sister Margaret shushed the young ones out of the car and exited herself.

She looked over at her friend and, when their eyes locked, Sister Marie had an answer. A slight shake of Sister Margaret's head confirmed the notion. She got some money but nothing close to what they needed.

"Did she raise the money," Joseph whispered.

"She has enough, Joey. We will be okay. We'll be grateful for whatever she does have. God will not let us carry our burden alone."

59

After a while, I left Cooper's side and walked to the entrance of the abandoned tin mine. I needed to breathe fresh air. I wanted to see the last wisps of sunset. I wanted to feel alive before killing a man. In a matter of minutes, evil would fill my heart and total darkness would dance in from the east, embrace the desert, and mask my revenge.

I leaned against scruffy beams at the mouth of the mine. Nearby, warped planks and a condemned sign, which had blocked entry and partially covered the pit, were in a neat pile. Before departing, I would reposition them. Cooper and his car would disappear for a long time, maybe forever.

Behind me in an auxiliary tunnel that would become his grave, Aaron Cooper was naked, supine, and unconscious.

He was about thirty feet into a narrow shaft that branched left off the constricted main channel. His arms and legs were spread eagle and bound tightly to steel stakes with yellow nylon rope. Four leather straps, spiked on either end, were taut across his body, holding him firmly against the ground. Cooper could not wiggle free or lift his neck, chest, abdomen, or knees. I had sledged each spike firmly into the hard ground. They were immovable. Regardless of effort, Cooper was immobile. He would die that way.

From where I stood, the mine's interior was as black as coal. The glow of a small lantern near Cooper's head was not visible. If I could not see the light, neither could anyone else.

I listened for Cooper's voice: nothing! He was still asleep and I would wait, resolute and patient. I had plenty of time to kill him. His death would come soon enough, surely before midnight. Afterward, I would drive away in the chilly night air, never to look back.

Two rabbits darted across the old dirt road, a wide path actually, that led up to and away from the abandoned mine.

Three jets, one heading east and two going south, drew contrails in the sky. The jets themselves were barely visible.

The rabbits and aircraft signified life's routine. Perhaps it was God's way of indicating that my actions meant nothing in the scheme of His grand design. Life would go on. The orb would spin. Winds would blow. Human hearts would beat.

We, Cooper and I, were a sideshow. Jill's death mattered only to me, Cooper, and, although she did not know about it, to the completely innocent Liza Mercer.

I felt bad for the woman I had never met. I had snooped on her and Cooper's conversations with the parabolic dish I purchased in Erie. I knew about their dreams and desires.

In years to come, she would sit and question what happened. I imagined her beside a fire conjuring what might have been, needing answers, wondering why Cooper disappeared just when their lives seemed perfectly aligned.

Such is life. One day everything is peaceful and the next turmoil devastates. Cooper cast his die, and mine, and Liza's at the precise moment he snapped Jill's neck.

In my experience, few people actually consider the residuals of their actions. However, residuals matter and sometimes they sting. I offered a silent apology to Liza Mercer because of what I was about to do. I hoped that, in time future, she would find love, peace, and laughter.

On my drive from Buffalo, suckled by the catharsis of the open road, I pondered the consequences of my actions. A few would surface but they did not outweigh what I needed to do. They, or Liza Mercer's sadness, would not stop me.

In Tulsa, I decided Cooper had to understand the lingering effects of Jill's death. Before he died, he would hate the day he placed a nightmare on my doorstep. He would die knowing that every action demands a reaction, that an improbable hell awaited him, and that I was the person who would introduce him to the devil.

In my travels, I concluded that no matter what Cooper did or said I would not yield. Like an agent-for-hire, I would not let him burrow under my skin. If that happened, it would spoil the honeyed taste of revenge I longed for with each passing mile of open road.

A cool breeze ruffled my shirt collar as I checked my watch: 5:18 p.m. Cooper would awaken soon. When he did, it would mark the beginning of his journey to perdition.

"Not too much longer," I said to Bailey, who was perched on a flat rock, beside the entrance. "I gave Cooper six of Jill's sleeping pills and those little bastards have a kick."

By my calculation, the sedatives I dissolved in juice and force fed to Cooper with a turkey baster would last about ten hours. Two pills made Jill, a woman who barely weighed a hundred ten pounds, sleep for six hours. Six pills should keep Cooper, a man nearly twice her size, out for ten or twelve. My guess was unscientific, but a good one.

I studied the lay of the land. Back during World War II, the old mine would have been a busy place. Now, with the rusting hulk of an old lorry, a ghost's deathbed, off to the side of the pit, the mine was a vague footnote of history.

The mine itself, a sliver cut into the base of a small cliff, neighbored truly majestic rock formations. I could see the hand of creation at work in the desolate design.

As accent, juniper bushes, scrub pine, assorted cacti, and other nameless bushes added to the raw beauty.

The desert in that part of New Mexico, at that time of year, was an ardent blend of browns, grays, yellows, and russets, with varying patches of light and dark greens.

The combination was compelling and, oddly, soothing.

My eyes flicked west. The sky mixed pinks, oranges, and purples. Eventually, the colors would merge into the hue of a good dark wine and, at some point, black would replace burgundy as night descended.

Pioneers on the old Santa Fe Trail would have seen similar skies from atop the rock-hard bench seats of creaking wagons. They sensed adventure and burst at the seams to fulfill the passion of their dreams. Brave beyond measure, many made that trip. Some found diamonds. Some found stones. Most made a living. Still, they persevered.

Maybe that was their reward; that they lived and grew old with those they loved beside them. I had hoped to grow old with Jill, too, but Cooper destroyed that dream.

For some mysterious reason, the face of the nun in the restaurant drinking vodka entered my mind. The look of desperation in her eyes was as desolate as the land that surrounded me. I thought about her, her orphanage, and Cooper's money.

An idea flashed in my mind and I nodded in agreement.

A cooler breeze swept in from the west, caressed the dry path, collected dust, and sped off to the east. The dust swung over an arroyo a few hundred yards away, out where I hid my pickup in the shadows of a small overhang.

To prevent reflections from the sun, I had muddied the chrome, thrown a tarp over the windows, and used clumps of brush and tumbleweed to camouflage the wheels. I had parked the pickup there the day before I dragged Cooper into the mineshaft and staked him to the ground.

I hid the pickup to avoid inadvertent discovery. I removed its license plates, too. I was overly cautious because of the way Murphy's Law tends to spoil human efforts.

I glanced at Bailey. He sniffed the air, as he sat on a flat rock near the mouth of the mine. If man or animal, approached, Bailey would tell me. He could hear and smell things, and always warned me about subtle changes.

"This was Indian country," I said to him.

I always spoke to my dog, as if he understood every word. At the sound of my voice, his ears lifted.

"Of course, these days the tribes are on their reservations or managing their casinos. Before Columbus crossed the Atlantic, the Apache, Comanche, and associated tribes roamed these rocks, hills, and valleys."

If I looked closely, I would see remnants, signs of the brave warriors who once ruled the land before the white man's ambition stole it. On this day, history had no bearing. Today, a man would die in his own misery.

Lifting worn binoculars, I did a three-sixty before full darkness descended. I was looking for hikers, or flashlights, or the glow of a cigarette, for a match, for anything that could kick-start Murphy's Law. Nobody was out there. I was alone. If people *were* looking for Cooper, they were not out there in that sparse land.

I glanced upward at the dark sky: no clouds. I studied the spreading jet contrails, backlit to a bright orange by the high rays of the setting sun. Unnamed men and women were on their way to dreams, and hopes, and maybe sorrows. I wished them well but my wishes did not mean a damn thing.

I could not help but wonder if it entered anyone's mind, as his or her plane flew by, that six miles below one man prepared to end another's life. Would any of those passengers have the guts to kill Aaron Cooper? Maybe! Push a person far enough and he or she will gouge out eyes, poison hearts, and laugh about it. I am a cynical bastard but bad days and regrets transform the human character.

Not too far away, a dry creek bed sliced through a small narrow. The scene fascinated me and I remembered a long-ago trip with Jill to the Grand Canyon...

...Come over here, you big chicken," Jill shouted, "There's a guard rail."

"It's a long way to the bottom, Jill," Jack replied, teasing her. "Despite jumping from planes, I dislike heights."

He walked over and kissed her cheek in the sunlight, squeezing her waist and the resting his hand on her hip. Jill's warmth seeped through her clothing.

Together they gazed at a horizon that seemed an eternity away. A nearby sign indicated the venue provided a glimpse of Utah, but, mostly, it was sky and canyon.

Jill pointed at the river, where people rafted. Others hiked an adjacent shoreline.

"Let's go there," she said, her voice filled with excitement. "I want to see the view looking up from the bottom of the canyon. I bet it is incredible. We need to see that, Jack."

See it they did and later that evening, after they ate cheese enchiladas and drank margaritas, they made love in their hotel room. Afterward, they held each other in the dark, looking out the window so Jill could see the moon above the canyon, and maybe wish on a shooting star.

"We're like explorers and this big old canyon is completely ours," Jill whispered.

"Am I your conquistador?" Jack asked with a whisper.

"Coronado's troops never had it better than this," Jill whispered, moving her legs, pulling him into her...

...As Bailey growled, a moan filtered out of the mineshaft. I turned to enter and Bailey started to join me. I gave him a hand signal, indicating he should stay. He settled quickly. A bark told me he had my back. Bailey would stand watch. Seconds later, I was beside Cooper.

"Do I know you?" Cooper asked groggily, as I stood over him. The thick paste of an uneasy sleep muffled his voice.

"We've never met," I replied. "We will spend some time together."

Cooper blinked hard, trying to shake the lingering bonds of an unwanted and manmade sleep.

"I'm thirsty," he whispered. "Do you have water?"

I nodded, filled the turkey-baster, and let him drink.

"Where am I?"

"In an abandoned tin mine," I said, south of Santa Fe."

"This has something to do with the cocaine, doesn't it?"

I nodded, saying, "Yes, in a way, it does."

"Why are you doing this? Is it about the money? Did that prick Sarcusi fuck me? I knew the buy went down too easy."

I knelt and patted Cooper's cheek. He had not shaved in a few days and I noticed a thin scar angling through his right eyebrow, maybe from a knife fight.

"Come on, shake it loose," I said. "Sarcusi, whom I'm guessing is one of the men you met earlier, did not send me. Nobody double-crossed you! They don't know me. I don't know them. They don't know where we are. They'll never know. The secret belongs to you, and me, and the desert."

Cooper breathed in air deeply several times, trying to collect his faculties. I could tell he was trying to place me.

"I can't move. Did you paralyze me with something?"

"You're tied down tighter than a submarine hatch."

Cooper strained so hard to free his arms and hands that his face turned an ugly purple.

"Motherfucker," he said, relaxing. He was breathing heavily, gulping for air, both angry and defiant.

"You can't free yourself. I tied your hands and feet with nylon rope. I draped four taut straps across your body. I used two-foot stakes...really high-quality steel. I pounded eighteen inches of each stake into the hard ground. You won't move, don't waste your time."

Despite my suggestion, he strained hard to free himself. This time beads of perspiration dotted his forehead. His breathing was heavy and uneven. The muscles in his arms, severely agitated, started to spasm.

I watched Cooper's carotid artery pumping vigorously.

I thought of a Ross MacDonald mystery.

In THE BLUE HAMMER, the carotid artery of a beautiful woman, pumped hard, too. As I recall, she died in that book and Cooper would die in the story I was writing.

"If it's not the money, then what is it?" Cooper asked.

"I'm here to even a score and send you away."

"A trip?"

"Yeah, you'll be leaving this world for the next."

He eyes darted in all directions and then met mine.

"Are you dumb? I'm a cop. When people find out about this, you'll be knee-deep in shit. You'll be screwed."

I laughed. Cooper still was not thinking clearly; he was having a hard time connecting the dots.

"You're a *retired* cop," I clarified, "and no one will ever know. You are naked and cannot move," I paused for effect, "and *I'm the one* who's in trouble? You're not a very good detective, after all." I slapped him across the face, hard. "Trust me; you're the one who's neck-deep in shit."

The slap and my words hit home. His eyes filled with alarm. He must have finally realized what being naked and vulnerable meant. His faux cool crumbled. Instinctively, he tried to sit upright, but could not manage.

"Goddamn it," he said. "Let me go, fight me like a man."

"You're fighting days are over, Cooper."

"How do you know my name?"

"Manny Tobias wrote a letter telling me all about you."

"Tobias? That little weasel, what does he have to do with any of this? Why do I feel so fucking sleepy?"

Cooper blinked fast, trying to shake his cobwebs.

"Tobias watched you on a very snowy night. As for being groggy, I gave you a sedative—six sleeping pills. I dissolved them in orange juice and squirted them down your throat, after I knocked you out."

"Now I remember. You're the stiff on the bicycle."

Cooper finally made the connection.

"A 10-speed acquired in Albuquerque, it came in handy. I rode it to Santa Fe during the night after I left my truck and dog here. It was only thirty miles." I held up a turkey baster. "A buck forty-nine at Wal-Mart. You want more water?"

"Piss off."

"Have it your way. You know I'm not a big fan of Wal-Mart; however, you can get virtually anything you want there. I bought tent stakes and the fashionable yellow rope that's holding your wrists and ankles, everything I needed for this crucial day. I got batting gloves to, left and right; can't be leaving any finger prints."

"I'm naked?" he grunted, finally grasping my words.

I nodded and said, "Totally naked."

"Are you queer, is that it? You're a coke-sniffing fag."

I slapped him hard, imprinting my hand on his cheek.

"Show some respect for God's children. I'm not gay."

"Then, what the hell do you want?" Cooper's face turned crimson where I slapped him.

"I want you to know that you are on the precipice of hell." I spoke evenly. "I want you to know you are about to meet the devil. I want you to know it is payback time."

"Payback," he repeated, confused.

"Yeah, you killed my wife, Jill, in Pittsburgh."

Terror filled Cooper's expression but he recovered quickly. He had not yet fully accepted or comprehended his fate. I knew what was next: he would try to get under my skin.

"The drunken broad in the alley, I screwed her, a great piece of ass," he lied, showing too much false bravado.

This time I slammed the side of my fist into his testicles. He gasped for air, his body shook, and he shivered as waves of pain swept through his body.

"Don't test me, Cooper," I said.

He groaned and I added, "You and I know you did no such thing. You killed her in cold blood and you will pay."

He screamed. All of his instincts told him to fight, but he could not and it was triply frustrating. His screams loosened pebbles and dirt, which fell onto his sweaty chest from overhead. I did not attempt to brush the debris away.

"Scream all you want. No one can hear you," I said. "My guess is we are fifteen miles from any living soul, in a condemned and abandoned tin mine outside of Madrid, New Mexico. I found it on the Internet. I needed an out-of-the-way place where we would not be disturbed. Using a computer at a library, I checked State of New Mexico and other Web sites. I found several locations. I liked this one the best because it is so remote and I could ditch your car. You know, you can find almost anything you want with a few keystrokes. That's how I learned about your career. Now, if you promise to control your temper, I won't gag you."

"They'll find the car, your DNA will be all over it," he was grasping at straws, anything to stall.

"No." My voice was cold. "Your car is in a pit, at least fifty-feet deep. I measured the depth with Wal-Mart rope."

He was still hurting from the punch to his genitals but managed another loud scream, calling me a son of a bitch. More silt fell. I lifted the lantern to study the beams. I guessed and hoped they would hold.

Turning to Cooper, I said, "Have it your way."

I lifted his boxers and tore several strips, muffling him with a section of the pee-stained fly.

"Maybe I'll give you time to respond, maybe I won't," I said. "But, I talk first." I paused to sip water. "Are you with me here, Cooper?"

Pure hatred filled his sad eyes; he did not react.

I jabbed the tip of my knife into his right cheek, drawing blood. Cooper winced when I showed it to him.

"I asked a question. Blink twice, if you understand."

Cooper blinked quickly. Tears rolled down his cheeks.

To show him I was in total control, I took cloth from his boxers and, using the highly corrosive acid from Theo Jefferson's basement, I demonstrated how quickly the acid destroyed it. I held the bottle above Cooper's genitals.

"Do you understand that you are not to make a sound?"

As he blinked, a stream of his urine shot out of his penis and away from me.

"Good thing it leans right," I said, laughing.

More tears filled his eyes. He was crumbling quickly and humiliation forced him to shake uncontrollably.

"Don't be embarrassed. I would probably pee myself, too. Now, breathe deeply a few times and pay close attention!"

Cooper blinked, inhaled, and eventually calmed himself.

"My name is Jack Redding. I am a retired Army colonel and I can be a mean son of a bitch. I spent twenty years fighting for my country, about as long as you were a cop."

Surprise filled his eyes.

"I know how to kill, Cooper. I've taken down probably eighty men in my lifetime and ordered the deaths of many more. I fought in Desert Storm. Before and after that, I was in Mexico, and Central and South America, mostly in Colombia, raining hell on drug cartels for several presidents. My teams and I were off the grid, so to speak. They call it Black Ops. Ours was the dirty war Uncle Sam will never acknowledge and, at times, it was brutal. I've tried to forget all of that; unfortunately, you brought it back.

"I tell you this so you understand that I know how to kill, that I am not afraid to take another man's life. If you think I'll hesitate, I will not. Cooper, when you killed Jill, you signed your death warrant.

"I'm from Buffalo, that's where Jill and I lived." I paused to breathe, adding, "We planned to grow old together. You destroyed our dream when you broke her neck. I left Buffalo late last week hunting you.

"For the past six days, I've been in New Mexico, stalking you. I've been a very busy boy preparing for this, finding a location to kill you and bury your body, and getting what I needed. I've learned quite a bit about you and Liza Mercer, your lovely friend."

He groaned through his gag, his concern for Mercer was obvious but unwarranted.

"Don't worry, she's not included in any of this. I'm sure she is as anxious as hell about where you are. I do feel sorry for her. She'll never know what happened. She'll think you deserted her. Now, where was I? Yes, I remember, I've been following you; we called it *basic recon* in the Rangers.

"Using an inexpensive listening device for bird watchers, I eavesdropped on your conversations, sitting up on the hill behind your condo. That's how I knew you were meeting two men and a woman at that storage center to exchange cocaine for money. I heard bits of that conversation, too.

"I've got to hand it to you. It was a perfect location for the exchange, isolated. It was ideal for me, too. I guessed you'd take your time leaving that storage facility. When I scouted it yesterday, a plan jelled. I bought the 10-speed, a cycling suit, the lantern, the rope, the spikes, and a few other things. Not the acid, the acid I got from a friend. It all fell together. It was simple and actually easier than I expected.

"By the way, the money from your drug transaction is stowed in my truck. That is a windfall. I knew you took Jill's and my money and, all the way from Buffalo, I knew it would be difficult to get my money back. My guess is your ill-gotten fortune is in safe deposit boxes. How the hell could I access those?" His eyes told me I'd just hit pay dirt. "But, I've got to hand it to you. Your timing was impeccable," I added. "I have those briefcases. Fate does exist, huh?"

If Cooper could have killed me with a human expression, I would have died right on the spot.

"I counted the drug money as you slept," I said, "a million three hundred thousand. I'll keep an amount equal to what you took from Jill and me, and a bit more. The remainder goes to charity. You will be an unnamed benefactor of the poor. Maybe the gift will buy you a cup of water in hell."

Cooper was furious but the ropes and straps held against his diminishing strength. More pebbles fell atop his body.

"Uh, uh, uh," I cautioned, shaking my finger like an old blue-haired teacher. I hit his inner thigh with a drop of acid, creating a nasty, inch-round blister.

"Not a sound, I will not tolerate any more attempts to free yourself. Cooper, you killed my wife. I think you killed Manny Tobias, too, probably before he told you what he knew. How many others; probably killed a few more, huh?"

Cooper's expression said I was right. His fear was torturing him. I decided to add to it. I punched the side of his neck and hit his abdomen with another drop of acid.

"You're a despicable sack of shit." I said calmly.

I removed a cell phone from my jeans and held the screen before Cooper's eyes.

"If you dare close your eyes, I swear I'll fill one with acid. Now, watch!" I pressed a button. "That's you, Cooper, with Jill. Manny Tobias made this recording the night you killed her. If you listen hard enough, you can hear her neck snap and her skull crack as it hits the curb."

I paused to gulp whiskey from a half-pint I removed from my hip pocket. It was a burden to stay calm.

"You are a bad man and a bad cop. I see it. Hell, you didn't even know Tobias was recording you."

Cooper started to weep and, again, urinated involuntarily.

"The truth is a hard chew when your life's on the line, huh? I want to tell you about Jill.

"In the last few years of our marriage, she became a drunk. She was probably drunk the night you killed her.

"Jill wasn't always an alcoholic. She was a vibrant, dynamic woman. She drank because we lost babies. Then, there were family deaths, some natural, others accidental."

His tears formed a steady stream.

"The deaths were hard for Jill to accept, so she started drinking to mask the sorrow. She told me the booze took the pain away. Actually, it only cloaked it."

I had another gulp of whiskey, my last until I was in Vegas. Cooper watched and waited.

"Here's where you must pay close attention," I stated. "I'm only going to say this once. I was helping Jill; we were getting past the problem. She would have made it. She would have come back to me, and we would have been happy for a long time. I planned to tell her that we would adopt a child, maybe two. She was coming back. I know it as sure as I know you will die. You took that away.

"Jill slipped and that slip took her to Pittsburgh for some reason only God knows. Are you following me, Cooper?"

He blinked twice, despite his constant tears.

"Good. When Jill drank, she became thoughtless. For example, for her trip to Pittsburgh, she withdrew nearly four hundred thousand dollars from our joint checking account."

Cooper's eyes narrowed.

"That's right, it comes back to the money," I said. "Jill took our money to Pittsburgh. As you heard on Tobias' recording, she thought she was bringing it to me. For all her good traits, Jill could be nosey, too. She overheard you talking about cocaine and, for that, you killed her."

Cooper's hands were balled fists. Blood pooled where his nails bit into the skin of his palms.

"Here's where you erred, Cooper. When Jill drank, she became forgetful. Odds are she would have forgotten about your conversation, but you didn't know that.

"You couldn't take that risk, so you broke her neck.

"Another mistake was telling you she had money. Where did she have it stashed, a locker somewhere? It makes no difference, because I know you took it. I saw you take a key. Tobias saw it, too. My bet, he wanted to shake you down but you wasted him before he mentioned the recording. Thanks to your recent cocaine sale, I have my four hundred thousand back, plus a whole lot more. Your actions will give me and others a very good life."

Cooper made a strong attempt to free himself, but his effort was futile. I slammed my fist into his abdomen.

"Calm down," I demanded. "You can't change the outcome of this. Before I kill you, I want you to know that your dream is over. I imagine you thought you won. You did not. The party is over. The orchestra has gone home.

"This past December, months after Tobias' death, which I eventually read about on-line, somebody sent me Manny's letter and a memory card. Manny told me all about you, about how crooked you were, and about how you killed Jill. The video proved it. He hoped I'd give everything to the authorities." I poked my chest with my forefinger for emphasis, raising my voice, "I don't know who sent that letter, but you are looking at the final authority."

I yanked the gag from his mouth.

"You rotten motherfucker," he shouted. Then, he started to weep uncontrollably. I waited. When he caught his breath, he looked at me.

I put the knife against his throat. "I want you to admit you did it, that you killed my wife."

"I killed her you asshole. Someone will find me," he said.

"No they won't."

"They'll connect your name with mine. They'll check hotel records; they'll see you visited Santa Fe. You will go down."

I laughed.

"I'm not here as Jack Redding."

He seemed confused.

"I have another identity, you ass: a driver's license and credit card. It's not me, of course, but a photo booth and lamination turned it around quickly. I used it at a motel where I stayed. When I checked out, I paid cash. I'm clean."

I could see him thinking.

"Come on, man. Don't do this. Don't kill me. I'll make it up to you. You can have three million."

"Can you bring Jill back?" I asked.

His silence was his answer.

"Then, how can you make it up to me?"

"I will kill you, you bastard," he shouted.

I grew tired of his bravado, shook my head, and walked away. I went outside to relieve myself in the darkness, listening to his screams dissipate.

I patted Bailey's head and noticed him rubbing the GPS collar from Rosemary Tomasulo; it was too tight. I had it on him as a precaution. I took it off, shoved it in my hip pocket, stooped, and opened a duffel bag. The time had come. I found the .45, slid one in the chamber, and walked back into the mine. I held the automatic in my hand, sans silencer.

"They will find you, man," Cooper was shouting. "Someone will find you just like you found me. They will hunt your boney ass down."

"They won't," I replied, standing near his left hand.

As I studied Cooper's face, I moved to improve my position and my foot bumped against a stake. I fell and discharged the weapon. It was a slip, a careless mistake.

I stood up, agitated. Wanting to terrify Cooper, I put another round into the beams above his chest. As I leveled the gun at his heart and prepared to pull the trigger, several rotten beams gave way, directly above his waist.

Rock and dirt started to cover him. I fired once at his chest not knowing if debris blocked the shot.

Then, I turned and sprinted for the exit.

I almost made it but that damned cave-in followed me as I ran. A falling beam hit my foot, tripped me, and I fell to the ground. To avoid burial, I started to crawl. It did not work. Falling debris held me in place and I could not move.

I thought I would die and hoped Bailey would survive. I could see the entrance and the moon in the distant sky. I closed my eyes and made a small pocket of air with my arms, hands, and the Colt. Soon, I was unconscious.

~

I awoke with Bailey tugging on my shirt, licking my face. He dug my head out with his forepaws. The moon seemed to be in the same position. Luckily, I was not out long.

I dug my legs out of the dirt and exited the mine. I pocketed the .45, dusted myself off, and found a bottle of water in the duffel bag. I drank, pulled out a flashlight, and crept back into the mine. This time, Bailey went with me.

I stood where I had slipped into brief unconsciousness. Using the flashlight, I peered into the narrow mine. Piles of dirt and debris had half-filled the main shaft.

Had Cooper survived? As I crawled over the rubble, I heard a slight beeping. I followed the sound and, using the light, found the shaft where I had bound Cooper.

Dirt and rotted lumber went back as far as I could see. The beeping persisted. I searched along the edge of the cave-in and finally saw the GPS collar.

Thankfully, it had fallen from my pocket and for some reason was beeping. Cooper had to be nearby. I positioned the flashlight on a broken beam and began digging furiously. Bailey sat beside me, waiting.

Minutes later, I noticed a streak of yellow: the nylon rope!

I paused slightly, dug some more, found Cooper's arm, and followed it to his wrist. I checked his pulse.

He was gone. Soon, his body would begin to rot.

I bowed my head.

A sense of dissatisfaction filled my body for a moment or two. Initially, I felt cheated. However, the feeling soon disappeared. I truly did not care. The son of bitch was gone, forever. No matter how he died, I had avenged Jill's death.

Cooper had admitted what I needed to hear.

He had acknowledged that he killed Jill.

Sure, I wanted to kill him but I told myself he was dead and I accepted the result. If not for me, he would be alive.

Whether he died from my gunshot or from a cave-in, he would never hurt another human being. That pleased me.

He showed abject fear.

He begged for his life.

Fear emanated from his naked body.

He was defenseless, dehumanized, and sick with terror.

He gave me what I wanted.

"Enjoy hell, you son of a bitch," I whispered.

I lifted the GPS collar and stopped the beeping.

Turning to Bailey, I said, "Let's get out of here."

I resealed the front of the mine. Afterward, I shined the flashlight into the pit. I could not see the STS.

I started the pickup and, using its bumper, inched the rusty old lorry into the pit atop Cooper's car. Next, I pulled longer boards across the open pit and used dead brush to erase many tire tracks. As Bailey hopped into the pickup, we heard a rumble and the ground shook slightly.

A massive cave-in had occurred. I cleaned the headlights, reaffixed the pickup's license plates that I retrieved from nearby rocks, and drove away in the scant moonlight.

~

An hour later, at a fast-food joint, we ate burgers and warm apple pies, and drank water. Next, I ran the pickup through a car wash. Gratefully, the odor of soap and hot wax cleared the stench of death and raw earth from my nostrils.

60

Liza Mercer was worried. Aaron Cooper was supposed to pick her up at 9:45 a.m. It was now midnight and she had not heard from him. Countless calls to his cell phone went unanswered. She called Tony Sarcusi and drove to the storage facility where Aaron kept his Thunderbird. Nothing!

Finally, she dialed the police.

"Precinct Seventeen, Officer Ruehl speaking," a cop said.

"Yes, this is Liza Mercer, a resident of Santa Fe. I'd like to report a missing person."

"Who and how long has he or she been missing?"

"It's my boyfriend, my fiancé. Aaron Cooper's been missing since about nine this morning. I'm really worried."

Ruehl wanted to ask the woman if her boyfriend was a drinker, usually when men went missing they were off drinking with their pals or shacked up with some bimbo. Instead, the cop turned official.

"Ms. Mercer, our policy is not to list a person as missing unless thirty-six hours have passed. Have you checked his clubs, his place of business, perhaps his friends?"

"I've done all of that, twice. I cannot find him. He's missing; I know it. I fear something bad has happened."

Ruehl hesitated.

"Did he have any meetings?"

"Yes, with a friend to try to sell a car. I talked to the man twice on his cell. Aaron was happy when they met. If fact, Aaron called me after the meeting; he seemed fine."

"Hmmm," the cop said, "I'll make an exception. Come to the precinct and I'll take your information. I will put it in the system and issue an alert to all officers on patrol. I hear the worry in your voice. Please, I want you to relax. I've seen these things before. They usually work themselves out."

This time, Officer Ruehl would be wrong.

61

Bitter winds buffeted the high plateau not far from the heart of Los Alamos as Bailey and I turned onto a long, graveled driveway. A weather-weary sign stating St. Therese of the Mountains Orphanage flapped back and forth, dangling on links of rusty chain.

The milky light of pre-dawn heralded the coming of morning, which was but moments away. A big gray farmhouse stood isolated in the distance, at the base of a red-rock cliff, surrounded by a crown of ponderosa pine. A lazy little creek meandered off to its right.

I shut off the truck's headlights and slowed my advance. The crunch of the truck's tires whispered my scant progress.

The sky seemed big and bold, celestial and seraphic. Streaks of pinkish-orange filled the eastern horizon; off, to the west, gunmetal gray faded to black.

Storm clouds festered and prepared to roll in.

The weather had shifted. Cold winds blew out of Canada, crossed Montana, sucked up moisture over Wyoming, and spread wide over Utah and Colorado. Eventually, rain would bore hard and true into New Mexico, spoiling the sunrise and dampening the bucolic landscape.

For as far as I could see, from north to south and probably all the way to Santa Fe, grey veils hugged the earth like lonely maidens hugging pillows. Wind would kiss rain, and there would be plenty of it.

If it got cold, snow would surely fall. In a matter of minutes, Bailey and I would see one hell of storm. I felt the moisture in my bones stirring the throb of old war wounds that whispered of memories I never could quite forget.

I braked, stopped, and turned on the radio. The forecast called for temperatures below freezing by mid-morning.

Definitely more snow, I thought.

Cottony drifts would lay cold and heavy in passes and valleys. The snow would cover the thick, sweet grasses of the mighty plateau.

Remnants of the storm could linger for days, like virgins hiding in shadows, covering the oranges, yellows, and russets that so enamor western artists.

"I need to be about my task," I told Bailey.

I released the brake, put the truck in neutral, and let its weight take me down the grade toward the orphanage.

I thought about Cooper, far to the south and, by now, cold in his grave. If snow fell around that old mine in Madrid, it would cover any tire tracks I might have missed. I decided to buy a different brand of tires in Las Vegas, just in case.

I checked the time. Bailey and I left the arroyo outside of Madrid nearly nine hours ago, after I covered the pit and re-boarded the entrance. I was sure Cooper's body would disappear by the time thawing winds carried the warm promise of spring. As for his car, I doubted its discovery. However, if discovered, no one could trace it to me.

I looked at the orphanage. "No lights," I said to Bailey, "Let's hope they don't see us." He looked at me and then at the sky. A subtle whine told me he was anxious about the storm and wanted to roll.

"I won't take long," I said, hesitating and thinking.

I flashed back on the drive to Los Alamos. About twenty miles out, I pulled off the side of the road and dropped the 10-speed in a dumpster. I also burned my *Cooper file*; tossing the ashes into in the air and watching them fly away and twist in the wind.

Using tin snips, I destroyed several memory chips, a spare DVD, and the STS's license plate. As I drove along without headlights, I tossed the small pieces onto the road, knowing they would scatter. No one would ever find them.

When I was finished, I hit the lights and headed north.

"He's gone," I whispered to Jill's memory. "I cannot do any more. Now, I live with the consequences."

My duty to my wife had ended. I wanted a new life. The first step in that journey meant giving some of Cooper's money to a despondent nun who drank airline bottles of vodka in a café in Elk City, Oklahoma. I hoped the gesture would clean a few marks off my blackened soul.

Nearing the orphanage, I stopped the pickup, behind red berry brushes. Thankfully, the house remained dark.

Wearing the batting gloves, I put eight hundred thousand dollars into a white plastic garbage bag. I wrote a note on the bag with a permanent marker telling the nuns to put the money to good use.

I signed my message, *St. Jude,* the patron saint of lost causes, thinking they would appreciate the irony.

I sprinted to the front door, set the bag on a welcome mat, rang the doorbell, hustled back to the pickup, and watched. Bailey's panting emphasized the growing tension.

A few moments later, a porch light came on and the front door opened. Two women peered out. They noticed the bag as they were about to close the door. One of the nuns opened it cautiously, peered inside, and made the sign of the cross.

Maybe the generosity would ease Cooper's and my journey through hell. I fired up the engine, turned around, hit the accelerator, and drove back to the main road.

Bailey and I were finally on our way to Las Vegas.

~

My thoughts turned to Jill, as we watched the sunset from a cabin on a mountain high above Lake Louise.

Back then, in July of some long-ago year, Jill crawled into bed next to me as I stared off into the night sky from a darkened bedroom.

On that night, I was fighting old memories, things that gnawed at me from my past.

Gunfire, screams, and too much blood were in the mix.

I was thinking of men lost, of children wasted, of men and women trapped as slaves by the cocaine that slipped onto our streets and into their bodies.

Sometimes, bitter memories hit me when I least expected them, and it felt like I could not shake them loose.

Jill, my dear, sweet love, always came to me…

…"What's the matter?" Jill whispered to Jack long ago. Her eyes sparkled with love.

"Old miseries, desperate moments," Jack replied.

She leaned over and kissed Jack's cheek.

"Jill," he continued, "sometimes I feel empty, and I wonder if it will ever change. I feel isolated and afraid. I would dearly like to know peace, peace that will last.

"I have done so many terrible things. I see images I hate and feel emotions that scare me. When I was a kid, I thought the world was a good place, that people were good, that life would always be good. Now that I am older and have done the things I've done, I realize how naïve I was and how terrible the world really is."

Jill kissed Jack's cheek again.

"Yes, she said the world can be a bad place. I believe that is why God gave you to me, so I could soften your days and make your life happier. Let me be your music. As long as I am with you, Jack, you are not alone," Jill replied, taking his hand in hers….

…I turned on the radio, scanning for music or news, for anything that would keep me awake, for anything that would fill my tired mind.

An all-night female disc jockey out of Los Angeles, but syndicated nationally, dedicated the next song to a woman in Iowa, but the words seemed to come from Jill.

Soon, Patty Griffin sang a haunting song. However, it was Jill's message and her voice, and it was for me alone:

She sees him laying in the bed alone tonight
The only thing a touching him is a crack of light
Pieces of her hair are wrapped around, and 'round his fingers
And he reaches for her side, for any sign of her that lingers
And she says you are not alone
Laying in the light
Put out the fire in your head
And lay with me tonight.

"Jill," I whispered. "The life we wanted is gone. I loved you beyond all measure," I said, driving on a dark road.

Put out the fire in your head...

I could not help but feel Jill's presence. I believed she was indicating to me that I should move on with my life; that it was time. I wanted to see new roads. I yearned for new songs. I welcomed new voices.

Sadly, I did not know that revenge would call again or that Murphy's Law and the chum of human failure would have both sad and glorious moments.

I have come to realize that a dark and aberrant strain in my DNA demands I even the score. I believe that every eye should negotiate for itself and trust no agent. I do not know from whence that impulse sprung. I just know it permeates my sinew and I cannot remove it.

Heart is a factor, too. At least, it is for me.

Heart wins more races than we humans can ever imagine. We call it luck or fate. A big heart is vital in the realm of human achievement. It is extremely special.

Heart, God's precious gift, gives us untold victories.

A single mom raises three children in a ghetto on guts and courage, working her fingers to the bone. She keeps her kids from the drugs and hate that fill many other lives.

Her children become a doctor, a lawyer, and a professor, respectively. The mother could have caved but her heart did not let her. Giving better lives to her three children mattered most. She struggled but she won because she had heart bigger than anyone could have ever imagined.

A blind man takes a bus every day to a job that barely pays minimum wage. Still, he is happy and joyful, and makes all those he encounters richer because of his optimism. That man's heart is as big as an autumn sky.

A mute girl grows up and, despite her disability, inspires the world. It has happened before and it will happen again.

There are countless stories like these and they all have one thing in common—the magnificence of the human heart.

Heart creates desire and from desire comes human achievement and, of course, unparalleled love.

I knew Jill was gone, forever. I wanted her but I could never have her, *not ever again*! I would have to pick myself up by the bootstraps and muddle through.

I hoped I had the heart to do it.

I truly needed a victory!

I needed to breathe new air.

I wanted to be happy.

I wanted to put the mess that filled my life because of what happened to Jill, far behind me.

I looked over at Bailey. He deserved a change. I knew his heart broke, too, because Jill was gone. I wondered what he would say if he could speak.

One day our lives were happy. Jill and I were planning for the kind of future that is rare. We were thinking of children and growing old.

Her parents were healthy and in our lives.

Her sister was successful and building a family of her own. She and Jill were close.

Then, for whatever reason, it all turned upside down.

We tried to fix it.

We tried to make amends.

We tried to get past it.

We failed.

Put out the fire in your head…

I wondered if I could ever do that. Was the cup half-empty or half-full?

The song on the radio came at me again…

It was good to be alive
But sometimes that can slip away as fast
As any fingers through your hands
So you let time forgive the past and
Go and make some other plans

I gunned the pickup through a curve, hit the high beams, and headed for Las Vegas.

The time had come to make some other plans.

Book 3

March-April 2013

Rebirth

We do not exist for ourselves.
—Thomas Merton

62

On my first day in Las Vegas, I packed five hundred thousand dollars into a safe deposit box. Jill's and my money, plus about one hundred thousand extra from Cooper, was securely under lock and key.

For a time, Bailey and I kept a low profile. I unpacked, settled in, and tried to unwind. I bought new tires, caught up on sleep, read a few books, talked at length with Bill Hawkins, and adjusted to my new environment. I did not consider gambling. I did not have the desire.

A few weeks in, I checked all my gear, making sure I had not overlooked any connection to Aaron Cooper. I believed I was clean, that everything was gone. Tobias' letter, which I slipped behind Jill's photograph the day I departed Buffalo, never entered my mind. My oversight would eventually taint what I had hoped was a chance for a new life.

That aside, I took long walks with Bailey and the days and nights merged into one continuous interval of renewal.

I ran every day and did calisthenics. I was pushing myself to purge whatever demons remained in my weary heart. I kept to myself. I acknowledged other residents, nodded and waved, but I did not really know or care to know anyone.

Then, it all changed with a simple telephone call.

"Jack," Hawk said, "Come over to the office. I want you to meet a friend of mine. He has baked us a lemon pie."

"I'll come right over," I replied.

Bailey and I walked to the main office, where Hawk introduced me to Isaac Turner.

"Everybody calls me, Ike," he said, as we shook hands. "You should, too."

"Ike, the pleasure is mine."

"Hawk tells me you and he fought the good fight."

"I don't know how good it was but we did it together."

"A certain comfort resides in that," Ike replied.

For the next hour, I sat in Hawk's office, with Bailey sleeping beside me. The coffee was as good as the lies Hawk and Ike told about life and fishing, about love and laughter, about highs and lows, about new and old, about wins and losses, about mysterious things seen in desert skies.

Ike had a hearty laugh and an endearing personality, primed with infectious mirth, deft sarcasm, and common decency. He was a solid, joyous, humble, magnificent, and picturesque man. He filled gaps in a conversation as easily as water fills the spaces between marbles in a jar. Once given, something told me his friendship would last forever.

We talked and laughed, and then, in an instant, fate tossed me a curve ball. Emma Cassidy opened two doors: the first, to Hawk's office, the second, to my heart. The latter came as an absolute surprise. I imagine the sensation was comparable to that of the first person to see Victoria Falls, a monster tidal wave, or the glorious hues of a sunset across the Pacific Ocean on a pristine and primeval beach. I knew instantly that she was a gift and a treasure.

I watched Emma close the door with a slight push of her rump. When it clicked into place, everything I had ever done in my life existed in two spheres: the old and the new. Emma seemed to separate time-past from time-future.

I liked her eyes. The appeal I saw in them danced on my skin. A glance, a smile, and a simple touch rekindled the sense of excitement that I had lost in a cold alley in Pittsburgh. I knew it immediately; Emma did, too. I was as sure of it as I was of the air created to sustain life.

I have often wondered if the sensation was extrasensory because words had no part in my reawakening.

A fire ignited. A switch flipped. A bond formed. Hearts joined. Emma's spirit warmed and comforted mine. I felt ebullient, excited, and reborn.

I do not understand what evokes this kind of weighty and immediate attraction. Yet, I know it exists and is as real as wind or sunshine. We recognize these natural phenomena immediately. Yet, we cannot fit or trap either one in a bottle. Still, they are as real as flowers or diamonds. Because we do not exist for ourselves, an unanticipated and unbreakable bond formed between a man and a woman.

Thinking back, I recall feeling eager and hopeful as Emma braced her hand innocently on my shoulder to keep her balance. That simple touch reminded me how much we need hope in our lives. Hope makes our existence valuable, giving us reasons to live, and, most assuredly, reasons to fear but accept the beauty that rests beyond death.

Emma leaned over to pet Bailey, touched me accidentally, and I felt animated for the first time in months. I looked into her eyes, as she studied mine. Slight nods and matching smiles hinted of an intimate future as clearly as a compass indicates true north. Was it magic, or chemistry, or physical attraction, or simply luck? Perhaps it was the nexus of each.

A dusting of freckles slanted across her attractive nose. I liked the reddish tint in her auburn hair and the sparkle in her blue eyes. Irish or Scottish, I thought, and average in height and size but solid and resolutely graceful. Her hands with their manicured and artistic fingers were wicks that drew me into her warm and vivacious personality.

She reminded me of a fair-skinned woman I once saw standing idly on a windswept beach beside the North Sea in Anstruther, Scotland.

That was long before Jill, long before my life bumped awkwardly over ice cubes and empty bottles of booze.

A long-overdue military leave took me by train from London to Edinburgh, and to venues north for rounds of golf on famed old courses. Before heading back to England, I spent a day sightseeing in the Scottish countryside.

On a misty day beside the North Sea, a man and a woman nodded as they passed; their eyes met. Had that mysterious but beautiful woman asked me to go with her, I would have gladly taken her delicate hand. I remember her turning and looking at me as if she had heard a whisper from heaven. For just an instant, she owned my heart.

I think about that woman from time to time and hope she remembers me as fondly as I remember her.

Jill captivated me in much the same way and, thereafter, I tumbled head over heels. Now, some supernatural directive told me it was Emma Cassidy's turn. I heard the music; only a fool would ignore the dance.

For a second or two, pure satisfaction rushed through my body and then, as quickly, the thrilling sensation receded. I felt enough to know I wanted more. To deny its existence was naïve and insensate. Emma's touch was a hint, an intimation of days to come and nights to remember.

I guess the melding of hearts works that way. If we search too hard for intimacy, it is illusive and seldom, if ever, surfaces. When we drop our guard and void our expectations that transitory yearning disappears. Invariably a special person steps in, touches a soul, and changes a life completely. It happens in an instant, the whole world in a grain of sand.

Jill's death no longer tied me knots; I was gaining on it. I still had rough patches and bad nights. Thankfully, since Cooper's death, that gap had widened. The pain was softer, its poke not as acute. More than a year had passed since her death. Whether a person likes it or not, wounds heal, hearts rest, and rough waters subside.

A different venue and the quiet of the desert helped. I was turning away from darkness and angling toward light. A different life was out there on the fringe. If only I could find the courage to step in the proper direction.

For the past year or so, I had muddled through each day on base instinct. In any given evening, I tried to make it to the next morning. In the morning, I hoped to reach the afternoon. After that, I aimed at evening again. Then, the cycle repeated itself.

My gut told me if I managed enough repetitions, I would eventually make it. My instinct had paid off. I was feeling better. I knew I would never forget Jill but I finally realized I could live without her. Then, unexpectedly, one door closed and another opened. Meeting Emma sweetened a soured life.

Bailey and I had arrived in Las Vegas in the midst of a warming trend. Hawk had the condominium ready. The place was painted, furnished, and comfortable.

Bailey took to it immediately. I liked it, too.

My life's touchstones, all the bitter memories, were in a carriage house back in Buffalo where they belonged. Scents, colors, or keepsakes remained there, too. At least at EL CORAZÓN I went to sleep and awoke without seeing fifty shades of Jill everywhere I turned.

As for Aaron Cooper, I rarely rendered his image. He seemed to vanish when I returned the driver's license and credit card I pilfered in an Elk City, Oklahoma, eatery.

I sent them back to the rightful owner, Fred Adkins of Flagstaff, Arizona. I did that in Los Alamos, after donating about eight hundred thousand dollars of Cooper's drug money to the nuns at St. Therese's Orphanage.

I clipped two one-hundred dollar bills to the credentials, my way of saying *thank you* to a stranger for the temporary loan of his identity. No harm and no foul.

I did think about God occasionally. I asked Him to guard Jill's soul. I asked for His mercy and I apologized for offending Him, if I had. I never sought forgiveness. I was not sorry about Cooper's death. If given a hundred chances, I would have ended his life a hundred times.

With that mindset, asking for forgiveness seemed disingenuous. Apologizing and seeking mercy was more honest.

A quick call to Vince told him I was fine. When asked, he said he would destroy my note and the DVD, and never mention the subject again.

He then asked a pointed question.

"How did everything go, Jack?"

"I'm alive," I replied. "That says a lot."

"I knew you would be," he said. "I never doubted it."

I switched subjects.

"How're you feeling, Vince?"

"Iffy," he responded. "But by some standards that's good."

He never told me his days were numbered. I guess he thought the burden of Jill's death, and my unspoken actions, was enough weight for me to carry. We talked some about my trip, and sports, and old memories, his land and lake, and ended the call.

Thereafter, the days passed quietly. Hawk and I had some long talks about our experiences and the future. Something in his eyes told me he believed my trip west was not solely about escaping old memories. However, he never asked.

Knowing Hawk as well as I did, I knew he never would. True friends do not ask; they abide. That alone brings them ease. Hawk was a man of great worth and reliability. I loved him beyond all thought. In many ways, our souls were one.

He thought my idea about novels based on our experiences had merit and decided to help me frame some stories. He even knew a literary agent, to whom he sent an email. Hawk was restoring a vintage cabin cruiser for the woman, replete with fixtures of silver and mother of pearl.

"She's a card," Hawk said. "She has money to burn. If she wants a gold commode and can pay for it, I will install it. If she likes your books, you've hit the big time, bud."

Hawk and the agent had developed an unlikely friendship. The agent agreed to read whatever I wrote, based solely on Hawk's recommendation. Things seemed positive and moving upward.

Thus, the days passed for Bailey and me.

Then, on a sunny afternoon, as Ike and Hawk laughed and joked, the office door opened and the shadows at the fringes of my life grew lighter. Ike's scratchy voice found enthusiasm and my life gained new momentum.

"Oh my, it's the pretty lady from Kentucky," Ike said.

"Ike, you know Emma?" Hawk asked, surprised. Turning to me, Hawk asked, "Jack, have you met Emma Cassidy?"

"I have not," I said, smiling at a lovely woman.

With his thumb, he motioned behind his office.

"Emma's in a studio apartment out back. Sadly, her Aunt Amanda died recently. She had your condo."

"Sorry for your loss," I said.

Emma nodded a silent thank you.

"Ike, are you going to answer my question?" Hawk continued. "Or, are you going to sit and grin like a damned dime-store wooden Indian looking at a naked mannequin?"

"It's a small world, Hawk. Emma and I met on the flight from Cincinnati," Ike explained. "Ain't she a dish?" To Emma, he said, "Did you hurt yourself," referring to her slight limp. He lifted the coffee pot and poured her a cup.

"My knee throbs when the weather changes," she stated. "I hurt it skiing about a year ago and recovery has been slow. Storm's coming; it's never wrong about rain."

"Rain, you say?" Ike asked.

"According to my knee," she replied.

We all laughed.

"My friend, Jack Redding," Hawk said, introducing me.

"Nice to meet you, Jack," she said. Her smile seemed only for me and I liked it.

She held out her hand, I shook it, feeling the first stir.

"Any luck on your job search?" Hawk asked Emma.

"Yes, I've accepted a contract assignment, which should last about a year," she replied, running her fingers through her thick hair. "The initial timing is odd, but I took it anyway."

"Odd," said Ike, "How so?"

"I'll work for two weeks. I'll help finish an ongoing assignment. Then, I'll have three weeks off at half-pay, after which a full-year assignment begins. It requires some travel and it seems I'll be busy."

"Explain your schedule again," Hawk said.

"Different contracts with different companies. I'm coming in on the end of the first. The second begins three weeks thereafter. I'll be off with the exception of some marginal training. I said what the hell, and took it."

"So, you're staying in Vegas?" Ike asked.

"It's as good a place as any," she replied.

Ike looked at me. "Emma owned a newspaper in Northern Kentucky, near Cincinnati. She retired from that business and has decided to scale new mountains."

"Retired is not really accurate, Ike. I failed," she clarified.

"*C'est la vie*," Ike whispered, "cycles of learning."

"Are you here because of your aunt?" I asked.

She nodded.

"Yes, I've settled most of her estate. Papers signed, deeds given, as they say. Her life insurance covered her bills and burial. Now, I have to decide what to do with her artwork. Some of the pieces, according to a local appraiser, are worth thousands. She owned hundreds of wonderful pieces. I have the task of understanding and evaluating each. Many are highly valued. Still, I would rather have her with me."

"She could really dance," Ike said. "She won two Tony Awards on Broadway, and many other awards, too."

Emma nodded. “It really stinks. Anyway, the art appraisal is in process. I must decide what to keep and that requires talent. Art is singularly appealing. She was a fascinating woman. I have learned things I never knew.”

“Such as,” said Ike.

“She corresponded with some famous people and she was a pack rat. She never discarded any documents. I'm going through everything.”

“Life is full of its mean little injustices,” Ike noted. “Say, how about joining us for a piece of lemon pie?” He pointed to a pie tin on the table, “I baked it this morning.”

“Sure,” Emma replied.

Ike nodded and gestured to a small table behind me.

“Hand me the plates, would you, blossom?”

Emma walked behind me and paused when she noticed Bailey sleeping beside my feet.

“What's this handsome lug's name?” she asked.

“Bailey,” I replied. “He's my sidekick, goes where I go.”

“He looks like a charmer.”

She leaned to pat Bailey's head, resting her hand on my shoulder. The innocent touch was light, its warmth heavy. It was as if she touched the back of my heart. I studied her face. He smile said she found something, too.

Seconds later, she placed the plates in front of Ike.

“Did you need something, Emma?” Hawk asked, as Ike sliced the pie.

“Yes, a helping hand.”

“Fire away,” Hawk replied.

“It's the artwork. I need help wrapping about twenty pieces, Friday evening. They are big and are too heavy and cumbersome for me to lift and wrap by myself. A local gallery will take whatever I want to sell on consignment and for a commission. Anyway, they are holding space for me and I want to get some artwork to them.”

"By Friday evening," she added, "I should have a few pieces I want to sell selected. I need to wrap them for pick-up on Saturday morning. Can we meet about seven p.m.?"

"Not a problem," Hawk replied.

"Just for an hour or two," Emma clarified.

Hawk nodded, adding, "My guys and I will help."

"Perfect," she said.

"We can do it sooner, if you wish," Hawk offered.

"Complications," Emma replied. "I have responsibilities for the new job. I get back late each day. Friday is best."

"Now," Hawk said, rubbing his hands together. "Let's have that pie."

"I'm with you," said Ike cheerfully, as he dished quarter slices for each of us.

Emma tasted hers and said, "This is wonderful. Only one pleasure is better."

I smiled.

"And what's that, Emma?" I asked.

She looked at me, knowing what I was thinking.

"Why pecan pie, of course," she said, giggling.

"Next time, that's what I'll make," Ike added. "My mama's recipe is from heaven. I know you'll like it."

Emma looked at me and winked.

Hawk noticed me studying Emma's smile.

I felt his stare and glanced over. His expression seemed to say I might want to get to know Emma.

I nodded to tell him he might be right.

Bailey scored the crust.

63

Rosemary Tomasulo glanced out the front window of her Buffalo home, searching for her mail carrier. He was four doors away and coming in her direction. At the same time, two thousand miles away, Jack Redding opened his laptop in Las Vegas for his first attempt to outline a novel.

Rosemary turned to her purse and removed a nearly four-thousand-dollar money order, proceeds from the sale of select pieces of Jack and Jill Redding's furniture.

She opened the desk drawer, found a personalized note card, jotted a few lines telling Jack she had more to sell, sealed, and addressed the envelope. She applied a small strip of scotch tape to secure the flap.

As she looked out the window, her carrier turned into her walkway. Good, she thought and smiled as she opened the front door.

"Hello, George," she said.

"Hi, Rosemary, you look lovely, today." He handed her a few magazines. "That's all I have for you."

She gave him the card and a ten-dollar bill.

"Would you arrange postage and tracking for me, George, and give me the receipt and tracking number tomorrow?"

"Not a problem," he replied, 'two-day delivery?"

She nodded. "Do you think a ten-spot will cover it?"

He checked the address.

"Las Vegas," he said. "It should. If there's a difference either way, we'll settle up tomorrow."

"Make sure you ring the bell. I'll be in the kitchen making cakes. Do you have a favorite flavor, George?"

"A guy can never go wrong with chocolate."

"Chocolate it will be, with vanilla and coconut icing."

"God bless your heart; I'll bring a basket."

"You do that."

64

Emma Cassidy read poetry every night after she prayed. She learned her prayers from her mother who was a decent and loving woman. Her love of poetry came from her father, an intuitive journalist, a marvelous writer.

"Poets respect the language," he would often tell her. He loved the manner in which poets toyed with words, the way they turned a phrase.

"Emma," he would say, "poetry is like a day in Paris. No matter where you turn, you discover beauty and feel a sense of new excitement. Like great painters who create masterpieces from basic colors, poets use simple words to capture a person's heart, to describe the essence of life, to reveal human sorrow and elation."

Emma and her father read poetry together almost every night, a father-and-daughter ritual. Poetry and THE COVINGTON STAR were his two greatest gifts to her. She lost the newspaper but vowed she would never lose her love of poetry. It was one way of honoring her father.

Emma liked all poets, but she was partial to William Butler Yeats, Christopher Marlowe, Lord Byron, T. S. Eliot, William Wordsworth, and Pablo Neruda.

On this rainy night in Las Vegas, after a moderate sprinkle predicted by her throbbing knee, Emma settled on Marlowe. His poem, THE PASSIONATE SHEPPARD TO HIS LOVE, was the selection. Because of her recent meeting, Jack Redding was the motivation.

Emma read the poem twice, closed her book, dimmed the light, and looked out the window, thinking. Moonlight drifted in through scattering clouds, angled across her pillow, and helped frame her thoughts.

She had seen Jack Redding a few times since their introduction but she had not talked to him.

She would have gladly conversed with him, but the chance never arose and that was too bad because she liked him, a lot. How could that happen so quickly?

She did not know, but she knew the attraction was real and exciting.

Jack Redding was handsome, physically attractive, and emanated self-assurance and inner strength. He seemed like a man with a big heart, caring and resourceful.

She could not help but think about him naked beside her, touching her, teasing her, making her soar, gentle yet bold. She wanted to caress him, teach him things, and please him. Could she make that happen? Maybe, she could.

His reaction to her touch supported her yearning.

She glanced at her book of poetry.

"Come with me and be my love and we will all the pleasures prove," she whispered the opening line from THE PASSIONATE SHEPPARD.

Jack's whole manner shifted in her direction from the moment she entered the room. It was as distinct as a cold wind on a warm face.

When she placed her hand on his back, she knew a connection had existed from the first tick of creation.

Why was that?

Had fate joined their souls in another time? Perhaps, it had. Why else would she feel as she did? Why else would she be lying in bed enamored when new romance was the last thing she ever expected?

Jack Redding was not typical of the men who usually entered Emma Cassidy's life. For one thing, he was older and seemed much more grounded. He was introverted and reserved. The past loves of her life had been anything but.

Still, there was that connection, an unexplained river of emotion that poured from his heart into hers. The mystery of it all was exciting and unexpected.

It was a pleasant contradiction and diversion.

Emma gravitated to extroverts—actors, singers, or journalists—men and one woman who craved the spotlight. Now, here she was, filled with moist yearning on a damp night, pining about a man who made her lightheaded.

She pictured herself with him on a beach watching the sun dip behind still waters, with palms swaying and night birds singing pleasant songs. Somewhere in the dark, music played, soft and soulful, and a husky voice sang a love song.

As she stretched, a shooting star burned across the night sky high above the now-intermittent clouds and she whispered another line from the poem, "That hills and valleys, dale and field, and all the craggy mountains yield.

That star demanded a wish and Emma responded in kind, hoping for one intimate embrace. She believed that was all it would take to capture Jack's heart.

She wanted him to make love to her; she wanted her musky scent to mesmerize Jack, her beauty to hold him captive and capture his thoughts.

She visualized the rippling muscles in Jack's forearms as he gestured. She desired his most private touch. She wanted those arms around her body, holding her, never letting her go. Emma liked hugs because they explained people in ways words never could. A hug, she thought, let me have one hug.

Emma smiled. Intuition said the delight she would experience might be more than one person could bear. She was sure Jack Redding would like such happiness.

What did it all mean? Was some cryptic force at play?

Hers was not a rebound effect, because she had not been searching for anything remotely romantic.

Emma was more intent on finding a job and rebuilding the fortune she had squandered on a failed business. In the back of her mind, she knew, if given the chance, she would try to resurrect a new publication to honor her father.

The emotion that swept through her body because of a chance meeting did not align with her goals or expectations. Still, it beckoned her and she felt herself tipping toward it with all the joy one feels when love places a head where heels should be.

In passing, Bill Hawkins mentioned that Jack was single, that he was a retired Army officer, and that he had managed an advertising agency in Buffalo. He was a man hoping to explore a new career as a novelist.

Jack Redding was the complete opposite of Joseph Pidgeon. Pidge was a narcissist; Jack could never be one.

She laughed aloud.

"Blind," she whispered, "I was blind about Pidge and about all the others."

Two months ago, she would have shouted that she was madly in love Pidge but that passion had cooled quickly. From afar, she could not even recall the initial attraction.

With Jack Redding, it surely seemed quite different.

Emma felt it in her *heart's deep core.*

The line, one from Yeats, explained the gravity. The emotion she felt bubbling in her soul when she thought about Jack Redding was different from any wave of any emotion Emma had known, ever!

It dazzled her.

Emma fluffed her pillow, tucking her hands underneath. What to do was the question. Should she play it coy or advance and throw caution to the wind?

What would she do if Jack never acknowledged her or turned her way? Should she take the first step?

She watched trees sway in the night breezes.

A second or two later she dozed and dreamed she and Jack were dancing, that the music was poignant, and that it made her heart ache.

A drum of thunder forced her awake.

After a while, she remembered Walter Raleigh's response to Marlowe in the NYMPH'S REPLY TO THE PASSIONATE SHEPPARD.

"A belt of straw and ivy buds, with coral clasps and amber studs: and if these pleasures may thee move, come live with me, and be my love," she whispered. "But could youth last, and love still breed. Had joys no date, nor age no need, then, these delights my mind might move: to live with thee and be thy love."

Do not reject the feeling, Emma, this overwhelming sensation is real, not an illusion!

You must take a chance, Emma, she thought.

You will never know for sure unless you do.

In this case, the feeling of youth and love *would* breed and it would make all the difference in the world.

She rolled onto her back.

God, she prayed, you know I have had chances, let me have one more. For once, let something good fill my heart and my life. I promise you, I will not give up on this man.

As if given as a response, lightning briefly turned distant clouds orange. Then, quickly, the radiance faded.

Emma nodded a silent thank you.

She wanted her heart to mingle with Jack's heart. She wanted to place her head on his chest to hear his heartbeat. She longed to feel him listening to hers. She wanted to feel him inside of her and whisper warmly against his neck.

She wanted to breathe the same air he breathed as they sweated together in a night of unconstrained passion.

She wanted to hold him as his body quieted and he slept.

Jack Redding and Emma Cassidy, she thought.

It does have a certain appeal.

Soon, she was sleeping.

65

Kyle Shaw and Rosemary Tomasulo would never meet but they would forever be linked because of the money order Rosemary sent to Jack Redding.

A portion of that money used on a simple game of chance would lead to the death of two men, one of whom would be Kyle himself. He would die a horrible death for killing two innocent men: all because of his father's self-righteous indignation and condescendence.

As Rosemary blended eggs into cake batter in Western New York, Kyle sat in the sunroom at his Las Vegas residence, thinking. The sunshine was warm in the glassed-in room and he poured tea into a frosty glass filled with ice, adding a slice of lemon for flavor.

Kyle considered calling his brother but decided against it. He would not include Louis in his escapade. He thought about Honey Pszczoła, too, but knew Honey would blab to the old man because he buttered Honey's bread. Besides, Kyle trusted Honey about as far as he could throw his new Mercedes SUV.

I will do it alone, Kyle concluded. I will get the diamonds, place them in my father's hand, and walk away. For all I care, the son of a bitch can rot in hell. Amanda died because of him and I was too afraid to fight him. It stops now!

If he pulled it off, Kyle would never again associate with Gordon Shaw. Kyle had more than four million dollars in his name, four million that his old man's selfish fingers could never touch. Moreover, he owned his house and two others. Kyle could live a comfortable life. He did not need his father.

He examined the drawings on the table in front of him.

Reconnaissance had given him the company name and model number of the manufacturer of EL CORAZÓN'S prefabricated warehouse, and he might have found a way in.

It was through the roof, via a door behind vent fans, and hidden from the cameras that constantly monitored the front of the building, protecting Bill Hawkins vintage boats.

It was so simple that it seemed too good to be true.

A quick check would give Kyle his answer.

He picked up a disposable cell phone, called the manufacturer in Reno, and waited for an answer.

"Yes," Kyle said, "My name is Major Thomas McSorley; I'm the assistant chief with the Las Vegas Fire Department." The name and title were real; Kyle's use of them was not.

"How can I help you, chief?" a woman replied.

"I am hoping you can, it will save me some time and effort. I am doing annual building inspections and I need some preliminary information. I've noticed that we have a few of your buildings in the area." He checked his notes. "I am looking specifically at your drawings, from your Web site, for Building Model 1850."

"Yes, sir."

"My call regards possible roof access, should we ever have to enter one of those buildings. Your answer will save me a lot of time with site inspections."

"I'll help if I can," the woman replied.

"I see from your Web site you have two drawings for the 1850. The more recent drawing shows the roof trap with the hinges on the inside. The older drawing shows the trap with the hinges on the outside."

"Why is that significant, sir?"

"It's quite simple, actually. In case of a fire, if hinges are on the outside, my men can pop the hinge pins and gain access immediately. They would not have to cut. Hinges on the inside mean we have to burn our way through. Your drawings indicate the trap and ceiling are half-inch steel. That's a problematic burn with a fire raging below."

"I understand. May I have a moment?"

"Sure."

Kyle waited, listened to something from the SOUND OF MUSIC and, then, the woman was back on the line.

"We have fifteen Model 1850s in the Las Vegas area. Six are pre-2010."

"And the significance of that is?" asked Kyle.

"The roof trap design called for internal hinges that year. Owners had the option to re-fit with the new style door."

"According to your records, did you do any installations?"

"Two did, four didn't."

"May I have those four names?"

"Sure, they are ACE INTERIORS, CHARLES DISTRIBUTION, EL CORAZÓN CONDOMINIUMS, and LANGSTON AUTOMOTIVE."

"So, then, it's reasonable to tell my crews they can pull the hinge pins at those four locations?"

"Sure, they'd be able to pop the hinge pins, no problem."

"Wonderful, I'll put that in my report, thank you for your time Miss…"

"Hoffman, Elizabeth Hoffman. Chief, couldn't your men just go in one of the front doors?"

"Yes, they probably would, but it's my job to think about and create contingencies."

"That makes sense. I hope your men never have to go on those roofs. Let me add that we appreciate all that firemen do to keep us safe."

"You have a kind heart, thank you, Ms. Hoffman."

"My pleasure, major," the woman replied, ending the call.

Kyle hung up and slapped his hands together.

"People are so goddamned gullible," he whispered.

Now, more than at any time since Amanda's death, he knew he would finally be able to hand Louise Shaw's teardrop diamonds to his cagy and deceitful father.

He smiled at the thought, anticipating the satisfaction.

66

Out in Flagstaff, Arizona, Madison Adkins tilled the soil in her garden as her husband, Fred, strolled down a stone path. Maddie, as he always called her, could see her husband was perplexed. Something was bothering him.

"What's wrong, honey?" she asked, turning away from the dirt beneath pink knockout roses.

"It's the damnedest thing, Maddie," Fred said.

She smiled.

Being a retired editor, Maddie always told her husband he buried his lead. From years of experience, she knew the precise topic would surface in a few seconds.

"I decided to read my new bass guide and, as I thumbed through it, I found an envelope I hadn't seen before. It was stuck in between the pages of the magazine. I got my license and credit card, apparently from that fellow who phoned from Elk City. He attached two one-hundred dollar bills."

"Really?"

"Yeah, and then this strange receipt was in today's mail."

"A receipt, who is it from?" she asked.

"It's a receipt from a Motel Six in Santa Fe. I have a zero balance; it is from more than a month ago. When was the last time we were in Santa Fe, Maddie?"

"Four or five years ago," she replied.

"I think in was 2009, certainly no later. Why would they send me a receipt from this year?"

He handed it to her.

"It says you don't owe any money; I wouldn't worry about it." She returned to her rose bushes. She looked back at her husband. "Are the hundreds real?"

"As far as I can tell, they are."

"Good, you can take me to dinner tonight. We'll go to that new Italian place up near the university."

67

Madison Adkins continued to prune her rose bushes in Flagstaff as a doctor in Jamestown, New York, rechecked the results from a series of recent tests. A knock on the door interrupted him.

"Your appointment is here, Dr. Tanner."

The doctor rubbed his eyes and shook his head. He hated this part of being a physician.

"Send him in, LuAnn," he advised.

The woman nodded, turned away briefly, and held the door wide open to allow passage of a wheelchair.

Vince Redding, shrunken and grey-faced, rolled in. He seemed to have aged markedly since his last visit. The effects of the kidney failure and leukemia, the doctor noted.

"You asked to see me, doc?" Vince said. "From the look on your face, this isn't going to be a chat about bond rates."

A shake of the doctor's head said Vince was accurate.

"No, there's no easy way to say this. Your tests are bad."

Vince winced and was silent for a few moments.

"How long do I have," he whispered.

"Maybe two months, if you're lucky, but probably sooner," the doctor replied. "I know we thought more. Vince, I..."

Vince held up his hand to interrupt the physician.

"You can't do anything, right?" asked Vince.

"I've had two other doctors review the test results, one in Atlanta and one in Virginia. They agree with me."

Vince nodded.

"Then, I have to move on."

He turned to wheel himself out.

"Don't you want to discuss this?"

"What's to discuss," Vince replied. "I know where I'll die. I assume you will soften the blow with drugs. I have a Navy Seal to visit; he's in bad shape from Afghanistan."

68

The second time I talked to Emma Cassidy she pecked my cheek, which led to a deeper, more passionate kiss. From that moment, the hook we each felt drove deeper into our hopeful hearts.

Thinking back on that moment, I consider it pivotal. It most assuredly was the moment love issued its decree.

Earlier in the evening, after letting Bailey out, I became absorbed in a book by Hampton Sides. Several hours later, when a wall clock chimed and broke my concentration, I realized Bailey was adrift. I glanced at the patio door, thinking he would be there. He was not. He would not be too far away but I knew he was out roaming.

I bookmarked the page, exited through the patio door, and whistled. When Bailey did not come immediately, I knew he had found some bit of tomfoolery.

I began my search in the lingering twilight, comforted by breezes and surprisingly warm air. As I walked along, I was amazed again by the vivid colors of the sunset. I noticed things that would have slipped my view in the past. I could smell the desert and the hint of pine in the air as the wind whistled through nearby trees. Not far away a big old bullfrog bellowed what I hoped was a call to his love. Contrails of jets crisscrossed a high and wide sky. Off to the east, a few stars shown bright and unexpected. They were a sign of hope for dreamers.

Eventually, my walk took me past a hot tub where a woman's voice mentioned my dog's name. I stopped in shadows to watch and listen, feeling the warmth of a westerly wind on my unshaven face.

I split the branches of a willow tree to find Emma Cassidy in a black bathing suit, drinking wine, enjoying the warm water that bubbled around a thin scar on her left knee.

In the half-light, Bailey perched beside her, his head on his forepaws, his nose beside her thigh, listening intently to every word she spoke. His ears were alert, as they had been whenever Jill spoke.

I closed my eyes and listened to the soft lilt of Emma's voice, its timbre remarkably similar to that of Jill's. I remembered Bailey's ears lifting when he first heard Emma speak in Hawk's office. My yellow lab had recognized the similarity immediately; I had missed it.

I re-opened my eyes and studied Emma's pretty face caught in the glow of a spotlight, recessed above the tub. Her skin appeared flawless, the gentle cleavage of her breasts inviting. Interested, I listened to a one-sided conversation:

"I always try my damnedest, Bailey," Emma said, "in everything I do. I have failed so often it gets me down sometimes. My newspaper crumbled and Pidge, a man I believed loved me, told me he was moving on and going to Broadway! Actually, the son of a bitch said, and I quote, 'I'm out of here.' He said it as if I were diseased. Can you believe he would talk like that to a lovely, inviting woman like me?"

Bailey whined at her question and I smiled.

"Then," Emma continued, "He was off to the Big Apple and the role of a lifetime in a new musical. Afterwards, a friend told me he had been unfaithful many times, often with her. Bailey, that woman is no longer my friend."

The wind shifted and a slight breeze rippled across my back. A second or two later, Bailey smelled my scent. He sat upright and barked.

"Here you are," I said, stepping out from the shadows of the willow tree, as if I were strolling along and just happened upon them. I hoped Emma would not think I had been spying.

She stood up immediately, dried her attractive legs with a towel, and wrapped herself in a white robe.

She had an attractive figure, much better than I had considered. I was interested and, considering how I felt over the past year, I realized that was a good sign.

"Hi, Jack. Want a glass of moscato?"

"Half a glass," I replied. "I'm not much of drinker. I removed my glasses and rubbed my tired eyes.

"Working?" she inquired.

"No," I replied, "I was reading. I lost track of time and this big rascal," I patted Bailey's head, "did not come home."

She handed me a wine glass and, either by accident or design, her fingers brushed against mine. Again, unnerving warmth entered my body where our skin touched. She smiled sweetly; she must have felt the sensation, too.

"About his not going home, that's my fault. Bailey is a good listener."

I nodded and said, "He's the best listener when it comes to secrets. I saw you flexing your knee in the warm water, is it bothering you?"

She shrugged.

"The water feels good, therapeutic."

"Have you wrapped your art?"

"That sounds rather personal," she joked, then nodded.

Changing the subject, she said, "Bill Hawkins told me you're originally from Western New York; that you and he served together in the U.S. Army."

"The Buffalo-area, Lackawanna, actually," I replied, adding, "And, yes, we served together in the Army Rangers."

"Why did you come to Las Vegas?" she asked.

"A change of venue," I said, seeing Cooper's sweaty body shaking in the light of a lantern, sensing the cold emanating from Jill's corpse on a gurney in a morgue.

Knowing Hawk as I did, I knew he would have kept Jill's death confidential.

I changed the subject. "How's the training?"

"It's interesting. Twelve months of pay will help, as will the health benefits."

"Good." I smiled, recalling Rosemary Tomasulo's words and her admonition.

"Here's to warm days," she said, offering a toast.

"Warm days," I repeated. Unpredictably, I asked, "Who is this fellow, Pidge?"

Embarrassed, she ran her fingers through her hair.

"I guess you heard my one-sided conversation."

"Parts of it, I'm sorry."

"It's no big deal. Pidge, his real name is Joseph Pidgeon. He claims to be a distant relative of the late actor Walter Pidgeon. That might be bullshit. Anyway, I thought he was *the* love of my life. Turns out, he was not. He is starring on Broadway and I am learning process graphics, doing contract work in Vegas, trying to sell my aunt's artwork. We split up weeks ago, the day before my business closed." She sipped her wine. "Such is life," she continued. "It really doesn't bother me that we broke up, what bothers me is my naïveté. What you heard me tell Bailey was merely venting."

"I understand. Emma, I know from experience that things do improve."

"I'm not dejected. It was more like needing somebody to listen and Bailey filled the bill."

I finished my wine and set the glass on a nearby table.

"He's a good listener." I turned to Bailey, "Let's go, bud." To Emma, I added, "Maybe we can have lunch sometime or, at least, tea. Hawk said you drink lots of tea."

Her face brightened. "I *do* like tea. Lunch would be good."

As Bailey and I turned to leave, something sparkled in the scant light. I bent and retrieved a delicate gold necklace. I handed it to her, saying, "I doubt you'd want to leave this behind. Some scoundrel might keep it."

"Thanks, it was my mom's."

Emma slipped it around her neck, fastened it, and, then, kissed my cheek.

"What was that for?"

"For seeing my necklace, besides it felt right," she replied.

She started to walk away. I touched her shoulder, turned her around, and kissed her. She kissed me back.

Holding her in my arms, feeling her warm body pressed against mine, was more than thrilling, it was sublime. I knew immediately that I wanted more, that I wanted her.

She pulled away, looked into my eyes, and kissed me again. Her eyes opened a pathway to her heart, which gave me a floating sensation.

"That was lovely," she whispered, squeezing my hand. "I have to go, next time you should tag along with Bailey."

Next time, I thought. I liked that.

Before I could respond, she turned and walked away leaving me standing alone in the dark with my dog.

I watched her until she disappeared behind a fence and then I turned and walked away in the darkness, filled with a sense of promise I had not known in many months.

I thought about Jill as I walked home. She had been gone a long time and the only woman I had touched was Theo Jefferson. Those were intense moments. Theo needed them as much as I did but it was not love.

Emma was different! The air sweetened when I looked at her, when I heard her voice. I thought of sunshine, candles, long walks, and whispers. Vince's words echoed: *After what happened to Jill, you deserve someone who will love you and comfort you as easily as waves lap against a shoreline.*

Emma came into my life easily and I liked that. I found myself wanting her. I wanted to explore her body and her mind as I would explore a treasure chest. I had to let Jill go. That, I realized, was a good thing, and maybe a miraculous sign that God's mercy truly did exist.

69

Sister Margaret Bosko, from St. Therese of the Mountains Orphanage, waited in the anteroom of the Los Alamos office of the chief of police.

She stood at a window looking out at the Bradbury Science Museum, which housed Manhattan Project exhibits. As a door opened, she turned and smiled.

Monsignor Liam Feherty, with white hair and a perennially sad smile, entered the room. The monsignor, a retired priest, was the orphanage's chaplain.

"Sorry I'm late, sister," he said.

"Not to worry, monsignor," she responded. "The chief has not finished his meeting, besides we are..."

The office door opened, interrupting. Chief Miller smiled and invited the nun and the cleric into his office.

"I'll get right to the point," he said as they all sat. "No one in the state has reported a theft of eight hundred thousand dollars and there are no reports of large amounts of missing money. I called the FBI. Several agents examined the currency. It is negative from their perspective."

"Negative," the nun repeated. "Is that bad news?"

"Quite the contrary, I should think," the priest interjected.

"The monsignor is correct. Two weeks from today, the money belongs to the orphanage."

"We've been given a miracle," the nun whispered. "I thought all the Good Samaritans were gone."

"Clearly, not," Chief Miller said. "What will you do?"

"We will fulfill the mortgage and make much-needed repairs. The remainder goes into our general fund. Today and for the next two weeks we will say special novenas for the benefactor who manifested this generosity."

"I imagine a very special person," he said.

"An angel," Sister Margaret said. "It has to be an angel."

70

As a nun and a priest discussed a change of fortune with a police chief, Gordon Shaw and Honey Pszczoła sat down for another private meeting in an out-of-the-way restaurant, far to the east of Las Vegas.

Shaw was clearly irritated.

"It's been nearly a month, Honey. Where are my mother's jewels? I pay you well; am I wasting my money?"

Pszczoła was quiet, contemplative. No one had discovered the diamonds and he believed they were with Amanda Cassidy's personal items in the warehouse at EL CORAZÓN.

"I've been past the warehouse several times. I have yet to figure an easy way around the cameras."

Shaw was not happy.

"Cut the camera feed and force the door open."

"That's one way but not a good one, and it's risky. Do you want your name dragged into the middle of this? I'll do it that way, if you wish but it won't work."

Shaw faltered. "What about Amanda's niece?"

"It's a possibility but I doubt it. I think the diamonds are exactly where Amanda hid them the night she died."

"Have you talked to Kyle? He's been very silent. I imagine he hates me because of what I said about his dear Amanda."

Honey nodded. Frankly, he sided with Kyle.

"We've not talked." Honey noted.

"Maybe you should visit him. The longer we wait, the harder it will be to find my mother's diamonds. Louis tells me his older brother has studied that warehouse. He thinks Kyle is about to do something. Don't let him sully my family, Honey. Go and talk to Kyle and see what he's doing."

Honey nodded.

"I'll stop for a chat."

"Do more than talk; find out what he's planning."

71

Many men suffer physical pain when they die. Ted Jefferson also endured mental anguish, which made him desire and pray for a quick death.

He never had reconciled his actions in battle and it haunted him. Gordon Shaw or Honey Pszczoła would never know about Jefferson's agony at that precise moment in Tulsa, Oklahoma, yet it was as real as their desire to find Louise Shaw's teardrop diamonds.

Physically, Ted was in his hospital room. Mentally, he was in Panama, on a hilltop…

…Despite the beating, Jack Redding would not tell his attackers the location of his men, which is what they really wanted. The head of the Chico Cartel did not want one U.S. Ranger. He wanted them all. He wanted to tell the world that America could never win.

"Have you got him," Hawk said over the radio.

"Roger that," Jefferson replied. "They are beating the living shit out of him, Sarge."

"A shot," Hawk replied. "Do you have a shot?"

"I don't have my rifle; I lost it when I jumped a waterfall."

"Where the hell are you?"

"I don't know, downstream from the falls…oh, God."

"What."

"Jack's been shot…they shot him in the leg."

"Is he alive?"

Jefferson was angry. "Yes, I think so," he said.

"I didn't hear a shot," Hawk stated.

"The bastard used a silencer," Jefferson replied, scanning the horizon through his binoculars looking for something, anything Hawk could use for a fix. In the distance, an airplane came directly at him.

"Hawk, can you see that aircraft."

"Let me get up high," Hawk replied. Seconds later, he said, "I got it."

"I'm at its twelve o'clock," he said, "about two miles out."

"Don't move! We're on our way, a half-mile on your six. We'll arrive ASAP."

Jefferson watched one of the men urinate on Jack's wound. Then, he punched Jack several more times. Jack toppled over, nearly unconscious.

Jefferson climbed a tree and looked to his six o'clock. He scanned the foliage and soon he had Hawk and three others.

"I got you," he radioed. "I'm dead ahead, three hundred-fifty yards."

~

Hawk had one of the Chicos in his scope, Willis the other.

"Jefferson, you make sure no one comes out of the bushes, if they do, light 'em up. Willis, aim for the chest, we want to kill these hombres," Hawk said. "Take a deep breath, count three, and fire."

Jefferson watched the execution through the scope of a sniper's rifle Hawk had handed to him. He heard two shots, almost simultaneously. Beneath him, a hundred yards away, the two Chicos fell. He scanned left, then right. Something caught his attention back on his left. He saw arms and legs and fired. A young girl of maybe twelve or thirteen years of age had just lost one-half of her face.

Moments later, he and the others were down the hill and dressing Jack's wounds. Willis was on the horn calling for evacuation. Jefferson walked over and, using the tip of his boot, turned the girl over. She had two weapons in her belt.

~

As the chopper took them out, Jack looked at all three men and nodded.

"Jefferson saved your ass," Hawk shouted.

Jack gave him a thumbs-up and passed out...

...Jefferson opened his eyes and he was back in his room at the hospice, alone and cold. Despite the room's uncommon warmth, he shivered.

"Take me now, Lord," he prayed, "I beg you."

He felt dizzy and in the next instant specs of white light sifted through his field of vision. Breathing became extremely difficult.

"Oh, Theo," he whispered, "I wanted you here with me."

He closed his eyes briefly and actually felt his heart stop beating. In the instant before his brain died, Jefferson saw Jack Redding's face from that day in a Panamanian jungle. Humility and appreciation filled Jack's eyes.

"Never give up, Ted," Jack whispered. "Especially not now, you are close to seeing God."

"I understand, Midnight," Jefferson thought, "God forgive me, I am..."

He never finished his thought.

In the next second, his brain stopped functioning.

He was gone and became a part of the eternal tapestry.

72

When Bill Hawkins entered IKE'S VEGAS CAFÉ, I knew he bore bad news. When you know a man as well as I knew Hawk, it was not hard to detect his moods. His disposition that day was gloomy.

I was at the counter drinking coffee and he plopped on the stool beside me.

Ike filled Hawk's coffee cup immediately.

"Something's bothering you," I said.

"Ted died," he replied. "I just got an email from his niece; she wanted us to know. He'll be cremated."

"No service?" I asked.

"She said it's his wish, going out like he came in, alone."

Ike had been listening, pulled out three shot glasses and filled each with JIM BEAM.

"To your friend," he said.

We each drank, in silence, to Ted Jefferson's memory.

Hawk looked at Ike and said, "Give us a minute, Isaac."

Ike nodded and walked away.

"Theo said her uncle has been mumbling about killing a young girl in Panama. Do you remember that?"

I rubbed my leg where the Chico had shot me. "How could I forget? I wouldn't be alive if not for Ted."

"Ted was always troubled by what he did in Central and South America, still he kept doing it. Why do you think he did that, Jack? I mean, he could have got out, several times."

"It was because of us," I replied.

"Us?" asked Hawk.

"He loved us like brothers." I motioned for another round.

After Ike poured, I said, "We cared for each other deeply."

"Still do. I killed to save you; I'd have died for you."

"Back at you," I replied.

We drank. Ike poured again, which seemed appropriate.

73

The third time I saw Emma Cassidy, we made love. Our union was like an unexpected gift from that place in the universe where God and pure ecstasy reside.

On a sunny, windblown Saturday afternoon, exactly four days after we first met, I looked up from the book I was reading and she was standing at the patio door. She waved awkwardly and entered, holding a bottle of wine.

"What's the occasion?" I asked, standing.

"A celebration," she said. "This is the day, the first time we make love."

She set the bottle on the table, closed the door, locked it, and drew the shades. Then, she took my right hand in her left and kissed me.

"Come with me and be my love," she said, heading to the bedroom. Her eyes glowed.

"What if I don't want to?"

"You will," she said and, as she walked along, she discarded her clothing. When I entered the room, she was on my bed wearing only lacey red panties.

"I want to watch you undress," she said, tugging at my belt. Her eyes never strayed from my body. After I was naked, she examined me from head to toe.

"Turn around" she whispered. As I did, she said, "I can live with the scars; you have a nice ass. I like the tattoo."

I turned and joined her on the bed and watched her remove her underwear. She was tapered, trim, and inviting.

"I need you," she said. "I can't stop thinking about your kiss. I loved it and I want more."

I kissed her and explored her body. I never thought about my past, about my lost love. This was a new chapter. I looked at Emma's pretty face, nudging her remarkable chin with my knuckle. She smiled, saying, "We're good to go."

"How long have you been planning this?" I asked.

"Since about a second after you kissed me," she replied.

"What has brought us together?"

"A force bigger than I can explain," she replied.

"I'm at least fifteen years older than you are, Emma."

"My youth or inexperience won't hinder you, in any way," she whispered. She held me in her hand to guide me.

I felt the world start to tip slightly and I wondered if, because of Emma's power, trees swayed in warm breezes, ships rose on splendid waves, and old women awoke from slumber to remember the smiles of lost lovers.

The sphere spun on an axis that bore through the center of Emma's heart and mine. As we locked in an embrace designed by heaven itself, the world as I knew it faded. That which resurfaced was one of newfound delight, ablaze with the colors commonly favored by Monet.

Emma's body shuttered when she climaxed and salty tears ran down her cheeks. I kissed them away and she held me until my body stilled, until my heartbeat normalized.

She put her warm lips against my ear and whispered, "I've come to understand, something T. S. Eliot once wrote."

"Tell me."

"You are the music while the music lasts," she whispered.

"Then, it will last forever," I replied.

"And one day longer," she added.

I placed my head on her warm breasts and listened to her gently beating heart.

The drum beat of a new life, the rhythm of heaven's everlasting kindness.

"What's next?" I asked.

"We should find out, we should get to know each other in the sunlight of coming days that we alone own."

"And, in the comfort of warm nights, too," I added.

She giggled and kissed me.

74

Two lovers, spent from an afternoon and night of discovery, were lulling in each other arms when Honey Pszczoła stopped to visit Kyle Shaw in North Vegas. Suspicion surfaced immediately in Kyle's eyes.

"Your old man asked me to look in on you," Honey noted.

"I guess he lacks the courage to do that himself."

"Goddamn it, Kyle, he feels bad. He doesn't know what to do. He's upset about the diamonds, with you, and with his actions. He feels inordinate guilt about Amanda's death."

"Ya think? Honey, it will be a frigid day in Satan's domain when he and I talk."

"Is it really that bad?"

"After he has his precious diamonds, I'll never see him."

"What's your guess?" Honey asked.

"About the diamonds…they are with Amanda's things."

"That's my guess, too."

"Have you figured a way into that building?" Kyle asked.

"Not yet."

"I was about to fix a drink." Kyle stood. "You want one?"

Honey nodded. "Sure, whatever you're having."

As Kyle departed, Honey whispered, "He's hiding something." He went to Kyle's desk and found the folder Kyle had placed in a drawer when Honey knocked. Seconds later, when Honey found the drawings, he realized Kyle had discovered a way into EL CORAZÓN'S warehouse.

He decided to watch Kyle daily, but from a distance. If Kyle took a risk, Honey would be there to ward off the consequences. After all, Gordon Shaw expected it.

A moment later, Kyle handed Honey a glass of ginned lemonade.

"Will you find the diamonds?" Honey asked.

"Yes," Kyle replied. "I'm sure of it."

75

Louis Shaw, Kyle's younger brother, was about to cast off when Honey Pszczoła stepped onto his boat at a Lake Meade dock.

It was indeed a rare visit. Honey and Louis only talked when Gordon Shaw needed a go-between, and usually in the dark of night. Louis suspected Honey was prying.

One, Honey hated the water.

Two, he never came directly to Louis for anything.

Three, the old man paid him to be a sneak.

"Have you talked to Kyle lately?" Honey asked.

"We talk daily, why?"

"How does he seem to you?

"Subdued, his break with my father is real."

"Do you think it will last?"

"This time it might. He's not as big a pussy as the old man thinks he is. Kyle's in tremendous shape, he rock climbs, he's strong, and he has made a great deal of money on his own. He doesn't need my old man. He doesn't want anyone. He can survive quite well."

"Tell me again, what was his major in college?"

"Kyle has a degree in mechanical engineering with a master's in business, why do you ask?"

"He knows how to read plan drawings and blueprints?"

"Are you shitting me? He loves using his mind and hands. Since childhood, he's been into anything mechanical." Louis studied Honey's face. "Why are you asking these dopey questions? Why are you here, sniffing around?"

"Watching out for him and helping your old man."

"Bullshit, I don't believe that for a minute."

Honey smiled. "Will he take matters into his own hands?"

"If Kyle is pissed, Honey, get out of his way."

"Then, I'll keep watching him, in case he needs my help."

76

The weekend had stretched into Tuesday and Emma Cassidy leaned over and kissed my cheek. I opened one eye and looked at her in the morning light. She handed me a mug of coffee and I sat up.

"What time is it?"

"A few minutes past seven, why?"

"You're up early and dressed already?" I said.

She nodded and smiled. If we were not already in love, it was only a matter of time. I liked every quality: her mind her smile, her voice, her scent, her jokes, her laughter, her lovemaking, the way she held me, and our conversations. For a year, I had been languishing but not any longer.

"I got a text," she said. "I have to go to Boulder City to work. They need me for a few days. By the way, because you gave me a key, I put some of my clothes in your closet."

I nodded, leaning against the headboard with the coffee.

"I'll be back Friday evening, about six," she added.

"We'll have a late dinner, maybe seafood."

"I'll come right here and shower," she said, checking her watch. "I have to go. I wanted to wake you and tell you that these last few days have been..."

"Wonderful," I said, finishing her statement.

"Yeah, we're doing something right. I want more."

"That is a deal."

She kissed me, "Will you miss me?"

"Absolutely," I replied.

She nodded, "I'm off to do some process mapping."

"And the reason for that is?" I asked.

"To eliminate waste because in any business time is money. If a company can eliminate wasted time and resources, it saves capital, which can be applied elsewhere."

"It's like editing a bad sentence for better meaning."

"Yeah, like that."

"I'll see you Friday night...dinner and a movie?"

"Sounds like fun," she replied, "One final kiss." Afterward she said, "You taste like coffee." She caressed my cheek. "Do you think you'll shave by Friday?"

"You want me clean shaven, too?"

"Why not, live a little." She put a note on the nightstand. "They booked a room for me at a Boulder City motel. Fourteen hour days but you can always text me."

"Is the pay good?"

"Nearly two grand a week," she replied.

"Have they paid you yet?"

"Thursday, I get my first check."

"Good, then you can buy dinner."

She smiled.

"Hey, why not save a buck if I can. I'll be here waiting. By the way, you make a good cup of Joe."

"That, among other things," she said

Emma blew a kiss, waved, and was out the door.

~

I placed the cup on the nightstand and rested my head on the pillow. I remember fading off to the lingering scent of Emma's perfume. I fell into a rare sleep that numbs reality, where every cell in the human body falls luxuriously into the depths of pure relaxation...

...Jill turned toward Jack in hushed light. She seemed like an angel. Yellow neon seeping through a crack in a curtain turned her skin to gold as it slanted crossed her naked body.

"Sometimes, you seem hesitant," she said. "That's not the Jack I know and love."

Jack rolled over and studied her eyes.

His fingers danced on her skin.

"It's hard to let you go, Jill. You owned my heart."

"I lived there and I understand but you have a profound capacity to love, Jack. You loved that woman by the sea before me. There is room for yet another. Let her in."

He kissed Jill as he always did, slow and soft at first, then with intensity and passion. She moved beneath him.

"One more for the good times," she whispered, guiding him, taking him fully. She shivered with pleasure.

"You were the only man I ever loved, Jack," she said as a rising passion arched her back. "Make me soar once again. Warm my cooling heart; we'll each feel better."

"And what happens afterward?" Jack asked.

"I return to the light and you live again to follow your dreams and your heart. Humans live by heart, Jack."

"The light, is that where you live now, Jill?"

"We all will. I like it. When I'm there, I find it very warm. I feel alive. The light showed me how badly I treated you and how weak I let myself become."

"I never stopped loving you."

"I know. Now hush, enjoy the moment. I am yours alone."

They were in a place where nothing else mattered. Jill shuttered and Jack trembled. The waves of pleasure seemed endless; they drifted high above the earth. Sadly, without warning, Jill disappeared and the neon coming through the curtain was yellow on the pillow…

…I opened my eyes. Now, what seem like Jill's favorite perfume lingered in the air. I rolled over and hugged the pillow. Was it really Jill or merely a dream?

I looked out the window. A golden canary perched on a branch, watching me. A ray of sunlight broke through the clouds and the bird flittered upward into it, disappearing.

"I loved you beyond all comprehension, Jill. You are correct. I must move on. Be well and be warm."

77

Kyle Shaw studied EL CORAZÓN for nearly a week. He had parked on several streets in different cars where, from behind tinted windows, he observed patterns at Bill Hawkins' complex.

On this particular morning, he observed Emma Cassidy, dressed for business. She walked to her car with a briefcase and a laptop, pulling a suitcase. Obviously, she was going out of town.

He nodded, thinking now or never. If he could get inside the warehouse, he could find the diamonds. He would be free from the mess his father created.

He watched Emma Cassidy drive away and thought about next steps. Several times in past days, from nearby residential streets, he watched vans from a local art gallery drive away carrying framed posters and paintings.

He even went to the art gallery and inspected all the artwork from what they were calling THE CASSIDY COLLECTION. He did not find the diamonds.

On this day, after Emma departed, Kyle started his car and drove away. A few minutes later, he parked at a casino and went inside to find a pay phone.

"JANUS GALLERY, how may I help you?" a voice said.

"Hi, my name is McSorley. I need a favor," Kyle stated.

"If I can, Mr. McSorley," the agent replied.

"I really like THE CASSIDY COLLECTION, do you have more? Perhaps I could arrange a private viewing. I would happily pay you a commission for the privilege."

"Let me call the owner. Would you hold?"

He was immediately on hold. The agent must be dialing Emma Cassidy's cell phone. Minutes later, he was back on the line.

"The owner can see you on Saturday about 9.30 a.m."

"Not until Saturday," Kyle said, his voice filled with faux disappointment. "I don't think that works."

"She'll be out of town and will not return until late Friday evening," the agent clarified.

Bingo!

"It cannot be sooner?" Kyle asked, continuing the ruse, even though he had the answer he needed.

"She said Saturday morning."

"Damn, I have a conflict. I'm out of town this weekend," he lied. "Are you sure she can't do it sooner?"

"No, I'm sorry, Mr. McSorley. Am I correct, you do not want me to make the appointment for Saturday?"

"I cannot do it. I will call next week and try to set something up for a better time. Thank you."

"Good day, sir."

Kyle Shaw hung up; the time had come.

Emma Cassidy would be out of town. She would not be in the warehouse in the evening. Typically, no one was. Bill Hawkins was always out by five p.m. Kyle had actually charted patterns.

This being Tuesday, he would double check all his plans and go for the diamonds on Thursday night. He would stay until he found them, and he was hopeful he would.

Back in his car, he spent a few moments looking at a series of photographs and he made a list of the things he needed to do. He, then, drove back to EL CORAZÓN.

The rear of the warehouse abutted landscaped mounds, about ten feet from the roof. A grappling hook, a rope, a quick climb, and he would be on top in seconds.

"Pop the hinge pins and I'm in," he whispered.

He turned up the air-conditioning in his nondescript rental, sipped water, and departed.

He did not see Honey Pszczoła watching hidden from view, not too far away, behind thick foliage.

78

Weary faces stared back at Jeff LaMont from MAGNA PROCESS SYSTEMS. The group had been mapping best practices in Boulder City, Nevada, for two days straight. The employees of SYMMS ENERGY, a growing solar company, needed a break. They were near the end of an intense six months of cultural change and LaMont had pushed them hard. Each employee did his or her regular job during the day. Each spent evenings mapping and analyzing processes, finding ways to eliminate corporate waste.

Less waste had two benefits. It freed up resources, both human and capital, for application elsewhere in a business. It made the company's "to-market" time faster, tighter, and more efficient, which meant they would likely clobber the competition. A term the government did not like.

"I think we'll modify Friday's session and get all out by Noon," LaMont said. "We've been going hard and strong. We'll use tomorrow morning to analyze our progress."

"You want a long weekend at home in Sacramento, Jeff?" a SYMMS manager asked.

LaMont smiled. "It can't hurt us to be with our families." He turned to Emma Cassidy. "Are we good?"

She hit a few buttons. "Saved and copied, and sent to all appropriate emails."

"Emma, I'd like the process animation software. Tomorrow morning, before SYMMS associates leave, I want to focus on this week's mapping. The MAGNA team will work until early afternoon getting ready for next week's wrap up. I want MAGNA out of here by three on Friday. We should have plenty of time to do the animations."

"Sure," Emma said but, searching, could not find discs. Then, she realized the reason. She had removed the discs a few nights ago as she was searching for her calculator.

The software discs were in EL CORAZÓN'S warehouse, near the artwork she had been assessing.

"Damn it," she said, a bit too loudly.

"Is something wrong?" LaMont asked.

"I mistakenly left them at home. I forgot to put the discs back into my briefcase."

"Can we get them by morning?"

"Sure, I know exactly where they are. I removed them Monday night, got involved in something else, and forgot about them. I'll drive back and pick them up."

LaMont checked the time.

"Let's have the discs delivered in the morning. We won't need them until about nine-thirty. It's late. Let's have a bite to eat and get a good night's sleep. We'll come back fresh and at full force in the morning."

"It will only take two hours."

"Don't waste time driving, Emma. You need to relax. It's not a big deal. Rest and recharge your batteries. I want you primed for the summary session. Tomorrow will be very busy for all of us. If someone can access them, use delivery."

"I will," Emma said, "Which courier service? I'll make the call right now."

"We have an account at GREEN LIGHT DELIVERY and they deliver 24/7. Our account number is MPS77759. Request a delivery by nine o'clock."

Emma nodded.

LaMont noticed that Emma still seemed upset.

"Really, Emma," he said, "it's nothing."

Emma nodded, smiling.

"I'm cool with it."

Unfortunately, for every action a reaction occurs and what was about to happen would change lives forever.

79

Hawk and Ike were playing checkers and sipping whiskey when the telephone rang in Bill Hawkins' private office. Ike reached over and answered.

"EL CORAZÓN, Ike speaking."

"Ike, this is Emma. Is Bill nearby?"

"His smug and homely face is staring at me right now, sweetheart."

Ike gave the phone to Hawk, saying, "Emma Cassidy."

"Hello, Emma," Hawk said. "What's up?"

"Bill, I need a favor. I left a folder with two discs in the warehouse near the spot where we wrapped my aunt's artwork. A driver from GREEN LITE DELIVERY will arrive in the morning to courier those discs to me."

"I can get them and drive them to you," Hawk said.

"No, that won't be necessary. The courier is all set; cancelling would just add more confusion. GREEN LITE will be at your office at seven tomorrow morning. Just put the folder with the discs in the box he hands you and seal it. He'll do the rest."

"Consider it done," Hawk said, "Ike, Jack, and I are off early for a bit of morning fishing. We'll be up early enough."

"Good.

"Tulio is here at the crack of dawn, too. He or I will take care of it. Do you want me to call to confirm that the package is on its way?"

"No, the courier will contact me, but thank you."

"As you wish," he replied.

"Fishing tomorrow, huh?" she said.

"Yeah, it's a bit overdue."

"Be careful."

"You should tell that to the fish," Hawk said, chuckling.

"I'll see you soon, thanks," she replied and hung up.

80

At precisely 10:12 p.m. Thursday evening, as Emma was reading T.S. Eliot in Boulder City, Kyle Shaw used a grappling hook and climber's rope to scale the rear wall of EL CORAZÓN'S warehouse. Heavy clouds made the night sky pitch black—no stars, no moon.

He pulled himself silently onto the roof, soaked the hinge pins with penetrating oil, and quickly popped them with a punch and rubber hammer.

He pried the trap open with a crowbar and was inside and down the building's built-in steel ladder in less than thirty seconds. All told, from the time he entered the property through the woods to the moment he placed his feet on the warehouse floor, maybe four minutes had passed.

Nobody knew he was inside or so he thought.

He removed a flashlight, studied Amanda's belongings, and began an orderly search: boxes, drawers, furniture, garments, pillows, artwork, and more. He examined everything twice, leaving every item as he found it.

He was surprised when he checked his watch and noted the time: 3:22 a.m. He had been at it for nearly five hours.

"Damn it, where are they?" Kyle was angry, sweating, and frustrated. He hoped to be home in bed by this time. Yet, here he was still searching, with not much time remaining until sunrise. "The diamonds must be here," he said to himself, irritation evident in his voice.

He decided to give it two more hours. Then, he would get out and try again, another time.

Stay positive, he thought, and stay focused.

~

Two hours later, Tulio Garcia pulled into his slot at EL CORAZÓN. Tulio, usually the only early bird, was surprised to see Bill Hawkins talking to Jack Redding, who walked away.

"Hello, boss; why are you and Mr. Redding up this early?"

"Jack was out running. He went off to shower. He, Ike, and I are going fishing up in the rolling hills."

Garcia eyed Hawkins sidearm

"I get it, now," Tulio said. "Snakes, right?"

"I hate those slimy little shits," Hawk replied, giving a mock shiver. He patted his firearm. "I'll be ready. Listen, I got a call from Emma Cassidy last night and she left an item in the warehouse. I need to get it.

"She is sending a courier who will be here at seven to deliver it to her. Take a walk with me. I want to get what Emma needs and get a tackle box and a pole for Jack. I'll leave it up to you to make sure the courier gets what he needs for Ms. Cassidy."

"I can get one of the golf carts."

"No," Hawk said, "I want the exercise."

"I'm with you. Where are you going to fish?"

"Geneva Springs, I hear they're biting."

"Boss, I love that place. My wife and I fish it a lot. Be careful," Tulio teased. "There are many snakes this year."

"Are you busting my balls, Tulio?" Hawk asked.

"Of course," Tulio said, his eyes sparkling, in the pre-dawn light. "That's what makes it fun."

~

Honey Pszczoła was watching from the warehouse roof, hidden behind air conditioning ductwork.

Using Kyle's rope, Honey had been in position five minutes after Kyle disappeared inside the building on his quest for the diamonds. Honey was standing guard.

Honey saw two men approaching from about four-hundred yards away. "They are coming in this direction," he said. "Why can't this be easier?"

He knew he had to get Kyle out, and fast.

He might have enough time because they were walking.

Had they been driving he would not have enough time to warn Kyle. Damn it, he thought, they still might find us.

Honey quietly descended the ladder. Twenty feet below, he could see Kyle, removing a box lid.

"Come on, Amanda, show me a goddamned sign," Kyle said. "I need those diamonds, babe. People cannot know."

Kyle had just removed a tap shoe when Honey whistled.

Kyle jumped and dropped the shoe. He turned abruptly, pulled his firearm, and leveled it at Pszczoła.

"Kyle, don't. Jesus, boy, it's me, Honey."

"Honey! You scared the hell out of me. I could have shot you." Kyle's expression showed confusion. "What are you doing here? Did the old man send you?"

"I've been tailing you, covering your butt. Hawkins and another man are heading this way. I need to get you out now. You cannot be in here. Breaking and entering is a serious offense. It will ruin your life. If they discover me with you, it will add layers of complexity that you, your old man, or I do not want. Let's hustle, now."

Kyle glanced down, not really listening.

"I'll be damned," he said. "It has to be."

"What?" Honey asked.

Kyle set his weapon on a nearby box, ripped the insole from the dance shoe's mate, and let the diamonds tumble into the palm of his hand.

"Ingenious, Amanda," he said. "Jesus, you had the smarts to do this while you were having a stroke. You had it together, kid."

He turned to Honey Pszczoła.

"She hid the diamonds in a tap shoe."

They heard keys at the front door.

"Let's get the hell out, now," Honey said.

It was too late!

The door swung open.

Seconds later, Tulio entered, followed by Hawkins, who turned on the lights. Honey knew Tulio recognized him immediately.

"You," Tulio said, surprised.

"Oh, God," Honey said. "Hawkins let me explain."

"You better explain." Hawk said. "What the hell is going on? Why are *you* here?"

Instinctively, Hawk pulled his weapon.

"No, don't," Honey shouted.

Kyle, seeing Hawkins pull his weapon and believing he was about to be shot, lifted the glock and fired. Honey's shout of *no, don't* was wasted effort.

Kyle shot Hawk first, through the neck, severing his spinal cord. Hawk dropped dead immediately.

Tulio lunged for Hawk's weapon as Kyle's second shot stuck him in the abdomen. Tulio managed to discharge Hawk's gun into the concrete floor. The ricochet missed Kyle's head by a fraction, hitting a distant wall.

"Jesus Christ, Kyle," Honey said. He took the gun away from the younger man and checked Hawk. He felt Tulio's pulse and put a second shot into Garcia's chest.

"Get out of here, now," Honey demanded. "Go!"

Kyle scurried up the ladder. Honey ran to the door and locked it. On the way back, he picked up the tap shoes, reapplied the insoles, packed them in their box, and replaced the lid.

He rifled a few drawers near the cabin cruisers, and was up the ladder after Kyle. They were both out of the warehouse in less than sixty seconds.

"What do we do with the bodies?" asked Kyle, as Honey crawled onto the roof.

"Not a thing. You keep your mouth shut and we will get through this. We both were wearing gloves. There are no prints. Here, help me."

Together they reinserted the hinge pins, closed the trap door, gathered up tools, and exited the rooftop.

"My guess, they'll think it was a robbery gone sour. You have the diamonds. Anything else besides the flashlight and the tools you used?"

"Nothing," Kyle replied

"Then, we're out of here."

"Why'd you re-box the shoes?"

"Less for investigators to consider; now, we haul ass."

Kyle nodded, flicked the rope and the grappling hook fell to the ground. They gathered it in and were gone, running silently through a sparse patch of woods to a seldom-used road, an eighth-of-a-mile away.

"Do not drive fast, observe all road signs. Lights go on only when you hit the main road. You don't want a cop to stop you for doing something stupid. Get rid of the clothes, the tools, the rope, and the hook, and I mean get rid of everything. Do not tell a soul. I don't want to know. No traces, do you understand?"

Kyle nodded. "What are you going to do?"

"Clean up your mess. Listen, if it bothers you that a couple of men died, you'll have to learn to live with it. I know people who can help you, confidentially."

"I can manage, I think."

"I will get you out of town for a while. Kyle, keep your mouth shut! That is most important. What happened is strictly between you and me; nobody can ever know, not your father or your brother, no one. Do you understand?"

"They'll put it together."

"Let them think what they will, don't give them a thing."

"I thought Hawkins was going to shoot me."

"As, did I. Self-defense, it was pure self-defense."

"Here," Kyle said, giving the diamonds to Honey. "Tell my old man to put them in the bank. Tell him I saved his ass."

Honey took Louise Shaw's teardrop diamonds and slipped them into his pocket.

All of this because of some rich old man's pride, stupidity, and greed, he thought. Rich people really do dumb shit. Luckily, they pay me extremely well to cover their mistakes.

"Will he think *you* killed those men?" Kyle asked.

"I think so. Believe me, Kyle, your old man is not a stranger to murder. I will handle it. You keep quiet and live your life as if nothing happened. If he thinks I did it, that's a plus for you."

"I'm through with him, forever, you know. I never want to hear from him again. Tell him never to contact me. Will you stay on top of the investigation?"

Honey nodded, "Of course, I will. I'm paid to know these all about these kinds of things."

Seconds later, they were both gone, leaving only the dust from the wake of their vehicles to settle softly on the earth.

Each man believed no one would ever know what transpired.

Neither man knew Jack Redding.

They did not know he treasured Bill Hawkins as much as he loved and respected his brother.

They did not know he would never give up if he figured out who murdered his friend.

81

Four shots! I knew the sound. Three came in rapid succession and a fourth followed about ten seconds later. They came from the rear of the complex near Hawk's warehouse.

I dialed 911 and ran toward the warehouse on the street behind my condominium. My immediate thought was gratitude that Emma was down in Boulder City.

For an instant, I considered taking my .45 but grabbed my 12-gauge instead. I ran from the condominium in shorts, a tee shirt, and flip-flops. I moved swiftly but cautiously toward the warehouse; I loaded the 12-gauge as I jogged along. If needed, I'd be ready.

Ramon Lopez and I arrived together, coming in from opposite directions.

"No lights, no open doors," he said.

"You got a key?" I asked.

He nodded and removed a key chain, eyeing my shotgun.

"Did you shoot?" Lopez asked.

"It wasn't me," I said. "Those were handguns, my guess the shots came from inside."

In the distance, sirens blared.

I waved Ramon to the left side of the doorway; I took the right. After he unlocked the door, I turned the knob and peeked inside. The warehouse was dark.

When Ramon flicked on the lights, we saw two bodies on the concrete floor.

"Hawk and Tulio," I said. "I think they are dead."

We entered cautiously and went to look at the bodies. The pungent odor of gunpowder was thick.

Hawk was clearly dead, shot once through his neck. Tulio was gasping for air; we heard a deep sucking sound as bubbles foamed around his pale lips. He would not make it.

"He took one in a lung and another in the stomach," Ramon said, kneeling beside his friend. "It's really bad."

Tulio's skin was chalk-white.

He looked at Ramon and whispered something to Lopez, words that were inaudible to me.

"What did he say?" I asked.

"He said *A.B.*," Tulio whispered. "Then, he died."

"*A.B.*, what the hell does it mean?" I asked.

"His wife's name is Aletta Beatriz. He always calls...ah, called her *A.B.* I'm guessing he wanted to say something to her, maybe that he loved her."

I nodded, looking at Hawk's body. The shot through his neck probably severed his brain stem. He died instantly.

We had been through dozens of firefights and he never had as much as a scratch. Now, this, I thought. What a horrible and hideous way to die.

"Son of a bitch," I said.

"I agree," Ramon added.

Seconds later, EMTs and the police arrived.

They ushered us to the door, where we stood watching.

I heard footsteps behind me. Someone came up the road in a golf cart. I turned, looked at Ike, and shook my head.

"Hawk and Tulio," I said. Ike bowed his head and started to sob.

"Hawk is dead," he cried, adding, "Oh, my lord."

I nodded.

"Mercy," he said. He kept saying it again, and again.

His plea was a cry to the heavens. A prayer asked countless times throughout the course of humanity, when good people died for no good reason.

~

A detective spoke with the EMTs, checked out the bodies, and chatted up two uniformed cops, who were on the scene first. They gave him a sheet of paper. He nodded.

He turned in our direction and walked toward Ramon and me. He looked tired and drawn.

"My name is Detective Harry Stanton. Mr. Redding?"

I nodded.

"Thanks and," looking at Ramon, Stanton added, "you are Mr. Lopez?"

"Yes," Ramon said.

Stanton nodded.

"My partner, Lieutenant Stola will be here shortly and he might have more questions. I assume you knew the deceased?" Stanton asked.

Ramon offered a weak smile. He seemed nervous.

"Why are you covered with blood, Mr. Lopez?"

I gestured toward Garcia's body, under a yellow sheet, as Ramon replied, "I tried to save Tulio's life. I was an Army medic. It's *his* blood...he was too far gone."

"What about Hawkins?"

"I checked him, officer," I added. "I touched his neck for a pulse. He was dead. It's the only thing I touched."

"I appreciate that. I want each of you to tell me what you saw and heard. Mr. Lopez you go first."

Tulio spoke. "I was near the tool shed, filling the mowers with gasoline. Today is our mowing day. I heard four shots. Three real fast like pop, pop, pop. After a few seconds, then another shot."

As Tulio finished, another cop joined us.

"My partner, Lieutenant Jacob Stola," Stanton said, introducing us. "What was the time between the third and fourth shots?"

"I didn't time it, but I'd say no more than fifteen seconds," Ramon replied.

Stanton nodded and wrote in his notebook.

"Did you talk to the deceased before they entered the building," Stola asked.

"No," Ramon replied. "I didn't even know they were here. Tulio usually comes in early, but I did not see or talk to him. I drove in and went straight to the mowers."

"What about Hawkins?" Stanton pressed.

"No, I did not see him or talk to him."

Stanton nodded and wrote in his notebook.

Stola looked at me.

"Tell us what you heard and saw, Mr. Redding."

"Same as Ramon, three rapid shots, maybe ten or fifteen seconds later, a fourth," I replied. "I didn't see any of it."

"Where were you?"

"On my patio," I said, "getting my dog back in. I live one street over and four doors down, to the east. I saw Bill Hawkins this morning, after my run. We talked briefly about some fishing we planned to do later this morning. I saw Tulio arrive but did not talk to him. I went to take a shower."

"Do you know why Hawkins was armed?" Stola asked.

"He hated snakes and, if he was going fishing, he always wore it," Lopez replied. "He had a carry permit."

"Did either of you see anyone?" Stola asked

"No," we answered, simultaneously.

"Did you hear anything, other than the shots?"

I indicated I did not. Ramon said the same thing.

"Whose shotgun is that next to the door?" Stanton asked.

"Mine."

"Why the gun?" he asked.

"Four shots, I heard four shots. I thought I might need it. It was precautionary."

"You would have used it?" It was Stola.

"For self-defense, yes," I replied.

"You a cop?" he asked.

"No, former Army Ranger, a colonel," I clarified.

"Is the shotgun loaded?"

"Yes," I replied.

"You really would have used it?" Stanton asked.

"If fired upon, you're damned right."

Stola smiled and studied my eyes.

"I believe you," he said. "So, four shots, each of you came running, did not see anyone, or hear anything else."

Ramon raised his eyebrows.

"Did you hear something?" Stanton asked.

"Before he died, Tulio said, *A.B.*"

"*A.B*?" the cop asked.

"Yes, his wife's name is Aletta Beatriz. He called her *A.B.* all the time. I think he was trying to say something to her."

"That doesn't help us much," Stanton said.

"Not much info," Stola added. "Stay a while, would you?"

He told a cop to unload the shotgun, return it and the shells to me, and escort us onto the road and away from the crime scene.

"Get them coffee or whatever they want," he said, as we walked away.

While we waited, I sent a text to Emma and told her what happened. When I finished, I went over to Ike.

"Why did they have to die like that?" he asked. He was standing, his eyes still teary.

"I don't know. It came unexpectedly."

"Do you think it was kids looking for gold or silver?"

"Gold or silver," I repeated.

"Hawk was doing something with gold and silver on one of the boats he was remodeling."

"You should tell the cops," I said.

He nodded, adding, "Sometimes life sucks."

~

Later, after the coroner released the bodies, the crime scene unit went over the building.

I overheard a forensics officer talking to Stola.

"They came in through the roof. Other than that, it's a clean crime scene. Whoever did this wore gloves, maybe coveralls, too. We'll check what we did find; however, if I were a betting man, I'd say you won't have much to go on."

"What makes you say that?" Stola replied.

"Just a hunch, after twenty years on the job, I can tell almost immediately. My guess, the only blood is the victims, no fluids, no trace; we really don't have a ballbuster."

"Ballbuster?"

"You know: something to crunch them with."

Stola turned and nodded toward Ike.

"That man said Hawkins kept some gold and silver in the warehouse. Did you find it?"

The forensics man checked his inventory.

"We found a safe, we cracked it. Gold and silver were inside. Nothing seems disturbed; nothing is broken. A few drawers were open...could be someone was looking for gold. One of the victims fired, we found the slug."

"Not much to go on," Stola admitted. "More than likely it was some crack-head looking for something to pawn to make a score. We'll check the pawnshops. Anything else?"

"We're CSI in Vegas, but we ain't the TV show. No prints, no trace, no motive, no suspects. I'll bet a fiver we don't find a thing and that you won't ever solve this one."

"You're on," Stola said, telling a uniform to let us go.

I shook my head and walked away, with Ike and Ramon.

Cops are all the same to me. If they did not have a lead, the investigation would end quickly.

I still despised cops.

Because of Jill, my prejudice was apparently more ingrained than I realized.

82

Gordon Shaw was in his office east of Las Vegas when Honey Pszczoła walked in and placed Louise Shaw's teardrop diamonds on the desk. Shaw smiled a tight smile.

"So, now, they truly are conflict diamonds. Men have died because of them," Shaw whispered. "Is my secret safe?"

Honey nodded. "That's one way to look at it."

"Did you kill those two men or did Kyle?"

"I have no idea how those men died," Pszczoła said.

Shaw smiled knowingly and asked, "Have you seen Kyle?"

"He's doing fine, if that's what you're asking. He's a lot tougher than you may think."

"Do you think he and I will ever reconcile?"

"In a betting town, I'd bet no."

Shaw retrieved an envelope from his desk and handed it to Honey. "It's fifty grand for your retirement fund."

Honey nodded and put the money in his pocket.

Shaw searched Honey's eyes.

"Can Kyle be trusted to keep his mouth shut?"

Honey nodded. "Kyle will be fine. He's out of town for a few weeks. It will do him good to spend some time with a lovely woman who only wants to have fun."

"He has a new girlfriend already?"

"He will when he gets to Carson City...I've arranged it."

Gordon Shaw laughed and opened his wallet.

"Here's another grand."

"For what?"

"I like the way you think, Honey. I always have. You seem to be in the right place at the right time. You help me, a lot."

"That's what you pay me to do."

"And you do your job well. Do you want a drink?"

"Scotch, the best you've got."

"I only have the best."

83

Tulio Garcia was buried first. His simple ceremony, offered in English and Spanish by a Franciscan priest, was only for family and close friends.

Ike, Ramon, Emma, and I attended. Tulio was a good kid who died because he chose to help his boss.

We stayed and joined the family for coffee and sat quietly by ourselves, watching and listening.

A woman in her late twenties, carrying a baby, stopped.

"Hello, Mr. Ike," she said.

"Mrs. Garcia," Ike said, taking her outstretched hand.

"I am sorry," Ike stated, then looking at us, he added, "We are all disheartened."

"Who are your friends?" the young woman asked.

Ike introduced us. He explained the woman was Tulio's wife, Aletta Beatriz. She shook our hands and her eyes held mine for a few seconds longer than they did the others.

"Why did this happen?" she said tearfully. "No one can tell me. I have two babies without a daddy. The police tell me they have no leads. Who will give me justice? More so, will justice ever give my babies their daddy back?" She paused for a few seconds and added, "If you can help me, please do so. Tulio was a decent man. God bless you for coming. Pray for me, for Tulio, and for my children. We will need much help."

~

Hawk's wishes called for burial in the military cemetery in Fernley, Nevada, which is near Reno.

I stood holding Emma's hand, feeling the wind on my face, remembering all the good years he and I had served together. He was my subordinate in those days but I thought of him as a brother. He would have died for me back then and I would have died for him, too.

It was a silent agreement we had, never spoken, but very real. Most people never understand the bond. I treasured it.

Afterwards, as we drove to Las Vegas in Emma's company car, the mood was subdued. I could tell she was hurting.

"What is it, Emma?" I stated, already knowing what she was feeling and what she would say.

"I asked him to get my software discs. I keep thinking that if he or I had gotten them the night before, he would still be alive. He wanted to drive them to me. If he had, he and Tulio would be here today."

"Ifs and ands, Emma...you cannot blame yourself," Ike stated, from the back seat.

"Ike's absolutely correct," I added. "You had nothing to do with their deaths. You had no way of knowing about the break-in. If we knew the outcome of our actions, we would not do many of the things we do. Understanding the rationale is for a higher source.

"You got that right," Ike agreed, patting Emma's shoulder. "You did nothing wrong."

"Still...," she whispered.

I took a deep breath and exhaled softly.

"I once loved a woman who died a tragic death and I blamed myself for not helping her," I stated.

I then spent a good portion of our drive telling Emma and Ike about Jill, explaining how bad I felt for leaving her alone when I went to Syracuse. As I spoke, Emma took my hand in hers and squeezed it. I did not look at her, but I knew tears were rolling down her lovely cheeks.

"I'm sorry," she whispered.

"You did yourself and us a service by telling this account, Jack," said Ike. "I appreciate it."

I nodded.

"I've learned we cannot worry too much about the past."

"That is truthful," Ike added.

"We do the best we can in life," I continued. "We cannot change any of it, and worrying about things after the fact, thinking we had or have the power to arrange a different outcome, is pointedly useless. People make their own decisions. We have free will. We exercise it. We move on."

"You really loved her, huh?" Ike said.

"Yes, I did. When I lost her, I felt pain I never knew existed, and hatred, too, for the longest time."

"What helped you heal?" Emma asked

"Time," I replied. "And you."

"Amen," Ike whispered, "and halleluiah."

I looked in the rearview mirror and he smiled at me.

"Death hits us all," he said softly. "But it can only defeat us if we let it. If we live good lives, honor those we loved by living good lives, we pay them tribute. I plan to do tribute to Tulio and Hawk. I hope you and Emma will join me."

I smiled back at him.

With a sideways glance at Emma, I caught a slight smile and an even slighter nod.

~

Surprisingly, the next few days blended into a steady stream of pure joy. Newly found love's questions received honest answers, and the bond hardened

Of course, I never mentioned Aaron Cooper. He had destroyed one life. I would not let him destroy another. It is best to leave some things unspoken and not tempt fate.

Emma and I dreamed, made plans, fell into each other's arms, churned moments of sexual bliss, sang together, took long walks, and read books long into the dark of night. She read poetry to me and I read things I wrote to her.

She was critical of my work but never disparaging, and I loved her. She and I became one, and we were friends.

Nonetheless, one difficult hurdle remained for a love that I truly believed was unbreakable.

84

I was making a salad for lunch mid-way through Emma's hiatus from her contract work and ten days or so after we buried Hawk up in Reno.

Although we did not discuss it, we each experienced moments that felt like we had taken one in the stomach. The emotion was evident after we talked to Ike that morning during breakfast at his café.

"I talked to the police," he said.

"And?" asked Emma.

Ike swallowed his coffee and took a bite of toast.

"The investigation is proceeding. In other words, they don't have a clue about who committed the murders."

"Doesn't surprise me," I said, thinking about Jill's case.

"My guess," Ike added, "the cops will never know. I feel it in my gut as sure as we three are here in my café."

I looked at the sadness in the old man's eyes. The pain on his face was the identical to the pain I saw in mine after I answered a call from Pittsburgh.

"I will never understand those murders," Ike said. "It is a useless waste of life."

Emma and I agreed.

Ike said he wanted to go to church. Emma and I took him and sat with him as he prayed.

"I'm finished," he said half-an-hour later. "Let's go."

Now, back in my condominium, Emma perused a magazine as I set the table. She noticed a pile of mail that had built up and began to sort it for me.

After a few moments, she asked a question.

"Who is Rosemary Tomasulo?"

"Rosemary? She owns the carriage house where Jill and I lived. Why?"

"You have two letters from her."

"I do?"

"When's the last time you checked your mail?"

"It's been a while."

I walked over and she handed Rosemary's letters to me. I opened each, read them, and smiled.

"What is it?"

"Money orders, one for four thousand dollars and another for twelve hundred."

"Fifty-two hundred bucks," Emma said.

"Before I left Buffalo, I asked Rosemary to sell my things. The checks are the proceeds, less a commission she took for a few charities."

Emma continued sorting the mail as I sat, thinking.

"Let's take a trip, Emma."

"A trip?" she asked.

"Yeah, you still have a few weeks before you start your next assignment, right, and all your training is done?"

She nodded.

"Let's get out of here. Have you ever been to red rock country?'

"Red rocks?"

"Yeah, let's drive to Sedona and commune with nature and make love and drink wine and leave all of this bullshit behind us for a while. We'll use this money for some fun."

~

Each of us deserves good in his or her life.

We need to take time to love another person, to breathe fresh air, to feel the wind on our faces, to dance in the moonlight, to study the horizon, and to plan and dream.

That is what Emma and I intended to do.

We wanted to fill our lives with magic, and leave the sorrow and the bitter taste of death in our wake.

In Sedona, we filled days with laughter, and nights with intimacy. The closeness was immeasurable.

Each day was a mixture of all that makes love good.

We took long walks to cleanse our souls in ancient vortices that Indians claim carry healing powers. We rode horses. We tried new foods. We swam naked in a deep spring we found pooling in red rocks a few hundred yards beyond DEVIL'S BRIDGE.

During those moments, we talked about our lives, things we had seen and experienced.

I told her about my parents and my sister's death.

I told her about Vince, Vietnam, and his subsequent life.

I told her about killing men, and perhaps women and children, in Mexico and Central and South America.

I told her about Jill's humor.

I explained how I never believed Jill slipped and fell.

I never mentioned Cooper or Manny Tobias. They were my secrets and my burden. I did not want to tax Emma with that composite misery.

She told me about attending Dartmouth.

She told me how she lost her virginity to a college chum from Elwood, Indiana, who lost his life in one of the twin towers. They had been lovers and good friends.

"I once loved a woman, too," she told me. "That was never destined to last. Still, she was sexy and it fit the moment but never again. Once was enough. I prefer men."

She told me about the pain of losing her parents' business.

"Someday, I'll own a publication, making it a success in their honor," she said, seeming committed to that goal.

She danced for me one night, naked around an open campfire, her oiled skin shining a yellowish-orange in the pivoting flames.

As we made love, she smelled of baby lotion and laughed when my body slid awkwardly against hers. She laughed harder when wind blew ash from the cold fire. It clung to our bodies and we seemed tarred and feathered.

Fortunately, the deep pool in the red rocks was nearby. We washed and made love again, and washed again.

All of it solidified a truly matchless union. We seemed invincible to the movement of life and the qualms of the outside world.

We laughed, we cried, we made love. We shopped. We danced the Texas two-step at a country bar, and we sang, hiked, and took long walks.

The night before we planned to return to Las Vegas, we were watching the sunset, far in the west, from atop a high plateau. The colors—gold, yellow, orange, and purple—were breathtaking as if from the palette of a master.

Emma squeezed my hand, turned, and studied my eyes.

"If Jill was murdered, do you ever wonder who did it? Did you ever want justice?"

I felt a chill crawl up my spine.

"What provoked that question?"

She shrugged.

"I used to think about that a lot," I replied, honestly. "I don't anymore, not since I left Buffalo. I left my life, that part of it, behind me. Frankly, I hope the ruins and wounds remain there, too."

She opened my hand and kissed my palm.

"You don't seem like a man who would accept it."

"It's in God's hands," I replied. "I don't know who did it."

"Whoever killed her, if that is true, should pay."

"Maybe that person already has," I whispered.

She looked at me oddly. Maybe she felt some vibe in my hand, maybe some errant emotion fired through my skin into hers to say I was lying. I hated being untruthful, but Cooper's fate was my secret and my burden.

"I guess anything's possible," she said. Questions filled her expression. I thought I saw doubt flicker in her eyes.

I nodded.

"Which means everything is possible," she added.

"That, too."

Emma remained quiet. I kissed her forehead and held her close. Then I whispered, "I love you, Emma, only you."

"Let's make love, I want you inside me," she said.

"You mean right here and right now?" I asked.

"Why not, let's be bold."

"Then, bold it is."

~

The next evening, after we returned to Vegas, I counted the money in my billfold.

"We still have more than two thousand," I said. "Let's hit the tables...if I win big, we'll give the money to Tulio's wife."

"That's a great idea."

Half an hour later, we strolled into the BELLAGATO CASINO. I had designs on playing Blackjack for the first time since arriving in the Las Vegas area.

As we entered the casino, loud cheers attracted our immediate attention. A man rolling dice was on an enormous hot streak.

"What's going on?" Emma asked a woman who was leaving the table.

"Some guy is on a fantastic run. I'm telling you the son of a bitch cannot miss. If I didn't have to pee, I'd stay and watch."

"Let's go, Jack," Emma said.

Interested, we walked over.

~

The gambler, an older man with a gray mustache, rolled three straight sevens, winning what appeared to be fifty thousand dollars.

He pulled the money aside, bet fifty one-hundred-dollar chips, rolled, and won again. The applause was deafening.

He let it ride and won again.

The applause this time was thunderous.

Again, he sorted his chips and bet another five thousand. With the next roll, his luck ended. Still, everyone cheered. He received several pats on the back and smiled broadly.

"I've just paid off all my debts," he announced. His newfound fan base cheered again.

"How much did he win?" someone asked.

"About three hundred fifty thousand dollars," a man said.

"Wow," a woman added.

I watched the man fill tray after tray with one-hundred-dollar chips. The dealer called for assistance and two casino employees came to help the man. As he lifted his chips, two fell onto the floor and one of the casino employees stooped to pick them up. I immediately recognized him from the murder investigation but could not place the name.

As the man extended his hand, Tulio's words echoed in my mind. I saw the tattoo of a bumblebee above his right wrist, halfway up his forearm.

Then, it hit me.

Tulio was not saying *A.B.* for his wife. He was telling Ramon he saw *a bee*; I knew it! I was stunned. The same speck of hatred I felt when Jill was murdered came into me again at full force. From that moment forward, it was as clear as the most expensive crystal. I knew he was the man who was present when Hawk and Tulio died.

~

The mustachioed man and the employees walked over to the cashier. As a pit supervisor passed, I asked if he knew the taller of the two employees. My pretense was that I knew him and was trying to place the name.

"That's Jake."

"Jake?"

"Actually Jake Stola, he's a lieutenant with the Nevada State Police. He helps us with security."

"Yes," I said. "Now, I remember."

Emma heard my question and saw something register in my eyes.

"You don't really know the cop, do you," she asked.

"Not really, but he is the man investigating Hawk's and Tulio's murder. He talked to Ramon and me the night of the murders. I didn't remember his name."

Emma seemed to sense I had just discovered something very revealing, a fact never before disclosed.

"What's this about, Jack?" she asked.

"It's not really important," I said. "I recognized him and could not remember his name."

I turned to Emma and smiled.

"Let's go, I feel lucky. Let's go win some money for Tulio's wife."

85

Jake Stola was tired and thirsty and needed sleep. He wanted a cold beer and then it would be lights out. He turned into his driveway of his Vegas home, saw a cat scurry away in the wash of his police cruiser's headlights, stopped, and turned off the ignition. He exited in the darkness, yawned, and walked to his door, fumbling for his keys.

Before unlocking the door, he looked skyward: no moon, no stars, some cloud cover, and a chilly breeze. He thought about rain. His flowers could use it.

He reached for the door and felt a sting in the side of his neck. Labored breathing, dizziness, and nausea took over. He tried to put his hand against the doorframe for support but his arm did not move. He wondered who was tying his hands behind his back.

He felt someone behind him. Even though his mind was shutting down, Stola knew a man was supporting him, preventing a fall.

Every instinct told him to shout, but he could not. He tried to remember how tape covered his mouth but had no recollection. Panic consumed him. Who did this and why?

A man's voice and warm breath filled Stola's ear.

"It's a fast-acting sedative. You can't fight it."

Stola nodded slightly.

"We are going into the desert."

Those words and a dog barking in the night were the last sounds he would heard for quite a while.

~

A few hours later, Stola awoke staked and spread eagle in the desert, vis-à-vis Aaron Cooper. He would be the second cop to die that way in less than two months.

A dark figure removed the tape from Stola's mouth.

"Who are you?" he asked, groggily.

"Who killed Hawkins and the kid?"

"I have no idea what you are talking about."

In the sparse light of a lantern, Stola watched the man open a bottle of acid. He poured a few drops onto Stola's abdomen. It burned, and hissed, and hurt like hell.

"Honey is what some people call you. You are going to die, you won't see the sunlight; however, you will tell me what I want to know before you take your last breath."

"No, I won't."

"Yes, you will."

A healthy dose of acid and Stola screamed.

A few seconds later, a rag in his mouth stifled Stola's groans and screams.

"We can do this all night. The next drop is in your left eye. You will tell me and you will beg me to kill you."

Stola and his attacker went back and forth for maybe an hour. The cop was blind in one eye, had lost both testicles, and was fading in and out of consciousness but he gave it up. He whispered a man's name and address in Carson City.

Then, without a prod, Stola told an unbelievable story about rich people and conflict diamonds, about lies and tax evasion, about deceit and a woman's stroke, and about a bonus of fifty-thousand dollars in a wall safe.

"Two good men died because a rich prick lost diamonds. Why didn't he just knock on the door and explain it?"

"Tax and legal issues, you dumb fuck."

"You're in the desert dying and I'm the dumb fuck," his attacker said. "What a tragedy you helped create."

Stola watched as the man affixed a silencer onto his .45. Next, Stola felt it pressing against his temple.

"Do you want me to pull the trigger or do you want to punch your own ticket into eternity?"

Stola nodded and soon his right hand was free from its tight restraint. He longed to end his agony.

He reached out, put his finger atop his assailant's, and applied pressure. The sound of the shot, despite the silencer, still filled in the night air.

Would heaven recognize his suicide as a last minute act of repentance?

The assailant pushed Stola's body into a shallow grave, prepared while the cop was still unconscious. Next, the body was covered and the desert was silent. No one would ever find the remains.

~

The morning was still dark when the cruiser returned to Stola's house. The streets were empty. Everything was quiet. The neighborhood was in slumber.

A man entered the house, found money in a wall safe, and departed. He was not inside very long.

Next, the cruiser stopped behind an empty restaurant several blocks from Stola's residence. Quickly, gasoline saturated the inside of the automobile and, after the last few drops, the can sat on the back seat.

A lit cigarette went into a partially opened window and the driver disappeared in the darkness.

A few miles away, near the Las Vegas Strip, a man unlocked the door of a pickup and drove away.

He passed several fire engines racing to quell a car fire.

Kyle Shaw was next.

86

Kyle Shaw enjoyed his daily climb, one of moderate difficultly. He was always alone. The sun always seemed high in the sky, the breeze gentle. He loved the solitude. No pressure, no one to coddle, it was his time to explore his talent. The sense of peace he experienced was as astounding as was the scenery south of Carson City.

Kyle's routine was methodical. He would stretch, jog half a mile, and then climb one of two cliffs: the east cliff on Mondays, Wednesdays, and Fridays, the west on Tuesdays, Thursdays, and Saturdays. On Sundays, he rested.

The image of Amanda Cassidy flashed in his mind. He paused for a deep breath. He believed he should miss her more than he did.

He would always love her, always be grateful he knew her, and always value the joy she gave him. He had to say, the revelations spouted by his old man had tainted him more than he wanted to admit. The abortions did not bother him; however, the venereal disease did. If that were true, he wondered about residual problems. Sometimes it was an overwhelming emotion! They had been very active sexually.

He breathed deeply, cleared his mind, and concentrated. With an 80-foot drop, he could die without focus.

Kyle never suspected scrutiny. The shooting investigation in Las Vegas had stalled. Honey had worked his magic; in fact, they had not talked in days. Self-defense was Kyle's rationale and he could live with it. Now, that the infamous diamonds were back with his old man, Kyle felt his life was finally unfettered. He was rich, independent, and confident. He considered himself untouchable; however, he was not.

His routine did him in. Each morning, at seven, he would leave his condominium and drive to a series of cliffs in an isolated area south of Carson City, some twenty miles away.

Kyle whistled as he climbed. He seemed not to have a care in the world. He was in his zone, in that magical place climbers cherish. He could not get enough of the rush.

On this day, Kyle did not know a man waited patiently above, searching the land with binoculars, looking for any sign of human activity! The landscape was vacant and supportive. They were there, alone.

Kyle reached the top of his climb in twenty minutes. His left hand came first, then his right, then a leg. The man lifted a rock and prepared to roll it. However, as Shaw leveraged himself over the edge seeking the proper grip, a snake coiled in a crevice, lunged, and bit Kyle's cheek.

Shocked, he lost his concentration and fell immediately.

~

Minutes later, the man who disturbed the snake when he dislodged a rock examined Kyle Shaw's body, with its broken neck and limbs. The snake was an unexpected participant.

"You, Stola, and Cooper," the man whispered. "There's really no difference. Perhaps, I'm no better but I'm alive and you're not, and you will never kill again."

The man turned and walked out of the wilderness. He took his time and drank two bottles of water when he got to his pickup truck. He decided to dispose of the bottles somewhere else. He would not leave a clue.

As he departed, he wondered if, as he fell, Kyle Shaw had time to ask God's forgiveness. Frankly, he did not care. He thought about killing Kyle's father, Gordon, the man Stola said created this mess. No, he decided, I will not kill again. Let Gordon Shaw's memories be his constant torture.

Too much death, the man thought, as he passed a school bus. I have to start living again; I have to take time and do deeds that will clean the dark stains off my soul.

He knew, at times, he had not led a very good life, and he wanted to change that. He hoped it was not too late.

87

As Jack Redding entered his condominium in Las Vegas, the lives of people he had encountered, directly or indirectly, during his westward trek spun in their own way:

Sister Margaret lit a candle in Los Alamos, New Mexico, for the stranger who gave St. Therese orphanage a fortune.

~

Liza Mercer sat alone in Santa Fe, New Mexico, drinking port and feeling betrayed. Where was Aaron Cooper? Did something happen? Is he dead? Was it all a farce?

~

An aging waitress in Elk City, Oklahoma, served eggs to a blue-eyed trucker who admired her figure. She liked to flirt.

~

Rosemary Tomasulo sipped coffee in her Buffalo, New York, kitchen and decided to take cookies to a young priest.

~

Henry Bosko read RODEO NEWS in Clinton, Oklahoma. Then, he nodded off to sleep, dreaming about his glory days.

~

A female cashier in Erie, Pennsylvania, kissed a boy for the first time and it felt thrilling. Her spirit brightened.

~

In Pittsburgh, Pennsylvania, Casmir Kwiatkowski signed retirement papers. His considered Jack Redding, wondering if the man ever found the peace he richly deserved.

~

A few miles away from Kwiatkowski's desk in Pittsburgh, Frank and Ruth Kropinak went to a Mass for the repose of the soul of Manny Tobias. Kropinak thought about the letter he mailed to Buffalo. It remained his secret.

~

Sam Toliver ate a sandwich with a pal from Vietnam at a sub shop in Fayetteville, North Carolina, near Fort Bragg.

"The people you met in your travels, Sam, were they good or bad?" the friend asked.

"Mostly good," Toliver said. "A guy in Ohio gave me a handful of money. I bought food and a bus ticket here."

~

Theo Jefferson brought home a yellow lab puppy in Tulsa, Oklahoma. The dog, named Bailey, followed her everywhere.

~

In Flagstaff, Arizona, Fred and Madison Adkins ordered furniture for their new condominium in Wichita, Kansas.

~

Amos Talley smiled when his wife told him about her promotion. They lived near Fort Leonard Wood, Missouri.

~

In Detroit, Michigan, Tony Sarcusi called Aaron Cooper for the fifteenth time. He never got an answer. Across town, Tito Claroni met with Patsy Domico. "We're already up three million from the Santa Fe buy." Domico smiled.

~

In Henderson, Nevada, Aletta Beatriz Garcia opened a Fed Ex package containing fifty thousand dollars.

~

Vince Redding thought about a woman in Saigon and remembered a thin line of perspiration on her upper lip.

As he looked out the window in Jamestown, New York, a pickup truck passed on a distant road and Vince thought about his brother.

"Give him peace, Lord. Peace and good days, and someone to love," he whispered.

A searing pain in his back forced Vince to turn slightly and, as he did, he yawned, groaned deeply, experienced a tremendous calm, and died.

88

The next morning I received a telephone call from an attorney in Jamestown, who informed me about my brother's death.

As I hung up, Emma walked out of the bedroom.

"I heard the telephone," she said, drying her hair with a towel. "Was it import..."

She paused, seeing a pained expression on my face.

"What is it?"

"My brother died in his sleep, I have to go back."

She tossed the towel and came to me.

"How?"

"Leukemia, he never told me."

Tears in my eyes brought a kiss to my cheek.

"More death," she whispered.

I nodded.

"I have to take care of Vince. I'll call the airlines. Will you watch of Bailey for me?"

"Of course," she replied. "I'll come with you, if you want."

"Thanks, but you don't have to do that. I will bury him beside my parents and sister, sign a few papers, and come back. I'll feel better knowing you are taking care of Bailey."

"I have my key. He'll be in good shape."

"I knew Vince was going downhill, I didn't anticipate his death this quickly," I whispered.

"It seems to happen when we least expect it."

I nodded.

She kissed me again and helped me pack.

~

A few hours later, Las Vegas was a dot on the horizon and far behind the tail of the Boeing 757 that took me back to Buffalo. Vince was gone. Now, I was the only one left of my immediate family.

89

The captain turned from his window as Detective Stanton entered his Vegas office. They nodded and sat down.

"Any news on Stola?" the detective asked.

"The same, we found his cruiser gutted by fire a few blocks from his house. Crime scene doesn't have a clue. We've paged him, but nothing. His cell phone was in the cruiser. CSI did find that."

"You think he's dead?" asked Stanton.

"That would be my guess," the captain replied. "When a cop goes missing, usually it's bad. No leads. No motives. No suspects. I'm thinking the mob or somebody tied to the casino. I worried about that sideline job of his. Do you think it could be connected to the murders at EL CORAZÓN?"

"It crossed my mind," Stanton replied. "But that's a mystery, too. We got nothing to go on there, either."

"Was Stola getting close to anything on that one?"

"Not to my knowledge and I knew him as well as anybody. My guess, it was some druggie looking to score."

"What do you suggest?"

"It's clearly murder, which occurred in the midst of a robbery. Garcia and Hawkins surprised the thief or thieves and shot it out. Nothing seems to be missing. Some minor damage, it's as empty as a dry well."

The captain shrugged. "What a pointless mess we have! Stanton, EL CORAZÓN stays open but unless something pops, it'll eventually go on the back burner. The newspapers have dropped the story. Nobody gives a shit, especially with Stola missing. And that, I'm not happy to say, is just another sad commentary on life in the big city."

"These killings won't be the first murders we haven't solved," Stanton whispered. "I cannot figure it out. If he's dead, who in hell would have killed Jake?"

"That's the question everybody's asking. My gut tells me, we will never know and my gut is seldom wrong."

Stanton nodded.

"You don't think Jake was into something bad and decided to pack it in and make it look like somebody took him out?"

The captain took a deep breath.

"These days, nothing would surprise me. I asked Internal Affairs to take a look at him; the guy was clean."

"Yeah, they talked to me."

"We have talked to more than a hundred people. Nothing has surfaced: no connections, no threads to anything else; it's all very cold."

"The same with the deal at EL CORAZÓN, my gut tells me that's a dead end, too."

"Another issue," the captain said, standing. "You have a new partner, she'll be here tomorrow. Her name is Janice Likens. Keep going with EL CORAZÓN, but we just got another case. Looks like a heroin bag exploded in a mule's belly. Young college kid over at UNLV, she was probably trying to pay off her MBA. Get on it."

He handed Stanton the assignment sheet.

"Keep me posted," the captain ordered, "and don't give Likens any shit."

"Why would I?"

"It's your nature. She is a former Marine, with a black belt, who can break your neck."

Stanton paused at the door.

"What is it?"

"You know," he said, "I'm not a religious guy, but lately I've found myself praying for Jake."

"I have, too," the captain replied. "Somehow, I don't think our prayers will be answered."

"That would be my guess."

90

Jack buried his brother Vince in Our Lady of Victory Cemetery in their hometown of Lackawanna, New York, on a chilly day in the month of April.

Two hours later, as Jack was meeting with Vince's attorney, Emma Cassidy opened a closet door in Jack's bedroom, looking for a red blouse. She wanted to wear it for a new-client meeting she would be attending.

She removed her sweatshirt and tossed it up on a shelf, where it rested on Jack's duffel bag.

Bailey was beside her on the floor, watching.

She checked the time: 9:02 a.m. Her meeting was still some two hours away.

She moved a few garments aside, found the blouse, slipped it on, and reached for her sweatshirt.

As she pulled it, Jack's duffel bag tumbled to the floor. She picked it up and tossed it back on the shelf; it did not catch and, again, fell to the floor. This time a framed photograph fell out and banged against the wall. The frame separated, the backing came loose, and a hand-written note flittered out, resting beside her foot.

She picked it up and, not thinking, read eight words.

Jack Redding, I know who killed your wife.

Emma felt a terrifying chill.

She quickly remembered her conversation with Jack in Sedona. Jack had been quite specific; he said he did not know who killed Jill.

He had obviously lied. The letter was proof, addressed to Jack and tucked in behind a photograph of his deceased wife. Jack had to have read it.

There was only one logical conclusion: Jack did know!

Curious, she read the letter twice and, afterward, she felt queasy and had difficulty breathing.

She looked at Bailey.

"You were with him, you know, don't you?"

The dog stood and put his head against her thigh. His whine seemed to say he understood.

She refolded the letter, reassembled the frame, restructured the backing, inserted the letter, and returned it to the duffel bag, which she positioned on the shelf.

~

Back in her studio apartment, Emma sat at her computer and googled the name *Aaron Cooper*.

She found a series of laudatory articles about his service and retirement from the Pittsburgh Police Department, about ten months after the death of Jack's wife. Pittsburgh! Seeing the city's name in print gave her an odd sensation. Jill Redding died in a Pittsburgh alley.

Emma sat, trying to make sense of it all. She remembered something her father had taught her when she would go with him to the newspaper on weekends.

Her father had great instincts and she never doubted his experience or intuition.

"In the news business, in the guts of a story, coincidences rarely occur. Usually something bigger is at play...smoke usually means fire, Emma. Always remember that, the truth usually hides in the smoke."

She perused the search hits and an item at the bottom of the second page caught her attention. She clicked on and read the article.

Santa Fe (AP) Local portrait artist, Liza Mercer, has announced a five-thousand-dollar reward for information leading to the discovery of the whereabouts of Aaron Cooper, her fiancé. Cooper vanished mysteriously in February.

Cooper, 49, a Santa Fe resident and a former narcotics officer in Pittsburgh, was last seen by a friend who was interested in purchasing a vintage automobile.

Emma stopped reading. The man the letter accused of killing Jill Redding was missing. Next, she searched for Manny Tobias, the man who wrote the letter.

She found references to the police finding Tobias' body in a warehouse in Pittsburgh. He was a recovering drug addict. Cooper was a narcotics cop for nearly twenty-five years. Jill died in Pittsburgh! Cooper missing in Santa Fe around the same time Jack came west

"Oh, my God," Emma whispered, "no!"

Several moments later, the tears stopped and she wiped her nose. "This cannot be true," she stated. "Please, Jack, tell me you are not involved in any of this!"

She picked up the phone and called her supervisor begging out of the meeting. A fever was her excuse.

~

An hour after intensive reading, fate took Emma to Ike's café. She needed to see a friendly face and clear her mind.

"Is anything wrong, Emma?" Ike asked, adding, "You seem a bit down."

She nodded. "I'm not feeling a hundred percent. I'd like a cup of hot tea with honey, please."

A moment later, Ike brought her beverage and a ramekin of honey.

"Did you hear anything from Jack?" he asked.

"I got a text; he's meeting with his brother's attorney today. He'll be back tomorrow."

"Good."

Still numb, Emma merely nodded. Then, Ike mentioned another dreadful detail.

"Have you read the paper today?" Ike asked.

Emma indicated she had not.

"A story in the paper...Jacob Stola, the cop investigating the murder of Hawk and Tulio, is missing."

Emma looked at him.

"He's missing?" She asked. Fear filled her heart.

"Yeah, the cops found his vehicle out behind an abandoned fast food joint; somebody burned it."

Emma felt like she had taken a punch in the stomach and began to shiver. Two cops were missing, one in Santa Fe, and another in Las Vegas! Both connected to Jack.

Emma felt lightheaded. She placed a five-dollar bill on the counter and tried to stand.

"Emma," Ike said her name, concerned.

"I just need to rest," she replied. "Everything is tumbling about and I'm feeling dizzy."

"I have a couch in the back. You should go there."

He came around the counter and took her arm.

"The restroom first," Emma said. "Please."

~

Ike wanted to call a doctor, but Emma argued against it.

"If I get off my feet I'll be fine."

"You want me to get the tea and honey?" Ike asked.

Emma nodded and placed her head on a throw pillow. She wondered if the spinning would ever stop. She wondered if she would trip and fall and the stars would come crashing down around her.

No, Jack, please.

Unaware of her thoughts, Ike spoke softly, encouragingly.

"If you don't mind my saying so," Ike said, "You and Jack fit nicely together, you might consider keeping him."

"What if I learned something from his past that was terribly difficult to accept?"

"Hell, child, a skeleton or two can be found in every closet in this big land of ours," Ike said. "Wait, I'll be right back."

91

Emma's text said she would see me in the evening of the day I returned from my trip to attend to Vince's death.

When she entered through the open patio door, I knew immediately something was bothering her. I gave her a kiss but some part of her resisted, and she pulled back.

"What's wrong?" I asked, seeing her fighting tears.

"I have something to say. I saw the letter, Jack."

"What letter?"

"The letter behind Jill's photograph," she whispered.

At that moment, time stopped and I went cold.

"I wasn't snooping," she added quickly. "I went in the closet for a blouse and your duffel bag fell. The photograph came out, hit the floor, and separated. I saw a letter and happened to read the first line."

"And," I said, hating that this was happening.

"Aaron Cooper, a Pittsburgh narcotics cop, is missing in Santa Fe. Kids found Manny Tobias' body in a warehouse in Pittsburgh. Jill died in Pittsburgh. Manny wrote to you about seeing Cooper kill her in Pittsburgh. The cop you saw in the BELLAGATO is missing, too. His car burned. You're the common denominator, Jack."

I sat down.

"Jack, my dad was not the best businessman but he was one hell of a journalist. He always said that when it comes to the news, coincidences rarely happen. Usually there's a story and it's a big one. I came across another bit of information, a man my aunt knew intimately fell to his death about the same time the cop, Stola, disappeared."

"I don't know what to say," I replied. I was truthful.

"Maybe or maybe not," Emma replied. "You knew Hawk, you also knew Tulio. Jack, tell me the truth!"

"I do not like what you're asking," I replied. I did not.

"Have the police talked to you?"

"Yes, they did, after Hawk and Tulio died. All I know is what Ike tells me. They don't have any leads."

"Nothing else?" she asked.

"I don't know what to say to make you feel better."

"So then, what comes next?"

"I would like you to come with me."

"Where are you going?"

"I thought it through after I buried my brother. I belong where I spent many days growing up, on the land Vince left to me. I intend to live there. I want you with me."

She stared at me for a moment, removing a news article.

"The article says Jacob Stola had a bumblebee tattooed on his forearm. I did some research; his real name is Pszczoła, which means *bee* in the Polish language."

"So?"

"You told me when Tulio died he looked at Ramon and he said *A.B.* Ramon misconstrued it as a statement to Tulio's wife, but he was saying *a bee*, wasn't he, Jack? That's what went through your mind in the casino, wasn't it?"

"This is all circumstantial. Do you have proof?" I replied.

"I have instinct! Tell me that you do not know anything about the men who died…tell me," she said. "Say it."

"Why," I whispered. "It seems you won't believe me. Either you love me or you don't. Either you will come with me or you won't. Either you have proof or you don't." I would not lie to her again.

She shook her head.

"How can I do that? This changes everything."

"Does it? What you *think* you know changes nothing."

She shook her head, "I need to think, to do what's right."

"Do what you must," I whispered.

Without a goodbye, she turned, walked away, and took my shattered heart with her.

92

For the next week, I stayed to myself, half expecting the police to show up. They never did. That gave me hope. My love for Emma told me to visit her but I knew it best to give her space, that if she loved me, she would surface in time. I did call her office. I learned Emma was in Seattle on assignment for a month or so. I declined to leave a message.

Instead, I wrote a letter, gave it to Ramon, and asked him to hand it to Emma, when she returned. He said he would.

~

Dear Emma,

In life, we do things others do not understand. I am not ashamed of anything I have done for those I have loved. I would do the same for you. Please, know: my love for you is honest and true. I would never hurt you, in any way.

I am not a perfect man but I am a good one. I love you deeply, as deeply as I have ever loved anyone. I have decided that if I do not spend my life with you, then I will be alone.

I am going back home. My brother Vince said I would and he was correct. My grandfather built a cabin beside a small lake. Take Route 17 west out of Olean, New York, and turn right on Old Buck Lane. Find room for me in your heart, Emma. The human heart has an infinite capacity for love.

I will be waiting. Please, come for tea sometime.

~

I signed my named, printed my new address, and, on a morning where a pink dawn filled the eastern horizon, Bailey and I drove away.

I loved two women in my life. One died. As for the other, I believed I had lost her forever.

Bailey whined as we hit the open road and soon Las Vegas disappeared behind us in the warm haze of a new day.

The trip back to Western New York took me about a month. I was in no hurry to get there.

I stopped whenever the spirit moved me.

In the beginning, whenever I saw a police car, I really expected the cops to pull me over. They never did. After a while, I put them out of my mind.

Apparently, whatever Emma thought about me she kept to herself. I did not want her to carry my *so-called* sins, but that was her decision.

I never received any calls or texts from Emma on my cell phone and, when I did stop at a library or some other place to check my e-mails, there were never any messages.

I did a lot of thinking on my way back. I talked to Bailey all the time, too.

I decided to put past hate and terror behind me. It was time to move in a new direction and develop whatever talent I had as a writer.

Somewhere in Kansas, I made a call to Hawk's friend, the literary agent. She said she wondered why I had not sent her anything.

I used Hawk's demise and my brother's death as a pretense and told her she would have something from me in the next few months.

"Sorry about your brother," she said. "Hawk's murder was a tragedy. Do you know if they ever found the person or persons responsible? Will these people pay?"

I nodded to myself seeing Stola's acid-burned face and hearing Kyle Shaw's screams as he fell to his death.

"I don't know, maybe they already have," I replied. "I'll start writing and I promise to stay in touch."

"I'll look forward to your submissions. I think you have a bright future."

"Perhaps," I said, knowing it would be brighter if Emma were with me. Emma had all I needed to make me happy.

Book 4

October 2013

Renewal

The glory and the freshness of a dream
—William Wordsworth

EPILOGUE

On a warm day in Allegany, New York, in late October, I spent the afternoon watching a work crew thin and remove trees and undergrowth from the land I inherited from my brother. The woods and lake were peaceful. Emma was still missing; Jill was always with me.

Since leaving Nevada, I kept to myself, living quietly. Bailey and I sorted it all out, heading east. My money was safe. Tobias' letter and memory card were gone, forever.

I read the bible daily, a new practice for me. Some passages brought me solace, others I did not understand. I prayed, too: for those I loved and lost, for people who died because of me. However, I never prayed for Cooper.

Each day, at sunrise, I thought about Jill, Vince, Hawk, Ted, Theo, my parents and sister, and that wonderfully mysterious woman beside the North Sea. I wished their souls comfort. I thought a lot about Emma, too. I missed her smile. I longed as much for her as I once did for the glory and freshness of a dream that was my Jill.

Bailey and I often returned to the cabin beside the lake at five. Before entering, I would stand on the porch and study the valley below, where the spires of my university, St. Bonaventure, seemed to give the world definition.

I liked the silence of my new life; it pleased me. Thomas Merton, a theologian, a philosopher, and a one-time lecturer at St. Bonaventure, once wrote, "There is greater comfort in the substance of silence than in the answer to a question."

I never fully understood that comment until I spent those afternoons with Bailey on a rough-hewn porch where my grandfather taught Vince and me how to live as men.

After a few moments of contemplation, I would usually work on my novel, as I did that particular October afternoon.

So far, Hawk's agent friend liked what she had read.

The story was about a best-selling novelist, a medal-of-honor recipient, who lived in the Virgin Islands. He loved and lost a woman from Indiana and chose to live his life quietly. If he ventured out, it would be in disguise to use his vast wealth to help the poor. The story touched on love and war, but was mainly about the joy found in helping others.

The agent called not long ago; a publisher had an interest.

Once inside, I made a pot of tea, and became absorbed in my work, which suspended time and nature.

Eventually, Bailey's whine broke the creative spell.

When I looked up, Emma Cassidy stood at the screen door bathed in sunshine, in jeans and a cashmere sweater, smiling her amazing and wonderful smile.

"I think about you all the time," I said, opening the door.

She replied, "As I do you. We must share one heart, huh?"

I paused and spoke the dreaded question, "My past, Emma, what about the wedge between us?"

"There is no wedge. I love you. Ike knew it, too. He said I was a fool not to be with you. Jack, I only care about us and the local weekly newspaper I bought."

"You purchased the ALLEGANY NEWS?"

"Money from my aunt's artwork, I bought it to honor my parents." She paused. "Jack, I have two conditions."

"Which are?"

"Always love me and, from this day, never lie to me."

"I will and won't. Would you like a cup of tea, Emma?"

"Tea sounds good," she said, entering. Soon, her fingers found mine. Holding her hand calmed my restive soul.

Her skin was warm. I kissed her and asked, "One heart?"

She hugged me tightly, kissed my neck sweetly, and whispered, "Yes, the heart by which we live."

The End

CPSIA information can be obtained at www.ICGtesting.com
Printed in the USA
LVOW08s1405130414

9 781626 466722